GNARLED HOLLOW

Visit us at www.boldstrokesbooks.com

By the Author

Palette for Love

Love in Disaster

Canvas for Love

Pride and Porters

Gnarled Hollow

GNARLED HOLLOW

by
Charlotte Greene

2018

CREDITS

Editor: Shelley Thrasher
Production Design: Susan Ramundo
Cover Design By Sheri (hindsightgraphics@gmail.com)

Dedication

For you, always.

CHAPTER ONE

Emily's sister Marion insisted on giving her the map that morning, and she'd taken it from her with a groan of impatience. Ever since their parents had retired to Costa Rica three years ago, Marion, though younger than her, had fashioned herself into the new "mom" of the family. The map was clearly "mom" behavior, even if, in truth, it was something their real mother would never have offered. Marion produced it, along with a packed lunch for the trip, as if Emily were incapable of stopping somewhere and finding food on her own.

"You never know," Marion had said. "You might not find anywhere to stop. And anyway, homemade is healthier."

Now, hours later, Marion's sandwich in one hand, peering down at the map, she had to quell a flash of resentment. Marion had been right, as usual. Not only had her GPS and phone quit functioning, but she also hadn't passed a single place suitable for lunch in the last couple of hours. A few minutes ago, she'd simply pulled over on the side of the road, barely off the edge of the pavement.

Having a map, however, was no real help. Emily was hopeless with directions and place names. She'd been driving for the last hour, but the place names along that road on the map were unfamiliar. Surely if she'd passed a town called Persistence, she would have remembered it. Or a river called Sorrow. Or a lake called Lost Hope. Her sister, clearly trying to be helpful, had made little black circles at points along the road where she could turn and save time on her journey, but at this point Emily was less concerned with saving time and more concerned with actually arriving at her destination. She couldn't even remember the name of that last tiny place she'd driven through. Something with Falls in the name? But that couldn't be right, as she saw nothing with that in the name on her map, unless she'd somehow managed to drive completely off course.

She peered up and down the road. Maybe she might spot a sign to suggest that she was on the road she thought she was on, but she didn't. It didn't help that the road was curved and steep, the woods dense, the trees hiding the horizon in either direction. She sighed. The map was next to useless. She would finish her lunch and keep driving. Something must be ahead of her, and if she didn't see anything in half an hour, she could always retrace her route. Even she could do that, as she'd been on the same road for at least an hour without turning.

She leaned back on the hood of her car, munching the apple slices her sister had packed. Despite being lost, she had enjoyed the beautiful drive almost from the moment she'd left town this morning. She was unfamiliar with this part of the country. She'd grown up in New Mexico, where the woods, even when thick, were nothing like this. She didn't recognize the trees here—oaks or elms, maybe. The leaves and branches above her were so dense, they cut off sunlight. Only a soft-green light filtered through, catching motes of pollen and dust as they floated through the trees. The road itself was strangely out of place, foreign in this setting. One season without maintenance and the woods would take it back. Water ran down the hill behind where the car was parked, gushing in a stream nearby. It was marvelous here, almost like a fairy tale.

Her sister was living in New England temporarily with her husband on a military base, and Emily didn't know another person besides her and her brother-in-law for hundreds of miles. It was a peaceful feeling. No one around here needed anything from her or was counting on her for anything. No one was disappointed in her. Here, in these dense woods, she didn't need to answer to anyone. Even lost, she felt better than she had in a long time.

As she stuffed the little plastic baggies into the larger paper sack, she heard it: a strange sound—both familiar and unfamiliar—as if she'd forgotten how that sound was made. She froze, cocking her head, her heart rate unaccountably increasing. The sound was coming from the woods.

She turned in that direction, suddenly afraid she would see it, but saw nothing. The landscape remained the same thick wall of trees in all directions. She felt as if she were being watched. Despite the warmth of the day, she shuddered, still peering into the woods. Movement caught the edge of her vision, and she spun toward it, almost cringing as she tensed.

A bicycle finally came into view, making that strange whirling sound she hadn't been able to recognize. The trees must have caught the sound and thrown it somehow, as it had seemed to come from the forest rather than the road, but there it was. The cyclist spotted her almost the second she spotted him and stopped pedaling. For a moment, Emily was frightened. She'd lost a lot of weight recently during her depression, and the man, though average, dwarfed her short frame by a foot or more. He smiled broadly a moment later and then aimed for her, pulling up a few feet away. He was an older man—her grandparents' age or close to it. White hair peeked out from under a checkered, woolen fisherman's cap, and in his tweed blazer and flannel shirt, he seemed overdressed for both his activity and the warm summer day.

"I've been on this road nearly every day at this time for years, and do you know you're only the second person I've ever run into out here?"

She forced a laugh. "I haven't seen anyone in a while, too, if that makes you feel any better. I must have taken a wrong turn somewhere, and my phone's not working."

"No, it wouldn't, not up here," he said, as if that explained things. He glanced behind her and saw the map on the hood of her car. "Can I help you?"

Shame quickly followed Emily's rush of gratitude. She hated feeling helpless, hated depending on anyone for anything, but this was clearly a special circumstance. "Could you? I'm completely turned around."

He smiled and dismounted before setting his kickstand. The bike, like his clothes, was antique, strange. She couldn't imagine pedaling something that old and heavy up the hills around here.

"Let's see where we're at then," he said, indicating the map. Emily took a couple of steps away to give him room, and he peered down at it, then rooted around in his breast pocket and removed a pair of spectacles. He perched them on his nose and bent, staring at the map before leaning back and placing his finger on a spot.

"Here we are," he said.

Again, Emily felt a flash of relief. At least she was on the map. He moved his finger a little to the side, but once she saw where he was pointing, she looked up at him. "But that's impossible!"

His bushy eyebrows shot up. "How do you mean?"

Before the cyclist had shown up, Emily had been examining the lower right side of the map, at Persistence and Sorrow and all the other bleakly named places she'd been trying to remember. The man was pointing to the upper left corner.

She shook her head. "There's no way I'm there already. I timed it this morning on the computer and shouldn't have been here for hours."

"Yet here you are," the man said, again as if this explained things.

"But how can it be?"

He seemed baffled—clearly by her and not by her situation, and she made herself look at the map again to make sure she understood what she was seeing.

"But that would mean I'm almost there!" she said, still unable to accept what she was seeing. The man had taken a step away from her and the car, his face now troubled and wary. Emily held up her hands in a calming gesture. "I'm sorry—I'm having a hard time accepting what you're telling me. I believe you, of course. I just don't understand. I left this morning at eight and wasn't supposed to be in this area until three or four."

"Well, then, you're right on time," the man said, his posture relaxing a little. He glanced at his watch. "It's only going on four now."

Emily had to stop herself from grabbing his wrist to look at the time herself. Some of her doubt must have shown on her face, as once again the man took a slight step away. He held up the watch for her to see at a distance, confirming what he'd said. It was almost four in the afternoon. She'd stopped for lunch shortly after one. That had been, at most, half an hour ago, not three hours. She opened her mouth to say as much and then snapped it closed. Why would this man believe her? She didn't believe it herself.

The man had walked away and back to his bike. "Well, I'll be heading off then, if you're all sorted out." He kicked up the stand and climbed onto his bike.

"Wait," she said, holding out a hand. "Thank you. I'm sorry. I'm obviously more lost than I thought. Could you tell me if you know Gnarled Hollow?"

Again, his eyebrows shot up. "Know it! Of course. You can't live around here without knowing about that place."

"Can you tell me how to get there?"

"What on earth could you want with it? It's been closed for years now—decades even. They don't allow sightseers. I've never even been on the grounds. They've locked the gate like they're hiding the Crown Jewels in there."

His attitude seemed strange, almost hostile now, as if he resented having to admit this situation. Emily didn't want to have to explain why she was going to Gnarled Hollow—it was too complicated.

"I'll keep that in mind. But could you tell me the best way to get there?"

He studied her for a moment, as if weighing the option of denying her request, then finally sighed. "You're close to the main gate now. It's maybe five minutes from here. Keep going the way you're headed. You'll cross a small bridge at the bottom of this hill. Right after the bridge, you'll see a dirt road on the right. Follow that, and you'll come to the main gate. You can't miss it—there's nothing else down that road."

"Thanks again."

He shook his head, his face pinched with something like disgust. "You're wasting your time. You'll never get in."

"Okay. Thanks again."

He didn't respond beyond tipping his hat, turning his bike around, and pedaling off. Emily watched him for a moment, still confused and distinctly unsettled by what he'd told her. She looked at the map again and felt a strange dip in her stomach when she remembered where she was. And what time it was.

She pulled out her now-useless phone and confirmed that it was now after four. How had she gotten here? How had she lost three hours? She touched the hood of her car. It was cold now, but that didn't mean anything. Newer cars didn't stay hot like they had in the past—better engines, or whatever. And even so, forty minutes would cool any engine. Either way, she would have remembered standing here for three hours. She clearly remembered glancing at her phone and seeing 1:05 when she turned off the ignition. But she must have made a mistake. There was no other explanation. She'd stopped for gas around eleven this morning and had somehow driven for almost five hours without a break. She'd been lost in thought but apparently taking the right roads, as she was nearly there.

She shook her head again and tried to swallow her unease. None of this mattered now. She would be there soon and would forget all this nonsense.

CHAPTER TWO

Emily had been let go last December, three days before Christmas. That's what they called it now—"let go"—as if she'd been captive and released, as if she'd even remotely wanted her freedom. The phrase didn't reflect her awful panic when the chair of her department broke the news. It also didn't capture the absolute horror she'd felt when she finally accepted what it meant for her and her career. She'd had no idea the layoff was coming. The university she worked for had been threatened with budget cuts before, and she'd made it through the last batch of them.

But, as her chair had explained, these cuts had been deeper, more fatal. Whole departments were being lopped off, as were several junior faculty members from various non-STEM and non-business departments. Her friend Carol in engineering had survived, of course, but almost everyone Emily had started with in humanities and social sciences had been let go. None of them had achieved tenure yet, so their contracts were easier to terminate. She'd been given six-months' severance and a very good letter of recommendation, but that was it. Her career as an English professor was over.

Her chair had recognized this fact when he broke the news. He didn't even attempt to cover up his resentment with the powers-that-be, the nameless bureaucrats at the state level that didn't seem to understand that hiring poorly paid adjuncts to replace actual professors was not to the school's or students' benefit in the short or long term. Her chair was, in fact, livid—livid, but helpless. With universities making cuts across the country very much like the one that had "let her go," it was unlikely Emily would see the inside of a university classroom anytime soon, or possibly ever again. It also didn't help that most new academic jobs were posted in the autumn, which meant that when she was terminated, Emily had missed her best yearly, if very slim, chance to get something for the next school year.

The months that followed her layoff had resulted in a serious existential crisis. Who was she if she wasn't a professor and a scholar? Why had she suffered through twelve painful years of higher education? She'd done well at her three-year review, she'd had all her ducks in a row for her tenure review next year, and all that torture had been for nothing. The crisis had quickly devolved into a serious depression that, by March, had settled into a quiet, apathetic sort of nihilism. For a while, she found no point to anything. She spent most of the early spring binge-watching bad television shows, avoiding the phone, and hiding from her neighbors.

Then something strange happened. Two years ago, unaware of her career's impending doom, when she'd first proposed her book, she'd naively sent off a letter to the only living relative of an author she studied and taught in her American-literature courses.

Margot Lewis, the author, had been a tangential part of the Lost Generation of American writers in the years following World War I. While not part of the core group of (mainly male) authors living in Europe, Lewis had known most of them personally, and her work concerned many of the same themes as theirs. Her fiction, like that of other American and European modernists, was experimental, difficult, and often bleak. In part because of her femaleness, and in part because of her work's bleakness, Lewis had not enjoyed the same notoriety as the others in the Lost Generation. She was barely known then or now outside of feminist scholarly circles.

Lewis had returned to the States before the outbreak of World War II, by all accounts disappointed and bitter by her lack of fame. She'd disappeared into her family estate, Gnarled Hollow, in the woods of upstate New York, and never publishing another word. During the decades she lived at Gnarled Hollow before her death, she refused contact with anyone, relied on deliveries for food, and apparently died alone, her body rotting in the family house for days before someone noticed.

The estate and Lewis's legacy had passed on to a cousin, the woman Emily had contacted in her letter. Her book explored several American, female modernist authors, including Lewis, and she had contacted the cousin in the hopes of seeing the house firsthand. Emily's scholarship focused purely on Lewis's literature, not her life, so she had no specific reason for wanting to see the house beyond what was perhaps prurient curiosity. Her naïveté at what she'd thought was an innocent request had been immediately shut down by a cease-and-desist letter from the cousin's lawyers, which promised a lawsuit if Emily attempted to contact her again.

She hadn't.

Then, three weeks ago, a new letter had appeared in her mailbox, this one written on plain, if expensive, stationery with no return address. Emily almost hadn't opened the letter, addressed as it was to her at her former university. Someone on campus had forwarded it to her home address. She'd almost thrown the letter into the trash, unopened, sure it would simply be more salt on her wounds, but just before she let it drop onto the top of her coffee grounds and apple cores, she saw its New York postmark and hesitated. She'd applied for a grant in New York, which came with a small stipend and housing for the summer, but she'd forgotten all about it.

Hands shaking, she opened the envelope, but the letter she pulled out was not, in fact, in any way related to the grant. Instead, it was from another relative of Margot Lewis—a distant one—who had inherited the house after Lewis's cousin died the previous winter. This relative was contacting Emily after an inventory of the cousin's effects and after seeing the letter Emily had sent asking to see the house. This relative was opening the house that summer for scholars and wanted to invite her. A phone number was included in the letter, and Emily was asked to call as soon as she could.

Again, she started to throw the letter away, certain that if she followed up with this person and explained her new joblessness, the letter-writer would have to turn her down. Still, Emily was too curious to pass up the chance.

"Hello?" The voice was soft and shaky. Emily pictured a very old woman, wrapped up in a pale-pink, hand-knitted shawl.

"Hello. My name is Dr. Emmaline—Emily—Murray. I received a letter with your phone number. You asked me to call you regarding Gnarled Hollow and Margot Lewis."

"Oh, well, that's marvelous!" the woman said. "I was very much hoping I would hear from you."

Emily hesitated, surprised by the change in the woman's voice. It sounded stronger now, more certain. Perhaps instead of the hand-knitted shawl, she was wearing a silk blouse and holding a dry martini.

"I'm sorry," Emily said. "I didn't get your name—I couldn't quite make it out in the letter."

"Oh, forgive me. My handwriting's gone to shit. My name is Ruth Bigsby—and please, call me Ruth. I inherited Gnarled Hollow, though I couldn't begin to tell you how it happened. My lawyers tried to explain my connection to that family, but it's very distant. The Lewises had less of a family tree and more of a trunk, if you catch my drift. Lots of cousins marrying cousins and all that, and very few children. I know it was like that in those days, but it does give you pause to see people with the same last name marrying each other over and over again!" She barked with laughter that devolved into a hacking cough. Now Emily pictured a woman with a deeply plunging T-shirt showing off an overly tanned décolletage, a cigarette in one hand, a beer in the other.

"Anyway," Ruth said, "the house also came with a great deal of money, which is something I certainly don't mind, except for all the damn taxes." She barked with laughter again. "I've been working all spring to get things in order—figure out what to do with it so the damn government can't take it all from me—and one of my lawyers suggested setting up a kind of trust in the house itself, opening it up to scholars for study. The former owner had hundreds of letters over the years from people asking to see the house, and I asked my lawyers to find a few people in there who didn't seem like kooks. Your name rose to the top of the list."

"Glad to know I'm not a kook," Emily said, smiling.

Ruth barked again. "And how! You wouldn't believe all the weirdos out there trying to get inside. Bunch of whack jobs, let me tell you."

"I can imagine."

"Most of them want to see where she died. Want to touch her bed, that kind of thing."

"Right."

"Anyway, I had the place cleaned, top to bottom, and there's plenty of room for people to use it as a work space. Margot Lewis had a library, too, and she left all of her papers there, along with her family library."

"Her papers?" Emily asked, her heart pounding. No one had seen a single thing written by Margot Lewis in over fifty years. It would be a significant boon to modernist scholarship to find new work.

"Yes—and there's a ton of it. Stacks and stacks, journals and folders of things, some of it handwritten, some of it typed. I don't even know where to start. That's why I want to get some experts out there to start going through it all. Experts like you."

For a moment, the last few months fell away, and Emily felt a tremendous surge of hope and triumph. While her own scholarship had been well received in modernist-studies circles, she was too junior to have made much of a mark before she'd been let go. Being the person to release and study new work by Margot Lewis would certainly put her back on the map. Her hopes died a few seconds later when she remembered her changed circumstances. Ruth would be much better served, after all, by someone with a university to back up her work.

Ruth must have taken her silence as hesitance. "I can pay you, of course. Whatever you would normally be paid at your university, I mean. That's what the lawyers suggested. That way you could take a leave of absence, or whatever, and not be out anything."

Emily hesitated again. This was the chance of a lifetime. In fact, had she been in her old position at the university, it would have been very difficult, if not impossible, to accept the offer. Junior faculty were very rarely given leave or sabbatical. Her joblessness, in fact, would allow to her to go—if Ruth still wanted her. Emily decided to see what the offer would involve before she confessed to her current situation.

"When could I start?" she asked.

Ruth barked again. "As soon as you wanted! In fact, the sooner the better. The house is so old, it doesn't have air conditioning or central heating, if you can believe it, so working there in the summer would be much more tolerable. It's in the woods, you know, so it doesn't get very hot there, even in July. I don't know how people in those days stayed warm with only fireplaces, but that's all you'd have come October or so."

"And how long would the project last?"

"Heck if I know!" Her bark was more of a yipping chortle now. "Like I said, I need the experts to tell me that. I imagine you'll spend the first couple of months getting a handle on the situation before you can determine how long it'll take."

The temptation to accept pushed at the back of her tongue. Not only was this offer a lifesaver—her savings would be depleted by July, at best—but she would find the project itself incredibly fascinating. She had completed and submitted her latest book last autumn, but her chapter on Lewis had been the most interesting part of the whole project. Now that she knew what would be required of her—something she was, in fact, uniquely qualified to do—she didn't want to confess that she was currently without an institution. Ruth would likely turn her down if she fessed up.

Accepting the wild impulse that rose in her heart, the one that closed off all good sense, Emily said, "I'd love to do it. And I'd like to start as soon as possible—early June, if that's okay."

Ruth barked so loudly Emily had to pull the phone away from her ear, and they spent the next half hour covering the initial details. At no time was Emily tempted to admit that she was unemployed. The opportunity was simply too good. She would have to hope Ruth would forgive her omission later.

As they wrapped up their conversation, Ruth said, "Oh, before I forget, I wanted to mention the others."

"The others?"

"The other scholars that will be there with you. I wouldn't want you to be surprised when they show up. Most of them won't get there until after you, but don't worry. You won't be by yourself all summer in that big old place."

Emily's hopes sank. Very likely one or more of them would know who she was and what had happened to her. After all, academia was a very small world. Her charade would be up before she'd even had a chance to prove herself.

"Now let me see," Ruth said, and Emily heard her shuffling papers. "I have a note around here somewhere. Ah, here it is. First, there's a man from New York, Dr. Mark Somner."

"Dr. Somner? I've never heard of him."

"He's in architecture, if I remember correctly. An historian. He'll be studying the house. Then there's a Mr. Christopher Wu—I don't think he has a title, but I could be wrong. He's a landscape engineer, and he'll be studying the gardens and grounds. There's a Dr. Juniper Friend—what a name!—an art historian. And another one of your lot—Dr. Jim Peters, an English professor."

Emily's hopes had risen with the list of people from other disciplines, but they crashed on this last one. She and Jim had been on panels together at various conferences over the years. He knew her and would have heard about her layoff. Still, she decided to let this adventure play out. Perhaps she could, if it came to it, pass herself off as an independent scholar, should Ruth actually ask.

"Finally, there's my niece, Lara. She'll be there for a few days, sometime in mid-to-late June, I think. So you'll have company, but believe me, in a house that big, you'll barely notice each other."

This last addition made Emily pause. Would the niece be there as a kind of spy? She couldn't think of a way to ask about this possibility politely, however. She would wait and find out. A niece seemed like a very minor obstacle, especially since she apparently wouldn't be there very long.

"I might stop by once or twice myself, but you'll all have plenty of warning when I do. And as I said, the others won't join you until after you've gotten there. You should have the place to yourself for a few days, maybe more."

"It all sounds wonderful, Ruth. I can't thank you enough for this opportunity."

"The pleasure is all mine. What good is money if you have to give it all away to the IRS?"

CHAPTER THREE

The gravel road to the estate was exactly where the cyclist had said Emily would find it—just beyond a little stone bridge. She didn't find a marker of any sort from the main, paved road. Without his directions, she would never have discovered the road to the house, so she was grateful to him despite the strangeness of their encounter.

Much to her surprise, the road leading to the gate was well maintained. When the cyclist had told her it was unpaved, she'd expected a rutted, muddy mess out here in these wet woods. She'd grown up on a dirt road, and it had always been in a state of sloppy disrepair. If you don't take care of dirt roads—and their father rarely had—they quickly devolve into something most drivers have second thoughts about. This road, on the other hand, had been carefully raked recently, with new gravel laid down, although she didn't see a mark on it to suggest anyone had driven here recently. The trees had been trimmed back enough that they didn't brush her car, another monumental task with a road this length. Clearly Ruth was paying a lot to keep it in good condition.

A few minutes later she arrived at the gate, where she could finally see the large fence that encircled the estate. From the road, it had been hidden behind the trees, but here she noticed that the fence was high and formidable, a black wrought iron with tipped points. The gate was locked, of course, and she had to park and get out to unlock it. Ruth had sent her a large package the previous week containing keys and information, and it took her a moment to find the right key on the ring. The lock opened easily, and she released the chain that held the gates closed. It took a great deal of effort to swing the heavy gate, but she needed to open only one side to make enough room for her little car. She got back in, drove through and past it, then got back out and closed and locked the gate and chain again. Ruth had been very particular with her warnings about keeping the gate locked, to avoid the "kooks" getting in.

The gravel road past the gate was even nicer, made of what appeared to be crushed seashells. It was bright and white, and, as Emily neared the house and the trees began to thin, the road seemed to glow in front of her in the sunlight.

Later, when Emily tried to remember the feeling that came over her upon first seeing Gnarled Hollow, she wasn't able to pinpoint exactly what made her slam on her brakes and stop. At first, for less than a full second, she experienced something like fear—even horror. Turn around, she thought desperately. Turn around right now. Forget you were ever here. Leave and never come back.

Seconds later, she was hit with a surge of joy and exhilaration, a happiness so hot and sweeping that she had to blink back tears. Her heart began to race, and she flushed with heat and excitement. She could no longer see for the tears and clasped her hands to her chest, gazing at the house with blurry eyes.

She had expected Gnarled Hollow to be awful and ugly, hideous in a terrible, Victorian style of neo-Gothic or neoclassic. Despite its age and a vague kind of notoriety, she hadn't found any pictures of the house, so she shouldn't have been surprised to find something different out here in these woods. Yet she was. The house had been built in the late 1870s by a family with an unimaginable amount of money. Usually rich Americans in that era modeled their homes on European classics, sometimes going so far as to copy them outright. Gnarled Hollow was something else and totally, unexpectedly original.

White and stately, it had none of the trappings of other horrible large houses of the era: no columns, no marble, no flying buttresses or unusual gables. It was, in fact, something like a large, English-style cottage. However, the enormous windows made it entirely different—huge, eye-like squares across the entire façade of the house, seemingly hundreds of them at first glance. The wide lawn in front contained no fountains or statues to disrupt the open, empty green, and the white road curved around it in a graceful arc. The house was, in a word, one of the most beautiful things Emily had ever seen.

Embarrassed now, and glad she was alone, she put her shaking hands back on the steering wheel and followed the road around the green on the right, parking directly in front of the main door. Ruth had told her about a converted carriage house somewhere that she and the others should use as a garage, but she decided to find it later. She was compelled, somehow, to look at the house now.

Emily got out of her car and walked across the large lawn, back to the road where she'd stopped upon seeing the house. She turned around to take it in again as a whole, holding her breath. She wanted, in part, to feel that same rush of happiness she'd experienced when she first saw it. The sensation was weaker now, but still there, and heat and gratitude rushed through her. This is mine, she thought. I live here now.

Movement caught her eye, high up in one of the windows on the right, and she sought out the spot. The trees were far away from the house, the whole yard and some surrounding area on both sides leveled completely, but for a moment she was certain she'd seen merely the reflection of a branch or a cloud. She couldn't make out anything through the sunlight's glare, and she stepped to the side to avoid the direct path of the light.

A woman stood there in the window upstairs, staring down at her.

Emily's heart leapt, and she froze, so surprised she had to bite her lip to keep from crying out. She put a hand to her chest and laughed a little before lifting it in a wave. The woman continued to stare at her without moving or responding. Emily let her hand drop down at her side, confused, and a moment later the woman turned and disappeared into the room behind her.

Puzzled by this behavior, and curious to see who she was, Emily walked back across the lawn and to the front door, rooting through her key ring for the one to the front door. On impulse, she turned the knob and found the door unlocked. She pushed the door wide and went inside.

She was in a large foyer, and the marble she'd expected to see outside lay here on the floor. It stretched out from the foyer and around a main, central staircase. Near her toward the front of the house stood two sets of double doors, one to her left and one to her right. Farther away, to the left and right of the stairs, she could see more doors. All of them were closed. The stairs that led up were covered in a thick, pattern-less, maroon carpet. She closed the front door behind her, but the huge fanlight transom window over the door and two smaller windows on either side of it let in ample sunlight. She'd left the instructions for finding her bedroom in the car, but she wasn't concerned with that right now. Before she settled in, she wanted to find the woman she'd seen in the window. Clearly one of the others had arrived earlier than expected.

After climbing the stairs, Emily reached a landing from which two smaller sets of stairs led off to the left and right. She took the set to the right, in the general direction from which she'd seen the woman. It led up to a balcony-like platform that ran the length of the house. A short railing on the side overlooked the main foyer and stairs, and four doors to her left were spaced evenly the along the length of the house. Turning around, she peered across and over the main staircase and spotted another balcony at the top of the other set of stairs, to the left of the main landing. It seemed almost identical to the one she was standing on now, but she saw a fifth door on that side. The carpet here on the balcony was, like the stairs, thick, maroon, and fairly new, judging by its condition.

Unsure which door the woman was behind, Emily knocked on every one she walked past, and after she'd hit the last door at the end of the balcony, she tried to open it. It was locked. Confused, she glanced at her key ring but saw only four keys there—one to the front gate, one to the front door, one that was probably for her bedroom, and a smaller key that might be for a mailbox. She didn't have any others.

Emily decided to try the third, larger key, and when it slid into the lock, she somehow wasn't surprised to find that this was the key to her bedroom. She unlocked the door and opened it, once again nearly blinded by the light streaming in from outside.

Hers was a large corner room, with a comfortable sitting area and four chairs around a small round table, a tall wardrobe, and a huge canopied bed. The big, square, purple area rug on the floor complemented the lilac canopy and bedding. The light, canary-yellow walls had been papered with cloth in a paisley design. She touched the wall nearest her and pulled her fingers away a moment later, afraid she might damage it. Velvet paisley on top of silk.

Walking across the room to the window facing the front lawn, she realized she was in the room where she'd seen the woman—from this very window, in fact. The perspective matched completely. But where was the woman? Further, how had she gained access to a locked room unless she had a key? Ruth had told her a couple of staff members would be in and out of the house to tidy up and bring supplies, so that must have been whom she'd seen.

"Hello?" Emily called out. She walked out of her room onto the balcony. "Hello? Is anyone here? I'm Dr. Murray." She felt stupid using her title. She walked farther, back toward the stairs. "But you can call me Emily."

She was at the top of the stairs now and paused, listening. Had she heard footsteps, or were they her own?

Nothing.

"Hello?" she called, louder this time. The house wasn't so big that whoever it had been couldn't hear her—Emily was certain of this. Still, no one replied. Maybe she wasn't supposed to be in my room, Emily thought. Maybe she's afraid she'll get into trouble. From the little she'd seen of her, she'd been fairly young, so maybe this was a new job for her, too.

Emily turned around and tried opening all the other doors along the balcony. The first two were locked, but the third, the one next to hers, opened easily, and she found a small, old-fashioned bathroom, likely the only one on her side of the house. Unlike her bedroom, it had clearly not been renovated, or possibly it had been kept in its original condition for the sake of preservation. A small, stained tub—no shower—and a green porcelain toilet and sink hunched together. An overhead light consisting of a harsh, uncovered bulb hung from a bare wire in the windowless room, its peeling paint a pale, sickly gray.

Considering how nicely the rest of the house had been refurbished—at least what Emily had seen so far—this room seemed out of place, strange. She hoped there was another bathroom somewhere nearby, as she couldn't picture herself using this one except in an emergency. The thought of bathing in this creepy room—naked in that hideous little tub—made her shudder, and she closed the door behind her when she left.

Back downstairs, she decided to explore the rooms to the right of the main stairway first. She found only two doors: one a double set, the second a single close to the back of the house. The doubles led into a nicely decorated sitting room that featured a small upright piano in one corner and a sofa and chairs arranged in various configurations for group gatherings and smaller, more-intimate conversations. Two chairs near the windows faced each other across a little green card table. A well-stocked bar cart stood in a nearby corner. She saw no TV, the only type of media an old record player on a tiny wooden cabinet. The walls were covered in paintings in heavy frames, some portraits and some land and seascapes, all of which looked older, pre-Impressionist. Everything had been done in maroon and gold, with silk wallpaper behind all the paintings.

A small door connected to the only other room on this side of the stairway, and rather than go back through the foyer, Emily walked through it and into the library. It was much darker in here, the windows tiny and high. Bookshelves covered every wall and stretched from floor to ceiling. A wheeled ladder could be pushed around the room to reach the books above.

A surprisingly large, rolltop writing desk sat in the center of the room, but when Emily reached the front of it, she found it closed. She tried to open it and then pulled out her key ring again and slid the last of her keys, the small one, into the lock. It opened easily, and she rolled up the top of the desk to reveal a miracle.

Ruth had prepared her for the Lewis papers, but it was one thing to picture them and another thing entirely to see them firsthand. She found stacks of green file folders stuffed with paper covered in tight, small handwriting. There were also stacks of notebooks, the kind used in schools in the forties and fifties, and flipping one open, Emily saw that these too were filled with handwriting, covering every inch of blank paper inside. This hoard was a treasure trove—so priceless to Lewis scholarship that studies of her work would be forever changed.

She sat down on the old desk chair heavily, exhilaration making her, for a moment, feel almost faint. This project would be a huge undertaking. Despite her misgivings about Jim Peters, the other English professor that would be here this summer, she was suddenly glad he was on his way. She couldn't possibly do this project on her own, not unless she had years to work on it.

The door swung open with such swiftness and silence, Emily wasn't aware it was happening until it did. She had to bite her lip to stop from crying out, and she tensed, digging her fingers into the arms of the chair.

The woman who stood in the doorway was older than Emily by some twenty years, her dark hair striped with gray and piled onto her head in a loose bun. She was wearing a long skirt and a dark blouse, both fine and well-made. Emily knew instantly this wasn't the woman she'd seen in her window. This woman was much older, her hair markedly different. The woman seemed unsurprised to see her here, and it took Emily a moment to realize she was waiting for her to say something.

"Hi?" Emily finally managed, her heart still pounding.

"Hello, Dr. Murray," the woman said. "My apologies for being late. I didn't anticipate that you would be here so early."

"No problem at all." Emily rose and held out her hand. "Please, call me Emily."

The woman shook her hand. "I'm Mrs. Wright, the general housekeeper. Mr. Wright is the gardener. We come on Mondays and Fridays, normally, but Mrs. Bigsby asked me to be here today to greet you and show you around. I take it you've found your bedroom?"

"Yes. It's lovely."

Mrs. Wright turned without comment, and with a small gesture of her hand, she suggested that Emily follow her. Emily got up, but Mrs. Wright paused in the doorway and looked back behind them.

"You might want to lock that," she said, pointing at the desk.

"Of course!" Emily returned to the desk and did as suggested. "Thanks."

The woman continued without further comment, and Emily trailed her silently out of the room and back into the foyer.

"Does your assistant normally come today? On Tuesdays, I mean?" Emily asked.

Mrs. Wright paused and turned her head toward Emily, her eyebrows lowered in apparent confusion. "My assistant? You mean Mr. Wright?"

"No—the younger woman I saw earlier. In my room. Is she normally here on Tuesdays?"

Mrs. Wright turned more fully around to face Emily. "I don't have an assistant, Dr. Murray. No one else works here."

Chapter Four

"B ut you must be mistaken," Emily said, then felt foolish. "I'm sorry. I mean it's just that I saw her. In my room."

"In your room? But how on earth could anyone she be in there? You're the only one with the key besides myself and Mrs. Bigsby."

"Well, the front door was unlocked. Maybe she has her own keys?"

Mrs. Wright's eyebrows lowered even further. "The front door was unlocked? But that's impossible! I locked it myself yesterday."

Emily shrugged. "It was unlocked."

"Was your room locked?"

"Yes."

"What did this woman say? Did she explain why she was in your room?"

Emily hesitated. "I didn't speak to her. I saw her from the front lawn. I waved and then she left." She didn't use the word "disappeared," though that was more or less what the woman had done.

Mrs. Wright's face cleared a little, her expression now a little knowing and skeptical. "I see. Well, perhaps you were mistaken, Dr. Murray."

"How do you mean?"

"Maybe no one was there at all. The light on those windows makes it fairly hard to see inside the house this time of day."

Emily laughed, incredulous. "I know what I saw. And how do you explain the front door?"

Mrs. Wright sighed and shook her head. "That I have no explanation for. I'll have to ask Mr. Wright. Maybe he came inside and forgot to lock up after himself when he left."

"But I saw her!" Her chest felt tight—panic warring with something like anger. Her excitement was obviously making her seem ridiculous, but she was desperate to be believed.

Mrs. Wright seemed impatient now. "And what did this woman look like?"

Emily paused again. She'd seen the woman from a distance, and at an angle, but she'd had a fairly good glimpse of her head and shoulders. "She's pale, maybe in her twenties or early thirties, with dark, long hair. She was wearing a gray shirt, I think. I couldn't see her outfit very clearly, but it was dark and plain."

Mrs. Wright shook her head decisively. "There's no one like that around here, Dr. Murray. It must have been a trick of the light." She turned again and started walking toward the set of double doors on the left side of the stairs. "Please follow me. I'll show you around the dining room, the pantry, and the kitchen."

Emily stood unmoving for a moment until she realized Mrs. Wright had effectively ended the conversation. Either she genuinely believed that Emily had imagined the woman in the window, or she simply didn't want to deal with the repercussions of having, perhaps, left the door unlocked. Either way, for Mrs. Wright, the discussion was over.

"I'm sorry to hurry you, Dr. Murray," Mrs. Wright broke in, "but as I said, this is not my usual day here, and I'm anxious to go home."

Emily let it go for now and followed her into the dining room. The older woman closed the doors behind them, but, like the sitting room and library, the dining room wasn't locked.

The room had a large, twelve-place table made of heavy dark wood that had long since become unfashionable. An enormous, electric chandelier hung above the center of the table, a small serving table was set up on the side, a towering grandfather clock stood in one corner of the room, and a full-length portrait topped the fireplace. Smaller paintings dotted the walls between the windows, very much like in the sitting room.

"The table's a bit grand for regular use," Mrs. Wright explained, "but this room hasn't yet been fully restored. Mrs. Bigsby plans on replacing this table at a later date. As far as I understand, most people in the past, when this house was built, would have eaten their breakfast in their rooms. This room would have been used only for supper."

"Do you know much about that time period? For the house, I mean? What the family was like back then?"

Mrs. Wright shook her head. "I'm not aware of the history, I'm afraid. I'm not from around here. My husband and I were hired long after the writer lady died."

"And no one in town talks about the house?"

Mrs. Wright's eyes darted away from hers. "No one says anything about this place, Dr. Murray. They wouldn't know." She looked strangely guilty.

Emily opened her mouth with a follow-up question, but Mrs. Wright had already turned and was walking toward a door to the right.

"The dining room connects through the pantry into the kitchen. Mr. Wright and I will keep you stocked with basic foods here and in the icebox in the kitchen. If you require anything else, simply let one of us know, and we'll bring it when we return. Of course, you can always pick things up in town yourself if you prefer. I don't do any cooking, and all of you will have to keep the kitchen somewhat tidy. I can do only so much, coming twice a week."

The pantry lay off to the left of the little connecting hallway between the kitchen and dining room. Given the tall ceilings in the house, it too required a ladder to access its various baking, boxed, canned goods, and bread. They walked farther, into the kitchen, which, while clearly updated in the last century, was still old and dark—the kind of room the people who actually lived here would likely have never frequented. The dark-slate floor sloped slightly toward a drain in the center of the room. She noticed a large butcher-block table, an old fridge, an even older gas oven, and no microwave. Two new appliances sat on the counter: a coffeemaker and a toaster.

"Dishes are in those cupboards there," Mrs. Wright pointed, "silverware in the drawers below." She walked toward a small back door that led outside and waited until Emily approached. "Your key to the front door also unlocks this one. You'll find the garage in the back of the house, where you can put your car."

About fifty feet away from the back door, Emily saw an old carriage house with three doors that had been converted to allow entry for cars. With six visitors planned this summer, Emily couldn't imagine how they would all fit.

Mrs. Wright turned around. "Past the gardens, you'll see the path to the greenhouse and the pool. The main house key also opens those locks. I can take you out there if you like." She said this last part with a clear note of reluctance, and Emily had to bite her tongue to keep from laughing. This woman didn't hide how she felt about things.

"That's fine, Mrs. Wright. I'm sure I can find it on my own. It all seems very straightforward. Thanks for the tour."

Mrs. Wright indicated the third doorway in the kitchen before she walked through it. It led back into the main foyer, and they walked together to the foot of the stairs. Mrs. Wright pointed at the third, middle door to the left of the stairs. "You'll find a small powder room there."

Remembering the grim bathroom by her bedroom, Emily asked, "Where are the other bathrooms?"

"Two are on your floor, one on each side of the stairs. There is also one in the attic, but it's not in very good shape."

"There's an attic?"

"Yes. You can access it on the men's side of the house. But I wouldn't recommend going up there, especially alone."

"Is it unsafe?"

Mrs. Wright seemed momentarily confused and shook her head. "No—I wouldn't say that. Dirty, but not unsafe. It hasn't been renovated yet, and it's full of a lot of the old furniture and fixtures from the rest of the house from over the years. No one goes up there."

"I see."

Mrs. Wright paused and then moved toward the front door. "Well, I'll be off then. I trust that you can give the others the same tour should anyone arrive before Friday, when I'm back. I collect laundry on Fridays and return it on Monday. You'll find a laundry bag in your wardrobe."

Mrs. Wright's hand was on the front doorknob when Emily said, "Wait." The woman turned toward her with a look of wariness. "I did see someone in my window, Mrs. Wright. In my bedroom. I didn't imagine her."

Mrs. Wright shook her head, her face pinched with impatience. "It's impossible, Dr. Murray. No one else is here."

"She was here."

Mrs. Wright shook her head again and left, closing the door behind her with more force than necessary. Emily assumed she was angry with the implications of this mystery woman. It meant that she'd been neglectful and left the door unlocked. But Emily could give a damn about that. Someone had been here and left. Or, worse, someone was still here. Hiding.

She shuddered and rubbed her arms to dismiss the goose bumps on them. She was not a superstitious person, had never believed in anything like ghosts or spirits, but she did have an acute phobia of being watched or listened to without her knowledge. And, now that she was alone, she couldn't stop that feeling from creeping over her, a tingling suggestion that someone stood just behind her, staring at her back.

"Get it together, Murray," she told herself. Whomever she'd seen would eventually appear and explain herself.

All of these closed doors didn't help matters. Anything—or anyone—could be behind them. And they blocked the light. She opened the two sets of double doors—those into the dining and sitting rooms, and the effect was immediate. The feeling of being watched disappeared, and the light was much better. Both rooms had seemed a little stuffy, as well, so this would help air them out.

"That's better," she told the rooms.

She decided to get her luggage and then park her car in the garage. She at least had the benefit of not worrying about parking since she was here first. She grabbed her small suitcase and laptop from her trunk, put them inside the main door, and then drove over to the garage. The door rose from the ground and was difficult to hoist it on her own, but she managed. Her car barely fit inside the tiny stall, and she had to turn sideways to scoot around it and back outside. Anyone with a larger car would be out of luck, anyway. She closed the garage door and walked around to the front of the house again to get her bags.

She was halfway up the stairs, luggage in either hand, when she stopped, her heart seizing. For a moment, she stood there, frozen. An icy sweat broke out on her arms and neck, and she hunched over as if to protect herself. Slowly, moving a fraction of an inch at a time, she turned her head and peered back down into the foyer below her, afraid to see what her brain had registered a few seconds late.

The doors to the sitting and dining rooms were closed.

CHAPTER FIVE

Juniper Friend made a mean G&T, just the way Emily liked it. The flavor of the tonic was there, but not overwhelming, the strength of the drink relying entirely on gin and lime. She'd also added the right amount of ice, neither too much nor too little. Normally, when Emily ordered this cocktail in a bar, she prepared herself to be disappointed, but this one was better than any she could have made herself.

Juniper raised her eyebrows. "Is it good?"

Emily almost made a joke linking Juniper with gin, but she stopped herself. "Mmmm. Perfect."

Juniper responded with a wide smile, dazzling on her pretty features. This type of woman usually intimidated Emily—classically pretty, effortlessly graceful, tall and athletic. She had high cheekbones, creamy café-au-lait skin, dark eyes, and thick, enviable eyebrows and lashes. She dressed well, looking every bit like a woman cast as an art historian in film. But instead of making her nervous, Juniper had managed to put Emily immediately at ease. In the hour she'd been here, she already seemed like an old friend. She was intimate without being probing, nice without seeming phony. In a word, like her name, friendly. This smile, however, was disarming, and Emily's face heated. She looked away.

"I'm glad you like it," Juniper said. "I was a bartender once. In college."

"Oh?" Emily had a hard time picturing this woman—a lady if there ever was one—inside some dirty bar.

Juniper laughed. "For a summer. It was awful. But it paid for a study-abroad trip, so it was worth it."

"Where did you go?"

"Italy. Florence, mainly, but Rome and Venice, too. It was wonderful. All that art…"

Her eyes grew distant, and she stared out the window, clearly remembering the trip. It was hard not to stare at her.

"Have you been abroad much?" Juniper suddenly asked.

She shook her head and then shrugged. "A little. I did a semester in London in college. I've been back a few times to visit friends. I went to Paris for a few days. Not much besides that. That's the problem with studying American literature, I guess." She laughed to cover her embarrassment. She didn't want this woman to consider her some kind of rube.

Juniper didn't seem to notice her discomfort. Her face was grave. "That's a shame. I think you'd love Italy." Juniper peered at her closely. "You actually kind of look Italian—a lot of women over there are petite like you. Are you? Italian, I mean?"

Emily shook her head, almost reluctant. "Irish."

Juniper's expression cleared. "That explains your complexion."

"My pallor, you mean?"

Juniper grinned. "I wouldn't say that—pale, maybe, but not pallid." She stepped closer. "And gray eyes. Pretty."

Emily flushed and looked away, too embarrassed to acknowledge the flattery. She turned her attention to her drink and the window. Juniper's car was still parked in front of the house. When she'd heard the car's engine on the road, she had raced downstairs, flinging open the front door before Juniper had even parked. She'd been so happy simply to hear another person that she hadn't thought how she must have appeared when Juniper finally got out of the car. Desperate, maybe.

"How long did you say you've been here?" Juniper asked.

"A couple of days. I got here Tuesday." It seemed longer. Thinking back on the last two days, Emily could hardly believe it had been less than forty-eight hours since she first saw the house.

Juniper shivered dramatically. "I can't imagine how you stayed here on your own."

"Oh?" Emily's heart rate picked up. Maybe she knew something. "Why?"

Juniper shrugged. "Oh, no reason. I just hate being by myself."

After Juniper had gotten out of her car and they'd introduced themselves, Emily had helped her find her bedroom—the one closest to hers, in the end—and given her the penny tour of the house. She'd been rattling on about it, answering questions about herself, and asking almost as many. If Juniper had noticed anything strange about the manic way she was behaving, she hadn't let on. They'd finished in the sitting room, and Juniper had immediately offered to make cocktails.

"So how is it?" Juniper asked. "The house, I mean. It doesn't look like a haunted house, with all of these windows and sunshine, but it is in the middle of nowhere. Have you heard any bumps in the night? Seen anything strange?"

She opened her mouth to reply and then closed it. What should she say? After the first evening, with the mystery woman in the window and the doors closing on their own, things had calmed down. She'd thrown herself into the Margot Lewis papers immediately—the same evening she arrived—and hadn't stopped since. She found the library too confining and dark and had carried the journals up to her bedroom, where the light and space were better. After a deep sleep her first night, she'd worked all day yesterday. Except for the occasional sensation of being watched, nothing had happened after the doors had closed on their own. Until this morning.

After her experience with Mrs. Wright, she wanted to hedge her bets, so she lifted her shoulders. "Nothing really happened. Nothing that can't be explained, anyway."

Juniper's eyes lit up, and she leaned closer. "But something did?"

Again, she shrugged, unable to meet Juniper's eyes. After a long, awkward pause, Juniper laughed. "I'm sorry. I don't mean to pry. Forget I asked."

She stared at her, suddenly desperate to tell her everything, afraid now that she might not get another chance, but Juniper had looked to the side, out the front window. She was squinting against the sun, as if trying to see far away, and then Emily heard it, too. A car, somewhere in the distance. The sound was very distinct on the gravel road on this side of the gate—a kind of popping snap in addition to an engine.

"That's strange," Emily said. "No one else is supposed to be here until Monday."

"Maybe they decided to come early."

Emily couldn't help but feel a little disappointed. Having met Juniper, she'd already begun to look forward to the next couple of days on their own. She was suddenly hot with shame and glanced at Juniper again to see if she'd sensed her thoughts. She was still watching the driveway.

The car appeared a moment later and paused at the far side of the lawn, just as Emily had done when she'd first seen the house. A moment later the car started again and drove around the lawn and parked behind Juniper's SUV. She and Juniper got up and walked into the foyer. Emily had found a heavy umbrella stand she used to prop open one of the double doors for the sitting room, and it was working. So far, the door stayed open.

Juniper opened the front door right as two men climbed out of a large sedan. Both of them stretched, and Jim, whom Emily recognized immediately, jumped up and down a couple of times as if to wake up. Both men spotted them simultaneously, and Jim broke into a broad grin.

"Emily Murray, as I live and breathe." He waved a hand in front of his face and then laughed. "I saw your name on the list of guests this summer and almost didn't believe it."

The others were watching them, clearly confused, and Emily forced a laugh. "Nice to see you too, Jim."

"Hello," Juniper said, holding out a hand to him. "I'm Juniper Friend. You can call me June. Everyone does."

Emily felt a stab of betrayal. June hadn't suggested that Emily use her nickname.

"Hi, June. Nice to meet you." Jim shook her hand. He used his free hand to push his sunglasses on top of his shaggy, blond head, revealing the rest of his handsome face. While Emily would call Jim more of a colleague than a friend, she had been around him socially enough at various conferences and gatherings in their field to know that he was something of a ladies' man. At one Modernist Studies meeting a few years back in Las Vegas, if she remembered correctly, she'd seen him head back to his room with no less than four different women on different nights. Emily glanced at June to see how she'd react to him, but she seemed simply friendly, not interested.

Jim's face fell, but he quickly recovered. "Oh, sorry," he said, sweeping his hand toward the other man, "this guy is my old friend, Mark Somner, architect-historian extraordinaire."

Mark walked around the side of the car to shake hands. He was a little older than the rest of them, perhaps in his late forties, the hair gray around his temples. He was black and enormously tall and broad, his hand so large it encircled Emily's completely. He had a short beard and a stylish pair of thick-framed glasses.

"So very nice to meet you both," he said, his voice low, quiet.

"Mark and I decided to head up together a few days early," Jim explained. "I was already in New York, visiting my sister, and he'd already offered to drive us here. I was going to go to a concert this weekend but decided to sell my tickets instead. So here we are."

"How do you two know each other?" Emily asked.

The men shared a glance, and Jim raised an eyebrow. "Friends of friends, I guess. My sister married an architect, and I think we met at a party. We've known each other for years. When Ruth asked if I had contacts with anyone in architecture, I knew Mark was the guy."

"This house is incredible," Mark said. He walked away from them a little and stood looking up at it. "It's not at all like I expected. How is it inside?"

"Bright," June said.

"Big," Emily added, and everyone laughed.

Jim grinned. "Well, let's go inside and get acquainted, and we can let the expert get his first look at the place. I detect a note of gin in the air, and I can't say I'd mind a little tipple myself."

"I think that can be arranged," June said, grinning.

Emily's heart sank. June seemed to be flirting with him after all. She swallowed her hurt, ashamed of herself, and made herself say, "She makes the best gin and tonic I've ever had."

"With a name like Juniper, one would hope so!"

At this joke, June let out a long, pealing laugh, her head thrown back. Emily kicked herself for not making that joke earlier.

Jim seemed to take this laugh as due credit, his face bright and grinning as he watched June. He gestured dramatically at the door. "Shall we? Mark and I've been on the road all day."

Emily started to follow them inside but paused, waiting for Mark, who was lagging behind. He'd walked some distance away and was standing in the center of the lawn, staring up at the house. Emily saw something strange in his expression, but he shook his head a moment later and walked toward her.

"It's funny," he said as they went inside.

"What?"

"I could have sworn I saw…" He shook his head again and met her eyes. "It's only the four of us here so far, right?"

Emily's heart leapt, and she stopped in the doorway to the sitting room. "Why do you ask?"

"No reason, really. I thought I saw someone. Up in the corner room on the second floor."

"What's this?" Jim asked. He held out a cocktail for each of them.

Mark took his and drank half of it at once—a small mouthful for a man his size, Emily supposed. "I'm sure it was nothing, but I thought I saw someone in the window upstairs. A woman."

June and Jim glanced at each other and then back at Mark. Already, there seemed to be something between them. Emily's stomach dropped with disappointment, and she looked away quickly and back at Mark. "I've seen her, too."

All three of them were turned to her, and she swallowed before continuing. "The first day I was here. In the same window. That's my room, actually."

"You never said!" June said, seeming put out. "You said everything had been normal."

Emily shrugged. "I didn't know how to tell you. I didn't want to sound—"

"Crazy?" Jim laughed and held up his free hand. "Sorry. But really, how could someone be here? How could she get in? Have you seen her again?"

"No. And I haven't heard her, either. I only saw her that one time, the first time I saw the house from the lawn."

Mark's eyebrows were low, his face pinched with concern. He lifted his palms. "I'm not sure what I saw, really. It was brief—a glimpse of a woman's face, or what I thought was a face. It could have been a trick of the light."

June sighed and grabbed Emily's hand. "Don't listen to the skeptics, Emily." She pulled her over to the sofa, and they sat down next to each other, their legs touching. June put a hand on her knee, and Emily jumped. "Tell us everything that's happened. I knew you were hiding something earlier."

The men had taken the two armchairs across from the little table in front of them, and Emily glanced around at them. Mark seemed interested, solemn even, but Jim's face was a mask of incredulity. June's expression was open and attentive, and Emily decided to look at her as she told her story.

"Well, first it was the face in the window. A younger woman—maybe in her twenties, early thirties. White, dark hair." She glanced at Mark, and he nodded as if in agreement. She turned back to June. "Of course, the housekeeper said I must have imagined it, that no one could get inside without a key, but the thing is, the front door was unlocked."

"What did the housekeeper say about that?" Mark asked.

"She claimed it was impossible. She locked the door when she left the day before."

"She would say that," June said, rolling her eyes. "What else happened?"

Emily hesitated. It was one thing to tell them about the face in the window—Mark had seen it, too. The rest of it, however, was a little harder to describe. She met June's eyes, and June smiled at her, giving her courage to go on.

She swallowed. "Next it was the doors."

"What happened with them?" Jim asked.

"They closed on their own."

Jim laughed and leaned back in his chair. "I can think of a million explanations for that."

"Which doors closed, Emily?" Mark asked, ignoring him.

"The ones to this room," Emily said, pointing, "and the other double doors into the dining room. That's why I have the umbrella stand there."

Mark got to his feet and walked over to the door to the sitting room. The double doors swung inward from the middle. Mark leaned down and moved the umbrella stand, and all them sat there, silently watching. Nothing happened.

"Strange," Mark said, swinging the door experimentally. "It's weighted here on the edge, so it should stay open."

"So the wind closed it," Jim said, rolling his eyes. "Give me a break."

Mark shook his head and then pulled the second of the double doors, leaving both open. "We'll leave these like this for now. Then we can see what happens."

"You'd have to do the same with the ones across the hall to make it a true experiment," Jim said.

Mark gave him a level stare and then did as suggested before sitting down across from Emily and June again. Emily couldn't help but stare at the doors for a moment, and when she glanced at June, she saw concern there—pity, almost—and realized this had been a mistake. She shouldn't have said anything about the doors or the woman in the window. They were all going to think she'd lost her mind. She could give a damn what Jim thought of her, but she liked Mark instinctually. As for June...

"Go on, Emily. You're holding back." June gave her hand a quick squeeze, and Emily couldn't help the rush of happy heat that flashed through her.

"Well, it was quiet after that."

"What was quiet?" Jim asked. "The house?"

"Give it a rest, Jim." Mark frowned. "Let Emily finish."

Jim looked as if he might object, but he sighed and went back to his drink.

"It was quiet," Emily said, "until this morning."

"What happened this morning?" June asked.

What had happened? Emily wondered, and not for the first time. She had gotten into bed last night, closing the canopy around her. She'd made the mistake of skipping that step her first night and had been woken very early yesterday by the incredibly bright sunlight streaming into her room at six that morning. Last night, she'd been sure she shut it—certain of it. She remembered using her reading light before she turned it off, the one that clipped onto her book, and feeling like she was inside a cozy little tent in the woods.

She'd gone to sleep, and then what? Had she gotten up in the middle of the night?

The others waited for her to continue, and Emily laughed nervously. "The canopy on my bed opened on its own."

There was a long pause. Now even June looked skeptical. Once again, Emily kicked herself. They were going to think she was, in fact, insane.

"You can't be serious," Jim said.

Emily sighed. "You'll see when you go into your own rooms. The curtains on the windows don't block the light. All the beds have canopies—at least mine and June's do, so I'm assuming yours will, too. Last night I made sure I closed the canopy. When I woke up this morning, all three sides of it were wide open."

"You didn't hear them open?" June asked.

Emily shook her head. "That was the worst part. They're pretty loud and heavy, and I'm a light sleeper. I should have heard something."

The others shared a glance before looking at Emily again, as if waiting for an explanation. She held her hands up. "That's it. That's all that happened."

"Christ," Jim said, getting to his feet. Everyone jumped at his curse, but he didn't apologize. He walked across the room to the little bar and poured himself another drink—straight gin. He turned back to them, smiling broadly. "You really had me going there for a minute, guys." He laughed. "Damn! You're a fast one, Emily. I leave you alone outside with Mark for what, two minutes? And the two of you come up with this? I'll give you both credit—you're good actors."

June was looking back and forth between Mark and Emily, plainly confused, and Emily went hot with anger. She jumped up, hands clenched, and Mark touched her arm. She met his eyes, and he shook his head, almost imperceptibly. Her anger died. Perhaps he was right. Maybe letting Jim believe this was all a gag was better. After all, she had to work with him this summer.

Jim set his drink down on top of the record player and clapped. "So. Are you two ladies going to show me around this place, or do I have to do it on my own?"

June threw Emily one more probing glance and rose. "I'll show you. It's a big house, but not so big you'll get lost. You'll need your key if you want to get into your room."

Jim turned to Mark. "What say you? Want to get our stuff in and poke around a little? Get the lay of the land and all that?"

"Sure." Mark got to his feet. "Give us the grand tour. Let me grab my bags and the keys."

Emily and June followed them outside as they unpacked the car. Jim had apparently brought his entire wardrobe with him, as suitcase after suitcase was retrieved from the trunk. All of them, including Mark, were forced to grab a bag or two to help.

Once they were back inside, Jim said, "Ha, ha, very funny."

"What's funny?" June asked.

"You closed the doors," he said, gesturing with a suitcase.

He was right. All four of the doors had closed again.

"But I didn't do that!" June said. "And neither did Emily. I was with her the whole time."

"Sure you didn't," Jim said, rolling his eyes. He headed toward the stairs. "Any idea what side our rooms are on, Emily? You've been here the longest."

"You should be on the left. Men on the left, women on the right."

Jim laughed and took the second set of stairs to the left off the main landing. Emily started up, and June touched her shoulder.

"I know you didn't close the doors, Emily."

A rush of gratitude swept through her so deep, she felt like crying.

"I didn't even hear them," June said, her face troubled. "And we were right there. The front door was open the whole time. We should have heard them."

The two of them looked at Mark, who had heard this exchange, and he raised his eyebrows. He set the three suitcases he was holding down on the ground and walked over to the dining-room doors. He opened one of them as wide as it would go and then pushed it gently closed from the inside. The sound of the door latching was loud and distinct. They couldn't have missed the sound from just outside the front door. Mark came out of the dining room a moment later and shut the door gently behind him, but again, that latching sound was harsh and echoed in the empty, marble foyer.

"I don't understand," June said.

Mark frowned. "I don't understand it myself. Those doors aren't even easy to move. I'll have to examine them closer once we've settled in a little. Maybe some kind of cross wind pulls them closed when they're both open." He met their eyes. "For now, however, let's keep this to ourselves, if you don't mind. Jim doesn't seem to want to hear about any of this."

Emily and June reluctantly agreed and then followed him up the stairs with the various suitcases to the men's rooms. Emily couldn't help but glance behind them a few times. If she didn't watch the doors, she might miss whatever or whoever was closing them. She managed to wrench her eyes away only when she was safely at the top of the stairs.

CHAPTER SIX

Before the others arrived, Emily had taken to eating in the sitting room. The first day, she sat down with her dinner in the dining room and felt ridiculous and dwarfed by the huge table. She'd picked up her plate and moved it into the sitting room and had eaten every meal in there since. The morning after the others arrived, however, Emily came downstairs and heard the three of them chatting and eating in the dining room without her. She opened the door, and all of them stopped talking and turned her way. There was a long beat of silence.

"Good morning."

"Good morning!" June said. "Had a bit of a lie-in?"

Emily glanced at the grandfather clock. It was just after eight—hardly what she'd call sleeping in. "I guess so."

"Mark and I were up with the birds. You were right about the canopy—I should have closed it before I went to sleep. We've already taken a walk. Jim cooked breakfast while we were out."

"Quiche Lorraine," Jim said, gesturing at the side table. "Help yourself. You'll find some toast, fruit, juice, and coffee there, too."

Emily was more of an oatmeal or cereal person in the morning, but it would be rude to turn down the food. The others continued their earlier conversation, and a strange sense of loneliness settled over her as she served herself. She'd always had difficulty making friends, but she'd somehow believed this summer might be different. Everyone here was an expert of some kind, and all of them were academics, if from different fields. She'd felt a real connection with June, too, and that was unusual, especially with women. But, as usual, she was an outsider.

When she turned around, June was watching her, and Emily thought she saw pity in her expression, similar to when she was telling them about the strange goings-on at the house. The pity disappeared a moment later when their eyes met, and June smiled at her and patted the seat next to hers.

"Sit here, Emily. Like the bedrooms—boys on one side, girls on the other."

"You have to wonder what that's all about," Jim said, buttering a piece of toast. "It's like someone's worried we'll fraternize out here on our own without chaperones."

"Won't we?" June said, one eyebrow raised.

Emily went cold and peered down at her breakfast to avoid watching this exchange. She could hardly stand to watch them flirt. The food, already unappealing, was now completely unappetizing, but she made herself pick up a piece of plain toast and eat it.

"Oh, say, Emily," June said, laying a hand on hers. Emily jumped, and June removed it, looking startled.

"Sorry," Emily mumbled.

"That's all right. I was going to ask if you'd like to go exploring. Mark and I walked around the gardens a little, but I still haven't seen the pool or the greenhouse."

Emily opened her mouth to decline, the Margot Lewis work already commanding her attention, but when she met June's smile, her refusal died away. After all, she had the whole summer to work.

"I'd love to."

June's face lit up with her dazzling smile, and Emily warmed from within. "Great! I'll go grab my sweater. It's a little chilly out there today. You should be okay, though, in those heavy clothes."

Emily glanced down at herself, having forgotten her outfit, and then watched June, clad in only shorts and a T-shirt, leave the room. She hadn't realized she was staring until she looked back at the men. Mark was absorbed in his breakfast, but Jim was watching her, a smile twisting his lips.

She broke eye contact and tried to go back to her food, her stomach now a knot.

"Have you seen the Lewis papers already?" Jim asked.

She managed to smile. "They're incredible. You're not going to believe how much material I found." She paused. "I forgot to mention that I took the papers up to my room."

His face darkened and he leaned forward. "You did what? Why?"

Startled, she stammered, "It's hard to see in the library."

"Why didn't you take them into the sitting room?"

Emily hesitated. She didn't have a good explanation. "Didn't think of it, I guess."

"Well, I want to see all of them." His voice had risen now, and Emily was surprised to see his fists clenched around his fork and knife. "It's our project, Emily, not just yours. I have a right to see all of it. More, even, considering."

"What's going on?" June said behind them. She held a cardigan in one hand and her keys in the other.

"Emily has commandeered Margot Lewis's papers in her room." His face was cold, and he was glaring at her.

"I did no such thing!" Emily couldn't keep a note of petulance from her voice. "Really, Jim, I meant nothing by it. I'll bring all of them back downstairs, if that's what you want."

"There, Jim," June said, her voice soothing. "Problem solved. She'll do it when we get back."

"I want to see them now." He still sounded upset.

"Jesus, Jim, are you serious?" June asked. She gave Emily an incredulous look. "Do you have your keys, Emily?"

She dug them out of a pocket. June took them from her and handed them to Jim. "There. Satisfied now?"

Jim seemed a little shamefaced, but he didn't apologize. Instead, he asked Emily, "You don't mind if I go in your room without you?"

Emily did, but she wasn't about to say so. "Help yourself. Everything's on the table in my room."

He grunted without saying another word, and she shared another look with June and Mark. They both had their eyebrows raised, clearly wondering, like she was, what the hell that was all about.

June rolled her eyes and grinned. "You ready, lady? Let's get going before it starts raining. Want to come along, Mark?"

Emily noted that she'd pointedly not invited Jim, but she was disappointed that Mark was included. She'd hoped they would be on their own.

Mark shook his head. "No. I want to start on my sketches today, but I have a couple of phone calls to make first. I need to figure out where the architectural plans for the house were filed."

"Your loss! Shall we?"

Triumphant, Emily rose and followed June outside through the front door. The day was, in fact, much colder than she'd anticipated, and she almost asked June if she could run inside for her own sweater, but she didn't. She wouldn't want to inconvenience her. June was still holding her sweater, clearly not cold enough for it, so Emily simply hurried along after her as they walked around the edge of the house. She realized, as they rounded the corner, that she hadn't been outside since she put her car in the garage. She hadn't, in fact, explored at all, and she might never have thought of it if not for June.

They both stopped at the sight of an older man digging in the dirt in one of the formal gardens. He spotted them and got slowly to his feet before walking over, removing a dirty leather glove and holding out his hand. His face was kindly, warm, and open.

"Hello there. Sorry if I startled you. I'm Mr. Wright, the groundskeeper."

"I'm June and this is Emily." They all shook hands.

"Glad to meet you. The wife's running behind today, but she'll be here soon to tidy up inside."

June glanced around. "I didn't hear you arrive, Mr. Wright. Where did you park?"

"I always ride a bicycle. Nice to get a bit of exercise." He glanced down at her cardigan. "The two of you off on a walk, then?"

"We're going to check out the greenhouse and the pool. Just exploring."

He pointed off into the woods. "You'll find both of them out that way. Can't miss the trail."

"Strange that they're so far from the house," Emily said.

He shrugged. "I don't know why myself. The pool was a later addition, but the greenhouse, or a version of it anyway, has been here from the beginning. Might have something to do with ruining the view from the house, but I'm not certain."

Emily and June excused themselves and headed off around the edge of one of the formal gardens and toward the woods. As they approached, a sickly sense of dread suddenly clenched Emily's stomach. From afar, the woods simply offered a green background to the yard and the house. Close up, when she could see individual trees, all of them appeared to be bunched together and broke the line of sight. They resembled menacing sentinels, a wall to ward off trespassers.

Emily paused, and June turned around, one eyebrow raised. "What's up?"

She shook her head. "Nothing. I had a strange feeling. The woods are different here."

June looked back at them. "They are. Wilder. Older, somehow. We are pretty far north. I don't think this area has ever been cultivated or trimmed back. Some of these trees are probably older than the state of New York."

They stood there a moment longer and then started walking again. The path to the greenhouse and pool was almost impossible to see until you were on it. A few steps farther and the house and gardens completely disappeared behind a curve. The sunlight, which was already pale today because of the clouds, nearly winked out, and Emily and June shared a wide-eyed glance in the near-darkness.

"Jeez," June said, slipping on her sweater and shivering. "It's like a cave back here."

"At least the trail is maintained," Emily said, and it was. Like the road leading to the main gate and beyond, the trail was nicely groomed with clean gravel, the trees cut back well away from the path. The path itself was about five feet across, white stones on black earth, the woods trimmed back about that distance on either side and above.

"That old guy has his work cut out for him," June said, shaking her head. "He must have help. I can't imagine how he could do all this on his own."

After less than a minute's walk, they reached a wide clearing. Two large, glass-ceilinged structures had been erected here about fifty yards apart, but it was clear which was which. The greenhouse had been constructed of large, frosted-glass panels on the sides and top, each piece of glass divided by heavy black lead. The pool house had wooden walls with frosted-glass panels for a roof.

"Wow!" June said. "Imagine these glass buildings surviving out here in the woods like this. Too weird!"

Emily was too surprised to respond. With the summer storms and snow this area must get, it was hard to believe these structures had lasted so long.

"Want to look at the pool first?" June asked.

Emily nodded, happy to go along with whatever June wanted.

"I didn't bring my suit, but I'm excited to get in later when it warms up again. I love swimming."

"Me too," Emily said, lying. She hadn't been swimming in over a decade.

"When I heard there was a pool, I wasn't expecting anything like this big place. I thought maybe we'd find a little ten-footer somewhere out here."

"It's unexpected, that's for sure."

June used her key to unlock the door to the pool house, and they entered a large, light-filled, atrium-like room. The ceiling, almost entirely glass, let in a dazzling amount of sunshine despite the clouds. The pool was in the center of the room, the bottom tiled in a beautifully colored mosaic of blue and yellow floral patterns. A wide area around all sides of the pool contained Adirondack and lounge chairs. On the far side of the room was a door in the center of the wall, but that was the only other door besides the one they'd walked in.

"Holy shit," June breathed.

Emily was too awestruck to speak. The place was dreamlike and gorgeous, almost difficult to absorb.

June walked over to the pool, slipped off a sandal, and dipped a toe into the water. She smiled at Emily, her face lighting up. "It's heated!" She took off her other sandal and sat down at the edge of the pool, dangling her lower legs in the water. "Come on, Emily, join me! The water's amazing."

Emily looked down at her shoes and pants, not sure how this would work, but she automatically started untying her laces. She slipped off her socks and shoes, embarrassed a little to show her pale feet, then rolled up the bottom of her pants. She could hardly get them up to mid-calf, but she went directly to the water and sat down, dipping her feet in as far as she could without soaking her pants.

June shrugged off her cardigan, flinging it onto a nearby chair, and then leaned back onto her hands and closed her eyes. She tilted her face at the ceiling as if to soak in the light, and her lips curled into a happy, lazy smile. Emily followed the edge of her exposed neck with her eyes all the way to the top of her T-shirt. With June's head and shoulders thrown back and her chest thrust out, Emily couldn't resist gazing there for a second before looking away, her face hot. She'd relaxed her legs too much, and now, as expected, the rolls of material were wet.

Suddenly one of June's hands found hers, and Emily jumped, startled. June was grinning at her, her eyes twinkling merrily. "I regret not bringing my suit now." She gestured around them. "But then again, it is just the two of us. We could get in anyway."

"In our clothes?"

June laughed, her head thrown back. "No, silly. I mean, we could get in anyway. Without our clothes."

Emily went cold and then hot, a sweat breaking out from every pore. She opened her mouth and then closed it, her throat too dry to speak. Some of her shock must have shown on her face, as June laughed again and squeezed her hand. "It's okay, Emily. I was only joking."

Emily felt the chance slipping away, and again, she opened her mouth to reply, desperate now to salvage the situation. She was always like this—she always let what she wanted elude her.

A crash from somewhere to their right made them jump and look in that direction.

"What the hell was that?" June asked, now clutching Emily's hand.

Emily shook her head, her heart racing. "I don't know. I think it came from behind that little door over there."

"Is it a bathroom, do you think?"

"Maybe."

"Should we go check it out?"

Emily made herself nod. June seemed as scared as she was, but Emily could be brave, when needed. "We should. If something's broken, Mr. Wright will want to know."

June's eyes were wild and frightened, so when Emily stood, she helped her up. "I'm sure it's nothing."

June frowned. "If you say so."

Emily led the way, still holding June's hand. She would continue to hold it as long as June let her. As they approached the door she slowed, suddenly afraid of what they might see in there. The sound had been loud, like something big falling over. Maybe a bear or another animal had gotten inside. It would be stupid to open the door.

She was about to suggest this precaution and then hardened her resolve. June was counting on her. Using her free hand, she tried the door handle. It was similar to the ones found on industrial refrigerators. She had to pull on it to release it from the latch, but it opened easily. She paused again and then yanked the door open with all her might. Rather than slamming back against the wall, however, the door opened only a couple of feet. It was heavy and thick.

It was a relatively large, tiled room, and it took her a moment to understand she was seeing a steam room. Opening the door had triggered a light inside the room, and it flickered a few times before shining brightly from above. A drain lay in the center of the floor, and the far side of the room had two tiers of built-in seats. A large metal object, a little like a large cooking pot, was lying on its side next to the floor drain. One look at it explained the noise they'd heard.

"What is that thing?" June asked behind her.

"I don't know." Emily stepped farther into the room. She looked up at the ceiling and pointed at a chain hanging from the center of the room. "I think it was attached to that and fell."

"It fell? Just like that? Right when we were in the other room?" June shook her head. "That's a strange coincidence."

Emily walked farther into the room, and June released her hand, staying in the partially opened doorway. She leaned down and picked up the metal pot, surprised by its weight. She carried it back to June, and the two of them examined it closer. After a moment, June took it from her and peered at it carefully.

"That's strange," she said.

"What? What is it?"

June shook her head. "It's funny, but I think it's a bronze hanging bowl. I've seen a few of them over the years in museums. I took a class on Celtic art in graduate school, but I can't imagine what it's doing here." She pointed out a relief punched into the metal. "It even has the patterns characteristic of some Celtic peoples—flowers and waves in this case. La Tène influence, if I remember correctly. Usually that kind of piece has three rings for hanging, but this one has only this one in the center." She frowned at Emily. "Why on earth would this be in here?"

Emily walked back to examine the chain more closely. "There's a hook here at the end. The bowl must fall off all the time, given how heavy it is."

June's fear had dissipated with the mystery, and she entered the steam room. She lifted the hanging bowl and set it back on the hook. It swung there for a moment before coming to a stop, hanging in the center of the room at about chest level.

June looked at Emily, her eyebrows up. "What on earth?"

"I can't imagine. I mean, it's metal, right? Wouldn't it rust in here?"

"Too weird." June peered around the room. "Still, this place is really great. I love steam rooms. I wonder how you turn it on." She walked across the little room and sat down on the tiled seat, resting her arms on the step behind her. She patted the spot next to her, and Emily immediately went and sat down.

June grinned. "I could get used to a daily swim and steam. Sure beats teaching summer classes. This is the life." She closed her eyes again, relaxing backward, resting the back of her head on the step behind her.

Emily was perched on the edge of her seat, staring around her curiously. The mechanism for the steam hung high above on the ceiling next to the neon lights. The ceiling in this room was the only part of the building she'd seen that wasn't glass. It was covered with the same tile they were sitting on and seemed much closer than the glass ceiling in the atrium with the pool. They had entered the pool house on the far side from where they were now, so she hadn't seen the steam room from the outside. Sitting here, she imagined that it would look like a little brick building next to the larger pool house. It might have been added later, as an afterthought, or perhaps it was simply necessary to build it this way to trap the steam.

The two of them were only perhaps ten feet from the door, the hanging bowl about midway between them, and Emily might still have had a chance to stop it if she'd reacted right away, but, as she watched the door swing shut, she felt rooted to the spot. When she'd opened it, the door had swung into the pool house, away from where they sat inside now, so in order to close it, you would need to push it closed from the outside. It had been partially closed since they came in, so it didn't have far to move. The sound of the door latching made them both jump.

June clutched her chest and laughed, weakly. "Jesus. What is it with the doors around here?"

Emily's heart was still racing. June obviously hadn't seen the door close. Anyone that had would realize that it simply couldn't have done so on its own. Someone must have pushed it from the outside. June didn't need to know this.

"Let's get out of here," Emily said, jumping to her feet. She tried to keep her voice calm. "I need to get to work sometime today."

June sighed. "Yeah. I guess you're right. Now, in addition to all that Romantic art in the house, I'm going to have to figure out what the heck that thing is doing in here." She pointed at the hanging bowl. "It couldn't possibly be genuine. If it was, it would be locked up inside the house. No one would keep something so priceless out here hanging in a stream room. I'm sure it's a replica, so that will mean some digging to figure it out." She stood and stretched. "Think we have enough time to poke inside the greenhouse for a minute?"

Emily's heart was still tripping around in her chest. She kept seeing the door close, as if on a mental loop. More than anything, she simply wanted to get out of here and back to the safety of the house. Still, she didn't need to make this little outing a complete disaster. She needed to stay cool, collected. "Sure. We can check it out."

She'd seen door mechanisms like the one on the inside of the door in a restaurant she worked at in college. Instead of a pulling handle, like the one on the outside, the handle in here was a large circle intended to be pushed to unlatch the door. The door, on the whole, had been designed very much like a large refrigerator, probably in order to seal in the heat. She reached for the handle, and when she touched it, she suddenly knew what would happen next.

It wouldn't move. They were locked in.

She turned to June and must have looked as frightened as she felt. June's eyes grew larger, and she moved Emily, none too gently, out of the way and tried the door. She pulled and pushed at the knob, desperately, then turned back to Emily.

"We're locked in!" she said.

Emily had taken a few steps away from her and the door. Her palms were damp and her heart wouldn't slow down. A tingling numbness that started in her fingers quickly spread up her arms. The air around them seemed to constrict, and she gulped, painfully, for breath. Her vision dimmed a little, and she swayed. A moment later June launched herself forward and grabbed her by the shoulders.

"Whoa, there," June said, and directed her over to the tiled bench.

Her knees hit the edge and she sat down heavily, almost collapsing.

"Hey, Emily, hey," June said, her voice low and calm. She'd sat down next to her and taken her hand. "It's going to be okay. Take some deep breaths, all right? Put your head between your legs."

Emily obeyed, and June mimicked breathing in and out in deep breaths, rubbing small circles on Emily's lower back. Having her head down and breathing did help, and the world came back into focus again.

She sat up to see June watching her critically, searchingly. Apparently satisfied with what she saw, she said, "Better? You look better. You went as white as a sheet for a minute."

"Much better. I'm sorry."

June shook her head, dismissing her extreme reaction. "It's fine. I am glad you didn't actually pass out. I thought for sure you were going down. That would have hurt like hell on this tile."

"I've never fainted before," Emily said, feeling foolish. "I don't know what came over me."

"Are you claustrophobic?"

Emily lifted one shoulder. "Not really. I think I was just startled."

June's eyes searched the room for a moment or two, and she sighed. "Well, there's no other way out of here but through that door."

"Do you have the key?"

June laughed. "It's in my cardigan, and that's out in the pool room. And anyway, I think it locks from the outside."

Emily's courage was returning, and she squeezed June's hand. "Someone will come for us eventually. They knew where we were going, or Mr. Wright did anyway."

"I suppose you're right. It's not the end of the world." June's expression turned a little sly. "And it gives us a chance to get to know each other a little better."

Emily couldn't help but smile, and June returned it. "You should smile more often, Emily. It's really pretty."

Emily looked away, blushing. "Thanks."

June laughed. "You're pretty when you don't smile, too. I mean that it suits you."

Emily met her eyes to see if she was being genuine and found June grinning at her. They were sitting very close together, and June was still holding her hand. Not stopping to second-guess herself, Emily leaned forward, and June's eyes fluttered closed. Their lips almost brushed, and then the sound of the steam turning on made them flinch and pull apart.

June laughed. "Are you fucking kidding me?"

The steam was coming out in billowing waves from the mechanism near the lights, and Emily leapt to her feet in panicked desperation. "How did it turn on?"

June stood up and searched the room before shaking her head. "I have no idea. It couldn't have been from in here. There's probably a switch outside the door."

Their eyes met, and they both looked at the door. June walked over and slammed on it with her fist a few times. "Hey! Is someone out there? We're locked in!"

They waited, listening, but the sound of the steam was loud enough that, even if someone was out there, they probably couldn't hear them.

Emily had to raise her voice almost to a shout to be heard. "Who do you think it is?"

June frowned. "It could be Jim, fucking around. He seems like the type."

Emily wanted to agree, but she couldn't. "I don't know. He was so dead-set on working today. You heard him. I'm sure he's in my room right now, knee-deep in paperwork."

"But it couldn't be Mark. He's not like that."

Emily thought for a moment. "Maybe Mr. Wright is doing maintenance or something."

"Could be. But why can't he hear us?"

The steam was coming out so fast it was getting hard to see. Emily waved a hand in front of her face a few times, coughing, and stepped a little closer to June.

June laughed. "This is ridiculous! We're going to steam to death before someone finds us."

Emily frowned, suddenly terrified, and June squeezed her hand. "Hey, we'll be fine. I'm sorry. I shouldn't joke about it. But really, it's fine. We just have to wait a little longer. Someone will come for us eventually." She pulled on Emily's hand and led her back to the seat. "Let's sit. We'll feel better closer to the ground."

It was better, but only a little. The heat was tremendous, and both of them hunched over, nearer the floor.

"How long do you think the steam will last?" Emily shouted.

June raised her shoulders. "Ten minutes? That's how long the one at my gym runs. It should turn off on its own."

They sat quietly for a while, Emily breathing in and out of her mouth. The heat of the steam hurt the inside of her nose.

"God, you must be roasting in those clothes!" June said.

"I am."

"Well take some of them off, for God's sake. Everyone will understand if we come out of here half-naked. It must be a million degrees."

Emily was about to object, but June started unbuttoning her shirt. Emily froze, startled, and June stopped what she was doing and laughed.

"Hey—don't get any funny ideas. I'm helping you cool off here. For now." She winked at her.

Emily tried to smile back at her and raised her shaking fingers to help.

They heard the door unlatch almost the moment the steam turned off, and then Jim came into the room. He waved an arm in front of his face, coughing.

"Jesus Christ! What in the hell are you two doing in here? We've been looking all over for you!"

June's hands dropped from Emily's shirt, and she jumped up and rushed past Jim and out into the pool room. It was all Emily could do not to run after her. The two of them paused next to the pool. June was waving a hand in front of her face dramatically, and Emily bent at the waist, taking deep lungfuls of cool air.

Jim watched them, his face crinkled with apparent confusion. "What they hell were you doing in there with all your clothes on?"

June walked toward him, fists clenched. "Do you honestly think we'd go in there on purpose dressed like this?"

He gave her a nasty grin. "What the hell do I know? It seems like you were getting ready to get a little more comfortable."

"Fuck you," June snarled. "We were locked in there, you jackass."

Emily pulled her shirt closed and held it that way, suddenly realizing that it was almost completely unbuttoned. The movement caught the eyes of the others, and they both looked at her and away. Jim's face colored with embarrassment or anger.

June wiped her face with a hand and grimaced in disgust. "Thank Christ you finally came. I thought we'd be stuck in there all day."

"You nearly were," Jim said. "Like I said, we've been looking for you guys for hours."

June's head snapped at him, eyes blazing. "That's impossible!" She stared at Emily. "We haven't been in there that long. Right, Emily?"

Emily considered. "Maybe thirty minutes. We left the house an hour ago, tops."

Jim shook his head, his face cloudy. "At noon, lunchtime, Mark noticed that the two of you weren't around. I was still working, but he came up and found me. We didn't think you were still out on your walk—this was hours later, after all, so we checked the house first. We checked the garage and saw both of your cars, and when we ran into him, Mr. Wright said both of you had headed this way, to the pool and greenhouse. He hadn't seen you come back, and he was in the gardens all morning. The three of us came out here and looked for you, and we didn't see you in either the pool room or the greenhouse.

We went back to the house, made a few phone calls, and we were getting ready to call the police, but then the housekeeper remembered the steam room. I came right out here to check." He glanced at his watch. "It's going on four now."

"In the afternoon?" June shouted.

"Of course, in the afternoon! What the hell else would I mean?"

Emily lost track of their back-and-forth argument as she was swept into an overwhelming sense of déjà vu. Three days ago, on her drive here, she'd also lost time. She had been unable to account for three hours, and she hadn't let herself think about it since. Now it had happened again, and, like the last time, she'd returned to reality just before four o'clock. She was sure that if she looked at Jim's watch, it would be the same time she'd seen on the watch of the helpful cyclist on the road.

"Emily? Back me up here," June was saying. "There's no way that's the right time. I'd have gone crazy if we were in there for hours and hours. It was thirty minutes, at most—less, really. What do you think? Can you think of any other explanation?"

Emily licked her dry lips. "I think…" She was suddenly confused. Her thoughts were muddled, her tongue thick in her mouth. She shook her head and tried again. "I think…I think I need to lie down."

She felt a curious sinking sensation, and then everything went black.

CHAPTER SEVEN

Emily felt sunlight on her face. The canopy was open again, and she sat up, a scream rising to her lips.

June pushed her back onto the pillow, firmly. "Whoa, there. Take it easy. You're okay."

A wet rag had fallen onto Emily's lap, and June picked it up and put it back on Emily's forehead. "Lie back. Relax."

June was sitting next to her on the bed, and that side of her body felt distinctly hot. "How did I get here?"

June grinned. "Jim carried you, if you can believe it." She looked behind her, and Emily saw Jim and Mark sitting in chairs facing the bed. "My hero."

Jim rolled his eyes and got to his feet, wincing for a moment before walking closer. "And I'm going to feel it in the morning, let me tell you."

"Oh, don't exaggerate," June said. "She can't weigh more than a hundred pounds."

"You try lugging a hundred pounds half a mile and see how your back holds out."

"Enough, you two," Mark said, getting up. He walked close enough to peer down into Emily's face. "Are you okay? Do you want us to call a doctor?"

She considered his question. She didn't want to seem like a victim. She also hated having all this attention. "I feel fine now. Really." To prove her point, she sat up again, setting the rag down on the table next to the bed. Her head felt strangely light and detached from her body, but the feeling faded after a few seconds. She scooted up a little in the bed to get more comfortable and then winced from a pain in her side. She touched it gingerly and raised an eyebrow at June.

June made a sympathetic face. "You must be pretty bruised up. You fell on the tile."

"Like a bag of hammers," Jim said. "One second you were up, and then you were down. Never saw someone fall like that."

"I'm just glad you didn't hit your head," June added. "At least I think you didn't. Does it hurt?"

She lifted a hand and gingerly explored her scalp under her sweaty, damp hair. "Feels okay."

"Small favors, anyway."

Emily made as if to get up, and all three of them held up their hands. "Hang on a little longer," Mark said. "You need to rest."

"I feel fine. Really."

June put a hand on her shoulder and gently pushed her back into the pillows. "Please. Just stay there for a while, okay? It was really scary seeing you fall like that."

Emily met her eyes, ready to argue, but her retort died in her throat. She would never be able to deny her anything.

June, seeming to realize she had let it go, smiled at her gratefully and got off the bed. "At least she's okay," she told the men. "But it still doesn't solve the problem."

"What problem?" Emily asked.

They glanced at her and then at each other. Mark shook his head, wearily. "While you were unconscious, we talked about your excursion today."

June met her eyes. "I told them our side of the story again, but they don't believe me."

Mark shook his head, sighing. "It's not a matter of belief, June. It's a matter of fact. The two of you left the house at, what, eight thirty? Jim didn't find you until four. That's almost eight hours."

"But I'm telling you, it's impossible!" June said. She turned to Emily. "It's impossible, isn't it?"

"Time can be funny when you're panicking," Mark suggested.

Emily shook her head. "Yeah, but if anything, time slows down when you're upset. It doesn't speed up."

Mark raised his hands. "There's no argument here, ladies. You were gone all day."

June groaned. "Look—I'm not crazy. I can see the clock. I understand the reality of what you're saying. I'm trying to tell you that, at least to us, we left the house, we made it to the pool room maybe ten or fifteen minutes later, and we were in there for maybe the same amount of time before the hanging bowl fell in the steam room. Then we were locked in there for maybe twenty or thirty minutes. That's what happened."

Mark sighed. "And again, I don't doubt that's how it seemed to you." He raised a hand when June opened her mouth. "Let's not argue about that for now, June. You also said something about someone locking you in there? What did you mean?"

June threw Emily a guilty look. "I mean, I'm not sure. The doors around here close all the time. But someone had to turn the steam on, right? It didn't just turn on by itself."

Mark shook his head. "We don't know that, June. Maybe the mechanism is faulty. I'll have to ask Mr. Wright to examine it." He paused. "But if it was someone, who do you suspect?"

June frowned directly at Jim, and he laughed. "Why the hell would I do that?"

"I don't know, Jim. Why would you?"

His expression darkened, and he took a menacing step toward her. "Are you actually accusing me?"

June lips curled into a snarl, but her expression softened a moment later. She shook her head. "No. I'm sorry. I don't know what I'm saying."

Jim appeared somewhat mollified, but he turned around and walked across the room, possibly to cool off.

Mark looked back and forth from June to Emily a few times and shrugged. "I don't know what to say. I can see that it was a traumatic experience for both of you. I'd avoid the steam room for now until we've had the door examined."

June laughed. "Christ! Do you think I'd ever go back in there? Not for all the money in the world."

Emily shook her head adamantly. "No way."

They were all quiet. Jim stared out the window at the lawn, Mark absently down at the floor, and June watched Jim. Emily couldn't help but fidget, twisting her hands. How was this going to play out? Like her experience with the cyclist, she couldn't find any explanation for the missing time. It seemed useless to try to make sense of it, but that was only her opinion. She didn't know how the others would deal with it.

"How about a cocktail?" Jim turned around and held up his watch. "It's five o'clock, after all."

Mark sneered with something like disgust, but June laughed. "I could use one. What about you, Emily?"

She nodded, and before anyone could stop her, she scooted off the bed and stood up. "I'd love one. A double, if you don't mind, June."

Mark looked around at the three of them and threw up his hands. "Fine! But make mine a Manhattan, would you please? I hate gin."

June and Jim walked out of the room together, laughing already, and Emily followed with Mark. When the others had disappeared down the stairs ahead of them, Mark put a hand on her arm. "Are you really okay? You can tell me if you're not."

His expression was earnest, and she blushed at the implication. He clearly understood that she wouldn't want to seem weak in front of the others.

"I'll be fine. I am fine, I mean."

He met her gaze. "Okay. But if you're not—later, I mean, tell me. I can drive you into town."

When they reached the sitting room, they found Jim rooting through the small record collection and June making drinks at the bar. Emily tried to decide where to put herself. Sitting on the couch would invite someone to sit next to her—June, preferably—but that might be too obvious. She wasn't sure June would like that.

Not able to decide, she walked over to the windows that faced the front lawn and peered out at the long, unbroken green. It had been freshly mowed sometime today and was strangely shorn, naked almost. The sight, however, gave her pause. Mr. Wright had claimed he'd been in the back gardens all day, yet this lawn was proof that, at least for a while, he'd been on this side of the house. She and June could have come back during that time, but he'd told Mark and Jim otherwise. But perhaps he'd forgotten.

She heard a loud screech behind her and spun, startled. Jim made a face at everyone. "Sorry. Haven't used one of these in a while." He fiddled with the needle on the record player, and a piano sonata started to play. "Not much of a selection, I'm afraid. There's classical, and there's classical."

"It's nice," June said, handing him a cocktail. She turned and walked over to Emily with hers, and Emily took it from her gratefully.

"Go easy on that drink," Mark told her. "You had quite a shock. Heatstroke, at the very least."

June and she shared an amused glance, and June returned to the bar for the other drinks.

"Say, Emily," Jim said. "I want to apologize about this morning." She almost choked on her drink.

He looked distinctly uncomfortable and wouldn't meet her eyes. "I tried working in the library, and like you said, it was way too dark. Who knows why they put the library in the only dark room in the house. And you're right—it wouldn't make sense to bring the stuff in here." He gestured around the room, with its little coffee and drink tables, but no work surfaces. "Your room is much better. I was thinking we should keep working in there. I mean, if you don't mind having me come in and out."

Still surprised, Emily nodded. "Of course. If you think that's best. I don't mind moving to your room, if that would be better."

He laughed. "No way. I've been put in the nursery. You should see my bed—tiny, and there are no tables, either. I think you have the biggest room of any of us."

"Really?"

"Yes, really," June said. "How did you score that room, anyway? You should see mine. It's a shoebox."

"I'm actually rather surprised by the size of this house in general," Mark said. "The bedrooms are especially small, even given the time period this place was built. I was expecting a much larger house."

Jim suddenly walked over to the front window and pointed outside. "Hey, guys. What's that?"

All of them walked over, and Emily saw something sparkling at the far side of the lawn. It was small and shiny, indistinct at this distance. She hadn't seen it when she looked out the window earlier, but the light had changed in the last few minutes, so she couldn't be sure if it was new.

"Maybe a sprinkler? Or a piece of trash?" Mark suggested and took another sip of his drink.

Jim's eyes lit up. "Or maybe it's buried treasure!"

June laughed and swatted his arm. "You goof. I'm with Mark. It's trash. A balloon, I think. One of those foil ones."

Jim set his drink down. "I'll go check it out. But I call dibs! If it's treasure, it's mine."

June laughed again, and Jim dashed from the room. They watched him race across the lawn and then bend down. He held it up for them, but it wasn't clear from this distance what was in his hands. He started walking back toward them and then stopped about halfway across the lawn. He was close enough that Emily could see his expression change as his face turned up and to his right. He stood there for a long moment, his eyes wide. A second later he was running again, and the three of them moved to meet him by the front door.

"I saw her!" he said, his voice high. He looked at Mark and her. "I saw her! Up in your window, Emily, watching me. Let's go catch her! She can't get far if we're quick."

Without waiting for a response, he bounded up the stairs, and she and the others, caught up in his excitement, raced after him. She slipped on a stair and banged her knees painfully, but she was right behind the others when Jim unlocked her door and flung it open. He stopped a few feet into her room.

"She's gone," he said. He walked farther into the room and peered behind the curtains, then got down on his knees and looked under the bed. He got up again, his face pale and angry. "She was just here. I swear to God."

"What did you see?" Mark asked. His voice was quiet, serious.

"It was like both of you said. She was standing right there," he pointed at the spot by the window, "watching me on the lawn. I don't know what made me look up here—she must have moved or something.

She was right there!" He pointed again. "Then she turned around, and I couldn't see her anymore. That's when I came back inside."

"What did she look like?" June asked.

Jim hesitated, and Emily sympathized with him. The woman was hard to describe. In addition to seeing her at a distance and at an angle, at least in her case, she'd been in sight for only a few seconds at most, and nothing was very distinct about her appearance.

"She was younger—twenties, thirties, maybe. Shoulder-length, or longer, dark hair. Pale. I don't really remember what she was wearing, or I didn't see it clearly, anyway. A dark shirt, maybe." He shook his head. "Guys, she can't have gotten far. Let's find her. She must be somewhere in the house."

Mark touched his shoulder. "Jim, there's no way she could have left this room. We would have seen her leave. She didn't have time to go anywhere."

"Well, what other explanation do you have?" Jim said, almost shouting. "She can't have disappeared." He looked at Emily. "Is there another way out of here? A hidden passage to the attic or something?"

She shook her head. "Not that I know of."

"Then she can't be far. Did you lock your room, June?"

"It locks on its own, Jim, just like all of the bedrooms."

"Let's check the bathroom," Jim said, pushing past them.

Emily and the others shared a glance and followed him out into the hall. He flung the bathroom door wide, turned on the switch, saw an empty room, and continued down the hall to the next door.

"This is your room, June?"

She nodded.

"Open it."

June sighed and pulled out her keys, fiddling with the key ring long enough that he grabbed it from her and opened the door himself. Once again, they watched him riffle the curtains and check under the bed, his frantic frustration clearly mounting.

Again, Mark stopped him before he charged out into the hall. "Jim, calm down, please. We're not going to find her."

"What do you mean? Of course we'll find her!" His eyes narrowed. "Unless she slipped outside while we were in your room, Emily. But we would have heard her, right?"

"That's not what I mean, Jim," Mark said, but Jim was obviously not listening.

"Let's go check our bedrooms, and then, if we have to, we can check the attic. That would make the most sense, right? That she's been hiding up there all this time?" His eyes were wild, almost rolling in their sockets.

"Jim!" Mark said, this time grabbing both his shoulders. He made Jim meet his eyes. "She's not here."

Jim looked mutinous, his face flushing red, and for a moment, Emily was certain he would push Mark away. He shivered all over, and then the anger died in his eyes. His body relaxed, and a moment later he appeared embarrassed, but calm.

The four of them stood and caught their breath, all of them breathing hard from running. Emily's heart was still racing, and the others seemed shaken.

She took the opportunity to peer around June's room, curious. She'd seen inside, briefly, when June was moving in, but this was her first time past the doorway. It was less than half the size of her room, with no sitting area, a much-smaller bed, a tiny wardrobe, a night table, and a single chair. It didn't even have a carpet on the floor.

After a few moments, June walked across the room and stood staring out her window. She stayed there by herself for a long moment, her back to the others. Finally, she turned around. Her face was pale, haggard in this light. "I need to be alone for a while. Please."

Mark and Jim shared a glance before walking out into the hall. Emily stared at her, wanting to object, wanting more than anything to think of a way to make her feel better.

"Please, Emily. Give me some space, okay? I need to be alone."

Realizing she couldn't say anything, she nodded dumbly and left, closing the door after her.

The men were standing at the top of the stairs, their faces grave.

"Will she be okay?" Mark asked.

Jim's laugh was bitter. "What do you think? She was locked in a steam room all day, and now this, this—" he gestured feebly at Emily's room, "this whatever it was. I'd be surprised if she didn't pack her bags and leave."

Emily's stomach dropped, and she stared at June's door, desperately fighting the urge to go talk her into staying.

Mark sighed. "Maybe she'd be right. It might not be safe here."

"What's that supposed to mean?" Jim asked, his voice rising.

Mark met his eyes. "It means exactly what I said, Jim. Nothing more."

Jim laughed again. "You mean that the house is haunted? Are you seriously telling me that, Mark?" He looked at her. "Do you think it's haunted?"

She shrugged. "I don't know what I think. But you have to admit that something strange is going on."

Jim pointed at her and then at Mark. "Listen. I don't know what all of you are talking about. Everything that's happened has a logical explanation."

This time Mark laughed. "Then please, explain it to me, Jim. How do two perfectly sane women lose track of most of a day? How do doors that should stay open, close on their own? How does a strange woman appear and disappear in front of our eyes?"

Jim's eyes were wide with disbelief. "Do you hear yourself, Mark? Christ, you sound like a kook! There is no such thing as ghosts, for God's sake."

Mark shook his head. "I never claimed there was. And might I add that *you're* the one using the words haunted and ghosts, Jim."

Jim let out a short, bitter laugh. "You're not making any sense. Either it's haunted or it's not—it can't be both."

Emily had taken a couple of steps away from them, tired of this conversation. None of it mattered, anyway. The house and everything that had happened was inexplicable. Perhaps that was what Mark was trying to say, but Jim would never be able to hear it.

"I'm going to lie down for a while, guys. I might stay in my room for the night and read."

They both looked at her, seeming surprised, almost, that she was still here.

"Can I have my keys back, Jim?"

He frowned and dug them out of a pocket, also removing the thing he'd picked up from the lawn—a piece of a Mylar balloon. The three of them grinned when he held it up, and Emily took her keys back.

"I'll try to get up earlier tomorrow so we can work, Jim," she said.

He shook his head. "It's fine. Sleep as late as you like. No reason to kill ourselves over it."

"Good night, then, if I don't see you later," Mark said.

His eyes were dark and concerned, and she tried to reassure him by smiling. "Good night."

Her room was still surprisingly bright, dazzling her in the doorway, and when she closed the door behind her, she'd never felt so relieved to be alone.

CHAPTER EIGHT

Emily wasn't sure where the sound was coming from. She'd been sitting by the table, trying to read one of the journals, and at first the pounding seemed to come from below. The house was well insulated, so even if the sitting room was technically right below her, she'd never heard anyone down there before. She cocked her head, trying to locate where she heard it, and then it became a little louder. It was coming from the wall she shared with the bathroom.

She got to her feet and walked closer to it, pressing her ear against the velvet wallpaper. Listening carefully, she detected a kind of knocking sound—rhythmic and even. It seemed a little like something was hitting the wall directly on the other side, over and over. She glanced at the clock—nearly midnight. She'd heard June go in and out of the bathroom about an hour ago, but nothing since. Still, she might be in there again, doing who knew what to thump on the wall.

Maybe she's in trouble, Emily thought, then shook her head. The pounding was too rhythmic. If June was knocking on the wall for help, not only would she be calling out, but she also wouldn't be using the same, even pattern. Emily looked over at her bedroom door and hesitated. She should go see what was making that sound, but she didn't want to. She avoided using that bathroom as much as possible, and after the day they'd all had, she wasn't ready for something else to happen. Still, it could be a pipe or gas line rattling in the wall, and they might need to let someone know about it.

She walked toward her bedroom door, and just as she reached for the knob, someone knocked on it. She paused, jerking her hand back in fright.

"Emily? Hello? It's me, June. Are you still awake?"

Emily opened the door, and June jumped a little, putting her hand to her chest. "Jesus, that was fast. Did you run over here?"

"I was coming out."

"Oh, I'm sorry. Were you going somewhere? To the bathroom?"

Emily shook her head. "Not to go, but to see what that thumping was."

"What thumping?" June asked, entering her room.

"The one coming from the bathroom," she said, and then stopped, listening. She could no longer hear it. She shook her head. "Never mind."

June smiled and then headed over to the chairs, sitting down in the one Emily had been in and glancing at the open journal on the table. She gestured at it. "So how is this Lewis stuff? Interesting?"

Emily sat across from her. "Very. This one's a personal journal, but I've been having trouble reading it. She used some kind of shorthand, not a standard one, but I think I've finally figured part of it out."

"Didn't she live out here on her own for years and years? What does her journal talk about?"

"I've only read the first two pages, but it's day-to-day stuff—what she did, how she filled her time. With little snippets of poems in there, too. Those have been harder to figure out, but I think I translated the first lines of this one." She pointed at the page.

June leaned closer. "What's it say?"

She picked up her notes and cleared her throat. "When the dusty day settles into sleep,/beware the watchful eyes of the moon." She paused. "At least I think that's what it says."

June smiled. "'The dusty day…' I like that! You'll have to tell me the rest once you translate it. But I thought she was a novelist?"

"She was. I guess she was also a poet."

"But no hidden, unknown novels here?"

Emily shook her head, unable to hide her disappointment. "Not so far. But even if there isn't any fiction in this pile, it's still an amazing find."

June leaned back into her chair. She was wearing a short, silk bathrobe the color of crushed rose petals. It hitched far up on her thigh, and Emily had to look away to keep from staring at her exposed leg. June seemed oblivious to her own exposure and was digging around in the little pocket at the front of her robe. A moment later, she pulled out a joint and held it up for Emily to see.

"Do you mind? I was going to smoke it in my room, but I was getting a little edgy in there on my own. I don't smoke often, but I will when I can't sleep."

"Go ahead." Emily hadn't smoked pot since college, and she wasn't friends with people who did, but in theory she had no problem with it. She wasn't about to tell June that she hated the smell.

"Have something I could use for the ash?"

She thought for a moment and then walked across the room and grabbed a little glass tumbler off her nightstand. June had already lit the joint and taken a drag, her eyes closed as she held it in. She let out the smoke in a long, shaky breath, filling the room with the stink, grinning and coughing lightly.

"Damn," June said. "Tastes terrible. It's been in my purse too long." She held it out. "Want a hit?"

Emily started to shake her head, hesitated, and then took it. "I can't remember the last time I used this stuff." It had been once, at a party, over ten years ago.

June smiled. "Don't worry. It's like riding a bike."

Emily puffed on it, weakly, and, finding it wasn't as terrible as she'd feared, took a longer pull and burst out coughing. June stood up and sat in the chair closer to hers, pounding her back until she stopped. They grinned at each other, and Emily handed the joint back to her.

"Clearly a novice," she said, her throat raw from coughing.

"It happens to the best of us," June said, taking another hit. This time she held it in longer, and when she blew it out, she managed a smoke ring. She raised her eyebrows up and down. "But then, some of us are experts."

Emily was pretty sure it was too early to experience the effects of the joint, but her head felt light from coughing, and she leaned back into her chair, surprised to find herself relaxing. Being around June earlier today and yesterday had been a little nerve-wracking, scary in its own way. She'd been terrified lest she say something, do something wrong. Maybe now, after all that had happened, she could relax around her.

June gave her a funny smile, her eyes now red and watery. "I think you're starting to get a little stoned, Dr. Murray."

She laughed, much longer than she needed to, and shook her head. The feeling made her dizzy and she laughed again. "So fast?"

June shrugged. "You're probably a lightweight. I mean look at you—you're tiny. What are you, five feet nothing?"

"Five foot one," she said, pretending to be insulted.

June laughed. "Well, I'm five-ten, and let me tell you, it takes a lot to get me high. Or drunk." She shook her head. "I've always been envious of shorter women."

Emily laughed again. "You must be kidding me. Any woman would die to look like you." She knew she should be embarrassed to have said those words out loud, but strangely, she felt fine. She spoke slowly, emphasizing her words. "You're gorgeous."

June smiled and lowered her eyes. "You're not hard on the eyes either, Emily. You must have…people asking for your number all the time."

She noticed the hesitation and smiled. June must know by now, she thought. "Are you flirting with me, Dr. Friend?"

June smiled that stunning smile that disarmed her every time she saw it. "And what if I was? What would you do to stop me?" Her tone was coy, playful.

The question sobered her. She leaned closer to June, inches from touching her. "Nothing at all."

"Well, then," June whispered.

"Well, then," she repeated.

They continued to stare at each other, and June's lips curled into a lazy grin. Her eyes were mischievous, and Emily grew hot, tensing in anticipation. Any moment now, June was going to kiss her. She could see it in her eyes. Then, strangely, June's gaze flickered away from Emily's, and she leaned back into her chair.

"God, I'm so tired. This stuff is really doing the trick." She gestured with the joint. "After the day we had, I thought I'd be up all night."

Despite her excitement, sleep was now dragging at Emily's eyes, too. Her head felt heavy, her face hot, and when she leaned back, the room spun a little around her. She stifled a yawn and closed her eyes, suddenly sure she could sleep right here in the chair. A moment later she felt a hand on hers, and she opened her eyes and met June's. Her expression was dark, worried.

"Look. I didn't come in here to smoke pot with you."

"Oh?" Emily said, making herself sit up straight. It was hard to move. Her limbs felt heavy on her joints, difficult to control.

June was playing with the hem of her bathrobe, eyes averted. "I wanted to ask you something. It's going to sound stupid."

Emily's heart started pounding. The pot and their conversation had put what had happened today out of her mind for the first time all evening. She'd managed to get a little work done after she left Mark and Jim in the hallway, but she'd caught herself losing track of her reading several times, suddenly remembering her panic in the steam room or Jim's face when he'd seen the woman in the window. The work had absorbed her again before the knocking started, but she didn't want to talk about any of the earlier events right now. But of course she would, if June wanted to.

Emily made herself nod. "Go ahead. Ask me anything."

"Do you think I could stay in here tonight?"

She hadn't expected this question, and her face must have reflected her complete surprise, because June laughed. "That didn't come out right. I'm sorry. You must think I'm batty. I planned to ask more smoothly than that." She shook her head. "I guess I'm a little muddled. I don't mean to sound like I'm coming on to you or anything. I could sleep on the floor or whatever, if you're uncomfortable having me in bed with you. I'm afraid of being on my own. After today, I mean."

Emily steeled herself, meeting June's eyes. She wanted to get this right. "You can sleep in here whenever you need to, June. And you're not sleeping on the floor. I will if you want me to, but we can share the bed. It's big enough."

June gave her another sunny smile. "Whew. Thank you. I know I'm being ridiculous."

"Not at all."

"Okay. As long as you don't mind. Let me put this out and go brush my teeth." She shivered. "I hate that damn bathroom."

"Tell me about it."

"Right? It's a murder room if ever there was one. I took such a quick bath this morning, I don't even think I washed all the soap off my body. Tomorrow we should go see what the guys' bathroom is like."

Emily smiled. "It's actually worse. I already checked it out."

June made a face, and they both laughed. "Do you want to go in there first?"

"No. I'm okay. I can wait and go after you."

June left the room, and Emily continued to sit in the chair. Her palms were wet with sweat, a wave of excitement making her pulse race. She hadn't imagined it all. June had been flirting with her earlier today. After what had happened in the steam room, Emily had been afraid that nothing would come of it—that they'd never get a chance to follow up on their almost-kiss. And now June was going to sleep in her bed.

June came back a few minutes later, and Emily got up and went into the bathroom. She brushed her teeth and washed her face carefully, peering into the mirror before she left. Why June, of all people, would find her attractive was a little beyond her.

Emily knew objectively that she wasn't ugly. Her hair was nicely cut for once, chin-length and dark and, despite the activities of the day, still nicely styled. Her face, like the rest of her, was small, pointed. She'd always been a little underweight, always very slight—elfin, someone had once called her. She had nice, light-gray eyes, her most striking feature.

No, she wasn't ugly, but she also wasn't even close to June's level. She had dated different women off and on over the years, never seriously, and while it was true that men and women asked her on dates more often than she went on them, it had been a while since she'd slept with anyone. She wasn't even sure if June wanted sex. She was going to have to let June make the first move—no way was she brave enough to do it herself.

Half certain June would be asleep already, or pretending to be asleep, she returned to her bedroom and opened the door as quietly as possible. June had turned off all the lights except for the two dim ones on either side of the bed. She was still up, standing, and now wearing only a silk camisole and panties. Her long, gorgeous legs were completely exposed, her arms bare. The camisole was short enough that Emily could glimpse her stomach between it and her panties, and she swallowed, hard.

June gestured behind her at the bed. "I didn't know what side you wanted, so I waited."

Emily had to lick her lips to speak. "Thanks. The right, I guess."

June climbed into the left side of the bed, turned off her lamp, and then closed her side of the canopy. Emily shut the front canopy and then dragged her side halfway. She motioned at the light. "Ready?"

June looked very small inside the bed, the covers pulled up to her chin. She nodded. Emily turned the light off and pulled the canopy behind her before getting under the covers.

They lay in the darkness, a couple of feet apart. Emily hadn't realized how large this bed was. Somehow, with another person in it, it seemed bigger than it had when she was alone. Unless she'd known June was there, she would have been certain she was alone. Only the slight sound of June's breathing was evidence that she was actually here.

"Jesus. It's like a tomb," June said, sounding far away.

"I think that's the idea. No sun can get in here, that's for sure."

"Unless it opens on its own," June said.

"Right."

"Christ. I'm sorry. I shouldn't have brought it up." Emily heard and felt her twisting around, the covers moving on her body. June's voice was closer when she spoke again. "You must have been terrified when that happened."

Emily thought about it and then nodded, stupidly, in the dark. "I was. I could barely breathe."

"How awful for you." Judging by her voice, she'd inched even closer.

Emily's heart was pounding now. This was what she'd been waiting for. June was going to make a move, any second. She clenched her hands, terrified she would reach out prematurely. Nothing happened for a long time. She could picture June, turned toward her, maybe propped up on an elbow. Was she waiting for something? Should she do something now, before June had time to change her mind?

"Well," June said, and Emily heard her fall back onto the pillow. "Good night."

"Good night."

The disappointment was crushing, and Emily almost cursed out loud. She'd blown it again. June had come to her, waited for her to do something, and she'd lain there like a dead thing. All she'd needed to do was reach out—less than a foot—and touch the side of June's face, and June would have welcomed whatever came next. Why did she have to be so goddamn stupid all the time?

Hot with frustration and anger, she pushed the quilt off as far as she could, hoping she wouldn't disturb June. June had been silent for a while, so Emily was fairly certain she'd fallen asleep, but she was careful anyway. She was damp with sweat—her cotton nightgown clinging to her skin. For a moment, she imagined how nice it would feel to rip it off and throw it to the foot of the bed. But she didn't have anything on underneath.

She closed her eyes, remembering the glimpse of June's body. It had been everything she imagined it would be—long and lean, muscular but feminine, with cream colored skin. Emily could picture her own pale fingers running up and down June's arm. She bit her tongue, hard, to distract herself. Stop it, she thought. You're making it worse.

Suddenly June sighed, loudly, and flung back the covers. "God, it's hot."

Emily's heart tripped happily, and she licked her lips. "I'm roasting."

"Sleeping in here doesn't really help, does it? Either you're awake with the sun or you boil to death in your sleep."

Emily laughed, weakly, unsure what to say.

"Should we open the canopy? Maybe on one side?" June asked. "Then we could open a window or something."

"I don't think it matters what side we open—it will still be too bright in here. I say we open it completely or leave it closed."

"Let's open it, then. Maybe we can close it in the morning."

They both climbed out of bed, and Emily turned the light on again so they could see. Their gaze met across the bed once the canopy was open, and they grinned.

"Shall we open a window?" June asked.

"Let's. It might cool it down enough to close the canopy again."

Emily started struggling with one of the largest windows overlooking the front lawn, and a moment later June stood next to her, trying to help. They both cursed and fought with it before moving to a smaller window nearby, but that one didn't open, either.

"Damn," June said, stepping away. "Won't budge."

"They might be painted shut," she suggested. "Sometimes they'll do that on purpose to keep the weather out in these old houses."

June stepped closer as if to examine her more closely. "Your face is all red. And your hair is completely wet!" She placed her hand on Emily's forehead. "You're burning up!"

Emily leaned into the hand, closing her eyes. "I'm really hot."

"You might have a fever. Do you feel sick?"

She still had her eyes closed, and she shook her head, enjoying the sensation of June's cold palm. "I'm just hot."

She opened her eyes when June dropped her hand, and then they stood there looking at each other, Emily peering up at June's face. Nothing in June's expression told her anything different than it had before, but Emily brushed a lock of hair off June's face before tracing the edge of her cheek with her fingertips. June's eyes fluttered closed, and she leaned into Emily's hand. Emily used her other hand to pull her closer, and they kissed.

June's lips tasted like marzipan—sweet almonds. She moved closer, their overheated bodies now touching, and June threw her head back with a gasp. On tiptoe, Emily kissed her neck, feeling June shudder underneath her as she moved her lips and tongue across her collarbone. June's breath was ragged now, and she clutched Emily's shoulders, her grip almost painful. Emily pulled June closer and kissed her again and then stepped away, grabbing June's hand and pulling her toward the bed.

June followed.

CHAPTER NINE

The next morning, anyone might have thought it hadn't happened. Even Emily was halfway convinced she'd dreamt the whole thing. Except for the tender soreness in some unusual places, and the wrinkled, ruffled bed, she found no evidence June had been there except for the pink bathrobe she'd left behind. When Emily joined the others for breakfast, June greeted her like she had the morning before, warmly, but with no outward signs of affection.

Emily could understand this behavior. June would, of course, want to keep what had happened under wraps. They had to work with everyone this summer, and no one else needed to know about their private affairs. She wasn't even that hurt by June's deception, though she had fantasized about seeing Jim's expression when he saw them holding hands. But, without saying a word, June made it clear that wasn't going to happen, and Emily was fine with that.

She and Jim started on the Lewis paperwork right after breakfast, and the day passed quickly and without incident. Besides breakfast, everyone in the household ate meals haphazardly and alone, generally. In the early evening, when the four of them gathered again for a break, they shared their findings.

Jim was visibly excited, pacing the room as he talked and wringing his hands. "There's a gold mine up there. Emily and I solved the first riddle of her shorthand codes, and while it's getting easier to read the notes, it's slow going. I can't imagine how we'll get through all of it in one summer."

June and Mark were sitting together on the sofa. Emily didn't know which chair to choose and was waiting for Jim to help her decide by default. She wanted the one nearest June, but again, she didn't want to be obvious.

"What sorts of things did she write about?" June asked. "I mean, I don't really get it—keeping a diary when you live alone in isolation. I can't keep up with one, and I actually see people every day and go out once in a while."

Jim laughed. "That's the funny thing. You would think it would be deadly boring, but she managed to have a full life out here in the woods. Yes, she writes about her day-to-day life, but she also writes about what she was thinking about and reading. It's a fascinating look into her mind."

"What about you guys?" Emily asked. "What did you do today?"

While Mark was an architectural historian and June an art historian, it had been clear from some of their earlier conversations that some of their work overlapped, a little like Jim's and her own. The four of them, in a sense, were divided into two parties of interests.

"Not a lot," June said. "Without internet access, I'm a little out of my depth here. With one exception, I don't recognize any of the pieces in the house, but they're incredible. All the paintings are obviously from the same or similar time period, but without knowing the artists, I can't say much beyond that, except that whoever bought these was obsessed with Romantic art. It's a little funny, given the time period in which the house was built—at the height of Impressionism—but it's possible the works here were bought earlier, before the house was built. I can't find out without doing some research, and I can't do research without a decent library or internet access. I spent most of the morning and afternoon talking to internet providers, and we should be able to get a DSL line out here later this week."

Emily had a momentary pang of regret. She'd been happy to be off the grid for the last few days. It had been, somehow, restful to be away from the world—a little like camping.

Mark nodded. "I'm in a similar spot. I've done some more sketches, and I took some photographs, but I still need the internet for my research. I was, however, able to track down an historian at the university in Plattsburgh who's fairly certain he's heard of the house before, and he might know who the architect was."

"What's the architect's name?" June asked.

Mark laughed. "That's the thing—I don't know, and neither does the professor at Plattsburgh. But he swears he's read the name Gnarled Hollow before, so he's going to look into it. I would have done more work back in the city before coming if I'd known what it would be like up here."

"Were the plans for the house filed in town?"

Mark shook his head. "If they were, there's no digital record for them, so no one could tell me over the phone. The town historian, however, claims that if they were filed nearby, they'd be at the library in the archive. I'm going into town tomorrow to check it out. The library is open only a couple of hours on Sundays, but I thought I'd get a feel for their archive anyway. Anyone who wants to go to town is welcome."

"Have you been there before?" June said, turning to Emily.

She shook her head. It hadn't even occurred to her to go into town. She knew it was tiny—a couple of thousand people at most—but that was all. She couldn't even remember what it was called.

"Let's make an outing of it, then!" June said, clapping. "We could get lunch together and help Mark."

Jim sighed. "No, thanks. I grew up in a small town, and I've had enough of them. You guys go ahead."

June made a face at him. "Oh, come on, Jim. It'll be fun."

He seemed to want to decline, but he sighed with resignation. "Fine. But I don't want to be there all day."

June appeared satisfied, and Emily wasn't surprised that she didn't receive an invitation. June clearly already knew that Emily would go anywhere June liked.

"All right," Mark said, getting to his feet. "I'm planning to leave around ten in the morning." His stomach gave a low rumble, and he grinned embarrassedly. "I missed lunch, so I'm going to eat an early dinner. After that, I need to do some more sketches and reading. I might not make it back down here later, so if I don't, I'll see you all tomorrow."

After he left, June set her teacup down and stretched before glancing at the clock. It was nearly four. "It's way too early for dinner, but I need a nap." Her eyes flickered to Emily's and away. "I think I'll go take one now so I can work a little more after dinner."

Emily's face went hot. "Me, too."

They turned to leave, but Jim said, "Hang on a minute, June. I wanted to ask you something."

Having already committed to leaving, Emily was forced to continue toward the door, but June met her eyes as they passed each other. Once out of the sitting room, Emily paused in the foyer. If she waited for June, and then both she and Jim came out together, she would look ridiculous. But she also wanted to go up with her, and June had clearly wanted that, too. Emily hadn't imagined that furtive glance or its implications.

She sighed and headed up the stairs. The risk was too great that Jim would see her waiting, and anyway, she desperately needed a bath. She'd avoided it yesterday and this morning, and she was starting to feel grimy, particularly after last night. She retrieved her bath towel and soaps from her room and paused outside the bathroom, listening. Voices were coming from downstairs, so June was still down there. She opened the bathroom door, pulled the cord, waited for the light to flicker on, and then turned on the water in the tub.

It was grim and ugly in here, but at least the water was hot. The tub itself was about two-thirds the length of a modern one, but with much higher sides. It filled quickly as she undressed. She was always quick to take her clothes off in here. Invariably, when her shirt was almost off and over her head, she sensed someone standing there, right behind her, watching. Like the other times she'd undressed, she spun around, her heart racing. There was, of course, nothing and no one there, but the watchful feeling remained. She shivered despite the hot, humid air.

She slipped into the soapy water with relief, her body finally off display. The tub wasn't long enough for her to fully extend her legs, so her knees poked up above the water. She couldn't imagine how June, who was several inches taller, was bathing—she'd have to basically crouch in here to get clean.

After she washed herself with a rag, she slid a little lower, bending her knees, and her shoulders just fit under the water. She closed her eyes and dunked her head underneath before coming up again and then shampooed her hair. She'd cut it before this trip, not knowing what kind of stylist she'd find up here, and it was shorter than it had been in a long while. Her fingers ran through the ends more quickly than she was used to.

Her hair was, she knew, one of her best features—dark and thick, with hints of auburn when she stayed out in the sun for long lengths of time. It was snarled in places, and she had to pause once or twice and work through a knot with her fingers. She wasn't washing it enough and vowed to resume her usual hygiene routine. Creepy or not, it was only a bathroom. And, she thought with a grin, if she and June kept sleeping together, she would have to bathe more often, anyway.

She dunked down again to rinse her hair, and suddenly someone yanked her ankles up and out of the tub, pulling her farther under the water. Desperately, she tried to sit up, but the hands on her ankles were strong, pushing up on her legs, toward her head, making it impossible for her to get her face up. The water was deep enough that she couldn't quite reach the air, and she thrashed hard against the tub, trying to yank her legs back toward her. The grip on her calves was vise-like, holding her fast and painfully.

Suddenly whoever it was released her legs, and she sat up, sputtering and gasping for air. With soap and water in her eyes, she was temporarily blinded, but she thought she saw a shadow flicker off to her right, behind her. She was about to turn that way, but then she felt hands on her ankles again. She spun and tried to react, but it was too late.

Seconds later, she was yanked down again, back into the water. She screamed, once, but the water was in her mouth, and she choked on it, her panic making her thrash and splash at the water as she tried to grab the sides of the tub. Finding no purchase, she pushed on the bottom with her hands, trying to get her face up, but with her legs over her head, she simply couldn't bend her body that way. The grip loosened once more, and she came back up, gasping for air and screaming.

Distantly, she was aware of pounding on the door and could hear the knob turning back and forth, but the door remained closed. She spun around in the tub, looking into every corner of the room, but didn't see anything. This time, she had the wherewithal to tuck her feet up underneath her body to protect herself from being pulled under again, but, with her back turned to the door, suddenly someone pushed her shoulders, hard, and sent her back into the water once more. The back of her head hit the tub, but the pain was secondary to her panic.

She fought, finding the wrists that were holding her down. She clawed at them and twisted from side to side, trying to get the hands off her shoulders and neck.

And then they were gone, and she was sitting up, coughing and sputtering, a howl of terror escaping her lips a moment later.

The door crashed open behind her, but she didn't even turn toward it, the sound distant and removed from what had happened to her. A moment later, she felt hands on her, and she screamed, sure she was going back under the water again.

"Emily! Emily! It's me! It's June!"

Emily had closed her eyes, tightly, terrified to see what was coming for her, and when she finally opened them, she saw June's pale, wild face, inches from her.

"Jesus, Emily! What the hell happened?"

Emily spun around, staring into every corner of the room again, seeing the men but also not seeing them standing next to the tub.

"It's in here—it was just here," she said, spinning around again.

"What? What's in here?" June asked.

"It was here—it held me under the water. It-it wanted to kill me."

"What the fuck is she saying?" Jim asked.

"It's in here!" she said, again, and then burst out crying. She covered her face with her hands, shaking so hard it hurt to breathe.

The others were silent, and then Emily felt strong, warm hands reaching down and pulling her up to her feet. Someone wrapped a towel around her, but she was so removed from her body she wasn't even embarrassed. They helped her step out of the tub, and she opened her eyes enough to meet their faces. Jim seemed angry, June scared, and Mark was staring down at the water that had sloshed out of the tub.

"It was here," she said again, quietly. Mark met her eyes and nodded, though whether in agreement or simple understanding, she didn't know.

"Let's get out of here," June said.

She put an arm around Emily's shoulders and led her out into the hallway. Jim followed a moment later, holding her keys, and opened her bedroom door. It was still full daylight outside, and the room was strangely bright after the dark, windowless bathroom.

June released her shoulders and met her eyes. "Do you want a minute? To get dressed, I mean?"

Emily looked down at herself and finally felt the embarrassment her earlier fear had suppressed. She pulled the towel around herself. "Yes—but don't leave me alone. Please."

June turned around to the men. "Give us a second, okay, guys?"

Emily heard the door close behind her and started crying again, and June pulled her into an embrace a moment later. A moment later, June gasped, and Emily moved back, looking up into her startled face.

"What? What is it?"

"Those marks! On your shoulders and neck!" June said. She'd taken a couple of steps away from her now, her eyes wide and frightened.

"What marks?" Emily asked. She tried to see them, but the angle was awkward.

"Go look in the mirror!"

Emily let the towel drop and walked over to the full-length mirror on the wardrobe door. Dark red splotches stood out across her collarbones, the sides of her neck, and the tops of her shoulders. She stepped closer and could distinctly see that the marks were made by individual pressure points—what, even now, looked like hand and fingerprints. June was behind her in the mirror, and her expression changed as she saw them, too.

"And your legs!" The marks were there, too, on her ankles and calves where the hands had held her under the water.

Emily started to quake and tremble, her knees suddenly weak, and June grabbed her before she could sink to the floor. She steered Emily over to a chair and then raced over and grabbed the bathrobe she'd left last night, handing it to her. Emily held it, stupidly, for a moment, not knowing what to do with it, and June knelt to help her put it on.

"The others have to see, Emily. And they'll want to know what happened to you."

She nodded, vaguely, and struggled into the robe. June's eyes were hard, angry now, clearly determined. Robe safely on, Emily waved vaguely at the door, and June walked over to open it for Mark and Jim. Both men came into the room a second later, obviously anxious, and Mark walked directly to her.

"You have to see what's happened," June said. "Emily—show them."

"I saw some of it in the bathroom," Mark said, standing near her chair.

Emily pulled one shoulder of her robe down, exposing her neck on one side, and she heard Jim hiss between his teeth. Both of them bent closer, and June pointed at Emily's legs and ankles. "They're there, too."

All four of them exchanged looks, and then Jim cursed, storming across the room before pacing, nervously, back and forth from the chairs to the door. June and Mark sat down in the chairs on either side of her, and June took her hand.

"What happened, Emily? Can you tell us?"

Mark was watching her, his eyes careful and concerned. "You said when we were in the bathroom that 'it' was in there with you, that 'it' was trying to kill you. What did you mean?"

She frowned, thinking. She had meant something when she said that, but she wasn't sure now. She tried to piece together her impression of the thing that had held her under the water. It had hands, and arms—she knew that. So technically, it was human-like in shape. But she had also felt its skin when it was holding her by the shoulders. That last time it happened, when she'd been pinned back by her shoulders, she'd felt the arms pushing her down, and the sensation she'd had touching them made her shudder at the memory. The thing's surface hadn't felt at all like real skin.

She shook her head, meeting Mark's eyes. "I don't know what I meant. I think I meant that it could be either a man or a woman…" Tears rose to her eyes again. She choked on the sob and put a hand to her mouth, shaking her head.

"For fuck's sake," Jim said behind them.

"What?" June said.

"None of us saw anything! There wasn't anything there!" Jim said.

June launched to her feet, her fists clenched. "What's that supposed to mean? Do you have eyes? Can you see? How do you explain these bruises?"

Jim hesitated and then shook his head. "How the hell do I know? Maybe she already had them."

June's face drained of color, her face a mask of pure rage. "She didn't have them before, Jim, and you know it."

"I don't know! And how would you know? She dresses like a nun most of the time. They could have been under her shirt the whole time."

June didn't answer, and the two of them continued to glare at each other. Suddenly, Jim's face broke into a broad, sarcastic grin, and he laughed. "Oh! I see. You know because you've already seen what's under her shirt...and pants."

June's voice lowered with anger. "Fuck you."

"Jim!" Mark said, his face dark. "Shut up." He turned back to Emily. "Please—tell us what happened."

She swallowed, the memory already taking on the hazy edges of a nightmare. "I was taking a bath. The room was empty, but I felt like something—someone was watching me."

"Oh?" Mark asked. "How?"

She shook her head. "I don't know. I always feel that way in there."

"Me, too," June added.

Mark frowned. "Go on."

"Then someone grabbed my ankles and pulled me under the water."

"You didn't see anyone?" June asked.

Emily shook her head. "I had my eyes closed because of the soap."

Jim snorted, and the three of them turned to him, Mark's expression dark again. He looked back at her. "Then what happened?"

"The hands let me go, and I got my head out of the water, but I couldn't quite see yet. I thought I saw movement behind me, a shadow, and then it pulled me under again. It let go then, and that was when I heard all of you outside."

"The door was locked," June said. "Why did you lock it?"

She shook her head, confused. "I didn't."

Jim laughed, and when all three of them looked at him, he held out his hands. "I mean, come on! Are we supposed to believe this crap?"

"You think she's making it up?" June asked, her voice cold and quiet. "Why would she do that?"

Jim shrugged, dramatically. "I don't know—for attention?"

"You genuinely think she would do this to herself?" June asked, her voice still quiet. "That's your explanation?"

"There *is* no other explanation, June! No one was there! We all saw!"

"Enough!" Mark shouted. The two of them jumped and then looked sheepishly at Mark and her.

"I'm sorry, Emily," June said.

"It's fine."

"Go on," Mark said. "Tell us the rest."

"The last time I was pushed down by my shoulders."

"And you still didn't see anything?" June asked.

"There was nothing to see. I could feel it, but I couldn't see it. I felt hands here," she touched her shoulders, "but no one was there. I had my eyes open for part of the time, and I didn't see anything. When I was underwater, I was trying to get the hands off me, and this time I could feel them, but I didn't see anything."

Everyone was quiet. June was biting her lip, her eyes dark and worried, and Mark was staring at the table in front of him. Jim seemed to be glaring at the wall, but his eyes were distant, unfocused. Emily gazed back and forth among the three of them, wanting someone to say something, but no one did. There was nothing to say.

"I think we should leave," June finally said.

Jim laughed. "Of course you do."

"What the hell is your problem? Emily was attacked tonight, Jim. Yesterday she and I were locked in a steam room for hours."

"So now you admit you were in there for hours?"

"Damn it, you're not listening to me!"

Jim took a step toward her, his fists clenched. "I am listening to you, June. But I don't like what I'm hearing. Leave? Are you crazy? This is the chance of a lifetime." He looked at Mark. "And if the two of you are stupid enough to believe her," he gestured at Emily, "then by all means, hit the road. I'm happy to stay here on my own. Less distracting."

"She could have been killed!" June said, almost shouting.

"So she says," Jim said, shaking his head. "But I know what I saw when we opened that door, June. No one was there. It was just Emily."

"Well, I believe her, and I think Mark does, too. We should pack our bags, tonight, this minute, and go to a hotel. What do you think, Mark?"

Mark's brows were lowered, his expression thoughtful. He shook his head. "I don't know. I believe you too, Emily—" Jim snorted, but Mark ignored him and went on. "What do you want to do? Do you want to leave?"

Emily gazed around the room from face to face, and then she made herself look inward, searching her heart. The answer was already there, but she was surprised when she realized that she'd already known, even before she was asked.

She shook her head. "No. I want to stay."

June seemed stunned, but Mark had clearly expected her to say this. Jim laughed, once, in a kind of bark.

"Of course you don't want to leave. Having too much fun, I'd bet."

June gave him a dark look and turned back to her. "Are you sure? Don't you think it would be better—?"

But she was already shaking her head. "No. I refuse to let it force me out. Whatever it is."

Mark got to his feet. "I'm with Emily. I want to figure this thing out."

June had watched the two of them, clearly upset, but, evidently seeing their determination, she finally raised her eyebrows and sighed.

"Okay. If that's what you both think is best. But if something happens again, I'm leaving. I think we all should."

"It might be smart to avoid being alone. As much as possible, I mean," Mark said.

"I'm not going back in that bathroom alone. I can tell you that much," June said.

"You can use ours for now," Mark said. "Jim and I can use the one in the attic, if necessary."

"I'm going to my room," Jim said, sounding disgusted. "Some of us still have work to do today."

"I'll leave now, too, Emily," Mark said. "But you know where to find me. June, do you think you could stay in here with her?"

"Already my plan," she said.

"Good. In the morning, we can look closer at those bruises. When we go in to town, you might want to have someone examine them."

Emily wasn't about to talk to anyone outside of the house about her bruises. She knew how she'd sound. Still, she nodded. "Thanks, Mark. Good night."

None of them said a word to Jim, and he more or less stormed out of the room. Mark raised his eyebrows. "I'll try to talk to him, ladies. I don't know why he's behaving this way."

"If he lets himself believe, he'll have to be frightened," Emily said. The others seemed surprised by her matter-of-fact tone. She shrugged. "I can understand it if he doesn't want to feel scared. It doesn't bother me."

"Well, I think he's being a dick," June said. "I mean, my God, even if you had wanted to fake being hurt, anyone can tell you could never have done that to yourself—it's physically impossible."

"Stay safe now, ladies, and let me know if you need anything." Mark turned and left, closing the door after himself.

June and Emily stared at each other in silence for a long beat. June seemed worn out, a haggard cast marring her face again.

She forced a grin. "Sorry. I smoked the last of the pot this morning. Could have used it now."

"Would a drink help?"

June paused. "Have anything in here?"

Emily grinned and walked across the room to her wardrobe. She'd brought a small bottle of scotch from home, not sure what alcohol she'd find here. The bar downstairs was fully stocked, so she'd almost forgotten it. She held up the bottle, and June laughed.

"Of course you drink scotch."

"Oh? Why do you say that?"

"Oh—no reason. It suits you."

Emily decided to take that as a compliment and poured them both a small glassful. There was no ice in here, so they had to drink it neat, but June didn't seem to mind, and neither did she. They sat there, quietly drinking, until their glasses were empty. Emily got up to move the glasses to a safer table, away from the papers, and when she turned back, June was watching her with a slight smile.

"What?"

June shook her head. "Nothing. I like seeing you in my robe."

Emily looked down, having forgotten about it, and blushed. She'd been sitting there with her housemates, naked except for this short robe, for the last thirty minutes. June rose and walked toward her, then touched her face.

"I'm so sorry that happened to you, Emily. I'm sorry I wasn't there to stop it."

She shook her head. "You couldn't have done anything. I'm glad it was me and not you." She swallowed, a knot of emotion rising in her throat. The idea was dreadful. It would have been much, much worse had it been June in there.

June's eyes softened. "It didn't. It won't."

"You don't know that."

"I don't, but I won't let it. At the very least, I'm never taking a bath alone in this house again. I can promise you that."

She touched the side of Emily's neck at the shoulder, and Emily hissed a little in pain, flinching. The marks hadn't hurt before, or she hadn't felt the pain earlier, but now she stung all over. June made an alarmed face, and Emily tried to relax. June continued to examine the bruises closely, touching her lightly at times as she found them, and Emily bit her tongue when it hurt.

June shook her head. "They're horrible. I really think you should see a doctor tomorrow."

"And say what? How could I explain? Any doctor would think I'm being abused."

June sighed a moment later. "I guess you're right. But we should put some ice on them, anyway, to help with the swelling. I have some ibuprofen in my room." She turned as if to go get it, and Emily grabbed her hand. June turned back, appearing confused.

"Don't leave," she said. June looked at her for a long time as if she might not listen, and then she smiled. June turned to Emily's bed, and Emily followed.

CHAPTER TEN

Emily and Jim stayed home when Mark and June went into town the next day. Emily didn't go primarily because of her appearance. By morning, all the marks had bloomed into a purple so dark it was almost black, the edges of all the bruises red and painful. She couldn't hide the marks on her shoulders, collarbone, and neck with anything less than a turtleneck, and with such hot weather, that wasn't an option. After staring at herself with horror in the mirror, she told June she was staying and dressed in her lightest clothes, unconcerned with how she looked as long as she was here. Her shorts and T-shirt showed off the bruises in all their glory, but neither piece of clothing hurt to wear, which was key.

Jim refused to acknowledge her presence at breakfast, almost as if by seeing the bruises he would have to believe her. She detected a bit of regret in his eyes the couple of times their gaze met, as if, in the light of the morning, he was second-guessing what he'd said. Anyone could see what had happened—she simply couldn't have done this to herself. But Jim wasn't ready for what that meant, and she refused to try force him to change his mind. He was clearly the kind of man who needed to make his own decisions.

Jim and June were hardly civil to one another as they all ate, June snapping at him and Jim barking back at her. This fight was clearly the main reason Jim had decided to stay instead of go to town, but he also agreed that no one, especially Emily, should be left on their own in the house. The new rule was that, except for bedtime and bathroom use, they should move about in pairs as much as possible or stay in adjoining rooms. Last night, Mark made Jim prop his bedroom door open so they could hear each other if anything happened.

After June and Mark left, Jim seemed surprised when Emily suggested that they get back to work, almost as if he'd expected her to beg off. She didn't acknowledge his surprise, and, within an hour of starting, things between the two of them seemed normal again. She would show him a juicy tidbit from the poem she was working on, and he would point out an exceptionally interesting passage from the diary he was examining, and then they would go back to work. As far as she was concerned, he was the best kind of colleague to have—enthusiastic and hardworking. She didn't expect anything else from him.

Once or twice, she caught him staring at her or, more specifically, her bruises, but she always turned away first, not wanting to catch him. Again, she knew he needed time, and she wasn't going to force it.

The next few days passed in a similar pattern. While June waited for the internet to be installed, she helped Mark search the town archive. It was, they explained, as expected, a disorganized mess, and they were gone for most of every day searching in a dark basement of the library. Emily and Jim would start on the Lewis papers after breakfast and finish sometime in the early evening. By Wednesday, June and Jim were on speaking terms again, more or less, or at least civil to each other, and evening cocktails resumed. June spent every night in Emily's room, but they didn't talk about that arrangement during the day. If Mark or Jim knew what was going on at night, they didn't let on, and that suited Emily completely.

Nothing unusual had occurred after her near-drowning, and she couldn't help but feel like the house was waiting, somehow, almost as if it wanted them to forget and relax. Once or twice she saw Mark or one of the others out on the lawn, looking up at her window as if waiting for the woman to appear, but if they saw anything, they didn't mention it. They didn't even talk about the bathroom incident again. Everyone, including the house, seemed to be holding their breath.

On Thursday, a little restless after so many days of straight work, she and Jim decided to take the day off. He agreed to help Mark for a few hours in town, and Emily offered to help June do a photographic inventory of the paintings in the house.

"I can't keep twiddling my thumbs," June explained. "I can always label the paintings later, when I know who painted them, but I can do a lot of work simply examining them before I know who painted them."

"That sounds a little like some of my archival work with anonymous literature. I can make a lot of educated guesses about time period and literary movements without knowing the author."

June was starting the inventory in the sitting room, and Emily sat on the sofa watching her set up. She wasn't sure what help she could offer today, as the photography seemed fairly straightforward and solitary, but she was happy to get to spend some time with June outside of her bedroom. She hadn't asked June a single time why they seemed to avoid each other when they weren't sleeping together or having sex, and she wasn't about to start, but that didn't mean she didn't crave her company all the time.

"Right," said June, stepping away from her tripod. "I think that's good. Gosh. This is going to take forever."

"How many paintings are in the house?"

June sighed and looked up at the ceiling, counting silently. "Maybe as few as fifty? Possibly as many as seventy-five?"

"Wow. I hadn't realized."

"I've been keeping a running tally, and from what I've seen, there are at least three or four paintings in every room. More, of course, in here, in the dining room, and in your room. I haven't even been to the attic yet, so God knows what we'll find up there."

Emily liked the "we" in June's sentence and warmed from within. They might just be sleeping with each other for now, but she could tell that June also didn't seem to mind having her around. She hadn't annoyed her yet, at any rate, and she wanted to keep it that way by being helpful.

"So tell me the plan for today."

June perused the room. "I'm going to have to remove each painting from the wall so we can photograph both sides and the frames."

"Oh?"

She nodded. "It's fairly common for painters to make notes on the backs of canvases. They sign them there sometimes, and other times you'll see the title there. I find it very interesting that none of the frames I've examined have titles on them. It was common practice in the eighteenth and nineteenth centuries, but I haven't seen a single example here. And, aside from the Turner here—which is worth a fortune, I might add—none of the paintings I've seen are signed. I mean, a few painters don't put signatures on their work, but not many. It's a way of advertising your work, after all—almost like branding. Yet I haven't seen a single one except Turner's."

"Do you think the others are by the same artist?"

June immediately shook her head. "No. I've examined the ones in here fairly closely now, and I can see different brushwork and paint pigments. A lot of these paintings seem to be by different artists."

Emily glanced around the room, surprised. All of them seemed similar to her, all very like the Turner. His painting took up the largest space on the biggest section of the wall between the sitting room and library. Most of the other paintings were much smaller, both in here and in the rest of the house, but they all were in the same or similar style—sweeping vistas of nature and industry mixed with portraits. She shook her head, amazed. It must have taken a lifetime to accumulate this kind of collection. It represented a very specific taste and an enormous amount of money.

She turned back to June. "You also mentioned something about photographing the frames. Why are they important?"

June laughed. "It'll sound funny, but very occasionally, the frame is worth more than the painting, especially if it's period and especially if the artists are relatively or completely unknown. And even when it's a well-known artist, the frames can be almost as priceless."

"So what do you need me to do?"

"If you can hold the lights as I take pictures, that would be incredible. That's so much easier than using light stands, since I can tell you where to hold them and how high. I'll also need help getting some of the heavier pieces off the walls. We need to take all of them down before I can do the initial pictures, but we should do them one at a time."

"Sounds easy enough. Do you need me to take notes or anything else?"

June smiled and stepped closer to her, leaning down to kiss her forehead. "No, sweetie, though it's lovely of you to ask. I have a notebook and a little recording device, which I'll turn on soon. It will sound like a lot of gobbledygook as I speak, but please try not to talk when I'm speaking."

Emily saluted her. "Aye, aye!"

June's face broke into her heartbreaking smile, and she stepped closer to her again. "You're darling, you know that?"

She grinned. "Yes, I do."

June's expression became serious. "No, Emily, I mean it. I really like you, like being around you. I don't know what I would have done this week if you weren't here."

She blushed. "Thanks." She cursed herself after saying this, realizing too late that June was opening the door for a real conversation about what was going on between them. June raised her eyebrows and turned around back to her tripod, and Emily thought she'd seen momentary hurt in her eyes.

"And I do, too," she said, lamely.

June turned back, appearing confused. "What?"

Clearly the moment had passed, but Emily went on anyway, desperate to salvage it. "I like being with you, too."

June gave her a weak smile and turned back to her tripod to adjust the camera. Emily could have slapped herself for being so stupid.

"Okay," June said, pointing at a large light. "Pick that up and hold it about three feet to the right of the painting and about two feet from the wall."

Emily complied, and June had her move it several times by a few inches until she had it where she wanted it. Within seconds, Emily's arms started shaking, but she held the light as steady as possible until June let her relax. June muttered under her breath, and Emily realized she was talking into a little microphone on her collar. June looked at the photo she'd taken, made notes in her notebook, and read out a long series of numbers from the camera into her microphone before turning it off from the device clipped to her belt. She smiled at Emily.

"That's one."

It was backbreaking labor, and an hour later, despite what she'd thought earlier, Emily was starting to regret volunteering. She simply wasn't strong enough to do what June wanted her to do for long lengths of time. June snapped at her a couple of times for moving the light, despite her visibly shaking arms. After what was only the fourth completed picture, Emily finally had to ask for a break, and after June agreed, she collapsed onto the sofa.

When she opened her eyes a couple of minutes later, June was grinning at her and holding out a glass of ice water. She took it gratefully and chugged it down.

She let out a deep breath. "Thanks."

"No problem," June said, sitting next to her. "I'm sorry about earlier. I forgot what it was like to be an assistant. As an undergrad, I worked for a professor who was a complete asshole—always yelling and screaming at everyone when we did photos like this. I didn't mean to make you feel bad."

Emily shrugged, not willing to admit that she'd been hurt. June touched her chin and made her meet her eyes.

"I mean it. I'm sorry. You were helping me, and I was being a shit."

Emily finally met her eyes, and June smiled in response, her eyelids lowered. "I'm going to have to make it up to you," she said, her voice low. She scooted a little closer on the couch, her face inches away. Emily caught the scent of almond and leaned nearer.

"And how are you going to make it up to me?" she whispered.

June smiled coyly. "I can think of a few things."

Emily kissed her, and a moment later, June had her hands in Emily's hair, pulling it roughly. She stopped kissing her with a hiss of pained pleasure, her body instantly hot and trembling. June kissed her throat and then nibbled it, making Emily's blood sing in her veins, and she threw her head back for easier access.

"Oh, God, I'm so sorry," a voice said.

They both flinched and jerked apart, and Emily saw a stranger standing in the doorway to the sitting room. He turned away, but June called out to him.

"No, wait! Oh, I'm so sorry," she said, standing up. "We shouldn't have—"

He turned back, holding up his hands, his face red. "No, please, don't worry about it. I should have knocked."

The three of them shared awkward glances, and then, as if on cue, they all burst out laughing.

"Christ, what an introduction," June said, holding out her hand. He came into the room and shook hers. "Don't worry about it. I'm sorry to interrupt."

June laughed again. "I'm Juniper Friend, but call me June."

"I'm Christopher Wu—Chris."

Emily stood up and shook his hand. "Emily Murray."

His gaze traveled back and forth between them, and he squinted. "You're the art historian, right, June?"

"Yes."

"And you're an English professor," he said to Emily.

She hesitated. Technically, she wasn't, but she said, "Right again."

He seemed pleased to have remembered correctly. "Well, judging from the list I was given, I'm the only nonacademic attending this summer."

"You're a botanist?" Emily asked.

He shook his head and then shrugged. "Not really, but in a way. I studied history, botany, and gardening. Well, actually, I came by gardening through my parents. I should say I studied history and botany in school. I'm a landscape historian."

"Very interesting," Emily said.

He laughed. "You might be the only person I've ever met that responded that way."

"Well, you're going to be in a houseful of nerds, and we all have our hobby horses no one else knows a thing about."

He smiled. "The celebrated ivory tower." He clenched a fist in victory. "At last! I've made it!"

June threw her head back, laughing fully, and Emily saw Chris flush as he watched her. She wasn't surprised—she knew herself that making June laugh was one of life's most precious pleasures. And, despite the embarrassment of being caught together, at least he would know that June was already taken.

"Would you like a drink?" June asked.

He shook his head. "No, I'm sorry. I don't drink very much. Not because I can't—alcohol doesn't sit well with me."

"How about club soda? Water?"

"Sure—club soda. With lime, if you have it."

As June fixed his drink, Emily watched him check out the room, obviously curious. He paused at the sight of her camera and equipment.

"I'm sorry," he said, taking his drink. "You must have been working. I can go get unpacked if you want to get back to it."

June threw Emily a quick glance, smiling. "No, it's fine. We were taking a break."

"Is that what you kids call it these days?" he asked.

June laughed again and swatted his arm. "You're a riot. I'm glad one person out here has a sense of humor. The rest are sticks in the mud out here in the sticks." She winked at Emily.

He raised his eyebrows. "That so? I'm looking forward to meeting Mark Somner. I've read quite a lot of his research. There's a lot of crossover with what I do and architecture, actually."

"How interesting. So tell me, what exactly does a landscape historian do?"

He grinned. "If I had a dollar for every time someone asked me that…no, that's not really true. No one ever asks, because my job sounds deadly boring. But of course, I wouldn't do anything else. To put it simply, I work with historical homes and estates, restoring old gardens. I've designed some gardens myself, but generally an historical estate will hire me to help restore or, in some cases, replant old gardens based on original designs."

June and Chris sat down on the sofa together, and Emily was forced to sit in the armchair nearest June. Neither one of them seemed to even acknowledge her or attempt to include her in their conversation. It nettled her a little, but she was also used to this kind of treatment. It was easy to forget she was in the room.

"Where's the most interesting place you've ever worked?"

He paused. "Well, I did a lot of training in Europe, actually, and now I work there for the most part. After college, I started with a few years at Versailles, one at Hampton Court Palace, and most recently at the Schönbrunn in Vienna. I actually still work there, technically, but I've taken a leave of absence to do a study here for a month."

"Oh," June said, frowning. "So you're not here all summer?"

He smiled and shook his head. "No. But don't worry—you'll be sick of me by then."

"I doubt it," June said.

Emily had watched this exchange with growing concern. June had turned her body toward him on the sofa, her back to Emily, and Chris leaned toward her. Their arms—June's left, his right—were almost touching. She had never been a jealous person, and she certainly knew that what was happening was completely innocent, but she also couldn't help but feel a deep sense of misgiving. Chris was incredibly handsome—striking, in fact, more so even than Jim. He was trim and fit, with gorgeous cheekbones and thick black hair. Considering that he'd probably been in the car all day, he was dressed well, almost dapper in fact. With his self-deprecating humor and charm, he was also easy to like. He and June looked good together, natural, in a way.

Chris was talking about his plans for his study at Gnarled Hollow, and Emily focused back in as he finished. "So anyway, the gardens here are very small, but from what Mrs. Bigsby—Ruth, that is—told me, they're in the original design from when they were planted, with many of the plants grown from parenting clippings and vines. It'll be very interesting to see them and the old greenhouse. You don't find many formal gardens in this part of the world, and I'm curious to see what they decided to plant and grow."

He glanced at his watch and then stood up. "Anyway, I'll let you two get back to work. I want to unpack and maybe take a swim later. It was a hot ride here with this weather."

"Oh God, I'd love a swim, too. It's sweltering in here." June cocked her head. "That reminds me. How did you get here?" She gestured at the front window, and Emily saw what she meant—there was no car outside. "We, uh, might have greeted you more properly if we'd heard you coming." June glanced at Emily, her cheeks reddening a little.

"I rode a bike in from town. I took it with me on the bus when I came up here from New York. Little did I know the house was ten miles out. I should have hired a cab."

"I'm happy to go swimming with you, if you don't mind," June said.

"Not at all. I heard there was a steam room out there, too. I know it sound funny, but a steam on a hot day is really great."

June and Emily shared a look. "You don't want to go in there."

"Oh? Why?"

Emily shook her head. "Believe me. You just don't."

"It's...defective," June said, meeting her eyes.

Chris's face fell. "Oh, really? That's a shame. Well, anyway, the pool will be nice. When can you go?"

"Half an hour?"

"That's fine. I don't have a lot with me, so that should be enough time to unpack a little and get dressed. You wanna come too, Emily?"

She shook her head before thinking better of it. "No. But you guys go ahead. I want to get back to work."

"Oh, that's right, the Lewis papers!" Chris said, hitting his forehead. "Ruth mentioned them. You'll have to tell me all about them at dinner. Sorry I didn't ask earlier."

"'S okay."

After getting directions to his room, Chris left the sitting room. June held back, watching him leave, then turned back to Emily. Her face crinkled in concern.

"Are you okay? You seem, I don't know, upset or something."

Emily shook her head. "No. I'm fine."

"Are you sure? Are you embarrassed about what happened earlier? I mean, when he walked in on us?"

She managed a smile. "No—that's fine. It's funny, really."

"Okay. But I don't like leaving you here alone. I'd feel better if you came along, even if you don't get in the water." She paused. "Oh. Is that it? Are you afraid of going to the pool after what happened?"

That wasn't it at all, but she leapt at the excuse. "Yeah. I know it's stupid—"

June put a hand on her shoulder. "It's not stupid at all. I'm sorry for even suggesting it. Do you want me to stay with you?"

She wanted that more than anything in the world right now, but she'd never admit it. For one, she didn't want to seem needy, and for another, it would ruin June's fun, and she wouldn't have that.

"No, June, really. I don't mind at all. I might lie down for a little before dinner, anyway. I'm really hot."

"Yes, you are," June said, grinning at her stupid joke. "Okay—I'll leave you be. But if you reconsider, please come. I can't imagine we'll be gone that long, but if you get lonely, come anyway."

"Okay."

"Do you mind putting this stuff away for me?" June asked, waving at the photography equipment. "Just back in the cases. I'm going to leave it down here, for now, until I finish up on this floor, but I don't want it all lying around, either."

"I can do that," Emily said.

June kissed the tip of her nose. "Thanks. You're a peach."

She watched June race upstairs and then turned back to the equipment, sighing. She didn't mind helping. In fact, despite her fatigue, she would have gone on working all afternoon and evening, had they not been interrupted. She did mind feeling left out but knew she was being stupid. Both of them had invited her along, after all. So why didn't she want to go?

She finished by the time June and Chris came back downstairs. Both of them could have been swimsuit models. June took her breath away. She was dressed, surprisingly, in a modest one-piece, but somehow on June it was far sexier than any bikini would have been. It was solid red and contrasted nicely with her skin and hair. June had said she liked to swim, so it might be some kind of racing suit. Emily made herself look away and saw Chris grinning at her, as if he'd read her mind. She blushed, embarrassed to be so transparent.

"Are you sure you want to stay?" June asked again.

"Really, it's no problem to wait if you want to get your suit," Chris said. He had washboard abs, and despite her own preferences, she had a hard time not staring at them as he talked.

"Or you can come and sit with us as we swim," June offered, giving her a knowing stare. She thought, Emily remembered, that she didn't want to go because she didn't want to get in the water.

"No, really, you guys go ahead. I'm going to rest for a while."

They finally let the subject drop, and Emily watched them walk side by side outside, first past the front windows and then around the side of the house. June's face was lit up with laughter before Emily lost sight of her, and Emily had to fight a sickening sense of disappointment and dread after they disappeared.

June never laughed like that with her.

CHAPTER ELEVEN

Emily conjured up a thousand imaginary scenarios to explain why Chris and June were gone so long. Rather than nap, as she'd claimed, she spent the time pacing the ground floor of the house, looking at the paintings and out the windows. There were, strangely, no windows from this floor that revealed much beyond the nearest side of the gardens. The library's windows were high and small, and the ones in the kitchen were slightly angled away from the gardens, so she was unable to watch for their return. Hours seemed to pass, but the clock consistently showed her that it had been only ten or fifteen minutes since she last checked the time.

"You're being ridiculous," she told herself. And she was, but she couldn't help it. Her stomach kept dropping when she pictured the two of them together, swimming around and showing off their beautiful, athletic bodies to one another. She'd almost convinced herself to head out to the pool when she heard the telltale pop of the gravel road beneath tires. Mark and Jim had returned.

She went into the kitchen and watched Mark park his huge sedan next to the carriage house. Only June and Emily could fit their cars inside. Mark hadn't been happy about this discovery and had bought a tarp in town to cover his vehicle. She watched him and Jim struggle with it, and when they started walking toward the house, she opened the back door and waved.

Mark waved back, grinning, and Emily saw that he was holding several long, heavy cardboard tubes under one arm and a thick, large leather book under the other. Jim was likewise burdened, holding three more leather books, and she walked out to help them.

"Jackpot!" Mark said, still grinning broadly.

"What is all this stuff?" She took the leather book from him.

"I'll tell you when we get inside. Let's go in the dining room, since that's the only table big enough for the blueprints."

"You found them?"

Jim laughed. "We discovered everything, and I mean *everything*."

They set all their findings down on the far end of the dining table, away from where the four of them usually ate. Jim's face was a little red with exertion, and he fanned it a few times with a hand.

"Man, do I miss air-conditioning. Who knew it would be so god-awful hot out here in the woods."

Mark wiped his face with a handkerchief. "And it's only early June. I can't imagine what it'll be like in a month."

"So, tell me what you found," she said. The large books were old, giving off the musty scent of decayed leather and paper.

"Let me show you the plans, first," Mark said. He took off the plastic end of one of the cardboard tubes and shook out a wide roll of paper.

"I didn't know they made plans like this back then," she said as he unrolled it.

Mark and Jim pinned down the corners with two empty cups and two clean saucers.

"They didn't," Mark said, laughing. "Not like this, anyway. I found the original plans and scanned them. Then I blew them up and printed them so I could see them more clearly. The originals are in one of these books."

She leaned down closer to examine them. The first one he'd unrolled was a very clear rendition of the front, back, and sides of the house. She noted slight differences—the windows seemed smaller in these plans, but the house was recognizable.

Mark was grinning at her. "Notice anything different?"

"The windows, for one," she said. She looked back down at it, frowning. Something else was different, but she couldn't put her finger on it. She shook her head. "I'm not sure what else."

He smiled and held up a finger. "Wait a minute, and I'll get my own sketches. Maybe then you'll see it."

He left the room and came back a few minutes later, holding a large drawing pad. He flipped through it and opened it to his rendition of the front of the house. She took it from him and looked back and forth between the plan on the table and his sketch. Again, she could see a difference, but she couldn't pinpoint what it was.

"I can see and not see it," she said, handing the drawing back to him.

"What about you, Jim?" Mark said, holding out the sketchbook for him.

"Oh, for God's sake, Mark. Just tell us what it is."

Mark laughed and turned the page in his pad before giving it back to her. This sketch consisted of a detail of the ground-floor windows at the front of the house, and underneath, she saw numbers. Ten windows stretched across the front of the house in his drawing, and when she counted, twelve were on the blueprint.

"Bizarre," she said.

"It's like that on all sides of the house," Mark said, flipping to the next page.

Emily counted the ones in the blueprint, and he was right. In his drawings, every side of the house showed two fewer windows than in the plans. "Did the plans change later?"

Mark shook his head and took the sketchbook from her. "No, and that's the strangest thing about it. If they decided to make the house smaller, it would be in their interests to submit the correct plans. Tax payments were based on the size of the house, and these plans," he tapped the one on the table, "show a much larger house. Two more windows don't seem like a big deal, but it would actually mean much more space on every floor."

"That is weird," she said. "Why would they do that?"

Mark shrugged. "It's a complete mystery. Jim and I also found the builder's notes here, which is pretty rare, so maybe I'll discover why things changed when they built it, but it's definitely odd." He grinned. "But that's not the only evidence that the house is different from the plans."

He picked up a second cardboard tube, shook out a second blueprint, and he and Jim rolled it over the top of the front plan and weighted it down. This was the plan for inside on the second floor, where the bedrooms were now. This time, Emily saw the difference immediately. She looked up from the plans into Mark's grinning face.

"What the hell?" she asked.

"Right?"

Jim bent down to examine it and then frowned. "The rooms are completely different."

Mark pointed at him. "Exactly." He flipped around in his sketchbook again and set his drawing of the second floor down on top of the blowup of the original house plans. "You can see the missing rooms *in the plans!*" He sounded triumphant. "Instead of four bedrooms on either side of the stairs, as in the original plans, we have only three. The original also has an extra bathroom on either side of the staircase—but we have only the two, one on either side. The plans the Lewis family submitted were for a much larger house. Every floor, every room is significantly bigger in the originals, and you can see in the plans that these room configurations are different, too. Walls have been moved around, shapes are different. I haven't begun measurements yet, but I suspect the difference is going to be really, really significant. This house," he touched the plans again, "would make the one we're standing in look like a farmer's cottage."

"How strange!" Emily said. She felt strange, too. Seeing the differences made her stomach knot up. Comparing the two was like seeing a reflection in a fun-house mirror—distortions so different as to make the real house appear like something alien, twisted. "Why would they do this?"

Mark shrugged. "It's possible that the plans changed as they built. The family might have run out of money, or maybe they decided the upkeep on the larger house would be too expensive. It would take a great many servants to maintain a house as huge as the one in the plans. But why didn't they submit the new ones? Why would anyone want to pay higher taxes?" He shook his head. "There's no reason."

"So you didn't find the new plans at all?" she asked.

"No. Nothing else, and I've been through the whole archive. It's possible they were filed in a different town, but I doubt it, especially since we found these here. And we almost didn't locate these. Jim and I were about to give up, but the archivist remembered an old, locked trunk in a storage room in a different part of the library, and that's where we came across all this." He indicated the pile of things around the room.

"Too weird," Jim said. "This whole place doesn't make any sense." He blushed a little. This was as near an admission as he'd made that something was off here, and he knew it. "I mean architecturally, of course."

Emily and Mark shared a glance and then leaned back down to examine the original plans. After a while, she stood up, a shiver running down her spine. She didn't like seeing the differences. Jim was right—something was distinctly wrong with Gnarled Hollow. Even aside from what had happened to her, the whole place was off, somehow, and seeing it on paper wasn't helping her feel better about it.

Mark planned to start the inside measurements tomorrow and needed help, so Jim agreed to give him a couple of hours in the morning. The day after tomorrow, Mark planned to drive to Plattsburgh, which was several hours away, so he could spend the afternoon meeting with the professor he'd contacted at the university there.

Emily was only half listening to them, staring out the window. She wanted to figure out what she was feeling. She was chilled, yes, creeped out, certainly, but something else was there in her mind, something she'd felt before, after she was attacked in the bathroom. The realization, when it came, almost made her laugh. She was curious. Yes, she wanted to stay here and complete her work—she'd never get another chance like this. And yes, she wanted to be here with June—she'd also never have a chance with someone like her for the rest of her life. But mainly, she was also curious about this house. Why was it like this?

"Hey, Emily? Earth to Emily!" Jim said.

She looked at him, startled, and then laughed. "Sorry."

"I was asking you where June is. I thought we all agreed to stick together in pairs." He sneered as he spoke, as if he wanted her to know he thought the rule was stupid.

"She and Chris are swimming. Chris Wu—he got here earlier today."

"I can't believe she'd go out there again," Jim said, "after what happened to you guys."

Emily had no response, agreeing with him totally. She would never set foot in the pool house again, if she could help it.

"Chris is some kind of gardener, right?"

Emily explained what he'd told them earlier.

"Ah," Mark said, grinning. "I've seen his work before. I think I've even read some of his research."

"He's interested in meeting you, too," she said.

"Well, I'll start on a welcome dinner, then," Jim said. "It's been a while since we all ate together in the evening." He turned to leave and then swung back around, meeting her eyes.

"Say, Emily? I wanted to apologize." He had to look away from her, and he colored a little. "About the other night. I was wrong. I know you didn't do that to yourself. I knew it then, but I was being pigheaded."

Again, she was startled. He'd apologized to her before, and now, like then, it seemed completely uncharacteristic. Maybe he was less of a dick than she'd assumed.

"It's okay, Jim. I don't blame you. It's true what you said—there wasn't really any proof."

"Except the obvious," he said, his eyes falling to her neck.

She was wearing a light, gossamer scarf today to hide the bruises. They'd faded a little, but they were still dark and mottled in places, yellow or green in others.

She shrugged. "You saw what you wanted to see. You thought what you wanted to think. It's okay. I forgive you."

His face still appeared troubled. "I don't know what happened to you, Emily. I don't even think I *want* to know what did that to you. And I sure as hell hope nothing else happens. I don't believe in ghosts, or hauntings, or anything like that, but I do know that something's wrong here."

He left for the kitchen, and when she turned around, it was clear that Mark had overhead the entire exchange. He raised one eyebrow. "That was unexpected."

"No kidding," she said. She pointed at the other leather books. "So those are all the builder's plans?"

Mark shook his head. "No. Some of them are tax statements, and some are building contracts. There's more in the library, actually, but Jim and I couldn't carry it all. I'll start on what I've got here, and then I'll go back and get the rest." He paused. "Between this stuff and the Margot Lewis papers, we probably have enough material for a biography of the family and the house. I actually want to talk to everyone about doing something like that—maybe even together."

"Gnarled Hollow and its Captives," she said, grinning.

He laughed. "Something like that. Maybe we can discuss it at the end of summer, once we've all done some more research. I'm due back in New York in August, but we could still do a collaborative project when we're separated." He held up his hands. "Anyway— think about it. I'm just dropping the idea in your ear for now."

Emily's hopes rose and sank, and she shook her head. "Did Jim tell you? I mean, about me?"

Mark hesitated. "That you've been let go? Yes, and I'm sorry to hear it. That doesn't mean you can't still publish. And anyway, won't that mean you can devote yourself to a project like this?"

She smiled. "That's true. All I have is time now."

The front door suddenly flew open and banged into the adjacent wall. She and Mark jumped, startled. The double doors into the foyer were closed, but Mark opened one of them, and she followed him. June was standing in the front doorway, her hair soaked and plastered to her body. She looked around wildly, and when she spotted them, she sagged with obvious relief.

"Oh, Jesus, thank God you're here, Mark. Please, help me. I couldn't move him. I had to leave him there!" Her hands went to her face, her fingers hooked into claws. For a moment, Emily was certain she would tear at her skin. "Oh, God, he's still there! He's all alone! Please help! Help me!"

Clearly attracted by the noise, Jim had rejoined them. "What's happened? What's wrong?" he asked.

"There's no time," June said, almost screaming. "He's in the pool house. I got him out of the water, but I couldn't bring him here!

He's still there! Don't you understand? I had to leave him in there with…with it!"

Mark met Emily's eyes. "Stay here with her." He looked at Jim. "Let's go."

"Run, goddamn it! He was breathing when I left him, I think he was anyway, but that thing was still in there! I could feel it!"

Both men ran from the room, and June watched them for a moment before crumpling onto the floor, sobbing and shaking. Emily immediately went to her, kneeling and pulling her into her arms. June turned and hugged her with such ferocity, they almost fell over.

"It's okay, June," she said, rubbing her back. "You're all right now."

June pulled back a little, her eyes still wild. "It was there! It was in the pool with us!" She choked on a sob, and Emily pulled her back into her arms. June cried on her shoulder, her body hitching as she tried to catch her breath. Her feet were caked with mud and leaves.

"What happened?" Emily asked.

June shook her head against Emily's shoulder, still too upset to speak.

"It's okay. Shhhhhh. I'll take care of you. I won't let it hurt you again."

June snuffled against her, her face still tucked into Emily's shoulder. They were still on the floor, June's body twisted around hers. She continued to rub her back, trying to see out the front windows, hoping for the others to return.

She heard them before she saw them, and a moment later, they were spilling into the room, Jim and Mark holding Chris between them under his arms. Chris's head was lolling around on his neck, his eyes closed—clearly unconscious. She and June rocketed to their feet, and June opened the double doors into the sitting room. Jim and Mark dragged Chris in there, set him down on the sofa, his head thrown back, and then collapsed into nearby chairs, breathing heavily.

June knelt down on the sofa next to Chris, peering at his face, and then looked back at Mark.

"Is he alive?" she whispered.

Mark was still panting from exertion. He nodded. "His breathing is regular, and his pulse is okay."

"Oh, thank God," June said, covering her face with her hands. She dropped them a moment later, staring at them with red-rimmed eyes. "I got him out of the water. I don't know how. I couldn't, at first. He was stuck on the bottom."

"How do you mean?" Mark said, leaning forward, his forearms resting on his legs.

June took a long deep breath and let it out, shaking. "We were swimming. Everything was fine. We were goofing around a little. Racing, splashing, that kind of thing. Being stupid. Then, all of the sudden, he wasn't there behind me."

"What?" Jim asked. "What do you mean?"

She shook her head. "Exactly that. One minute he was there. He was laughing! Right behind me! And then…it was like his laughter was cut off. I turned around and he was gone. I swear to God—he just disappeared."

"How can that be?" Jim asked.

"I'm telling you what happened, goddamn it! He was in the pool with me, and then he wasn't!" She was still clearly terrified, but little spots of red colored her cheeks now.

Jim held his hands up. "Okay—he disappeared. Jesus."

She continued to glare at him, and then her face crumpled again. She shook her head to fight off the tears and went on. "At first, I thought he dove under. But I knew right away that couldn't be true. It's so bright in there, you can see the whole pool. But I dove down anyway to look. No one was there. I came back up and got out of the pool. I looked everywhere! I mean everywhere! I looked under seat cushions, for Christ's sake. I looked outside. He was gone, I tell you. Like he never existed!" Her eyes grew distant, welling with tears.

Mark touched the top of her hand. "What happened next?"

She shook her head to focus again. "I looked in the steam room."

Emily couldn't help but gasp, and June turned her way. "That's how desperate I was. But he wasn't there, either. I was about to run back here, call the police, do something, but when I came out of the steam room, he was there, in the pool, at the bottom."

"Jesus," Jim said, his voice quiet. "And you're sure he wasn't there the whole time?"

"Of course I am! Christ, do you think I could have missed him? I'm telling you—he wasn't there before!"

"Okay, okay, whatever. Damn, June."

Her face was so dark and angry she seemed ready to start swinging. She met Emily's eyes again, and her face relaxed a little. "When I saw him, I dove in immediately. I got down to him, but he was stuck. I pulled on his hand, but he wouldn't move. Nothing was holding him down that I could see, and I had to go back up for air and try again. The second time, I ran my hands over his whole body, trying to figure out what was holding him there. That's when I felt it."

"What?" Emily asked, her voice so quiet, she wasn't sure she was even audible.

June paled, her eyes darkening. "Hands. Arms. The hands were all over his legs, holding him down there. Dozens of them." She shook her head. "I don't really know what happened next. I was trying to pull them off him, but they wouldn't move. I remember that I needed to go up for air again, but I couldn't leave him there. Then, suddenly, the hands were gone, and he came up easily. I almost couldn't get him out of the pool, but I did. I saw that he was breathing, and then I ran back here."

Everyone was silent. The room was leaden with tension, all of them holding still as if waiting for something.

"Holy shit," Jim said. His eyes were big, round. He pointed a shaky finger at Chris, and, following the direction it indicated, Emily saw dark red marks all over Chris's legs. Already, some of them looked like handprints.

"Holy shit!" he said again, getting to his feet. "It's real! Christ almighty, you're telling the truth. This is happening! Holy shit!" He clutched at his hair, pulling on it in a way that would have been comically dramatic in any other circumstances. "My God! We have to get out of here! We need to leave—right now!"

"Jim, be quiet," Mark said. His voice, though soft, cut through the room. It carried enough calm authority that Jim shut up as if turned off. Some of the hysteria in his face seemed to seep away. His body relaxed, and he dropped his hands to his side again.

Mark, however, wasn't paying attention to him, and when Emily followed his gaze, she saw Chris stirring a little. All of them leaned toward him, and June, who was next to him on the sofa, took his hand. After a moment, he sat up and then groaned, his other hand going to his head in pain.

"Damn," he said. He blinked a few times, coughed, and then seemed to realize that he was being watched. He shook his head as if to clear it and scooted up on the couch, looking around at all of them with relatively clear eyes.

"Hello," he said, his face breaking into a handsome grin.

"Hi," Mark said, laughing. "Welcome to Gnarled Hollow."

CHAPTER TWELVE

After June and Chris showered and put on regular clothes, everyone gathered to talk over cocktails. The others had taken the four seats around the coffee table, so Emily was forced to drag over one of the chairs from the card table. No one noticed her doing this or offered to help. Even now, they seemed caught up with each other, especially June with Chris. She was holding his hand again, and Chris accepted it as if it were his due. He was calm, or seemingly so, though that might have been partly to do with the three stiff drinks he'd already downed. He drinks heavily for someone that claims not to drink much, Emily thought. She saw him occasionally wince when he moved too fast, and, like she had earlier this week, he seemed to avoid looking at the marks on his legs.

Chris remembered nothing of his ordeal beyond being in the pool with June and then waking up in the house. She was partly relieved for him, but also strangely let down by his amnesia. He was the only person who had vanished and come back when someone was watching, but he had no memory of his time away, wherever he'd gone. She was certain that, had he been awake the whole time, he would have experienced a shift in time, just as she had on the road and in the steam room.

As they sipped their drinks, Mark gave him a breakdown of the events of the last week. Chris listened, interested and polite, glancing at her once in a while during the story of the bathtub. She let Mark describe it, not offering any extra details. Mark might have thought she was too traumatized to say anything about it herself, as he never paused or suggested she jump in. June and Jim listened silently.

When Mark finished, Chris let out a long, low whistle. "Wow. An honest-to-god haunted house. I heard rumors at some of the places I've worked, but I've never actually experienced or seen anything myself. Crazy."

She and the others looked at each other. Despite what had happened, she was strangely uncomfortable calling Gnarled Hollow a haunted house, and she could tell the others were, too.

Seeing their faces, Chris laughed. "Well, how else do you explain it? Are you honestly telling me you don't think this house is haunted?"

"That's just it, Chris," Mark said after a pause. "None of us know what it is. 'Haunted' seems to suggest a presence, a being of some kind."

"What do you call this?" Chris said, indicating the marks on his legs. He pointed at her. "Or what happened to Emily? And June felt the hands on me, too."

"Exactly," Emily said. It was the first thing she'd said in a while, and everyone seemed surprised to hear her voice. "It's hands and arms without a body!" She shuddered.

June paled. "I made the mistake of trying to find the body attached to one of the arms, and nothing was there—nothing at all. I felt an arm that went on and on. And they don't feel like hands or arms—the skin is wrong somehow. They're hands, but they're not."

"Okaaay…So what about the woman in the window?" Chris said. "Isn't that a classic ghost? There one minute, gone the next?"

"If you'd seen her—" Jim stopped.

Chris laughed. "What? I'd think she was completely normal? Right. People can disappear when they feel like it."

Emily, Jim, and Mark shared puzzled glances, unable to explain what they meant. "It's something more than that," she said lamely. "It's almost like she's there and not there at the same time."

Jim and Mark were nodding. "Exactly," Jim said, pointing at her. "That's exactly how she is."

Chris huffed in impatience. "What's that supposed to mean? 'There and not there?' That doesn't mean anything!"

She frowned, trying to think of a way to put it into words. "It's almost as if, if you were looking at the right angle, she'd still be there. Like she didn't actually disappear—you just can't see her anymore."

Jim was visibly excited, his color bright and his eyes shining. "That's exactly how I felt when I saw her. Like if I could stand in the right place—"

"Or at the right time," Mark said.

She looked at him sharply. He'd put his finger on it. She met Jim's gaze, and he nodded again, his eyes slightly crazed. "Exactly. The right time. That's it exactly."

Chris laughed again. "Are you serious? You mean, like she's actually there, but in some other time?"

She, Jim, and Mark nodded at once. Somehow, the explanation fit precisely. Why hadn't she thought of it before?

Chris looked at June. "Do you agree with them?"

June shrugged. "I haven't seen her. I don't know. But the hands didn't feel human. That much, I know."

Chris rolled his eyes. "Fine. But regardless of when, who do you think she is? Margot Lewis?"

Emily shook her head immediately. "No. Margot didn't look anything like the woman in the window."

Jim was silent for a moment. "She's right. I don't recognize her, either. Maybe one of Margot's sisters? I think she had a couple."

"She had one," Emily said. "And one brother. They both died pretty young."

"Well, maybe that's her, then," Chris said. "Maybe it's her sister. Do you know anything about her?"

She shook her head. "No. I know her brother died in some kind of accident when they were all pretty young, but I don't remember what happened to her sister. I think she died when Margot was abroad." She tried to recall any details and then shook her head. "I don't remember anything else."

Chris sighed and then stretched, wincing again a moment later. He met her eyes. "Well, maybe that should be your part."

"What do you mean?"

He grinned. "Your part to solve, I mean. The family."

She frowned. "I don't follow."

Chris laughed. "That's what we should do, right? Isn't that what they always do in haunted-house stories? Find the cause? Isn't that how you rid a house of ghosts?"

Emily was uncomfortable again, and judging from their faces, the others felt similarly. She was curious, yes, but since the attack in the bathtub, she'd hoped to simply slide under the house's radar long enough to complete her work. The last few days of relative quiet had convinced her it was possible. She had felt, without putting it into words, that if she and the others simply did their jobs, didn't ruffle too many curtains, the house would let them stay here and then, when they were done, let them leave.

Chris laughed again. "Don't you want to figure it out? Aren't you all curious?" He looked around at each of them and shook his head as if disgusted. "Well, I am. And pissed off. At the very least, I'm banged up like I was in a hell of a fight. And if June hadn't been there, I think I would have been killed." He squeezed June's hand. "Thanks. For saving me."

Emily launched to her feet. She didn't like being put on the spot, but she had to convince them—had to get this right.

"It doesn't want us to solve anything," she said. "It wants us to leave it alone."

Mark's eyebrows lowered, but he didn't seem angry—only interested. "What do you mean, Emily?"

She was breathing rapidly, almost as if she'd been running, but she had to convince them. It was vital that they listen, that they understand.

"Everything that's happened is a warning."

Chris guffawed, but the others were looking at her as if they too had reached a similar conclusion. She held up a hand and counted off on her fingers.

"The woman in the window, for one. For me and Mark, she appeared before we even entered the house." She turned to Jim. "She also appeared to Jim, but think about how that happened. You were drawn outside first—almost as if something was trying to get your attention."

"It was a piece of trash," he said, frowning.

"But it wasn't there before. I was looking out that same window, and I didn't see anything. It was a little like the woman in the window—it was there, but I couldn't see it. It waited to show itself to you, Jim. To warn you."

The others seemed less certain now, and Jim was clearly unconvinced. Her opportunity was slipping away, but she continued.

"Then, when we didn't listen to the warnings, things got worse."

"You can say that again," Chris said.

"No, listen to me for a second! When I didn't heed the first warning—the woman in the window—the doors closed on their own. Then, when I still didn't listen, the canopy in my bed opened by itself." She thought harder, trying to piece it all together. "Then, after I told all of you about what had happened, it attacked me. I don't think it likes to be talked about."

Chris laughed again, but June was watching her. Jim had gotten up and was staring out the front window at the lawn. Mark was frowning at her, seeming halfway convinced.

"June," she said. "What were the two of you talking about? In the pool, I mean? Before Chris was attacked?"

June blushed slightly before shaking her head. "Nothing much. School, family, that kind of thing. Getting to know each other."

"Did you talk about the house?"

June looked at her sharply and shared another glance with Chris. "Yes, actually. I didn't tell him much—"

Chris broke in. "But she did say that you all had some stories to tell me later. About the house."

They were all quiet, and Emily could tell that she had, at least in part, convinced some of them. Chris, however, was clearly skeptical.

"So what do you propose?" he asked. "Should we leave?"

She immediately shook her head. "No. But we should leave it alone. We should do what we came here to do and not talk about the house. It doesn't want us to figure anything out."

Chris grinned, his mouth twitching as if he might laugh again, but when he saw that the others were starting to agree with her, he frowned deeply and got to his feet. He went over to the bar and poured himself some club soda. He hesitated for a second and poured a little vodka in his glass as well.

"Look," he said when he turned around. "I get it. You're all scared. I'm scared, too. But we can't have it both ways. As far as I can see, we have two options: either all of us go upstairs, right now, and pack our bags, or we stay here and figure this out." He paused, meeting their eyes. "Otherwise things are going to keep happening. It's not safe here, and it won't be unless we solve this thing."

"I'm not leaving," June said.

Emily was just as surprised as everyone else, and June colored slightly when they all looked at her. Her expression became more determined, and she shook her head. "I refuse to let it win. I wanted to leave. Before, I mean, but not anymore. Not now."

Jim let out a bark of laughter. "Agreed. Fuck this house and the ghosts, or whatever's doing this to us."

Mark was staring at her, his expression grave and thoughtful. After a long pause, he sighed. "I'm staying. And I agree with Chris. We can't have it both ways."

She went hot and then cold. Dread welled up in her stomach, and her heart fluttered with terror. On some level, she'd known it would come to this. The others wouldn't see it. She'd been here only a couple of days longer than they had, but she was right. If they left it alone, it would leave them alone. But people weren't like her. She knew that, too.

She sighed, accepting the inevitable. Whatever was going to happen, it seemed fated to happen. Everyone was determined. "So what do you want to do?"

Chris grinned broadly. "That's more like it."

Everyone looked at Mark. He was the natural, unspoken leader of the group. He seemed to accept this mantle without discussion, and she could see that he was already considering the question. After a while, he sighed and shrugged.

"In the long run, I don't know. But one thing I do know is something we can do together. We should go through the house, room by room. Now, if possible." He paused, and no one disagreed, so he went on. "I haven't been in the attic, and somehow I bet none of you have gone up there, either."

They all shared another look, and Mark nodded. "Isn't that strange? Not one of us thought to. Almost as if—"

"As if it didn't want us to," she said.

"Exactly."

"What else should we do?" June asked.

Mark paused. "Well, we have other mysteries to solve. Chris has already suggested one, Emily, and I think he's right—you're the person to solve it. We need to find out what happened to the Lewis family. I need to figure out why this house was built the way it is, completely different from the original plans."

"And I need to figure out who painted all the art in this house," June said. She seemed excited, her color high.

"And I need to figure out the gardens," Chris said. "Why are they here? Who planned and planted them?"

Jim was grinning. "And I need to keep working on the Lewis papers. With you, of course, Emily."

Everyone sat as if stunned. It all seemed so simple now. Every person here had a part to play that only he or she could do. Her stomach clenched again with fear. If they pursued this, they would be in a great deal of danger. Someone, she was sure, would be hurt again, and it might be worse this time since they hadn't listened to the warnings. The house wanted them to leave it alone. But they wouldn't—they couldn't. They had to know.

Everyone waited, almost as if each person wanted someone to back out or plead an excuse. Should one person change his or her mind, the whole project would collapse. They were either in this thing together or not at all. She glanced at Mark, willing him to say something, and he looked as if he was having second thoughts. The others seemed tense, even frightened. If no one said anything soon, the opportunity would pass.

She swallowed and squared her shoulders. Now that it had been decided, she didn't want to back out.

She turned to Mark. "Where should we start?"

As if she'd said the magic words, everyone visibly relaxed, their expressions changing from frightened to determined. Mark seemed to feel the shift too and laughed.

"Let's go to the attic first, then, ladies and gentlemen. I'll get my equipment before we head up there."

CHAPTER THIRTEEN

Unlike the side of the house that had been designated as the women's side, the men's side had five doors—three for the bedrooms, one for the bathroom, and one to the attic. The stairs to the attic were located between the bathroom and the corner room, which was partly why Mark, who was staying in there, had a much smaller room than Emily. Like the bathrooms, the door to attic wasn't locked, but it had clearly been unused for a long while, as it was difficult to open. The door was heavy and weighted, designed to close on its own, and Mark and Jim had to hold it open for everyone so they could get through.

The stairs were steep and dark, with no light switch, and when they reached the top of the stairs, after rounding a corner, they found a long hallway that stretched the length of the house. Several doors came off the hall on either side. Windows were located at the ends of the hallway, but no one could see any other lights. After the bright lighting in the rest of the house, the dimness seemed ominous and strange.

"Most of the servants would have stayed up here," Mark said. "I imagine we'll also find one or two larger rooms that male guests or older boys would have used after they graduated from the nursery downstairs."

"Up here with all the maids?" June said, grinning. "Seems a little risqué."

Mark smiled. "You're right. Generally, in a servants' hall like this, you'd have a door, perhaps halfway down the hall, with a lock for the women's side to keep the male servants and male household members out." He walked down to the approximate middle of the hallway and examined the floor and ceiling. "It doesn't even appear as if there was one here in the past. I can imagine taking out the dividing door after servants had become passé, but not to have had one? Ever?" He shook his head. "It would have been unheard of."

Emily and the others walked a little closer to him as he talked, mainly to avoid bunching at the end of the hall, and they left a series of footprints on the dusty floor behind them. No one had been up here in a long time.

"Let's start on one side, and then, if we have time, we can do the other," Mark suggested. He pointed at the door on the left at the end of the hall. "Once we see inside the rooms, maybe we'll get a better idea of how the household was arranged."

They had to force this door too, and when Emily finally saw the inside of the room, she was surprised how small and empty it was. Mrs. Wright had made it sound like the rooms up here were packed with junk and antiques from the past, but this little room held only a twin bed and a tiny dresser. It was much too cramped for all five of them to fit inside comfortably, but she, Mark, and Jim explored a little, opening the dresser drawers and peeking under the bed. They found nothing but the furniture and a single, small window, too high to see out of, caked over with grit and cloudy with age. Jim and Mark quickly measured the room with Mark's laser measure, and Emily took notes.

The next doors on the same side of the hall led to similar rooms, all completely devoid of personality. It made sense, in a way, that they would be plain and empty. It had likely been nearly eighty years since this house had any servants, but Emily couldn't shake the impression that they should have found something in at least one of the rooms—a mark on the wall, a button, anything. And, judging from the dirty floors, they were the first people in these rooms in years, if not decades. In each room, Jim and Mark measured and she took notes, while Chris and June waited in the hall, chatting or watching. Emily was grateful she had the notes to focus on, as she was finding June and Chris's camaraderie difficult to take. Their shared experience in the pool seemed to have shifted alliances.

The last doorway on the first side of the hallway led into a much-larger room—about three times as big as the servants' rooms they'd seen, and here they found some of the things from downstairs that had clearly been shifted up to the attic over the years: broken lamps, crooked tables, a few chairs with missing legs, trunks full of old linens, and other things clearly of little value. Large, white sheets had been thrown over much of the contents, and all five of them had to fight with the dusty material to uncover what was underneath.

Jim, Mark, and she measured and noted the dimensions of the room again, and Mark took the notebook from her when she was done. He cast a critical eye around the room and then handed it back.

"This was likely one of the gentlemen's rooms, if I'm not mistaken," he said.

"What makes you think that?" she asked.

"Well, of course it's much larger, and even though they're small like the others on this floor, there are several windows. If this was a servants' mess room, it likely wouldn't have as many windows. If they had a room like this of their own, it wouldn't be so grand. Also, as we're at the front of the house on this side, this room commands a lovely view of both the front lawn and the woods."

It was difficult to see through the dirt and grime, but Emily realized that Mark was, of course, correct. The view here, if the windows were clean, would likely be the best in the house.

"Anyone tired?" he asked. "Or shall we do the other side of the hall before we call it quits?"

"Might as well," Chris said, wiping at the dust on his sleeve. "No reason to get filthy a second time."

The door across the hall led into another larger room with dimensions equal to the one they'd just been in, but, as Mark predicted, the windows were much smaller. This room, like the other one, was stuffed with junk, but unlike the other larger room, most of the things in here were much older and in even greater disrepair. Some of the chairs and tables appeared to have been pulled apart, and others looked as if they'd been destroyed with tools. Splinters of wood covered the ground, almost as if someone had taken an axe to some of the furniture. Every bit of glass from the lamps and vases had cracks in it.

"This is strange," Mark said, walking over to the windows. He pointed. "These windows have bars on them."

"Why?" June asked. "We're on the third floor here. It isn't as if someone could break in."

Mark raised his hands. "That's why they're strange."

"Hey!" Jim said. "Look at this!"

Everyone turned toward him, and Emily saw he was holding a small wooden box. He dug into it and pulled something out, holding it up for everyone. She took a step closer and could finally make it out: a lead toy solider. Jim seemed incredibly pleased with his find.

"God, don't tell me there are creepy old toys up here," June said, looking around in horror.

Chris laughed. "No kidding. Nothing worse than old dolls."

June laughed, touching his arm lightly, and Emily almost flinched. The exchange had been cute, intimate even, and she forced herself not to run screaming from the room.

"I'm going to take them downstairs with me," Jim said, tucking the box under his arm.

"Why on earth would you do that?" June asked.

"Have you seen my room?" Jim asked. "I'm in the nursery— probably the ugliest room in the whole house. You should see the yellow wallpaper. The least I can do is put some toys in there. For the kiddies."

"Like you?" June said, grinning.

He stuck his tongue out at her, and she laughed.

"Did anyone notice this?" Mark asked. He pointed at the door. Emily hadn't noticed before, but it had several heavy locks on the hallway side.

"It's like a prison," June said, shuddering.

The words rang true, and Emily's stomach dropped. She immediately saw more evidence of what June had suggested. The walls, which were made of blank, grayish plaster, had deep gouges in them, almost as if someone had clawed at them. Emily walked a little closer to try to make sense of what she was seeing. She stopped when she saw something imbedded in the wall.

"Guys?" she said.

"What?" June asked.

Unable to speak, Emily pointed, and the others came closer. They all seemed to recognize it as the same time, as she heard a collective gasp behind her.

"Are those—"

"Shackles," Mark said. "I think you were right on the money, June. At some point, this room was a prison."

June put a hand to her mouth, going pale. "Jesus."

"Christ," Jim said. "What the hell? Who were these people?"

Mark shook his head, sighing. "It wouldn't have been completely unusual to have something like this in the nineteenth century."

"What? Why?" June asked.

"Some families in that era, if they had a troubled child, might have decided it was humane to keep the child at home. Certainly, in some regards, it was better than sending a child to an institution— they were notoriously hellish. They also might have been afraid of the notoriety a troubled child would have brought them should knowledge of it become public."

"Monstrous," Chris said, shaking his head.

Emily was listening to this exchange, but most of her attention was elsewhere. Suddenly, despite the safety she'd found before in the company of the others, she could feel that same watchful sensation she'd had before the attack in the bathroom. She felt first hot and then cold, and then a strange, suffocating sensation squeezed her chest. It was difficult to breathe. She peered around the room, fearful lest she could see whatever it was, but nothing was there beyond the piles of junk and debris.

"We need to get out of here," she whispered. The others looked at her strangely, but her face must have suggested more than her words, as everyone immediately moved toward the door. Unlike the other doors up here, which they'd left open for the light, they closed this one behind them. She wished they had the keys so they could lock it.

"Do you need to go downstairs?" Mark said, putting a hand on her shoulder.

Her heart was still pounding, but she felt better, and the air was moving in and out of her lungs with ease. Whatever had been watching her wasn't out here with them.

She shook her head. "No. But let's finish quickly. I feel…" She couldn't put the impression into words, but it felt again like a warning.

The house was letting them snoop a little, but its patience stretched only so far.

"I feel it too," June said. She held up an arm. "Look—goose bumps."

The men shared a glance, and Jim shrugged. "I mean, I'm creeped out, but I don't feel any different than before."

"I don't, either," Mark said, "but I'm with Emily. We should go back downstairs as soon as we can."

The remaining doors revealed a small bathroom with a tiny tub and toilet and two more empty servants' quarters, identical in dimension and content to the others across the hall. Jim and Mark hurried to finish the measurements, and Emily stayed in the hallway, too shaken to go inside any more rooms. She knew her reaction was completely irrational, but she was terrified that should she go inside any of these rooms again, let alone the one with the bars and shackles, she would be locked up here forever. She was grateful when the final room was measured, and she could tell the others were likewise glad to leave this floor.

Back downstairs, she didn't wait for June to act as bartender. Instead, she went directly to the whiskey and poured herself a large measure, tossing it down in one gulp. She shuddered a little at the heat of the liquor and poured herself another glass before turning around. The others had watched her do this, but seeing her face, they looked away quickly, evidently embarrassed to be caught watching her.

Mark sat down and began flipping through the notes she'd made. The longer he read, the more puzzled his expression grew.

"Sorry," she said, sitting down again in the extra chair. "Can you read my handwriting?"

He gave her a quick smile. "Your handwriting's fine. I'm just confused." He shook his head again and set the notebook to the side. "I'll need to measure the rest of the house before drawing any conclusions."

June sat down on the sofa nearest to them, and Emily saw that she too had poured herself a liberal, stiff drink. The attic had been unnerving on many levels, and not only for her. It was a relief, really, to see that someone else had been affected in the same way, though she wished for June's sake she hadn't gone up there. Regardless of what Mrs. Wright said, it wasn't simply dirty; it was dangerous in the attic. No one should go there.

Jim and Chris sat down, and she was a little relieved to see Jim seat himself next to June. He clearly didn't seem to think it was an issue to take the second sofa seat, but she thought she saw Chris give him a dark look before he sat in the other armchair.

"I'm not going back up there, I'll tell you that much," Jim said.

"That's exactly what I was thinking," June said.

Mark sighed. "You're right. Now that we've been up there, I think it's best we leave it alone. At least that's the impression I get now." He made eye contact with her. "Would you agree, Emily?"

She felt her face color. "Why are you asking me?"

He hesitated. "I don't know. It seems like you're more...attuned to the house somehow."

June nodded, but Chris and Jim also seemed puzzled by his statement. She shrugged and shook her head.. "I wouldn't say that—"

"But it's true," June said, her voice grave, her face pale. "It's like it's talking to you or something."

"What do you mean?" she asked. Her heart was beating faster, and she felt like standing up and leaving the room. She didn't want to hear this.

"Take that room upstairs—the prison," Mark said. "You were affected by it more than the rest of us. Wouldn't you agree?"

"Yes, but I—"

"You were the one who suggested that we leave. I found it odd, but I wasn't particularly bothered. You were. How about you guys? Jim? Chris? Did it affect you?"

Jim shook his head and then lifted his hands. "Well, no, not really. Not at first, anyway."

Chris thought about it. "Yeah, not really. Not until—"

"Not until we left the room?" Mark suggested. Everyone nodded, and her body clenched with fear. Again, she wished she could plug her ears to avoid what he was saying.

"When we were in the hallway, I felt relieved," June said. "I was glad when Mark closed the door."

Jim and Mark nodded immediately, and Chris, after a slight hesitation, agreed.

Mark looked at her again. "It was worse for you. I could see it in your eyes—we all could."

Her heart was pounding now, and a hot flash of rage swept through her. She didn't want to be special, and she certainly didn't want to be the one everyone turned to for an explanation. "But what does it mean? Why am I being singled out?"

Mark shook his head. "I don't know. I'm not sure if it means you're more sensitive to whatever is happening here, or if it's chosen you somehow, singled you out. What I do know is that you seem to pick up on it more clearly than the rest of us. You talked of warnings before, but I think *you* might be our best warning. You seem to be able to translate whatever the house is saying more clearly than anyone else."

She jumped up, her drink falling to the floor. She clenched her fists and felt a momentary thrill when Mark flinched.

"I don't want any of this," she hissed. "Can't you understand? I don't want to be singled out. I don't want to know more than any of you! I just want to be left alone!"

Mark grabbed one of her fists. At his touch, her desperate rage disappeared almost as quickly as it had come, and she opened her hand, taking his. She sat back down, covering her eyes with her other hand. "Why is this happening?"

"I don't know, Emily. But I do think you're in danger here. If you're going to stay—"

She looked up at him sharply, and he paused before going on. "Sorry, *since* you're going to stay, I think we need to be more careful. That goes for all of us. I'm starting to think we shouldn't be alone in this house or on the grounds. Ever."

They were all silent, considering the implications. So far they'd managed a kind of in-between in terms of safety, where they stayed together most of the day, but of course, except for June and her, they went their separate ways at night. But Mark seemed to be suggesting something more.

Jim laughed. "No way I'm taking a crap with anyone else in the room. Certainly not you, Mark." He gave June a wink. "Though I might make one exception—"

She hit him with a sofa cushion. "Ew! Gross!" She looked at Mark. "You don't really mean *all* the time, do you Mark?"

He frowned. "It would be best."

"Well, I'm not going for that, Mark," Jim said, getting to his feet. "And I'm not sleeping with any of you, either." He grinned at June again. "Unless—"

She flipped him off, and he shrugged. "Well, can't say I didn't try to follow the rules." He walked over to the corner bar to get himself another drink.

Mark's expression was troubled, but eventually, he shook his head. "Of course. I'm sorry. I shouldn't have suggested it. No one could expect to be with someone every moment of the day."

Emily felt eyes on her and saw June grinning at her. June patted the vacated spot on the sofa next to her, and her heart rose with relief. She got up and sat down next to her. June scooted closer, taking both her hands in hers. Emily saw Jim's face as this happened. He blushed and then rolled his eyes, sitting down in the chair she'd left. She was happy now and avoided meeting Chris's eyes, sure she'd see that same dark look from before. Instead, she met June's eyes, and June winked. Neither she nor June had said anything about what was happening between them, and they weren't demonstrative in front of the others, but their relationship wasn't exactly a secret, either. Chris knew about it, at the very least, and she was fairly certain Jim and Mark suspected. She and June didn't hide the fact that they spent their nights together, after all.

Emily looked back at the others and saw Mark watching her steadily, his expression grave. Mark, seeing her gaze, gave her a quick smile before his face grew serious again. "I don't want to upset you, but to tell you the truth, it's mainly you, Emily, that I'm worried about."

"Why?" she asked.

He hesitated. "I don't know. If you can somehow pick up on what the house is saying, it might get, somehow…" He seemed unsure how to finish.

"Louder?" Jim suggested. They all looked at him in surprise, and he grinned. "Isn't that the word you wanted, Mark?"

Mark's face was troubled. "That's exactly what I meant."

"If what you're saying about Emily is true," Chris said, "how do you explain what happened to me?"

Mark leaned toward him. "I can't—not exactly. But Emily was attacked first, in the bathtub. She told us earlier today that she thinks it was a warning—a warning we didn't heed. Then the house became more violent, and you were hurt, too."

Chris laughed. "How do you know? It could be completely random! It sounds like you're making the evidence fit the theory, not the other way around."

Mark wrinkled his forehead. "You might be right. All I have is a theory. But I do know—and I think we would all agree—that Emily is somehow involved in all of this in a way the rest of us aren't."

Her momentary happiness faded at his words. She was dimly aware of June's hands squeezing hers for reassurance and heard the others making plans for dinner, but mostly she was looking inside herself, considering. Ever since Mark had singled her out, she'd been angry and afraid. Now that she'd had a few minutes to absorb his conclusion, she was starting to accept it.

Mark was right—she knew he was. She was different, and the house knew it, too. She could either accept that position fully, or she could continue to deny it and stay frightened and angry. The others continued to talk as she made her choice, and by the time she focused on their conversation again, she knew something else: it was up to her to stop what was happening. Now that she'd accepted her part, she realized that deep down she'd known this all along.

But this was only half of it. She knew something else now, too—the house needed her. All the things that had happened had been a warning, yes, but also a kind of plea. Some part of the house was calling for her, begging her to do something.

The question now was not whether she would help it, but how.

CHAPTER FOURTEEN

The next day was ostensibly a workday, but Emily couldn't make herself sit down with the Lewis papers again. After yesterday, she was too hyped up to stay still. Jim didn't seem to mind her taking the morning off. In fact, before she left him to work in her room, she thought she detected a little relief in his eyes. It seemed like he didn't want to be around her.

She spent the first part of the morning helping Mark finish the measurements of the rooms inside the house. Mr. and Mrs. Wright were back for the day, and Mrs. Wright let them into the final, unused bedroom on the women's side so Mark could finish measuring. This last bedroom was larger, a little like Emily's, but it hadn't been completely renovated yet. The canopy was tattered and old, for one thing, and the walls were unpapered.

Back out on the balcony, Mark was studying his notebook, flipping back and forth between the pages for the attic, ground floor, and bedroom floor.

"Strange," he said.

"Hmmm?"

He shook his head. "I have to sit down with this for a while to figure it out. And I should measure the outside before making any conclusions."

"Do you need help?"

He shook his head and then gave her a quick grin. "No—I'll be fine. I'm going to use a measuring wheel." He glanced at his watch. "I should have time if I do it now."

"Oh," she said. "That's right. I forgot you were taking a trip today."

"At least overnight. My GPS says it takes a few hours to get to Plattsburgh from here, so I want to leave by noon at the latest. I might stay another day, until Sunday, but maybe not. Depends on what I find at the university there."

He must have seen something in her face as he touched her shoulder. "Hey, Emily. You might think of taking a break, too. You could stay in town or head to your sister's for a couple of days." He waved vaguely in the direction of the house. "This place is a little… trying, even for me."

She shook her head, firmly. "No. I'm staying."

He sighed and didn't argue, as if he'd expected her to say this. "Okay. But be safe. You hear me?"

She followed him downstairs. She thought of going outside to the gardens to see what Chris was working on but spotted June in the sitting room. They'd taken to propping open both of the double doors to this room with heavy objects, so these doors were always open now. Earlier today, June had gone to her bedroom to do research on her computer, but she was here now. She'd taken one of the larger paintings off the wall and propped it up on an easel. She was examining it with a magnifying glass.

"Find anything?" she asked.

June jumped a little and then turned around, smiling. "Yes and no. I'm telling you, I'm almost completely baffled."

Emily sat in one of the armchairs and leaned forward onto her legs. "What do you know so far?"

"Besides the Turner, I have nothing, and I mean no clue. I did a little more digging online this morning and sent out some inquiries a couple of days ago. I hoped someone would be able to track the sales of at least one of these paintings to give me some kind of idea as to their origin. So far, there's nothing, which is really strange."

"Why? Weren't they bought in the nineteenth century? Would records be around for that long?"

June laughed. "Actually, yes. That's one of the easiest ways to track the origin of a piece of artwork. Auction houses, especially in big cities like New York, keep detailed records and have for centuries. But normally, even if you can't find something in the auction logs, you should be able to find insurance records, at least in the twentieth century." She gestured around the room. "But I haven't located anything for a single one of these paintings, not even the Turner."

"That's strange."

June shook her head. "It's more than strange—it's unheard of. Most of the time people buy artwork as an investment, especially when an artist is well-known. The value rises astronomically over time with some artists." She stood up and walked over to the largest painting in the room. "Take this Turner here. If a Turner—almost any Turner—were to go on the market today, you're talking a sales price of tens of millions of dollars. The last time a private Turner went on the market, it sold for almost thirty million."

"Wow."

June held up her hands. "Who wouldn't insure something worth that much money?" She gestured again at the room. "Let alone the rest of the work in this house! Even if, as I'm starting to suspect, the artists for every other work in the house are unknown, that doesn't negate the fact that these are incredible pieces in their own way. Every painting in this house is a masterpiece, even the portraits."

She sighed and sat down again. "What's even stranger to me right now is that I can't find a single record of the one painting I can recognize—the Turner. It's almost as if it never existed."

"What do you mean?"

"Exactly that. No one has any record that Turner even painted that scene—no one. It's a complete enigma. For someone as famous as him, it's almost impossible. We have his notebooks, his sales receipts, for God's sake. We basically know every work he ever painted. But not this one—not the painting or the sale." She shook her head. "I can't explain it."

Emily glanced around the room at the other works of art, and a little shiver ran up and down her back. Ever since she'd started helping June, she'd been looking at the works in this house a little more closely. June was right. Every piece in the house was museum quality. Generally, when she'd visited stately homes in the past as a tourist, the quality of the artwork was mixed. The wealthy, like anyone, sometimes made poor choices when they bought things. But the artwork in Gnarled Hollow was, overall, impeccable.

The only paintings she didn't care for were the portraits, but even she could see that they were well done. Moreover, she had noticed that the portraits and landscapes were all of a type. To her eyes, anyway, they seemed to have been painted more or less in the same time period. This was also unusual, as it suggested that either they were all bought at the same time, or that the family had decided to keep buying paintings from the same era. This too was unlike any stately home she'd even visited. In most big houses, she'd seen a mix of eras, reflecting art trends over time. The art throughout Gnarled Hollow was uniform.

"Do you have any theories?" she asked.

"Yes, actually, though I don't have a lot of evidence yet."

"What is it?"

June grinned and stood up. "Come look at this painting first. It's a lot like the Turner but with some obvious differences. I was eating breakfast this morning, thinking about all the paintings, and suddenly remembered something I saw in this one a few days ago but hadn't really registered at the time. I got it down again to examine it up close, and I was right. See if you can spot it, too."

The painting showed the New York City harbor. The skyline was immediately recognizable, but the perspective of the piece put the city far in the background. Like Turner, this painter wanted, instead, to show the grand majesty of nature, primarily, and had focused almost entirely on the water and heavy storm clouds. A small boat threatened to wash under one of the turbulent waves, and the colors overall were dark and threatening. Emily peered at it closely for a long time and then at June for explanation.

June pointed at the boat, the sky, and the water. "If I were giving a lecture on this painting in an art-history class, I would tell my students that this is a perfect rendition of what artists in the Romantic era called The Sublime. The notion of The Sublime came out of philosophy in the eighteenth century and eventually influenced artists, primarily in Germany and England. The Sublime is, to put it simply, grandeur on a scale that inspires awe. In art, this usually means scenes like this one—where mankind, or the evidence of mankind, is diminished in the face of nature. Here, the sky and the ocean are so powerful that this little boat has no chance—it's miniscule and weak. When we look at a painting like this, we're supposed see ourselves—our own insignificance in the face of this storm. We, like the boat, are nothing to the ocean and the heavens."

Emily smiled. "Yes—I see."

June pointed at the distant city. "But here's where things get strange, and here's where I think we see Turner's influence in this painting most clearly. With some Romantics, we detect very little evidence of man. In fact, some of paintings don't even depict human figures—we see only nature's awesome force. But in this painting, we can see the city. If you look closely, you can see industry, smoke stacks from factories, that kind of thing. Turner did this a lot, especially in his later paintings, with London and other cities. Mankind, in this painting, has some power. For example, if this little boat can make it through the storm, it will be safe, because New York is safe. The storm hasn't affected it at all. People are working despite the rain. And then there's also this." She held the magnifying glass up to the painting. "What do you see?"

Emily bent down and peered at it closely before standing up again. "Is that the Brooklyn Bridge?"

June smiled and rolled her hands for her to continue.

"But wait," she said, confused. "When was the Brooklyn Bridge built?"

"The late nineteenth century."

"And when did Turner paint?"

June was clearly pleased that she was catching on. "The first half of the nineteenth. He died in the 1850s."

She hesitated. "So you're telling me that this painting is more recent than Turner?"

June nodded vigorously. "More than that—I think it was painted, at most, about a hundred years ago."

She shook her head, still confused. "But that would put it, what, seventy, eighty years after Turner?"

June smiled. "About that."

"But if the Brooklyn Bridge is built in what—the 1870s, 1880s?—that's not really that long after Turner. But you're saying this was painted later than that? How do you know?"

"Two things tell me, actually. One—the paint. I'm sending a sample to have it analyzed, but I'm fairly certain this is modern paint—early twentieth-century paint. The other clue is both obvious and not."

"What?"

"The skyline, of course!" June said.

Emily took the magnifying glass from her again and scrutinized the city. Some taller buildings stood there—clearly none of the awesome skyscrapers from the later twentieth century, but one stood out in vast relief against the cloudy sky.

"What building is that?" she asked.

"It's the Woolworth building. Completed in 1912, opened in 1913."

"Wow," she said. "That's incredible."

June laughed. "I almost missed it. I had to look it up. Some of the buildings in the late nineteenth century were pretty tall, but nothing like the Woolworth. It was the tallest in the city until the 1930s."

"So this painting was created between what, 1913 and 1930 or so?"

"About that, I'd say. And yet, if you didn't know any better, you'd think it was painted around 1840 or 1850. I've never seen anything like it. The 1910s and 20s were the first heyday of Post-Impressionism and Abstraction. No one was painting like this then."

"No one paints in an older style?"

June shrugged. "I mean sure, people try to do it all the time, I guess. Especially students. But it's one thing to try to paint your own Turner, and another to fill a whole house with them."

"So do you have any ideas who painted this?"

"A couple of them. The Lewis family could have hired people to do all of these. That would make the most sense. Maybe the Lewises that lived here originally bought the real Turner. That would have been about the right time to buy one, a couple of decades after he died. Even then, it would have been difficult to buy one. And then maybe they wanted more but couldn't afford them or couldn't get them for some other reason. He was and is very popular. Even if you wanted fifty Turners, you wouldn't be able to buy that many. Some of the paintings in here are definitely older than this one with the Woolworth. The portraits and at least some of the land and seascapes are more like 1880s or 1890s. And like I said, I think different artists did them, so they might have kept hiring people to paint this way over the decades after they moved in."

"What's your second theory?"

June paused, suddenly seeming strangely reluctant. "I don't have any evidence of it, so I can't really say."

Emily laughed. "Oh, come on. I don't care about evidence. What is it?"

June averted her eyes. "I think, except for the Turner, the family painted all of these on their own."

The air rushed out of Emily's lungs, almost as if it had been sucked out, and she turned slowly around in place, taking in the paintings here in the sitting room. At least ten works hung in this room alone, all of them masterpieces. She had several like them in her bedroom, and she'd seen paintings in every room except the attic, library, and kitchen. The house was like an art museum.

"You're right," she finally said, meeting June's eyes. "I know you're right. They did it themselves."

June smiled and then looked uncertain again. "Of course, there's no way to prove it yet. It's just a…feeling, I guess."

Emily thought for a moment. "Now that you've said it, I feel it, too."

"Imagine! A whole family of artists. I mean, maybe not everyone, but at least a few of them were. Just in here, I've found evidence of at least four different styles. That means, at the very least, four different people schooled in this technique."

"Incredible."

"I'll need more evidence, of course. I'm going to keep looking at the paintings, but maybe you'll find something when you and Mark start researching the family a little more. I've never heard of anything so crazy. If we can prove it, it'll be a sensation when I get the news out."

Her eyes were already locked onto the painting she'd been examining, and Emily decided to excuse herself and leave her to it. June kissed her briefly, clearly distracted, and Emily turned to leave. She stood for a moment in the doorway to watch June work. There's nothing sexier than a smart woman, she thought.

She tore her eyes away and then paused in the foyer by the front door. She should go upstairs and get back to work on the papers with Jim, but she couldn't make herself do it. She was about to go outside and find Mark when he came inside. He was holding his notebook and the measuring wheel, his face pale.

"What's wrong?" she asked.

He shook his head and then sighed, his expression changing from one of fear to resignation. He glanced quickly into the sitting room, held up a finger to his lips when he saw June, and indicated the dining room. Confused, Emily followed him, and he was careful to close the door after them. They both sat down at the far end of the enormous table, where the original house plans were still laid out.

Appearing grim, he drummed his fingers on the table before speaking. "Before we begin, I have a favor to ask. I want to keep this between you and me for a while, if you don't mind."

"Why?"

He shook his head. "You're more open to hearing it. And, well, I don't want to frighten the others unnecessarily."

She gave him a wry grin. "But you don't mind scaring me?"

He looked at her evenly. "But you're not, are you? I mean, not like the rest of us. Some of this has spooked you, at least for a while, but you're okay right now, aren't you?"

She nodded.

He smiled. "That's what makes you different, Emily. The rest of us are terrified. I don't know how the others are managing to keep up appearances, but if they're anything like me, they're hanging on by a thread. Most of the time I'm here, I want to run screaming from this house, drive away, and never come back."

She considered what he'd said. She'd obviously spent more time with June than anyone, and she knew he was right about her, at least. Last night, for example, June had been jumping at shadows, flinching at the tiniest sounds. When they'd finally gotten into bed, she'd been trembling. Emily had held her long enough for her to fall asleep, but it had taken a while. In retrospect, she'd thought at the time that she was being brave for June, but now she realized that she was genuinely not frightened—not then and not now. She'd been terrified plenty of times since she came to Gnarled Hollow, but Mark was right—she wasn't always scared.

"Okay," she said finally. "I'll keep it to myself for now."

He slid his notebook over to her, and she saw sketches with the outside measurements of the house, greenhouse, and pool house. "I noticed it first when we were in the attic. I couldn't be sure last night, but then we measured the rooms on this floor and the bedroom floor, and I was pretty certain I was right."

"What is it?"

He took the notebook back and opened it to his drawing of the attic. He'd put the room measurements she'd gathered into it in tiny letters and numbers inside the drawing of every room.

"What am I supposed to notice?" she asked.

"Just take a look those measurements." He pointed to the long and short length of the house.

"Okay."

"Now look at this," he said, turning back to the page with the measurements taken from outside the house.

"They're the same," she said.

He took the notebook from her and flipped it to his sketch of the ground floor before sliding it back to her. She examined it closely and saw the difference in the measurements immediately. She looked up at Mark, her stomach dropping with fright.

"They're different," she finally said.

He nodded, his face ashen and grave. He opened his notebook to his rendition of the attic. "The attic is the only part of the house that's right. It matches what I found outside when I measured it. The rest of house, however…"

"Is much smaller," she said. He stared at her levelly without saying anything, and she broke out in a cold sweat.

"But how can that be?" she asked.

Mark stood up, setting his notebook to the side, revealing the large, blueprint-sized plans of the house, still unrolled and pinned by glasses and saucers. "The original plans here match the measurements I took outside and those in the attic from last night. Even the windows on the attic floor are exactly the same as the plans. I should have seen that yesterday, but I overlooked it." He moved the outside plans and the attic plans under those for the ground floor. "But, as you can see, these original plans are very different from the actual measurements we took inside the house." He moved them and replaced them with the plans for the bedrooms. "And these are wildly different. In fact, the floor with our bedrooms measures even smaller inside than the ground floor."

"But how is it possible?" she asked.

He laughed. "If the walls were thicker in some places—and I'm talking much thicker, feet and feet thicker—we might have an explanation, but they aren't, of course."

"But how?"

Mark shook his head. "It isn't possible, Emily. There's no explanation. I'll need to go through it more carefully later when I get to Plattsburgh, but we're talking tens of square feet missing here on the ground floor, and even more on the floor above us."

The clock started chiming, startling them both, and Mark cursed. "I have to get going. I'm meeting the professor in Plattsburgh for dinner and need time to check into my hotel and get settled."

He starting putting things away, and she helped him roll up the plans and get organized. Then she helped him carry the plans, his notes, and the large leather builders' notebooks out to his car.

"How much are you going to tell him?" she asked. "The professor, I mean."

Mark shrugged. "As little as possible. I need a relatively local contact, but I'm starting to think we should keep all of this to ourselves for now. We'll need proof—lots of proof—before or if we decide to go public with what we're finding here, especially the more unusual things."

"Agreed."

He moved to get in his car and then turned back to squeeze her shoulder. "Be careful this weekend, would you? Call me if things get bad again." He glanced at the house briefly and looked away again.

She saw a flash of fear in his face, but it was gone a moment later when he smiled, gave her a brief hug, and got inside his car.

She waved as he drove off, and after he disappeared around a corner, she rubbed her arms despite the warmth of the day. She had her back to the house, and when she turned toward it, a feeling of foreboding so deep and powerful swept through her she almost moaned. She had to reach out to steady herself on the wall of the carriage house, certain she would fall over.

But the feeling passed and she walked inside.

CHAPTER FIFTEEN

Emily was dozing in bed. She'd gone up to her room early, too tired to play cards with the others. They'd all agreed to avoid being alone in the house, but they tended to do this only when it was convenient. Call it sloppiness or call it forgetfulness, but each of them spent time alone. Further, she had decided long ago that being together wouldn't help anyone. Things happened even in pairs and groups. The house would do whatever it wanted to do to them whenever it decided to. She hadn't shared this insight with the others, however, as she wanted them to have the illusion of control and safety.

She hadn't been getting enough sleep lately. Part of it was, of course, June. Last night, for example, after June had finally dozed off, Emily had lain there fully awake for at least a couple of hours. What she'd told Mark was right—she wasn't scared. She was excited to be here—curious to the point of distraction. She knew she should never tell anyone about this feeling of exhilaration. They would think something was wrong with her.

Now, lying in bed, her book on her lap, she was fighting sleep. She'd planned simply to lie down and rest, read a little before June came up, but though it was barely nine in the evening, she couldn't keep her eyes open. This far north, the sun had only recently set, and the room was still bathed in pale light.

She must have fallen asleep, as the next time she opened her eyes the room had sunk into utter darkness. She could see moonlight outside, but it barely penetrated the room. The other side of the bed was still empty, so it couldn't be too late, or June would be there. But perhaps June had decided to sleep in her own room tonight, maybe to avoid disturbing her.

She was about to sit up and investigate when the hallway door opened. She saw June's silhouette for a moment, and then she came in and closed the door after herself, plunging the room back into darkness.

"You can turn the light on," Emily said. "I'm still awake."

June didn't respond. Instead, she came directly to the bed and crawled up on it and over Emily, pinning her underneath the sheets. Her lips were on Emily's a moment later, and Emily relaxed into the pillow. June's kisses became more frantic, and Emily tilted her face upward to give her access to her neck. A moment later she was nibbling on her pulse point, making Emily squirm. She struggled a little, trying to free her arms from underneath the sheets, but June continued to pin her down.

"I'm stuck," she said, gasping for breath. "Let me get my arms free."

In response, June squeezed her breasts through the sheets. The sensation was intense and painful, and she hissed in pain. June continued to kiss her—quickly, desperately, wordlessly.

Something was wrong. This wasn't like June at all.

"June, stop," she said in a firm voice. June ignored her, continuing the onslaught. "June, please. I can barely breathe! Slow down. Let me get out of these sheets." The kissing continued, and her panic rose. She struggled harder, but still she was pinned.

"June—"

She was about to yell when the kissing stopped, instantly. The sensation of being pinned down vanished at the same time, and she was able to sit up. She put her hands out to find June, but no one was there.

The light in the room had changed. It was no longer pitch-black. Instead, remnants of dusky sunset filled the room. Out the window, she could see the tops of the trees again. Only moments ago, she hadn't been able to see anything beyond the dim outlines of large pieces of furniture, but now she could make out details again.

She heard the key turning in the lock, and a moment later a silhouette appeared in the doorway again. It seemed to hesitate for a second, and then the light came on.

June was standing there, her expression confused.

"I'm sorry. Were you sleeping already?" She glanced down at her watch.

Emily looked around, panicked, but again, nothing was here. June must have seen something in her face, as she rushed over to her and sat down next to her on the bed.

"What's wrong? What is it? You look like—" June paled.

"Like I've seen a ghost?" She shook her head. "I didn't see it—I mean I did, for a second. In the doorway." She pointed. "Like now, when you came in. Then I didn't see anything concrete. It was too dark."

"Too dark? What do you mean?"

"It was black as pitch in here. I couldn't see any details." She shuddered at the memory and clutched June's hands. "I thought it was you, June. It-it got onto the bed with me."

June gripped her hands even harder. "What happened?"

"It was on top of me—it was kissing me." She shook her head, her mouth suddenly sour and sick. "I thought it was you."

June pulled her into her arms, and they stayed that way for a while. Emily knew she should be terrified, horrified about what had happened, but shame, not fear, was twisting her stomach.

She moved back and met June's eyes. "I'm so sorry, June. I thought it was you."

June seemed confused for a moment, and then her expression hardened. "Goddamn it, Emily, you have nothing to apologize for. That-that *thing*," she spat out the word, "comes in here and does that to you, and you're apologizing." She got to her feet and started pacing. "Christ! The nerve! I think it's fucking with us now. Of all the people to do that to…" Her expression darkened even further. "It's like it knows how we'll react. Anyone else, if that happened, would be scared, terrified, maybe running for their car. But it knew you would feel like this." June met her eyes. "You feel guilty, am I right?"

She nodded. Yes, she was a little frightened, but that emotion was nothing in the face of her guilt.

June frowned, her face pinched with anger. "It's toying with us. It's getting something out of making us feel this way."

She came back and sat on the edge of the bed again, taking Emily's hands once more. She met Emily's gaze. "Emily—you do not have to feel guilty. I'm not upset with you. I'm angry with whatever's in this house—not you. Do you understand?"

She hesitated. "Yes."

"Do you believe me?"

Again, after a pause, she sighed. "I guess. I mean, I want to."

June was quiet for a long time before she burst out in anger. "Christ on his cross. It knows just how to push our buttons. I wouldn't be surprised if it wanted me to react this way. It made you guilty, and it made me angry. It's hitting all the emotional highs and lows with us—through us."

Emily was somehow sure what she'd said was right. The house, or whatever was here, was feeding on their emotions, manipulating them to get what it wanted.

"So how do we stop it?" she asked. "How do we avoid reacting to the things it does to us?"

June shook her head. "I don't think we can. I couldn't have been less angry or less scared with the things it's done to us. I can't stop my feelings. But I am starting to think we need to be more careful. No one should be alone anymore while we're here, especially you. I agree with Mark. Things have happened to the rest of us, but the house is focused on you."

"Why?"

June laughed. "How should I know? Maybe it's because you're the only person here not terrified of it. Maybe it has to try harder with you to get a reaction."

For the second time today someone had pointed out that she wasn't afraid of the house. When Mark had brought it up earlier, she'd accepted it with little thought, but now she couldn't help but feel a little ashamed. Why wasn't she scared? The others were clearly terrified, and she wasn't. Why not? Once again, she'd become an outsider.

The anger drained from June's face, and she put a hand on Emily's shoulder. "Are you okay? Did it…do anything to you? I mean, besides kiss you?"

Emily blushed and broke eye contact. "It touched my chest a little, on top of the sheets."

June was silent before she asked, "Can you talk about it? What made you think it was me?"

She shook her head. "A few things, I guess. It came into the room, for one thing, through the door." Early this evening, June had followed her into the bedroom and taken the keys with her when she went back downstairs. Besides Mrs. Wright's and Ruth's, there was only the one key.

"Did it unlock the door?" June asked.

She frowned. "No. I don't think so, anyway. I don't remember hearing the key. It just came in."

June went over to the door. She opened it and tried the knob from the outside. "It's definitely locked. But you didn't hear it unlock the door?"

She shook her head, firmly. "No. Definitely not. I didn't think about it at the time, but I'm certain now: I didn't hear it unlock."

"What else do you remember?"

She tried to piece the whole experience together. "It was a woman. That was the main reason I thought it was you."

"I thought you couldn't see it?"

"I couldn't—not really. I saw an outline, when it was standing in the doorway. I remember a skirt, like you're wearing now." She paused, blushing at the memory that followed. "Then, when it was on top of me, I felt hair—longer hair, like yours." The memories welled up, and she remembered her rising panic as she was pinned under the sheet. "But when it kissed me, it was different from you. Harder, mean even."

"But it seemed like me otherwise?"

She tried to picture the thing's size and weight in the dark. "Yes. I never thought it was someone—something else. But it did feel different, somehow."

June stared at her for a long time without saying anything, and again, Emily could see her face harden in rage. June finally looked away. She walked across the room to the wardrobe, threw open the door a little too roughly, and pulled out the scotch. Emily had taken a couple of nice tumblers from the kitchen, and June quickly filled both of them nearly to the rim. She came back and handed Emily the second glass, then drank most of hers without stopping.

"I'm so angry I could kill something," June said. "You don't deserve this, Emily. I think—maybe you should leave."

She flipped the covers off her legs and got out of bed to stand in front of June. June finally looked at her, still seemingly enraged, but Emily took her other hand.

"I'm not leaving, June. In fact, if anyone should leave, it should be you. I don't want it to hurt you. You'd be safer somewhere else."

June's laugh was bitter. "This damn house has us right where it wants us. Both of us want the other person to leave, and neither one of us is willing to." She grinned. "With the artwork here, it's given me a mystery to solve, one guaranteed to make me want to stay. And it's pissed me off—several times, but especially now. I've never been angrier in my life, and anyone that knows me knows I won't back down from a fight. This house knows me well. It knows all of us better than we know ourselves."

She finished her drink and then took Emily's full glass from her and set both of them on the nightstand. She turned back and took both of Emily's hands in hers and leaned down to kiss her. Her lips were gentle, searching, and Emily wondered dimly how she could have ever thought those earlier kisses were June's. She kissed her back, pulling their bodies tightly together, and their heat increased with contact. June gasped and pulled away for air, and Emily moved her hands up June's body, lightly touching her breasts.

June was breathing hard, but she put a hand on Emily's. "Are you sure you want to? I mean after what happened?"

In response, Emily slipped off her nightgown.

CHAPTER SIXTEEN

Emily recognized the sound immediately. She'd heard it before, the first night June came into her room: an even, steady knocking, coming from the wall she shared with the bathroom. At the time, she'd forgotten all about it. The sound was the last thing on her mind after June stayed over that first time. She hadn't thought about it or heard it since.

Jim looked over in that direction, his brow furrowing. "What the hell is that?"

"I don't know. I heard it before, but it stopped after a couple of minutes."

"That's the bathroom over there, right?" Jim asked.

"Yes."

"Maybe it's a pipe or something."

He went back to the notebook he was working on, clearly dismissing the noise. She didn't remind him that no one had used that bathroom since she'd been attacked in there—it wouldn't do any good. Jim was clearly a little under the weather the last day or two. His face, normally clean shaven, was marred by an unattractive, patchy five o'clock shadow. He had deep circles under his eyes, and his clothes were wrinkled and stained. He looked like a man fighting a bad night's sleep or maybe a hangover, and she wasn't about to ask him about any of it. He'd been testy all morning.

He'd taken to carrying around one of the little lead soldiers he'd found in the attic, and it perched on the edge of their work table. Instead of the usual gun or sword, this soldier held a telescope, and right now the scope was pointed at her as if it were looking for somewhere to land. As with Jim's disheveled appearance, she hadn't commented on the toy, expecting that should she do so, he would snap at her and become even more irritable.

It didn't help that what they were doing was trying and dull. Despite working steadily yesterday and this morning, both of them had yet to get through a single journal since they began last week. Yes, she had taken off part of yesterday and the entire day before that, but since she'd started before him, she and Jim were more or less at the same point in their current work.

One of the major obstacles for them was the shorthand Margot Lewis used in her notebooks. At first, Emily had assumed the same shorthand was used throughout all the journals, but, as she and Jim had found, Lewis often switched from one shorthand code to another. Once she or Jim came across a new code, they had to stop what they were doing and break it. This, too, would have been okay if it were an infrequent occurrence, or if Margot reused codes they'd already broken, but it could switch mid-page, seemingly at random, and was always new. They weren't terribly complex codes, but it could take upward of an hour to break a new one.

Further, the findings so far, at least in the two journals they were working on, were not revelatory, either. They'd found snippets of poems, yes, but the poems themselves were often incomplete and, if Emily was honest, not very good. Most of the journal she was reading described day-to-day activities. This had been interesting reading, at first, but grew tiresome by the hundredth day of basically the same thing.

She and Jim had started on the earliest journals they could find— 1934 and 1935—the first two years after Lewis came back from Paris. Even in 1934, the journal Emily was occupied with, Lewis was already isolated and alone, which, once you'd read more than a few pages, became boring. Occasionally, she would talk about her walks around the estate, a swim she took in the pool, or a book she read, but most of the entries traced the repetitive minutiae of someone living alone in the woods. Even when Lewis took longer walks, she only occasionally remarked on something interesting—generally she simply noted her route and the animals she saw. Emily had been hoping that even should they not discover new fiction hidden in these journals, they would at least find her memoirs—perhaps of her time in Europe or of her childhood—but they'd come across nothing like that here so far.

Each of the twenty-six years Lewis had lived here in Gnarled Hollow had a single journal associated with it, all of them written in shifting code. The folders of paperwork that had been put in the desk held things typewritten or handwritten in normal English, but they consisted of tax records and some letters to her lawyers and editors, nothing personal. So far, what they'd uncovered reflected the dull, lonely life of a recluse. Because of the codes, it was impossible to read ahead, so Emily could only hope that a novel, or at least some short stories, were hidden somewhere in the pile of journals.

"Christ!" Jim said, pushing the journal away.

"What?"

"Another entry about the fox in the herb garden. Goddamn! How many days can a person watch a fucking fox?"

"At least yours has a fox in it. The last four entries I read detailed cleaning a bedroom. First she did the carpets, then the curtains, and then sheets. And that was just one room. I think the next entry talks about a different room."

Jim barked a laugh. "And I thought the fox was bad!" He shook his head. "Can you imagine how we'll feel when we get to bottom of that pile, and all we have to show for it is Margot Lewis's cleaning schedule and a fox in the garden?"

She laughed. "That's if we finish the pile."

"What do you mean?"

"How much more do you have?"

Jim opened the journal again, found his place, and flipped to the end. "About fifteen pages."

"I've got about the same. We've both been working for about, what, ten days each so far? So it'll be maybe eleven or twelve days altogether to finish these first two journals."

"I mean, we might get a little faster with time."

"Not necessarily, but sure, maybe we will. Let's say we can get down to ten days per journal. There's still twelve journals for each of us after the ones we're working on now. That's a hundred and twenty days with no breaks—again, assuming we speed up."

Jim let out a low whistle. "You're right. I mean, I knew we'd be doing this all summer, but yeah—there's no way we'll finish before the school year." He blushed slightly, looking away. "I mean, before my school year."

They hadn't talked about her layoff, but it had been in the room with them since Jim arrived at Gnarled Hollow. He'd made a couple of snide comments about her in front of the others, though not enough to reveal her secret. June and Chris, as far as she knew, had no idea she was essentially unemployed. Jim had, however, told Mark, and she was still a little pissed at him for that. She stared out the window, breathing in and out of her nose in slow, deep breaths to calm down.

Jim touched her hand. "Listen, Emily. I'm sorry. About your university, I mean. I know it's not your fault. Christ—it could happen to any of us. If I hurt your feelings joking about it, I'm sorry. Sometimes I say things without thinking."

She was surprised and touched. She squeezed his hand and gave him a bright smile. "Thanks, Jim. And don't worry about it. Already forgotten."

He grinned and bent back over his journal again. She watched him briefly before going back to her work. Time and again, this man surprised her. He seemed like one type of person only to reveal himself as another. She needed to get better at letting people show their whole selves to her before judging them.

"Goddamn," Jim muttered a few minutes later.

"What?"

"That sound is driving me crazy."

She had forgotten about it or become so inured that she had basically stopped hearing it. She turned her head in the direction of the bathroom now, frowning.

"Is it louder?" she asked.

"I think so. At first I thought I was imagining things, but it's definitely getting louder now."

"What do you think it is? Some kind of pipe?"

He shrugged. "Maybe. Could be air in there. No one has been using that bathroom, so maybe that has something to do with it."

He got up, and she followed him a moment later, grabbing her keys at the last minute. He went into the bathroom, turned on the light, and they stood there listening for a long while. Distantly, she thought she could hear the sound, but it was so faint it seemed far away.

"That's strange," Jim said, frowning. He walked closer to the wall between the bathroom and her bedroom and put his ear to it. Then he leaned away and shook his head. "Can barely hear it in here."

"Maybe the plaster on my side isn't as thick?"

"Maybe. Let's go back in there and check it out."

They returned to her room, and the difference in the sound was immediately recognizable. Not only was it much louder than in the bathroom, but it was much louder than before they left to investigate. Now, rather than an insistent tapping, she would characterize the sound as something like a knock—dull and just shy of being loud. She and Jim went directly to the source of the sound, and she touched the wall. She quickly wrenched her hand away.

"You can feel it."

His eyes grew large, and he too felt the wall before jerking his hand back. He laughed a second later. "I mean, you can feel any loud sound, really, but it's definitely creepy. I can't even begin to imagine what it is. When do the Wrights come back again?"

"Tomorrow."

"Well, we should probably call them. If that's some kind of pipe, it might burst any second. If it's not, they might know what it is."

"Their phone number is by the house phone downstairs."

Jim grinned. "Top-of-the-line technology around here."

As they started walking toward the door, the sound grew noticeably louder. She flinched, and Jim reacted the same way. They both looked back at the wall, and he raised his hands.

"It sounds really bad. Maybe we should get the Lewis papers out of here." He had to raise his voice slightly to be heard over the sound.

She agreed immediately. If a pipe burst through the wall, the room might flood, and most of the journals and papers were piled on the floor.

"Do you have something to carry it all in?" Jim asked.

She went over to her wardrobe and searched until she found her messenger bag. It wouldn't be big enough to hold all the notebooks, but between it and their arms, they should be able to get it all in one haul.

By the time she returned to the table, she was fairly sure the sound had become louder again. The knocking, if you could call it that, was still steady and stable, each sound following the last after about a second. Each time it had grown louder, the pace had stayed the same, neither faster nor slower, never skipping a beat or hesitating.

Jim hurriedly crammed the notebooks into the bag, and she was annoyed to see that he bent the soft cover of one of the journals in his haste. She opened her mouth to chastise him and suddenly saw something that made her hurry as well: the water in her glass was shaking with the sound.

Before they could finish, the volume rose again. Each knock now sounded and felt like a deep bass drum. She couldn't help but react to nearly each beat, cringing away from the wall and expecting it to blow apart any second.

"That's all of it!" he yelled. He appeared to have spoken at the top of his lungs, yet she barely heard him. She grabbed the last six notebooks, he put the little lead soldier in his breast pocket, and they went to the door.

Just as in the steam room, she knew what was going to happen a second before her hand touched the knob. It was locked. She jiggled it, hard, twisting it, then gave Jim the notebooks in her other hand. She dug into her pocket and pulled out her keys, leaning down to see where the key went on this side of the door, but found no space for it. The door unlocked only from the outside.

Seeing her face and having watched what she'd done, he held out the notebooks in his hands and they traded. He jiggled the doorknob first and then bent to examine the lock. She saw him start slamming at the doorknob a second later, and then he stood up and hammered on the door. She could see his mouth moving, but the knocking from the wall was so loud now that her ears rang too much between the beats to hear his words.

After a while, he turned around, and she saw desperate panic in his eyes. He mouthed something at her, and she shook her head. She couldn't hear a thing. Jim dug around in his pockets and pulled out a little notebook and pen. He wrote something on it and held it up for her to read.

WE HAVE TO GET OUT OF HERE

She nodded as vigorously as she could but also raised her shoulders. How could they get out if the only door was locked?

He raced over to a window and struggled to raise it. She could have told him it was useless—she'd never been able to open any of the windows—but there was no point. He'd never be able to hear her. He tried every window in the room, pushing and pulling as hard as he could. The edges of his hands were bloody from pounding on the door, and he left little smears of red on every window.

After he'd tried to open the last window, he whirled around, his eyes crazed, not looking at her. He peered around the room, his head and body jerking with his gaze, and focused on one of the smaller chairs. He raced over and picked it up, and before she could even react, he heaved it at the largest window. The chair bounced back as if it had hit a rubber wall, and the window remained completely untouched. He picked up the chair again, and this time, rather than throw it, he swung it like an ax. His body absorbed the impact, and he dropped the chair, clutching his hands to his chest and doubling over. She dropped the notebooks and ran over to him. When she put her hand on his shoulder, he flinched away.

He stared up at her, his face wild. A second later, he touched her nose, and when he showed her his fingers, they were dabbed with blood. She could feel the wetness around one of her nostrils, now. Her nose was bleeding.

They both crouched down near the floor, and she covered her ears with her hands as tightly as she could. He followed suit, and both of them sat there, squatting on their feet, grimacing against the sound.

It was so loud now it seemed to be echoing through her. She could feel it in the air behind her—a deep bass-drum beat of noise that shook the room between breaths. She pressed on her ears more tightly and felt blood dripping down her chin from both nostrils now. She and Jim made eye contact. He seemed one step from losing it. Any second now, she thought, he would either start screaming or crying.

Fighting against the pressure of the noise, she struggled to stand and stumbled over to the window, hands still pressed against her ears. Outside by the lawn, she saw Mark's car parked in front of the house.

He had returned at some point and left it by the front door. She tried to see if she could spot him, but no one was on the lawn. The sight of his car, however, gave her hope, as he would no doubt come up here. He'd left for Plattsburgh on Friday, two days ago, so it would be strange if he didn't at least stop by to say hello, even when they were working. Any second, he would knock on the door, realize there was a problem, and get help. If they could hold on a little longer, they would be okay.

She turned back to where Jim crouched on the floor, eager to share this information with him in order to, at the very least, alleviate some of that panicked helplessness she'd seen in his eyes. While she'd been at the window, he'd collapsed onto the ground and was rolling around, his mouth open in an inaudible scream, hands still pressed to his ears.

Forgetting the sound for a second, she relaxed her hands and was nearly overwhelmed by the next booming knock. She tightened her hands against her head again and hurried over to him, kneeling beside him. She had to stop him. He was going to hurt himself. She hesitated and finally reached out for him.

The instant she touched him, the sound stopped. Jim stopped screaming a second later, the echo of it dying in his throat. He looked up at her, eyes glazed with shock, and then sat up into her arms, sobbing. She clung to him, squeezing him, realizing dimly that she was getting blood all over his shirt. She felt a hard lump in his shirt pocket, and it took her a moment to remember that he'd put the lead little soldier in there.

"Oh God, oh God, oh God," he repeated.

"Shhhhhh," she said, rubbing his back. "It's over. It's over now, Jim. We're okay."

After a while, he stopped sobbing, and when he moved away, his eyes were red and puffy. He snuffled once or twice and wiped his nose on his hand, making a face of disgust. He met her eyes and managed a weak laugh.

"I haven't cried like that in…Christ, I don't even know. Sorry."

He was, she knew, speaking quietly since they were so close together on the floor, but his voice sounded muffled, dampened. She remembered a similar experience after she attended her one and only rock concert in college—her hearing had been muted for days. She touched her ear and pulled her fingers away a moment later. It wasn't blood, but some kind of clear, slightly viscous liquid was leaking from her ears. She and Jim would be lucky if they didn't have permanent hearing damage.

"Can you stand?" she asked.

"What?"

She raised her voice. "I said, can you get up?"

He nodded, and the two of them struggled to their feet, swaying for a moment, legs shaking, clasped together for balance. She tried to walk and staggered. He held out a hand to steady her, and she took it, smiling at him gratefully.

"I'm a little dizzy," she said.

"What?"

She laughed and raised her voice. "Dizzy!"

He laughed. "Me, too. And clearly deaf now, on top of everything. Can we get the hell out of here?"

She was still unsure if she should be up and about. The dizziness made sense—the inner ear was responsible for a lot of the balance system in the human body, and hers had undergone a severe shock to its delicate system. She felt drunk.

Before they reached the door, they both heard a key turning in the lock, and a moment later Mrs. Wright came into the room. June, Mark, and Chris pushed past her soon after, all of their faces pale and terrified.

June rushed to her and gave her a rough hug before holding her out at arm's length. "What happened to you? Your face is covered in blood!"

"Nosebleed."

"Why wouldn't you open the door? We've been trying to get in here all day!"

"What's that?" Jim asked, cupping his ear.

Emily waved vaguely at her ear. "You'll have to speak up. We both can barely hear."

"Why?" June asked.

Emily sighed. "It's a long story. And what do you mean all day?"

"I came up here at lunch to see if you could take a break, and no one answered. It was weird, but I didn't think a lot about it at the time. I thought maybe the two of you were downstairs somewhere and I'd missed you. I was working on the paintings in my room today."

"I came home about an hour ago," Mark said. "I found June but not you guys. We knocked on the door, looked around the house, and then outside."

"They met me by the flower garden, and I told them I hadn't seen either one of you all day," Chris said. "It was like you disappeared. We checked the garage, of course, but your car was still here, Emily."

"I thought we should check your room—see if we could find any clues to explain where you'd gone," June added. "But we didn't have the key, so I had to call Mrs. Wright to come over and unlock the door."

"So what happened? Why is Emily's nose bleeding? Were you guys in here all day?" Chris asked.

"You keep saying that," Emily said, shaking her head. "What time is it?"

She already knew, so when Mark held up his watch and said, "Just before four," it came as no surprise.

"I need to get out of this room," Jim said, pushing past the others. When he reached the balcony, his shoulders sagged with apparent relief. "Goddamn. I thought we'd be in there forever. I'm starting to think we ought to take all the doors off the hinges."

"Oh, I wouldn't do that," Mrs. Wright said. They all looked at her, but her face gave nothing away.

"Why not?" Jim asked. "I know for damn sure that we could solve half the problems we've had if there weren't any doors."

Mrs. Wright shook her head again. "It wouldn't help, I assure you."

Mark walked closer to her and stood squarely in front of her. "What are you talking about? Do you know something?"

Her face remained impassive. "All I know is that removing the doors won't help you at all."

Mark's face clouded with anger. "And how, may I ask, do you know that?"

She raised her eyebrows. "I really couldn't say."

This was enough to compel Jim to come back in the room, and he stormed up to Mrs. Wright. She neither flinched nor backed down, only met his anger evenly. His face was red, fists clenched.

"You know plenty," he said. "And if you don't start talking, I'm going to make you talk."

"It's okay, Mrs. Wright," said a voice from the doorway. "You can leave now."

Everyone spun toward the new voice, and Emily saw a young woman standing beyond the doorway to her room. She wore somber, dark clothes, her hair tied back into a tight, unflattering bun. Her plain face was devoid of makeup.

Mrs. Wright inclined her head at this woman in a kind of bow, and, after a brief, almost triumphant glance at Jim, she left the room without a word.

They were all still staring at the woman in the doorway. She remained standing there without explanation, her expression bland.

"Who the hell are you?" Jim finally asked.

The woman looked at him as if stunned. "I'm Lara, of course. Who did you expect?"

CHAPTER SEVENTEEN

Emily's hands were shaking as she set her cocktail down on the coffee table, afraid she would drop it. Jim was likewise shaken, his face ashen, almost green. He was clutching his drink in both hands, but, like her, not drinking it. His eyes were glazed, and he stared into space, unblinking.

They were sitting on the sofa next to each other. After she'd had a few minutes to calm down and get the blood off her face, she had joined the others in the sitting room and told the story of the sound and the locked door. Now they had nearly identical troubled expressions. The only person who seemed unfazed was the newcomer, Lara. She'd broken in once or twice for clarification as Emily told the story, but otherwise she remained immobile, her expression serious and somehow knowing.

"That's it, that's all of it," Emily said. She glanced over at Jim to see if he wanted to add anything, but he was still staring straight ahead, eyes still glazed.

"We've done what you asked," Mark said to Lara. "You wanted to hear what happened, and now you have. You promised answers."

Lara's eyebrows shot up. "I did no such thing. I said I would tell you what I could. Whether I'll answer any of your questions is another thing entirely."

Mark huffed and lurched to his feet, walking over to the bar for a refill. They all watched him, and when he turned around, his face was still cloudy with rage. "At this point, Lara, I'll settle for anything you have. For one thing, Mrs. Wright said that removing the doors wouldn't solve anything. Do you know what she meant?"

Lara nodded. "We tried it. Six months ago, when my aunt inherited this house, we hired some workers to refurbish all the rooms. As you've no doubt seen, we haven't been able to finish, in part because of the doors. Workers kept getting locked inside different rooms. It was very inconvenient."

Chris laughed. "That's one way of putting it."

Lara ignored his sarcasm. "The doors locked, but nothing else happened. Nothing like what Emily described—just doors locking, making more work for everyone. I take it from the way you're all behaving you've experienced other things? In addition to this sound Emily described?"

Everyone agreed, and Lara's eyebrows went up. "I'd be very interested to hear the whole story. But to continue, after the workers had been locked in several rooms, they decided to remove the doors. They had other reasons to take them down temporarily, anyway, for moving the furniture and paintings, so of course we gave them permission."

"What happened?" June asked.

Lara looked at her. "The doors came back. Overnight."

Emily leaned toward her. "What do you mean?"

"Exactly that. The workers took them off the hinges one evening, put them in the attic, and by the next morning, they were back where they'd been, hanging up as if they'd never been touched. Ten men had spent most of the afternoon removing them, and it would have taken that many to put them back where they'd been. But there they were."

"Jesus," Chris said. He got to his feet and walked across the room, rubbing his mouth anxiously. He stood staring outside, his back to the room, before turning around. "Is that all?"

Lara nodded. "Yes. But it was enough. Every single person we'd hired quit that very day. That's why we haven't completed renovations. We're going to have to hire people from another county to finish once you've all left."

"Did anything else happen here? In the past, I mean?" Emily asked.

Lara shrugged. "We don't know. The woman that owned the house before my aunt—Margot Lewis's cousin—left no records of any kind related to the house, beyond tax records, of course. And, from speaking to Mr. and Mrs. Wright, it seems as if she never visited, at least not in the years they've worked here."

"And what do they say?" Mark asked. "Mr. and Mrs. Wright, I mean. Have they told you anything?"

Lara shook her head. "They were hired about ten years ago to replace the previous caretakers. According to the Wrights, they've never seen anything out of the ordinary. Except the doors, of course. You'll notice Mrs. Wright always carries her set of keys with her."

"And she always closes the doors behind her," Emily added.

Lara pointed at her. "Exactly. I'm not sure if they're lying, or if they really haven't seen strange things. Either way, I haven't heard about anything else happening before all of you showed up."

"What happened to the previous caretakers?" Mark asked.

Lara shrugged. "No idea. They were hired shortly after the cousin inherited in 1960, and they stayed on until the Wrights came ten years ago."

"That's a long time," June said. "Almost, what, fifty years? Jesus. I've been here less than two weeks, and I can hardly wait to leave."

"I wonder if anyone in town knew them, or of them," Mark said.

"One would think," Lara said, "but so far, no one in town will admit to knowing them or anything about the house."

Mark seemed surprised. "You've asked?"

Lara raised her hands in what looked like exasperation. "I've asked lots of people about everything related to Gnarled Hollow, but no one will talk."

After a long, tense pause, Emily felt suddenly as if, despite her earlier caution, Lara was in fact about to answer all their questions.

Lara looked around at each of them in turn, and then, as if satisfied they were all listening, she began. "Six months ago, when my aunt inherited this place, she and I immediately came out here to see it. I did a little research before we got here, but, as you've no doubt discovered yourself, I didn't find much.

"When we saw Gnarled Hollow for the first time, we were, of course, astounded by the whole estate. The house, the gardens, the artwork, and of course the paperwork and notebooks left behind by Margot Lewis. We knew once we saw it that, in addition to the sizeable amount of money that came with the place, we were sitting on something incredibly valuable. But, as you've probably found on your own, some mystery surrounded what we found here."

She turned to June, who raised her eyebrows. "Oh—the art, you mean? Yes. A houseful of art with no known artist."

Lara smiled as if she'd expected this answer. "Exactly. Except for that one." She pointed at the Turner.

June grinned. "A painting by a well-known artist with no known origin."

Lara smiled more broadly. "Yes."

She turned to Mark, and he smiled, obviously following her train of thought. "You also found a smaller house than you expected."

Lara laughed. "Much smaller. Based on the taxes paid since it was built, the house should be almost a third larger than it is." She turned to Chris. "I know you haven't been here as long as some of the others, but have you found anything strange regarding the gardens?"

He hesitated. "Well, a few things. The plants are unusual for the climate here. I spoke to Mr. Wright about them on Friday a little, but he was cagey about answering my questions. He seemed to think it was normal for orange and lemon trees to grow in upstate New York."

"Anything else?"

He seemed to think for a moment and then shrugged. "There's something else, but I haven't figured it out yet. It might have something to do with the layout of the gardens, but I need to study them more. They were laid out strangely, but I don't know how or why."

Lara grinned. "And I'm sure you'll figure it out." She turned to Jim and Emily on the sofa. "And the two of you have become code breakers, I take it?"

Jim smiled, grimly. "Code breakers, and little else. Before the noise started today, Emily and I were talking about what we'd found so far in the journals, and it amounts to basically nothing. Lewis wrote about a fox in her garden, cleaning the house, the books she was reading, but nothing important."

Emily sighed. "We keep expecting something more, but so far, there's nothing."

Lara leaned forward. "But isn't that exciting in its own way? After all, why did she go to so much trouble to put her journals into a code? I mean if it is, as you say, just her day-to-day life, why bother?"

Jim laughed. "Maybe because she was bored stiff. There's nothing else to do up here but make silly codes."

Emily was about to agree with him but paused. Something of what Lara was saying made sense. "You mean, maybe something else is in the journals? Something we haven't seen yet? Another code inside the code?"

Lara shrugged. "I don't know. I didn't even get through the first page of the one journal I looked at, but I wouldn't be surprised. Everything about this place seems to offer one mystery to solve, only to offer another beyond that."

They sat in stunned silence. Emily could see that the others, like she, were thinking the same thing.

June spoke first. "So you tricked us into coming here."

Lara laughed. "We did no such thing. We hired you, June, because you're an expert in Romantic art. We hired Jim and Emily because they study modernist American writers. Chris was an obvious pick, and Jim, after you talked up Mark, he too made a perfect fit to study the house itself."

"But you knew about this place," June said, her voice rising. "You knew something strange was going on here."

Lara was silent for a moment. "I knew."

"And you said nothing about it!"

"I didn't." Then Lara sighed. "What would you have thought? If I told you about the house? The little we knew at the time—doors locking on their own and reappearing by themselves. Honestly, what would you have thought?"

"I'd have thought you were off your rocker," Jim said. Everyone looked at him, surprised. He raised his shoulders. "What? It's true. I wouldn't have believed a word of it."

June shook her head. "It's still not fair. You and your aunt should have given us some kind of warning."

Lara leaned forward, meeting June's eyes. "We should have told you that the house is haunted? Is that what you're saying?"

The room was silent. Emily realized that while they'd used the word "haunted" a few times, almost in jest, all of them, including her, had avoided actually using it to explain what was happening. But really, what else explained this house? The word fit better than anything else, yet it also didn't. She didn't know what was happening here, but still, she wouldn't describe it as "haunted."

Lara had been silently watching them, and she finally nodded. "Either you would have thought my aunt and I were crazy, or you would have believed us and refused to come."

"So you actually believe it? That the house is haunted?" Chris asked.

She looked at him evenly. "Absolutely."

"And you invited us here knowing that it was?" June asked.

Lara nodded. "I did." Seeing their expressions, she held up her hands. "But I do freely admit that at the time, we didn't think anything was…sinister here. We had no evidence of that. Just the doors closing, locking, reappearing. Nothing more than that until now."

"So what's your explanation?" Mark asked. "Why is the house acting this way now?"

Lara shrugged. "I have no idea. Maybe something is different now. You're all living here, for one thing. Maybe your energy is feeding it somehow."

Emily and June shared a look. They'd reached precisely the same conclusion two nights ago.

Jim, however, laughed. "You must be kidding me."

Lara looked at him. "Do you have another explanation?"

He tried to laugh again and then looked around at them. His grin died a moment later. "You believe what she's saying?"

June threw Emily another quick glance, clearly suggesting they keep their conclusions to themselves. "I don't know what I believe, Jim," she said aloud, "but I do know that what's happening here can't be explained. Even you would admit that."

He seemed about to argue and then shook his head emphatically, not saying another word. Emily watched him touch his breast pocket and remembered the little lead soldier in there. She was about to say something about it when Mark spoke again.

"So what's your part in all of this, Lara? You've obviously brought us all here to solve your little mystery. Why are you here?" His tone was calm and restrained, but Emily detected a hint of anger underneath his words.

His question, however, didn't affect Lara, and she also didn't appear to find it offensive. She waited a moment before replying. "I don't intend to stay for long. Two days, perhaps, this time anyway. I'll come once a month. To check in on you."

"Are you too afraid to stay here longer?" June asked, her voice likewise dark with anger.

Lara looked at her, apparently surprised. "Of course! Especially now that you've told me it's attacking you. In fact, knowing what's happened, I'm surprised that any of you are still here."

Jim rocketed to his feet, fists clenched. His face quivered with anger, and his mouth worked on itself as he found his voice. One hand moved to his breast pocket, and Emily saw him clutch at the lead soldier through the material of his shirt.

"How dare you? Who the hell do you think you are? You think you can manipulate us like your own personal puppets?"

Lara didn't react beyond meeting his eyes. "You are all, of course, free to leave any time. Especially if the house becomes too much for you. We've found plenty of other people with exactly your skill set, all of whom would be interested in working on the projects I've hired each of you to do."

Jim opened his mouth, but Mark was already there, suddenly next to him, and he touched his arm. Jim spun as if to hit him, and then the fight drained out of him. He relaxed and made a noise of disgust before sitting down again next to Emily.

Everyone was quiet, Jim fuming, June and Chris staring fixedly in front of them, Mark staring at Lara. Emily tried to predict what they would do and then finally spoke to Lara.

"So you're here to check in?"

Lara shrugged. "In part. My aunt is quite busy, so I'm acting as a kind of go-between in her stead. This is not to say that we think any of you would shirk your duties, but to get more timely updates."

"Isn't that what the telephone was invented for?" Jim asked.

Lara gave him a weak smile. "Perhaps, but sometimes it's better to see things with your own eyes. If I come, you can show me what you're working on, rather than tell me."

"And if we solve one of your smaller mysteries, we might also solve the other," Mark suggested. "The house."

Lara smiled. "Exactly."

This conversation was very similar to one they'd had before, and most of Emily's resentment with the situation died. After all, they'd already decided to do precisely what Lara was asking—figure out the things they were hired to do and, hopefully, come to understand the house. Lara was merely saying that she'd hired them to do just that. The others seemed to be realizing the same thing, but Jim still seemed mutinous.

June spoke first. "So you want us to tell you about our projects—"

"And fill you in about what happens and what we discover about the house," Mark said.

Lara smiled. "Exactly. You see, once we heard about the doors, my aunt and I knew we had to figure this place out. She wants to live here, eventually, but of course she can't until…" She shrugged. "Well, you know. Until it's safe, I guess. We've only been able to spend a single night here."

"Did anything happen?" June asked.

Lara shook her head. "Not really. One of the doors closed on its own, but we both felt something. I feel it now." She looked around the room, as if she could see it, too.

"So you'll tell your aunt what you see and tell her what we tell you. That's all?" Mark asked.

"Nearly. I also want to do an experiment or two while I'm here."

"What kind of experiment?"

Lara met his gaze evenly. "I'm thinking of holding a séance."

Jim barked a laugh and got to his feet. "That's it, that's enough. I'm going to bed. The rest of you can sit around listening to this nut, but I've got better things to do."

"Wait, Jim—" June said.

"No, June, really. I have to get out of here before I lose it. You can tell your aunt I'm grateful to be here, Lara, and that I'm planning to stay, no matter what the hell this house tries to do, but I'm staying for the work I was hired to do, nothing else. If you want to figure out what's happening here, you're going to have to do it without me." He paused, staring at all of them. "And the rest of you would be wise to follow my example. If she and her aunt want to hunt ghosts, by all means, let them. I'm here to do my job."

He stormed out, slamming the door.

"I'm sorry. Maybe I should have put that a little more delicately," Lara said.

Mark shook his head. "It wouldn't have mattered how you said it. Jim doesn't want to talk about any of it, even when it happens to him." She looked confused. "Why?"

Mark shrugged. "I think he's hoping that if he ignores what's happening, he won't have to face it. At least that's my impression."

Emily considered this interpretation. "It's something like that, Mark, but it's more, too. I mean, he admits that something is going on—he's seen it and experienced it himself now, but he doesn't want to talk about it, either."

Lara nodded, slowly. "Some people are like that, I suppose. I can give him space, if you think it will help. The rest of you can fill me in if something else happens to him." She paused. "I think it's best for me to talk to each of you on your own. I want to get your version of what's happening. Would you do that for me?"

No one said anything, but no one disagreed.

Lara smiled. "Good. I think that's best."

"What about the séance?" June asked. "When are you planning to have it?"

Lara shrugged. "I'm still doing some research about techniques. Maybe tomorrow afternoon, or maybe the day after tomorrow."

June looked surprised. "Not at night?"

Lara laughed. "No, definitely not at night. Whatever's happening is strong enough during the daytime, let alone later."

Emily excused herself after this, too tired to face dinner and more questions. She and June decided that, at least for tonight, they would sleep in June's bedroom, but Emily was already halfway convinced that they could go back to her room at any time. True, things had happened in there, and kept happening, but never at night, except that weird hallucination she'd had about June kissing her. Daytime was the only time to worry about.

She took her toiletries over to the bathroom on the men's side and quickly brushed her teeth, washed her face, and changed into her nightgown and bathrobe. Although this bathroom was in even poorer shape than the one on the women's side of the house, she never experienced the same watchful feeling in here. Despite the peeling paint and tiny bathtub, it seemed perfectly benign.

She was about to head to June's bedroom but paused outside Jim's door. She very much wanted to check in with him, if only, at the very least, to make sure he was okay. She couldn't understand how he could be alone at such a time. She pressed her ear to the door, listening, but heard nothing. However, light was coming from beneath the door, so she felt justified in knocking.

"Who is it?"

"It's me, Emily."

After a long pause she finally heard him cross the room, and a moment later the door opened enough for him to poke his head out.

"What do you want?"

She caught a distinct whiff of sour sweat and alcohol coming from him and involuntarily took a step back. His eyes were even redder than before, glazed and unfocused.

"I wanted to check on you." She took another step away. This was obviously a bad time to bother him.

He laughed, bitterly. "Did that bitch Lara ask you to come here? What, are you her spy now?"

She held her hands up and took another step away and toward the stairs. "Never mind, Jim. I wanted to make sure you're okay. I'll leave you alone now."

He lurched toward her in one lunging step and seized the lapels of her robe, then dragged her closer, his face inches from hers. He shook her once, hard, making her teeth snap together, then pushed her, causing her to stumble onto the floor. She landed with a bone-jarring crash on her ass and one wrist, both hurting so much she cried out once before snapping her mouth closed. Jim stepped farther out into the hall, fists clenched, and she scooted away as quickly as she could, scrambling to get back onto her feet. He stopped a couple of feet from his doorway, and she thought she saw something flash across his angry face for a second—regret or concern—before rage replaced it once more.

"Leave me the fuck alone," he said, his voice quiet and low. "And tell that cunt Lara to leave me alone, too."

He turned and slammed the door behind him, plunging her into darkness.

CHAPTER EIGHTEEN

If Jim regretted what he'd done, he didn't let on the next morning. He greeted Emily just as he always did at breakfast— briefly and with a smile. He didn't even seem embarrassed, nor did he seem afraid she would tell the others. By the time she'd finished her buttered toast, she was fairly certain he either had no memory of the incident or he genuinely didn't think what he'd done had been as bad as it had been. She wasn't sure which of these options she preferred. If he'd forgotten, he'd been drinking enough to black out, and doing it on his own, which was deeply troubling. If he thought it wasn't a problem, his behavior bordered on psychopathic.

She hadn't told June what had happened last night, and she decided now that she wouldn't tell anyone unless necessary. She'd bandaged her wrist last night, but June hadn't inquired about it, probably thinking it had something to do with her ordeal with the sound in her bedroom. Still, she kept a wary distance from Jim, sitting as far away as she could at the dining-room table.

"So what did you discover in Plattsburgh?" June asked Mark, sipping her coffee. "It was so crazy here yesterday, I forgot to ask."

He frowned. "Very little. The professor I talked to did, in fact, find that reference he remembered again, but it was very vague. Gnarled Hollow was mentioned in an architectural survey of upstate New York, but by name only. So far, I haven't located a single source that names the designer or even the builders." He shook his head. "It's a complete mystery. The professor and I reviewed the plans for the house, but he too didn't recognize anything exceptional that might give us more clues." Again, he glanced at Emily, and she knew without asking that he'd shown the Plattsburgh professor only the original house plans, not the inside measurements he'd taken. Those discrepancies were still a secret between them.

June frowned. "Why were you gone so long? We expected you back Saturday."

Mark gave Emily another quick look, and she was reminded of the conversation they'd had before he left for Plattsburgh. The house unnerved him, and he'd needed a break. Another secret. To June, he said, "I did some digging at the library there before heading back."

"Any luck?"

He shrugged. "Not exactly. If anything, my research confirmed my conclusions about the oddity of the house. It was very unusual to build a house in this style at the time. In fact, I couldn't find a single example in the entire Northeast, and only two elsewhere in the States."

"What style is it?" Emily asked.

Mark set his juice glass down and folded his hands. "It's a little complicated. In the late nineteenth century, right around when this house was built, there was a movement called Queen Anne Revival. Like Neoclassicism, it took elements of any earlier architectural style and changed it. The original Queen Anne style buildings were early eighteenth century, in the 1700s and 1710s, but the revival took place after 1870 or so. Here in the States, Queen Anne Revival houses have very little in common with the original Queen Anne style in England. In fact, if you compare the original English Queen Anne buildings with American, you don't see much of an overlap at all— they're almost entirely different, alike in name only. It would make sense, then, if this house had been built in the American, Queen Anne Revival style—it was very popular then. But it's not. This house is in the original English Queen Anne style from the early eighteenth century."

Jim laughed. "Sounds like someone got their wires crossed."

Mark shrugged. "It could be that simple. It's possible that Roger Lewis, who commissioned this home, asked for a Queen Anne house and got this one. It's technically Queen Anne, yes, but the wrong one by one hundred and sixty years. I can't imagine how any architect could have bungled it so badly unless he was asked specifically to design it in the original English Queen Anne style."

Jim sat at the head of the table, so Emily had taken the seat across from Lara, as far away as she could. She noticed Lara watching Mark and the others closely, a slight smile twisting her lips. She seemed to sense Emily's gaze and looked at her, still smiling.

"You seem happy about something," she said.

Lara continued to grin. "It's simply that nothing in this house is easy. Everything is off and nothing fits. In fact, if you can count on one thing, it's this house not making any sense."

"And that pleases you?"

Lara hesitated. "In a way." She leaned forward, resting her arms on the table and lowering her voice. "When my aunt inherited this estate, we never thought we would find something so wonderfully strange. At best, I thought we'd find a money pit we'd either need to tear down or sell. Instead, this entire estate is like a revelation."

Emily went cold. While she wasn't afraid of Gnarled Hollow like the others, she did have a certain wary respect for it. Lara's amused glee seemed dangerous, even reckless. She was about to say something to this effect when Mark caught her attention.

"Hey, Emily?"

"Yes?"

"I'm heading into town today. I thought maybe I would check the census, birth, and death records for the town. I asked the town historian to get them out for us to see if we can find some more names. I also asked if we could see the town newspaper. Something else might be there, too. The last time I spoke to him, I told him to dig out whatever he could find related to the Lewis family. Want to come?"

She was about to decline, but she caught Jim's eye. He was staring at her evenly, coolly, and the expression in his eyes made her blood run cold. Seeing it, she was almost certain he remembered exactly what had happened last night. He broke eye contact first, and she had to suppress a shudder. The idea of working alone with him all day horrified her.

"Okay," she said, glancing at June. "Do you want to come, too?"

She shook her head. "No. I may head in later this week, though, if only to get a decent cup of coffee. I want to start examining the next painting in the sitting room today."

"Also, I was hoping June and I could talk this morning," Lara said. "If that's all right with you, June."

She hesitated. "Of course."

"And I'll talk to you, Chris, and Jim, afterward, if that's convenient."

Chris shrugged. "I'll be outside all day, but if you don't mind talking out there, by all means."

"I don't want to talk to you," Jim said simply.

"Jim, be reasonable," June said.

He shook his head, glaring at Lara. "The rest of you can do what you want. I couldn't care less. But I'm not saying a word."

Lara didn't seem perturbed. She spoke to June. "Shall we?"

June threw Emily a quick look and got to her feet. "Okay. Want to go to the sitting room?"

"That sounds fine."

June looked as if she wanted to kiss her good-bye, but as they hadn't yet done that in front of the others before, they hesitated long enough to make doing it awkward. She gave Emily a quick smile and followed Lara out of the room.

"You ready, Emily?" Mark asked.

She jumped slightly and blushed, sure she'd been caught staring at the retreating figures. "Sure. Let's go."

The day was stunningly hot, which surprised Emily until she remembered that the last time she'd been outside, it had been hot then, too. The house stayed remarkably cool regardless of the outside weather. She was about to ask Mark about this, but when she looked over at him, his expression, even in profile, silenced her. Like Jim, it seemed as if he hadn't been sleeping well. His eyes were ringed, and his skin had an almost sickly pallor.

They climbed into his large car, and he started driving them off of the estate at a quick pace, the little shells and stones of the road kicking up against the sides of the car. Turning in her seat, she watched the house disappear around the corner of the road and felt a strange sinking sensation of loss. She sat forward again and caught Mark watching her strangely before he looked back at the road.

"You're going to miss it, aren't you?" His voice was quiet.

She didn't respond, not wanting to admit it out loud. He sighed. "I can't understand how it doesn't affect you like the rest of us. I'm a nervous wreck, and the others aren't doing so well, either."

"Was it better when you were in Plattsburgh?"

He shook his head immediately. "No. In fact, if anything, it was worse. I think the idea that I was going to have to come back here… haunted me all weekend. In fact, except for going to town, I think I'll stay the rest of the summer, or I might never come back."

Before she could stop herself, she asked, "Why don't you leave?" She'd been wanting to ask everyone that question. Surely at this stage, despite the interesting findings at the house, everyone must be thinking about leaving. Everyone but her, anyway. She understood, or thought she understood, why June was staying—a kind of determined stubbornness—and Jim was like her, too. But she wasn't sure about Chris or Mark.

He didn't respond for a long time. They pulled up in front of the gate, and he turned the ignition off, shifting in his seat to face her. "Why don't you leave, Emily?"

She opened her mouth to respond and then shook her head. "I don't know what you mean. I've told you—I'm not going. Not until we have answers."

He stared at her a long time, his eyes narrow and searching as if he was trying to gauge her honesty. Finally, he sighed. "It's a little like that with me, too." He paused, breaking eye contact and staring out the windshield at the gate. "I guess part of me knows that if I left today, I'd always wonder."

"But you could stay in town," she suggested. "Everyone could." She meant everyone but herself, but she let him interpret what she'd said without clarifying.

Again, he shook his head. "It isn't that simple. I don't know how, but it wouldn't be enough. The house sticks to you—even when you're not there. At least that's how I felt when I was gone this weekend. I would have to give it all up, without intending to come back, and even then, I think it would still be with me for a long time." He looked at her and grinned. "And anyway, I'd hate to give up now and have some other architect solve the mystery. I feel like it's mine now."

They got out of the car, and she helped him unlock and open the gate. They drove through, closed and locked it behind them, and started driving again. Leaving was a strange sensation. She again felt an odd kind of desperate longing sweep over her, and she had to bite her tongue to not ask Mark to turn around. She'd never, in all her life, felt so connected to a place, and the power of the emotions swelling up in her chest left her shaken and frightened. For a moment, she was certain she would start crying, and she turned her face to the side window to hide her reaction from Mark, blinking back tears.

The village of Last Hope was much larger than she thought. She'd pictured a kind of pause in the road, with perhaps an old diner and bad antique market, but in fact the little town was charming. On the main street were a few cafes, a couple of upscale clothing stores, and a beautiful old school. She could see other establishments on streets branching off from this main one. On the whole, the place was prosperous, even cute.

Seeing her surprise, Mark said, "We're right on the road to a state park here. The town gets a lot of tourists on their way in and out, since Last Hope is the only place this big for a hundred miles or so."

They pulled into the parking lot for the tiny municipal building that seemed to hold all the government offices for the town, including the library. Mark led the way into a large, one-room affair staffed by a couple of middle-aged volunteers and a single librarian.

"Hello," the librarian said when he spotted Mark. "Nice to see you. And I see you have company again." He held out his hand. "My name's Jacob."

"Hi, Jacob—I'm Emily."

"What have you found for us, Jacob?" Mark asked.

"I have those census records you asked for—all the way from 1876, when the house was built, to 1960, when Miss Lewis died. I also pulled the death and marriage records for the same years. I haven't had a chance to examine anything yet, I'm afraid, because of the storm."

"Storm?" Emily asked. She didn't remember any storm. The weather had, in fact, been remarkably clear since she arrived.

Jacob looked at her strangely. "Yes. The storm yesterday. You must remember it. Took out the electricity in the whole area for hours."

She and Mark shared a glance, and she saw the same puzzlement in his face. Surely they'd remember a big storm yesterday, and the house was only a few miles away—they would have felt it, too. Admitting this, however, might raise questions they couldn't answer. Gnarled Hollow was isolated and separate from this town, yes, but the idea that it might have its own weather system would clearly suggest something more supernatural and possibly sinister than simple physical separateness.

"Oh yes, of course, the storm," Mark said, clearly trying to move on. "But anyway, don't worry about not finding anything. I'll go through the records myself today. Did you get a chance to read through the newspaper index?"

Jacob's face fell a little. "I did, but I haven't found very much. The index is, of course, incomplete. None of the papers before 2000 have been digitized yet, which means the index before that was typed or handwritten. It gets pretty spotty in some years. The librarians usually only note major events in town or worldwide affairs, like wars. But we have all the newspapers on microfilm, going back to 1900, when it began."

"There's nothing before that? No town minutes or anything?"

Jacob shook his head. "And it's a real shame. I've been the town historian for three years now, and I have yet to find a single thing before 1900. I've found evidence of a newspaper before that—a small, four- or six-page weekly—but none of them have survived, as far as I can tell."

"So there's nothing for the first twenty, twenty-five years the house was here?"

Jacob shook his head. "Nothing I've found yet, anyway. It's taken me three years just to start to get this place organized, and it still needs a lot of work. You wouldn't believe the state of this archive when I was first hired."

Mark looked at her. "What would you prefer—town records or newspapers?"

"Newspapers, I guess," she said.

"Okay. You start whatever year you think best while I begin reading through the census and town records. Those go back all the way to when the house was built, at least."

Jacob led her to a dusty area of the basement, where the only microfilm machine was awkwardly crammed into a corner. She sat down next to the boxes of microfilm he'd piled up for her and scanned their edges. Each box held about six reels, and each reel held about half a year's newspapers. The pile teetered from the floor nearly to the machine itself. She'd never be able to read every single newspaper between 1900 and 1960, even if she had months. And, as there was only one reading machine, it would be difficult for her or the others to split up the work beyond taking turns. She had to figure out how to speed up the process and read only what was important. She'd done archival work like this before as a student and as a professor, and it was always a matter of starting somewhere, finding clues, and skipping ahead or backward in time.

She decided to start with what she knew: Margot Lewis's death date. The *New Yorker* had included a small obituary for her, but she was fairly certain a local minor celebrity would also be written up in the town's newspaper. It took her a while to get a feel for the microfilm machine—it had been a few years since she'd used one—but she managed to scroll to the correct date fairly quickly. She saw nothing in the paper on the official death date, but when she scrolled forward a little, she found a notice when the body had been found. A week after the death date, she found a long obituary written by an English teacher at the local high school.

Loss of an Icon
Harold Arnett

March 21, 1960
The body of a local legend was found last week at her estate just outside of town. The author, Margot Lewis (1899–1960), may not have had the kind of notoriety some of her contemporaries enjoyed, but her work was every bit as important. In fact, I very much believe that future generations will wonder how people in her era and ours didn't seem to recognize her genius.

I had the great privilege to meet Margot, completely by chance, one rainy Sunday outside of town about two years ago. My bicycle had gotten a flat tire, and I was pushing it back to town in the rain. She appeared suddenly before me, almost seeming to come out of nowhere, and I recognized her on sight, having seen a few pictures of her over the years. People in town always said that she never left her estate, and yet there she was, several miles from it. She was surprised to find me there, yet she greeted me like an old friend. When I told her how much I admired her work, she was humble and gracious, and thanked me for reading. We talked for perhaps five minutes, and then she disappeared down the road. I wrote her one or two letters but stopped after getting no response. I never saw her again.

Margot's life was marred by tragedy. Her parents both died of tuberculosis, leaving all three of the Lewis children orphans at a young age. Relatives were brought in to help raise the children, but from what I have gathered from town rumor and memory, the Lewis children were essentially raised by tutors and governesses. Tragedy struck again when Margot's older brother Nathan was drowned when they were all still young, and Margot left for Europe soon after. Her sister Julia died of TB while Margot was abroad, so that when she returned, Margot was all alone.

I don't know if these tragedies fueled the awesome genius of her work, but Margot Lewis may quite possibly be one of the most important forgotten geniuses of the last fifty years. I think she was a pitiable figure, too far ahead of her time to be taken up by the literati of her day, and too old-fashioned to be recovered by our liberal times. Perhaps future scholars will do her the justice she deserves.

Emily read the article several times, the excitement of the first reading still with her each time. While the article provided very little she hadn't known before she read it, she did, at least, learn the names of Margot's siblings, which hadn't been in the *New Yorker* obit she'd found online again a couple of days ago. Nor had she known, until now, how Nathan had died. The fact that he'd drowned sent excited chills up and down her back every time she read that passage. It was important, but she didn't know how yet.

She heard footsteps and turned to see Mark walking toward her, a notebook in hand. "Find anything yet?"

She got up to let him read the obituary, and when he finished and turned back to her, she saw that same strange excitement she'd felt reflected in his eyes.

"Nathan Lewis drowned. It makes sense, somehow. I'm not sure how, but it does."

She thought it might explain something about the bathtub and the pool incidents, but she didn't want to say yet. She wanted to think about it until she could put her thoughts and feelings into words.

Mark handed her his notes. "If you want, I have some dates for you to try next: Nathan and Julia's death dates. I noticed each of them missing from the one town census to the next and then looked at the death certificates for the years in between until I found them. For some reason, only the months and years are mentioned, not the actual day. I'll dig around some more to see if I can find them. But Nathan died in July 1919 and Julia in June 1925."

"How old were they when they died?"

Mark scratched his head. "They both would have been about twenty-one."

"Margot's a little younger than Nathan, then. She was born in 1899. She must have left for Europe right after he died, since I know she was already in Paris later that same year, 1919." She frowned. "So she left her sister here? Alone? How old would Julia have been in 1919?"

"About fifteen."

They both sat quietly for a while, and Emily felt a strong, sweeping pity for the youngest sister, along with something like disgust for Margot. It was cruel of her to leave like that. Julia had been alone for the last six years of her life. And, as far as Emily knew, Margot didn't come back before Julia died. She'd still been in Europe in 1925.

Mark got to his feet. "I'll leave you to it, then. I'm going to do some more digging in the official records. I might find something like a coroner's report or something, though I doubt it. How long do you want to stay today?"

"Couple of hours? I can't read this kind of thing for very long before my eyes start to bug out."

"We could take a break for lunch around noon, if you like, and then decide if we want to come back after. I've been to all the cafes downtown and know the best one."

She agreed. "I also wanted to see if we could get in touch with someone from the school. He would be pretty old now, if he's still alive, but I wonder if this Harold Arnett, who wrote Margot's obituary, is still around, or if someone who knew him is still here."

"Good idea. I'll call around now and try to set something up after lunch."

It didn't take long to find Julia Lewis's death notice in the paper, but unlike what the obituary for Margot had said, the newspaper claimed she had died from an accident, not TB. Emily read ahead and back a few days in the paper but saw no other details.

It took her longer to find the notice for Nathan, and when she read it the first time, she almost shouted with surprised joy. She had to run upstairs to find Jacob to ask him for help, and he and Mark followed her back downstairs, caught up in her excitement. She wanted to figure out a way to print or scan the page she was looking at, but Jacob explained that they would have to send the reel away for a printout. This machine was incapable of it.

"Can I use your phone really quick, Mark? I want to call June and tell her the good news."

"Sure. Here you go. I have the house phone programmed in."

Mrs. Wright picked up, and it took a few minutes for her to find June and bring her to the phone. June sounded breathless when she picked up.

"Emily? Is that you?"

"Yes, June, and you'll never believe what I found today. Nathan Lewis, Margot's older brother, attended a prestigious art school in New York. I don't have any details yet, but it was mentioned in his death notice."

"What? That's great! But that means—"

"It means that, at the very least, we know one of the artists from the house."

"When did he die?"

"1919."

June was quiet, long enough that Emily was afraid they'd been disconnected. "June? Are you still there?"

"Yes. Listen—I have to check a couple of things. Could you print out that notice for me?"

"We have to send it to another library first, so it might take a few days."

"That's fine." June sounded distracted, and Emily let her make her excuses, hanging up slightly puzzled. Something about the year she'd mentioned had obviously bothered June, but she would talk to her about it later.

She and Mark left for lunch after this, telling Jacob they would either be back later today or tomorrow morning. She felt positively triumphant at their morning finds and couldn't wait to share their news with the rest of the household when they got back. She thought already that she would ask Mark to call it a day after lunch so they could go home early. She almost suggested it now but could tell that Mark wanted to delay going home for a while longer. She remembered then that she wanted to look up Harold Arnett and asked Mark what he'd found out when he called around earlier.

"Mr. Arnett is apparently alive, but retired. He still lives in the area, even. I left my number with the office assistant there at the school, and she told me she'd relay my number to him. Hopefully he'll call us back."

They found a parking spot directly in front of a café, and when they got inside Emily was surprised to find a business so chic and upscale in such a small town. The place seemed more like something someone would see in Northern California than in upstate, rural New York. The menu was likewise surprisingly varied, with a wide range of vegetarian and organic options. It was strangely crowded for a Monday afternoon, and it seemed from the conversations she overheard that it was mainly locals here today. Everyone seemed to know each other, and after strange stares at them when they came through the door, everyone more or less ignored them.

Several people were sitting at the front counter, so she and Mark took a booth. As he read the menu, she took the opportunity to glance around at the people in here. Something about one of the men at the counter gave her pause, and she watched him from behind long enough to remember him. It was the same man she'd met on the way to Gnarled Hollow—the helpful cyclist on the road. He hadn't seen her, or pretended he hadn't, and she frowned in concentration. She needed to remember something about him, but the harder she tried to think of it, the more distant the sensation became. Maybe it was simply that he'd been so dismissive of her experience, so certain she was wrong about the time, but that didn't seem quite right. There was something more—something important about him.

She stared at him long enough to see him reach into a pocket and pull out a cell phone. He held up a little slip of paper and peered at it for a moment before dialing, and a second later, Mark's phone was ringing.

The man turned, comically surprised, and Emily saw his eyebrows shoot up at the sight of her. Mark's back was to the man, so he'd missed this exchange, and he dug around in a pocket for his phone. The man hung up and got to his feet, walking the few feet over to their booth.

"Mark Somner?" he asked.

Mark looked up, startled. "Yes?"

The man held out his hand. "I'm Harry Arnett. You wanted to talk to me?"

CHAPTER NINETEEN

Harry Arnett was staring at the Turner, his shaggy gray eyebrows lowered in concentration. Like the last time Emily had seen him, he was unseasonably dressed in heavy tweeds, but whether for fashion or for warmth, he was, to judge from both occasions, used to dressing like this: something like a nineteenth-century gamekeeper.

Back at the café, she and Mark had introduced themselves, and strangely, without speaking about it, she and Harry had pretended it was the first time they'd met. Maybe he wanted to be polite and save her the embarrassment of recalling their awkward encounter, or maybe he had another reason—either way, the gesture made her like him immediately.

When she and Mark had explained what they wanted to talk about, and why they were here in town, he had asked if he could see the estate and the house. She and Mark had agreed at once, and now he was here in the sitting room. They'd left him alone in order to tell the others about their visitor, but as Jim was hard at work upstairs in her bedroom, and Chris outside with Lara, only June was available to meet him.

June carried in a tray of tea, and the rattling cups and saucers made Harry turn around, smiling at them.

"Thank you, Miss Friend," he said, sitting down on the sofa. "You didn't need to go through all this bother."

"Not at all," June said, sitting next to him. She poured him a cup of tea and handed him a small plate of cake. Emily and Mark sat down in the seats across from the sofa, and Emily watched Harry gaze around the room some more before he shook his head. "I can hardly believe I'm here after all this time. It's not at all what I expected."

Mark leaned forward, his expression serious. "Mr. Arnett—"

"Harry, please. Mr. Arnett is what my students called me."

Mark smiled. "Harry, then. We told you that we read the obituary you wrote for Margot Lewis. Could you tell us more about what you know about her, or about the house?"

Harry's heavy eyebrows went up. "Of course."

"You seem to be the only person in town willing to talk about anything related to the Lewis family. I've brought them up with several people, and the niece of the owner, Lara, has done the same. The conversation changes, or they deny outright that they know anything. My colleagues and I are all doing research here, but of course, sometimes the best information comes from word of mouth. It's never recorded."

Harry smiled. "I'm not surprised no one will talk to you."

"Oh?" June asked. "Why not?"

"It's kind of a local superstition. People around here claim this house is haunted—cursed, really." Harry shook his head in disgust. "Bunch of hogwash, of course, but there you have it."

Emily, June, and Mark shared a look before Mark asked, "Is there any reason people think that?"

Harry made a seesaw motion with one hand and shrugged. "Yes and no. A lot of it has to do with this estate's isolation. People will probably always think a place like this is haunted, if only because it's so far away from everything, and locked up like it is. That big fence around the place doesn't help, of course. I know when I was a boy, me and some friends tried to get inside the grounds, but we couldn't figure out how, so we gave up. There was also a rumor that someone tried and got impaled out there on the fence." He grinned. "But that's probably just a story."

"Why else do people think the place is haunted?" Emily asked.

Harry hesitated long enough that she almost regretted the question, but he finally sighed and set down his empty cake plate, leaning forward and clasping his hands.

"Okay. I'll tell you what I know, what I've heard, I should say, but keep in mind all of it is hearsay—a friend of a friend, the brother of a friend, that kind of thing. I heard stories when I was a boy and also when I was a teacher. It's something we all talk about around here—scary stories we repeat over and over again to frighten each other, like in any small town."

"We understand," Mark said. "Go ahead."

Harry leaned back on the sofa. "Most of it traces back to the people who worked here over the years. A lot of them lived in town. More recently, some of the men were hired to do renovations here at the house. I guess this was after the last owner died, last December or January—I can't remember which. One of these men is my nephew, so I heard it from the horse's mouth, as it were. He told me strange things about the doors—closing on their own, appearing overnight, all sorts of things that were hard to believe." Harry's eyes moved across the room to the heavy umbrella stand holding the door to the sitting room open. No one said anything, and Harry looked momentarily confused.

"Before that, various landscapers from town claimed they saw things in the windows—people, usually—when the house was empty. No one's lived here since 1960, yet they claim they saw faces in the upper-story windows."

Emily felt a chill. So far, they'd seen all the things Harry had mentioned for themselves. On the one hand, she was relieved others had seen these things, too. On the other, Harry's words seemed to make what was happening more real, more insidious, as his story suggested that whatever was going on had been happening for a long time.

Harry rubbed his eyes. "The rest of what I've heard happened much longer ago, before I was born, even, and goes back to the root of the problem, if you will. The cause, if you want to call it that. This estate employed a lot of people at one time, and while some of them lived here in the house, others lived in town. And, of course, the Lewis children sometimes came to town themselves when they were younger. They were privately tutored here at the house, but they would show up for carnivals, shopping, that sort of thing. People met them, liked them even."

"What did people say about them?" June asked.

"At first, they were pitied when their parents died. It would, in the end, have been much better for them had they been taken in by their parents' families in New York City and elsewhere. No one knows why they stayed here, or were left here, whichever it was, though there are some guesses. Various relatives would come for a while and then go home again, leaving them here, alone.

"After Nathan left for art school, only the girls were out here, and I think everyone in town was even more surprised that they were on their own. In those days, it would have been one thing if a man was around, even a very young man, to watch after the girls, but another entirely with them to be all alone with their servants. It was unheard of. Girls in those days, of that class, needed chaperones.

"But then Nathan came back after a couple of years in the city, and like any man of his class and age, he caused a few problems in town—drunken carousing, a pregnant girl, that sort of thing. I don't know how much of it is true, but the rumors are he was something of a hellion. Still, people were glad, at the very least, that he was home to watch after his sisters again."

"Was any of that true?" Emily asked. "I mean, was there a baby?"

Harry smiled slightly. "Yes. In fact, she and my father dated for a while before she and her family moved away. He wanted to marry her."

"Do you know her name?" Mark asked.

"Hilda," Harry replied, laughing. "I'll always remember that name, since my father used to tell me she was the one who got away—never when my mom was around, of course. I don't know her last name, but she was born when Nathan came back—late teens, maybe 1918 or 1919."

Mark made a note of her name. "But despite this hell-raising, people were glad Nathan was back?"

Harry hesitated, his face hardening as if he was reluctant to go on. Finally, he looked up and met their eyes. "Not exactly. Before he left for school in the city, one of the maids, a young thing, told someone in town that she'd seen something unnatural happening between Nathan and one of his sisters. No one wanted to believe her, of course, but then someone else—a gardener, I think—said he saw Nathan and one of the girls in the greenhouse together. Naked." Harry sighed. "The whole town turned against them. They had to send away for their groceries, even. No one in town would serve them.

"When Nathan died, a lot of people around here thought it was his just deserts, punishment for unnatural acts. Then, of course, Margot left for Europe, and only Julia was left out here in the house until she died."

Emily leaned forward. "You said in your obituary for Margot that Julia died of TB, but I read elsewhere that she died in an accident."

Harry frowned. "Yes, that. Well, you see, that goes into another thing people hint at but never say. There were a couple of attending officials at Julia's death, and they got their wires crossed, I think. They should have agreed on a cause of death they decided to share, because they put out to the newspaper that it was an accident and wrote TB on her death certificate. I didn't want to get into it in Margot's obituary, so I put down one of them there, even if we all knew better."

"Why would the officials do that?" June asked.

Harry sighed. "I'm sure a family like the Lewises has enough money to pay off people to cover up what really happened."

"Which was?" June asked.

"Suicide," Mark said quietly.

Harry nodded. "A lot of people said at the time that Julia hanged herself, though it might have been something else. Even before she died, there were rumors that she'd lost her mind when Nathan died. Some people have told me she was always a little off. They said the family had her locked up in the attic sometimes, though I never met or heard of anyone that actually saw her up there."

Emily shivered, remembering the shackles and the splintered furniture they'd seen in one of the larger attic rooms. She'd felt incredibly uncomfortable in there—confined and suffocated.

"So all of this is supposed to explain the doors, the faces in the windows, everything?" Mark asked.

She was surprised to hear that he sounded skeptical, almost as if he hadn't seen it for himself.

Harry raised his hands. "I guess so. At the very least, it's a good story. It's got incest, suicide, a murder, and a haunted house. It's no wonder people still talk about it."

"Wait—what murder?" June asked.

"Oh. I forgot to say. Some people believe that one of the sisters—Julia, probably, since she was the one who was supposed to be crazy—drowned Nathan. He was said to be a very good swimmer, so people of course make that leap." He shrugged. "But he might have been drunk. He was a heavy drinker, from what I've heard."

"Wasn't Julia much younger than him? Would it have even been possible for her to drown him?" Emily asked.

Harry smiled. "Scary stories don't have to make sense, Miss Murray."

"Did anyone else see anything here? I mean besides the doors and the faces in the windows?" June inquired.

Emily thought she sounded a little too eager and was afraid she might give something away.

Luckily Harry didn't seem to notice. He shook his head. "No one but the caretakers and the landscapers have been inside this estate since Margot Lewis lived here. And when she came back from Europe, most people in town felt sorry for her. She kept to herself, never came to town. She was alone for all those years. My father told me that something happened out here in 1940 or so, when the steam room was installed. Two men were killed in some kind of freak accident when they were working on it. The rumor mill kind of picked up again for a while after that, but I never heard many details about it. The Lewises are very good at hush-hush tactics.

"When I was a boy, there really wasn't anything new to hear. Most of the stories were old hat by then. You'd hear things now and again about the house, from gardeners and the like, but I don't know that many people actually believed the stories then or now. It's just something we talk about to pass the time."

"The previous caretakers never said anything?" Mark asked.

Harry shook his head. "No. In fact, if anything, Tom and Lydia—the caretakers before the Wrights—tried to shut down the stories. They would deny everything when people brought the subject up."

"Are they still alive?" Mark asked.

Harry shook his head. "No—they've been gone a while, now. Died of cancer, both of them."

"What have you heard from the Wrights?" Mark asked. "They've been here for ten years now. Have they said anything?"

Harry shrugged. "The Wrights don't talk to anyone. Quite strange, those two. Keep to themselves, barely say a word when you run into them. Definitely not adding to the rumors, if that's what you mean."

Emily and the others shared a look, and this time Harry noticed. "Wait a minute—has something happened while you've been here? I see the door propped open."

Mark hesitated and then shook his head. "They lock on their own sometimes—that's all. It's inconvenient to carry keys around all the time, so we've propped them open in here."

Harry seemed skeptical, but he let it go. "What is it that you're all researching out here?"

Mark gave a quick explanation of what he was doing, and Harry perked up with interest. Emily saw his eyes travel around the room as June went into more detail about the mysterious paintings, and when Emily told him about the Margot Lewis papers, his grin was positively gleeful.

"I knew it," he said. "I knew she was out here writing that whole time. I wonder that they haven't been transcribed before. Do you think I could see them before I leave?"

"There's not much to see, I'm afraid," she explained. "Everything is written in code. My colleague and I are having an awful time getting through it all."

"I'd still like to see one the journals, if you don't mind. I love Lewis's work. It would be like, I don't know, holding Elvis's guitar if you were a fan, something like that."

Emily laughed and stood. "Of course you can see them. You've told us more than we've been able to get from anyone we've talked to or anything we've read."

"Even if it is all a load of crap?" Harry asked, getting up more slowly.

"Even if," she said, grinning. "Come on. I'll show you upstairs."

Harry paused. "Do you think you could show me around first? I'd love to have a tour of the house."

Mark smiled. "There's not much to see, I'm afraid. Some of the doors are locked, and I don't have all the keys."

"That's okay—whatever you can show me." He looked sheepish. "I've always dreamt of coming here. Ever since I was a little boy, and then, when I was older and read Margot's work, I became even more interested. I don't think you can grow up around here and not wonder about this place."

"I'm happy to show you all I can," Mark said.

Emily turned to see if June was coming, but she was still seated on the sofa, her face troubled and drawn. She turned back to Mark. "You guys go on ahead—I'll catch up."

Mark glanced at June and then led Harry into the foyer. She watched them disappear into the dining room and then sat down next to June, taking her hands.

"Are you okay?"

It took June a couple of moments to respond, and when she met Emily's eyes, she looked as if she might cry.

"It's all real, Emily," she said.

"What do you mean?"

"All of it. I kept thinking that maybe, I don't know…maybe we were all hallucinating or something." She shook her head as if to clear it. "I mean, I knew it was happening—I was here! For most of it. But somehow, hearing all those stories, about the Lewises, about the people from town that worked here, it makes it real somehow." June met her eyes again, her brow furrowed. "Am I making any sense?"

"Yes. You are. I mean, I don't know how much of what he said was true, but while he was talking…" She shook her head. "It seemed like the truth. Especially after he told us about the doors and the face in the window. We've seen that."

"Do you think it's all true? The incest? The murder? I mean, my God, Nathan was drowned. I'd put money down that he was drowned in the pool."

What June said startled her, but she said nothing. When she'd first read that he was drowned, she'd immediately thought it had happened in the upstairs bathtub, the one she was nearly drowned in. But of course June and Chris had experienced something similar in the pool. She hadn't even thought of it.

"I don't know if we'll ever know what actually happened, June, but I'm going to try to find out."

June blushed a little, not meeting her eyes. "Maybe we can ask them later today."

"What do you mean?"

June grinned. "Lara's séance. She wants to do it this afternoon."

Emily laughed and then quieted when she saw June's grave face. "Wait a minute. Do you think that kind of thing is real?"

June lifted her shoulders. "Well, no, not exactly. But then, I also don't really believe in ghosts, or at least I didn't before I came here. I'm not sure what I believe now."

The front door opened, and Chris and Lara came in from outside. Chris spotted them, and his face seemed flushed and happy. Lara, too, looked excited, and they quickly entered the sitting room, both of them panting as if they'd run there.

"You guys have to come outside and see this," Chris said. "You'll never believe what Lara and I just figured out."

CHAPTER TWENTY

They stood at the bottom of the formal gardens behind the house. The three of them—Emily, June, and Mark—waited for Lara and Chris to explain why they were out there. Chris had left to find Mark, and Mark left Harry upstairs with Jim before joining them. The sun was oppressively hot, and once again Emily was startled by its power this early in the summer. The three gardens at the back of the house were separated by a footpath from one another, but arranged in a kind of fan shape. Each garden had been designed in a slightly different way, and each contained different plants.

"This is the herb garden," Chris said, gesturing to the garden in front of them, "that's the ornamental garden," he pointed to the right, "and that's the flower garden," he said of the final one to the left. "All of them are modeled on the English style, which aimed to be wilder, less regimented than the French style."

"English gardens were popular in the Romantic period, right?" June asked.

Chris grinned. "Yes. It went along with the Romantic ideal of letting nature inspire you through its untamed beauty." He shook his head. "Of course, it still takes a lot of care to keep things looking like this—it's a fake wilderness, at best. In bigger English gardens, you might see large, open lawns, untrimmed trees, that kind of thing, but in smaller gardens like the one here, that's not really the case. Of course, the woods here are untamed, so I guess that sort of goes along with the theme, and I know there are some hiking trails that might be considered part of the gardens, but as far as these three little formal gardens go, the only major thing that tells me that they're meant to be English gardens is the fact that the pathways between the plants aren't laid out in straight lines."

Emily saw that what he'd said was accurate. All the lines through the plants in each part garden were curving and, in some places, circular spirals. However, a single straight line ran through the center of each of the three gardens, bisecting the curves and circles awkwardly at times.

"It's in keeping with the artwork in the house," June said. "The Lewises loved their Romantics."

Chris smiled. "Yes. Anyway, I could tell that they were English. It's not hard to differentiate French from English, once you know what you're looking for. But I couldn't figure out this straight line here, the one that crosses through each part." He pointed at it.

"I was wondering about that, too," Emily said. "It's kind of, I don't know—"

"Ugly?" Chris suggested, then laughed. "It is, and it's also the complete antithesis of the design. At first, I thought it might be some kind of irrigation line, but it isn't. Then I thought maybe it was a result of having to dig up some kind of blight, but again, it wasn't." His grin turned into a broad smile. "Then, when Lara was out here talking with me, she wondered if it might align with something."

Lara jumped in, clearly excited. "We started thinking about star charts, ley lines, all sorts of silly things."

"But the most obvious explanation was the right one," Chris said. He turned to Lara to let her tell them.

"The winter and summer solstice," she said.

"Oh! Like Stonehenge!" June said, then laughed. "How funny!"

"Is it an exact match?" Mark asked.

Chris nodded. "As far as I can tell without measuring, yes. I could get some survey equipment out here and do the calculations, but I'd put money on it being exact." He pointed at the two ends of the straight line. "That's where it aligns. The sun should rise early in the morning on the summer solstice over there in the flower garden, and it would set over there at sunset on winter solstice in the ornamental garden. We'll be able to see it align with the summer solstice on the twenty-first."

"That's tomorrow," June said. She paused. "I guess the Lewises also liked prehistoric Britons." She described the Celtic-inspired hanging bowl they'd found in the steam room.

"Can I see it?" Lara asked.

June blushed slightly. "It's still out there, actually. I sort of forgot about it."

"Let's go get it now," Lara suggested.

June seemed reluctant, so Emily volunteered. "I'll come, too. That way, if the door closes, a few of us will be there to get help." She meant to speak lightly, but June paled a little. June had no more forgotten about the hanging bowl than she had. They'd simply avoided the steam room since they were locked in there.

The walk to the pool house was even longer than Emily remembered, and she was once again struck by how strange it was to build the pool out here in the woods, so far from the house. Anyone who wanted to swim would have to either walk out here in a swimsuit or change at the pool, where there were no changing rooms. She remembered the rumor about the Lewis children and the pool, and heat rode to her cheeks. If she managed to find evidence that Margot or her younger sister and their brother were having some sort of incestuous tryst out here in the woods, it would really change the way people thought about Margot's writing.

The trees suddenly fell away, and she, Lara, and June were in the clearing with the greenhouse and pool house almost before she was ready for it. Now, instead of interesting, the place was ominous, and she had to make herself keep walking. If only Lara had been here with her, she would have turned around, but she wanted to support June. June was pale and drawn, and Emily knew they were thinking the same thing. June had had two experiences out here—one with her and one with Chris—and Emily knew without asking that she would have happily gone the rest of her life without setting foot in the pool house again.

They unlocked the door, and the magnificence of the space once again struck her. Today the sunlight was even brighter, glaring even, and it made the water sparkle almost violently. She had to blink a couple of times against the light, squinting in order to see.

"I'll stay here," June told them, standing by the door.

Lara almost laughed, and then, probably because of their serious, frightened expressions, her smile faded. "It's okay. I'll get it myself."

They watched her head toward the steam room, and Emily walked into the pool house a little farther to look at the water. She was wearing sandals today, and she slipped one off and dipped a toe in. It was warmer than she remembered, but that might have something to do with the sunlight. She was about to turn back to June to comment on this warmth when she saw movement in the water out of the corner of her eye. She jerked her head that way and cried out in alarm.

Harry Arnett was floating, facedown, in the pool.

She screamed again and covered her eyes with her hands, bending over slightly in a low wail. June's hands were suddenly on her back, and Emily turned into her, clasping her tightly and crying. A while later—she didn't know how long—she finally realized that June was asking her something.

"What is it, Emily? What's the matter?"

She pulled back and turned toward the water, but saw nothing there. Harry's body had disappeared.

"He was there!" she said, almost choking on the words. She pointed at the water. "I saw him. Right there! I swear it."

"Saw who?" June asked. "Nathan?"

Lara had joined them now, and Emily saw that she was holding the hanging bowl in both hands.

"No," Emily said. "I saw Harry. He was floating in the water!"

Lara and June peered into it and then at each other. Emily saw Lara raise one eyebrow and suddenly felt anger overwhelm her. She took a couple of steps away from both of them and pointed at the water again.

"He was right there! I saw him!"

June shook her head. "But nothing's there, Emily." Her was voice quiet, placating.

"Then he must have disappeared!"

Again, Lara and June shared a glance, and that same frustrated rage washed through her. She had to get them to believe her. Maybe it wasn't too late.

"Why don't you believe me?"

June put a hand on her shoulder. "It was a bad idea for you to come out here. I don't even think I should be here." She looked at Lara. "We should leave."

"No!" Emily said, shouting. "We have to find him. We have to save him!" For a moment, she was tempted to jump into the pool, and June, likely seeing something of this intention in her expression, grabbed her arm, squeezing it painfully.

June made her meet her eyes. "Emily, we have to go."

She looked back and forth between Lara and June and saw pity. All the fight drained out of her, and she sagged with something like exhaustion. She let the two of them lead her out of the pool house and back down the little trail to the house. The whole way, she was oppressed with an almost crushing sensation of guilt. She had let Harry down, and she would never forgive herself.

CHAPTER TWENTY-ONE

Emily's bedroom was filled with that strange, golden light that comes just before sunset. It made the edges of the furniture in the room oddly stark and sharp, contrasting vividly with the rosy orange that permeated every corner of the room. She could see June and Mark sitting at the table, both of them engrossed in their laptops, and when she shifted to sit up, they both looked at her, their expressions strangely guilty.

"What am I doing here?" She hadn't been back in her bedroom since the experience with the knocking sound yesterday, and the room already felt foreign and strange.

June set her laptop down and came over to the bed, sitting on the edge. She took both of Emily's hands in hers. "You don't remember?"

She shook her head and then stopped. She had a vague memory of seeing the house after she, Lara, and June left the woods, and then nothing.

June patted her hand. "You passed out. One minute you were fine—walking along with us, and the next you simply fell." She frowned. "It was terrifying. I had to get Mark to carry you up here."

She shook her head to clear it and sat up a little straighter, wincing. Her neck felt stiff. "How long have I been out? And why did you bring me in here?"

June met her eyes. "Something happened while we were out at the pool house."

She could see the worry etched in June's face now, and she sat up straighter, scooting to support her back with the pillows. She looked back and forth between Mark and June, but neither of them said a word.

"What happened?"

June's eyes slid to Mark for a second. "I'm not sure we should tell you."

"What is it, for God's sake?" Emily asked.

Mark sighed and rose, walking the few feet between his chair and the bed. She was almost frightened by his expression. He seemed defeated, broken.

"Emily, Harry disappeared."

She hadn't expected this news, and it took her a second to process what he was saying. "Wait, what? How?"

Mark sighed and raised his hands. "We don't know. He was in here, talking to Jim. Jim said he wanted to look at the Lewis papers, and Jim showed him what he could. Harry even offered to help you and Jim get through some of the work, and Jim told him he would talk to you about it. After that, Harry left him to his work and then…"

She looked back and forth between them. "And then what?"

June's expression was still grim. "Apparently Harry left to go find the rest of us. This would have been when we were all outside with Chris, when he was showing us the gardens."

Mark frowned. "Somewhere between this bedroom and the gardens, he disappeared."

She held up her palms. "Wait—how do you know?"

"Well, we're guessing a little. We're sure he left this bedroom intending to find the two of us, or at least that's what Jim says. He was planning to head back into town, but he wanted to thank us first." Mark frowned. "I thought Harry was still up here with Jim, but when we carried you in here, we realized something was wrong."

Harry had brought his bicycle in the enormous trunk of Mark's car, and they'd taken it out when they got here. He'd said at the time that he wanted to ride home, since he liked to ride his bike every day.

"What about his bike?" she asked.

Mark shook his head. "It's still out by the garage. And anyway, he would have needed one of us to unlock the gate to leave." He paused. "Emily, we had to call the police. They're here now, and they've brought search-and-rescue."

As if he'd summoned them, she heard dogs barking in the distance outside. Ignoring Mark and June's alarm, she got out of bed and went to the window, looking down onto the lawn. Two police cars and several other vehicles were parked on the driveway. A group of men and women waited near the cars and trucks with several dogs.

"I thought you had to wait twenty-four hours to report a missing person."

"Not at all, especially if the person is elderly or very young," Mark said, "and it's different if woods are involved, too." He walked over to her and touched her hand. "Emily, the police want to question you. They've talked to all of us already." He glanced back at June. "We told them you had heatstroke. June and Lara didn't mention what you saw in the pool."

She looked at June quickly. "Why not?"

June hesitated and then shrugged. "I don't know. I wasn't sure what I should say. If I told them what you saw, it would sound—"

"Crazy?" she suggested and then laughed. She went back to the window and watched the searchers a while longer. "You're right, of course. It would sound crazy. I saw his body floating in the pool, and then it was gone. It sounds crazy even when I say it to myself."

For a moment, she felt a strong sense of frustrated hopelessness. Somehow, when it was just them—the researchers—all of the things that had been happening had seemed somehow personal, almost as if the house was doing those things only for them, to them. It had been dangerous, but they had also survived it all. What had happened to Harry was different, almost as if they were being punished for bringing in a stranger.

When she turned back to him, Mark's expression was troubled, and he took a step closer. "We had to call the police, Emily. You understand?"

She hesitated. "Yes. Of course." She looked at both of them. "It was a mistake to bring Harry here. This is on us."

Neither of them replied, and she took their silence as agreement. She gestured at the window. "They're never going to find him out there. He's here—somewhere in the house."

"They've already searched every room, including the attic," June said.

She looked at June. "But you know he's here, too, right?"

All three met each other's eyes, agreeing without saying it aloud. Mark sighed and rubbed his eyes. "This is such a mess."

June's face seemed haggard now. "We should have left after the first day. We should have gotten in our cars and never looked back."

Someone knocked on the door, and the three of them jumped. June opened it. Two police officers stood in the doorway, their faces strangely red from the dying daylight filtering in from outside. June gestured for them to enter, and she and Mark excused themselves.

Emily offered the officers seats, and they all sat down across from each other. One of the officers was a little older than her, the other so young he was ridiculous in his uniform. They both held wide-brimmed hats on their laps.

"Thanks for talking with us, Miss Murray," the younger officer said. "I know you're under the weather, so we appreciate your taking the time. We'll try to be as brief as possible. We're trying to develop a timeline for when Mr. Arnett went missing, so whatever you can add to what we already know would be helpful."

He consulted his notes. "According to Mr. Somner, you and he met up with Mr. Arnett around noon and agreed to bring him back here. Is that right?"

"Yes."

After a long, pointed pause, she realized they were waiting for her to go on. She said nothing.

Again, the younger officer spoke. "Why did you bring him here?"

"He said he wanted to see the house, and we were happy to show it to him."

Again, he consulted his notes. "Mr. Somner claimed he was the one to contact Mr. Arnett. He called the high school looking for him. Is that correct?"

"Yes."

"Why did he do that?"

"I asked him to. I'm doing some research here on Margot Lewis, and I saw that Mr. Arnett wrote the local obituary for her. I thought he might know something more about her."

"So, in exchange for seeing the house, you wanted to ask him about this Lewis woman?"

She shrugged. "You could put it that way, but I didn't think of it as payment, if that's what you mean. He asked if he could see the house, so we showed it to him."

"And this was the first time you met him?"

She hesitated, remembering their encounter on the road. The older officer's eyebrows lowered slightly—he'd seen something in her expression. She was going to have to be careful. She tried to smile. "Actually, Harry and I met before."

The younger officer looked up, clearly surprised. "Oh? How? When?"

"It was when I came here—two weeks ago. I got a little turned around on the road outside the grounds, and he happened to ride by my car on his bicycle when I pulled over to look at a map. He gave me directions to the house, and that was it."

"That's funny," the younger officer said. "Mr. Somner claimed it was the first time you'd both met him."

"He didn't know about our earlier meeting."

"Why?"

"I saw no reason to tell him. In fact, I didn't know that Mr. Arnett and the man on the road were the same person until I saw him today. We didn't introduce ourselves when we met."

Both of the officers seemed skeptical now, and both peered at her closely. The younger officer said, "Okay, let's move on. Could you repeat what Mr. Arnett told you about Margot Lewis once you had him out here?"

Emily didn't like the way he'd phrased that question—as if they'd brought Harry out here on purpose just to lose him, but she didn't comment. Instead, she decided that being honest at this stage was still safe, and she summarized, as best as she could, all the things Harry had told them about the house and the Lewis family. When she finished, she was amused to see that both officers were a little put out, almost as if they'd expected her to lie.

The younger officer hid his disappointment by shuffling through his notes again. "That pretty much aligns with what Miss Friend and Mr. Somner told us." He looked up at her. "What did you think of his story?"

She made herself wait a moment and took a calm, deep breath before replying. "I thought it was all of a lot of rubbish, to tell you the truth. And I think Harry thought the same thing. He told us what he'd heard, but I don't think he believed it."

"What gave you that impression?"

"Just the way he told it. He kept saying things like, 'this is what I've heard.'"

"So why did he tell you?"

She gave him a level stare. "I'm sure my colleagues have told you that we're all out here on an assignment, Officer. We're researching the house and the family. Mr. Somner and I have been discussing the possibility of writing a biography of the Lewis family and the history of this estate, so any information we can get is worthwhile, even if some of it is garbage. For example, Harry told us for the first time that Margot Lewis and her brother and sister might have been having an incestuous affair. That's worthwhile information, despite the rest of it."

She was amused to see the younger officer blush, and once again he buried himself in his notes. The rest of the interview went quickly. She explained how, after Harry finished his story and went upstairs with Mark, they'd all gone outside to the gardens, and then how she, June, and Lara went out to the pool house. She said she'd started to feel a little dizzy out there, so the other women had helped her back toward the house before she fainted.

"I think it was the sun. We were outside too long, and I'm sensitive to the heat. I should have worn a hat."

"So you've been up here all afternoon," the younger man said.

"Yes."

"And you didn't know that Mr. Arnett was missing until you woke up?"

"Correct."

"I think we can wrap this up now, Ben," the older officer said, speaking for the first time. He got to his feet, the leather on his belt and boots creaking loudly in the quiet room.

Ben, the younger officer, looked pissed off, but he nodded and got to his feet. Emily stood up with him, and they all shook hands.

"Here's our card," Ben said, handing it to her. "It has our cell numbers on the back, too. Call us if you think of anything. We're going down to check in on the search. We might have to bring some more volunteers out here later to help, but we'll let you know what's happening."

She followed them out of the room and downstairs, rejoining the others in the sitting room. Everyone seemed relieved to see her, especially June, who rushed over immediately and gave her a long, tight hug. She pulled away, and Emily almost kissed her, but stopped at the last second. Everyone had seen what had almost happened, and she had a momentary jolt of triumph at the police officers' startled expression.

"We'll leave you to it now," the older officer said. "Hopefully we'll find Mr. Arnett before it starts getting dark."

"Can we help?" June asked.

The officers shared a look, and the older one shook his head. "That wouldn't be the best idea, at least right now. We'll let the professionals do their thing."

He'd talked about getting some volunteers from town, and a quiet unease swept through her. She'd felt it when they were talking to her upstairs, too. They'd leapt on the discrepancy between Mark's story and hers, as if they'd suspected someone was lying to them. Something was off, and the police knew it.

The officers excused themselves and went outside, and Mark closed the front door behind them before coming back and shutting the sitting-room doors. All of them were standing around, everyone clearly anxious.

"Well, shit," Jim said. He walked over to the bar to refill his drink. From the high color in his cheeks, she could tell it wasn't his first or second of the evening.

"They know we're hiding something," June said. No one disagreed, and Emily saw the last remaining color drain from her face.

"Unless they find him, we're all screwed," Chris said.

Jim laughed, bitterly. "We're screwed if they find him, too. What do you think will happen if they find his body somewhere?"

"Maybe he's still alive," June said, almost whispering.

Jim shook his head dramatically. "How naive can you get, June? You know as well as I do that he's dead."

"But there's no proof!" Her voice had risen, and she was nearly yelling now. "I mean, how do we know for sure?"

Jim walked close to her and gestured, some of his drink sloshing out of his glass. "We don't need any proof, June! We all know it's true! Can't you feel it? I can. I know it." He looked at Emily. "And she saw his body. You know he's dead, don't you?"

She met June's panicked gaze and then Jim's before agreeing, reluctantly. "Yes. He's dead. I don't know where he is, but he's gone." She met June's eyes. "I'm sorry, June, but it's true."

It seemed as if June might argue, but her eyes suddenly filled with tears. She put a hand over her mouth to stifle a sob, and Emily went to her at once, putting an arm around her middle and leading her to the sofa. They both sat down heavily, and she rubbed June's back to calm her. Jim made them both a drink. She gave him a weak smile, and he sat down in one of the armchairs across from them, scowling and nursing his own cocktail.

Lara stood with her arms crossed over her chest, almost squeezing herself, and Chris stared out the window, ostensibly observing the search. Mark looked around at everyone in turn and then went to the bar to fix himself something. He sat down in the other armchair, his expression grave.

"What are we going to do?" June's voice was quiet, but Emily detected a hint of panic there, too.

"I don't know," Mark said. "On the one hand, I think it would be better if we found him ourselves. On the other hand, it might be better if there's no body."

Chris barked a laugh, whirling toward them away from the window. "So what, we're just going to let him rot somewhere in the house?"

"Or some time," Mark said, almost under his breath.

"What? What does that mean, 'some time'?" Jim asked.

Mark shook his head. "It's something I've been thinking about. I told Emily about it a little, about the house anyway, but I asked her not to say anything until I'd had time to think about it." He described the discrepancy between the inside and outside measurements.

June was looking at her strangely, and Emily gave her an apologetic smile. "I'm sorry. He asked me not to say anything."

June was clearly a little put out, but she seemed to let it go.

Jim asked, "So you're saying there's missing space in the house?"

Mark pointed at him. "Exactly. The outside measurements don't match what we're seeing inside."

"And there's no explanation?" Chris asked.

"None that I can find. The difference defies logic and sense. Somehow, when you're outside, the house is larger than when you're inside."

"Except for the attic," June said.

"Yes," Mark said. "The attic is the right size."

"So explain what you mean by 'some time,' then," Jim said.

Mark sighed. "It's just a theory." He paused, again looking around the room at all of them. Lara and Chris had drawn closer to the sofa and chairs, but they were still standing, both of them clearly too anxious to sit down. They stood behind June and Emily on the sofa.

Mark cleared his throat. "Let's assume, for simplicity's sake, that the house was normal when the Lewis children were here. Maybe it was even normal when Margot Lewis came back—I don't know."

"Why should we assume that?" Chris asked.

"Humor me," Mark said. He paused and got to his feet, walking across the room to pick up his laptop. He opened it and set it down on the table, facing everyone but him. "Here is the original plan for this floor of the house." He clicked a button and the image shifted. "And here is the plan as this floor is today."

"There are rooms missing," June said immediately. "We saw that already when you showed us these plans before."

"But like I said, the outside measurements match these original plans," he put them on the screen, "not these." He switched back to the new layout.

"So what are you saying?" Jim asked. "That the rooms are actually still there somehow?"

Mark held up his hands. "Something like that. But the theory I've been mulling over is that they aren't here—not really."

"Well, of course they aren't," June said, frowning. "We'd see them."

Mark leaned forward. "They aren't anymore, but they were there at one time. And maybe they are still there, but only sometimes."

"How do you know?" Emily asked. "There's no evidence."

Mark held up a finger. "Ah, but there is. It came to me yesterday, after you and Jim were locked in your bedroom together." He spun the laptop toward himself and scrolled through to find the right image before he turned it back to them again. "I've highlighted it, but what do you see in the original plans for upstairs?"

Emily reviewed the image on the screen and went cold. "There should be a room between my bedroom and the bathroom."

"Exactly. Your bedroom is supposed to share a wall with this missing room here in the original plans." He looked at Jim. "Yesterday, both of you told us that you went into the bathroom to see if you could find the source of the noise, but when you did, you almost couldn't hear it at all. That doesn't make sense, does it? If you could hear it on one side of the wall, you should be able to hear it on the other."

"Yeah, well, maybe the insulation is better in the bathroom," Jim said. He didn't sound like he believed what he'd said.

"Or, as I'm suggesting, you couldn't hear it because there *is* a room in between her bedroom and the bathroom."

Jim laughed. "But there isn't! We could go upstairs right now and you'd see—there's maybe what, two or three feet between Emily's bedroom and the bathroom door, not," he leaned forward and peered at the screen, "twenty feet or whatever. We'd be able to see it."

"Exactly," Mark said, "and we would see it, if it was 1918 or 1919, but it's not. Not always, anyway."

Jim laughed. "What the hell is that supposed to mean?"

"It means, some kind of slippage is happening here, something to do with time. Sometimes we're in touch with the past, and sometimes we're not." He paused. "That woman, for instance, the one three of us have seen now. Some people from town have seen her, too. She's there and then she's not. Who do you think she is?"

"The sister—Julia," June said without hesitating.

Mark looked around the room and no one disagreed. "Exactly—it's Julia. So why is she there sometimes and gone the next? When we were discussing her with Chris, after he was attacked in the pool, we all agreed that when you see her, it's almost as if, when she disappears, she goes back to where, or whenever, she's from."

Chris frowned, and Emily remembered that he'd been skeptical about this explanation. He was clearly still a little reluctant to agree with it, but he said nothing.

Mark continued. "I'm suggesting that the house is like Julia. These missing rooms are both here and not, and when they're not here, they're lost in time."

Jim guffawed and got to his feet. Emily saw him sway for a minute and then steady himself before walking, carefully, over to the bar again. He poured himself another drink, and when he turned back toward them, he raised his hand to his chest to touch his little pocket there. She was almost certain he was carrying the little lead soldier around again. No one else seemed to have seen this gesture, and he dropped his hand almost guiltily.

"The other evidence is the loss of time," Mark said. He gestured at June and her. "When you were in the steam room, it seemed like a few minutes to you, but to the rest of us, it was hours and hours. The same thing happened when you and Jim were locked upstairs in your bedroom."

"It happened when I was driving here, too," she said. She explained the loss of time on the road, leaving out the detail about meeting Harry. "I always come back around four."

"Chris reappeared in the pool right before four, and you were attacked in the bathroom about that time, too," June said.

Mark raised his eyebrows. "So four o'clock is important, somehow."

Lara, who had been silent this whole time, suddenly spoke up. "That's when we should do it, then."

"Do what?" June asked, turning around to look at her.

"The séance. We should do it at four tomorrow afternoon."

"It's the summer solstice tomorrow," Chris said, his voice quiet.

Jim snickered and then chugged the rest of his drink. He wiped his mouth on his arm. His eyes were bloodshot and sunken, even more than the night before. "You guys sound like a bunch of fucking kooks. Can you imagine what the police would say if they saw you holding a séance in here tomorrow? They'd lock you up and throw away the key."

Mark ignored him. "I think you're right, Lara. We need to do it, and soon." He glanced at Chris. "The Lewises seemed to have put some stock in this solstice business, so doing it tomorrow would make sense, too."

Jim slammed his glass down on the table hard enough that everyone jumped. "Can you hear yourselves? Jesus Christ!" He moved unsteadily toward the door, almost tripping. Mark raised his hands as if to help him, and Jim jerked away from him, glaring. "Don't touch me."

"Jim—" Mark said.

"And don't talk to me, either." He looked at Emily. "I'm taking half of the journals into my room. You can do whatever you want with the rest of them, but I don't want to be around any of you anymore." He frowned at Mark. "I thought we were friends, Mark. I feel like I don't even know you anymore."

"Jesus, Jim, calm down for a second—"

Jim made a cutting motion with his hand. "Shut up, Mark. If you keep talking to me, I'm not sure what I'll do." He took a wary step away from everyone. "And the rest of you should think about having your head examined if you go along with his bullshit."

With that, he stormed out of the room, slamming the door behind him. The five of them looked at each other in silence for a long moment.

"So," Mark said, finally. "Tomorrow at four."

CHAPTER TWENTY-TWO

Emily set her alarm to go off an hour before sunrise, but when it started blaring, she almost screamed. June also jerked awake, startled and peering around for danger. She finally laughed and reached across Emily to turn off the alarm before giving her a long, deep kiss.

"Good morning." Her voice was still scratchy with sleep.

Emily smiled. "Good morning."

June flopped back onto the pillows and threw an arm over her eyes. "Do we have to get up? We just went to sleep."

They had, in fact, been up very late. First, they'd been discussing the séance, and then the police had knocked, explaining that they were bringing in some volunteers for the evening search. Emily and the others had made pots and pots of coffee and given out sandwiches and water until about one in the morning, when the search was put on hold. It had taken a while for everyone to leave, so by the time they finally went to bed, they could only sleep a couple of hours.

"We have to get up, June," she said. "I want to see the solstice sunrise. Maybe we can come back to bed after it's over."

June flung her arm off her eyes and laughed. "Fat chance. Those search-and-rescue people will be back by then. In fact, we'll be lucky to get any sleep tonight, either." June turned her head toward her, frowning. "How long do you think they'll look for Harry? I mean before…"

"Before they give up?" She shook her head. "I don't know. Three days? Four? It probably depends."

June groaned and sat up, rubbing her eyes. "What a fucking mess. God, I wish we'd never brought him here."

She warmed with affection. She and Mark had brought Harry here, not any of the others, yet June seemed to be taking on the same blame as she did for herself. She leaned forward and kissed her again, and this time, when she moved away, she didn't see sleepiness in June's eyes.

June grinned, coyly. "Do you think Chris would mind if we took a few more minutes?"

"Is that all you need?"

By the time they joined the others outside by the gardens, the sky was already starting to light up with a warm, pink glow. She and June hadn't had time to shower or eat, and her hair was a snarl of tangles and sweat. Lara, however, was fresh and clean, her hair falling in soft dark waves on her shoulders.

Everyone was standing at the far end of the alignment line through the gardens, facing the point at which the sun would rise above the flower garden. Chris had imbedded a tall wooden pole in the grass on that end to give them a line of sight to watch.

He pointed above the tree line. "As you can see, the trees are completely filled in there, but I went out and poked around in the woods a little yesterday with Lara. At least at one time, they were cut back pretty significantly in that direction. A hundred years ago, when the Lewis children were here, it's probable there were no trees all the way to edge of their property. A line would have been cut straight through the woods to give someone a clear view of the sunrise on the horizon."

"These Lewises are getting weirder and weirder," June said, shivering. Without the sunshine, the morning air was surprisingly chilly.

"So what will we be able to see today?" Mark asked. "With all these trees, I mean?"

"I've adjusted the pole I put in the ground there to account for the trees, as best as I can, so when the sun clears the tree line, we should see it align there right above it." Chris pointed.

"How long will that be?" Lara asked, squinting.

Chris glanced at his watch. "At least another ten minutes. I had to approximate a bit. It could have been perfect if I had more of my surveying equipment here, but I didn't have time to go get it yesterday. I hope I didn't screw it up."

Mark clapped him on the back. "I'm sure it will be fine, Chris."

Chris smiled at him gratefully, and Emily felt a happy rush of affection for everyone here. Lara was still a bit of a newcomer, but Emily felt closer with June, Mark, and Chris than she did with her own family. Something about the situation had dissolved barriers between her and the others. She knew they felt it, too. Things would have been perfect if Jim was out here with them, but he hadn't come, and no one expected him to after last night. She frowned as she thought about him. They needed to reach out to him, but how? Wrapped up in these thoughts, she almost missed it, but she heard June gasp and looked up and over at the pole just as the sun cleared the trees.

The brightness of the sun immediately hurt her eyes. But for a second, before she was forced to look away, she saw an exact alignment between the sun and the pole Chris had planted in the ground. Suddenly, the gardens seemed to make sense in a way they hadn't before, and she stared at the spiraling paths with new interest. Whoever had designed them had been thinking of this moment, once a year, when the sun would fall on them precisely as it did now, and for a second she could see it. Each spiraling and curving path lit up, one by one, gradually filling with sunlight. A pattern formed there— something different than she'd seen before, something more beautiful because it was revealed only in the rising light. Finally, the sunlight reached the far edge of the gardens, and the impression she'd had faded almost before she was aware of it. Now everything looked like plants and flowers again.

"Incredible," Mark said.

"I've never seen anything like it," Chris said, tears in his eyes. She felt like crying herself, and she knew nothing about gardens or plants.

"But why?" June asked. She gestured at the gardens. "Why go through all this bother? That lasted what, five minutes? Now they're just like any other gardens."

"It must have meant something to them," Lara suggested. "This day, I mean. It's the solstice, and that might be enough, but it was probably something personal, too." Lara looked at her. "Was it someone's birthday today?"

She shrugged. "Actually, except for Margot's, which is in May, I don't know when their birthdays were." She turned to Mark. "Do you? Did you find them in the records in town?"

Mark shook his head. "I didn't get a chance. We found the years and months they were born and died, but not the birth days. Julia died in June of 1925, and Nathan in July of 1919, if I remember right from the obituaries. Maybe Julia died on the twenty-first. I don't know for sure."

"Well, the birthdays could be worth looking into, anyway," Lara said. "We might not find any reason for this elaborate setup in the end. They might have simply been interested in pagan ritual, but it's possible this date has special meaning for them."

Sounds from the distance made all of them turn back toward the house, but as it blocked their view of the road and driveway, Emily could only assume they were hearing the searchers returning. They'd given a gate key to the head of the search team so he could let himself and the others in and out at their convenience. She heard June's sigh and had to stifle her own. It had been so much better when it was just the six of them. This was, she thought, their punishment for bringing in an outsider.

She shivered, suddenly ashamed of herself. Harry was probably dead, and her first thought had been for her own comfort, not for his. She saw similar expressions of guilt mixed with dread on the faces of the others. She was certain they'd thought the same thing.

"Let's get this over with," Mark said, starting toward the house.

"Wait a second, Mark," Lara said. "We all agreed to do the séance this afternoon, but Jim's right, at least in one way."

"How so?" June asked.

"It's going to be hard to do it with all these people around. And he's also right about being caught. None of us want to have to explain ourselves."

"What do you propose?" Mark asked.

"We need a lookout, maybe more than one."

Everyone seemed equally puzzled, and Mark frowned. "You mean one or two of us would sit out of the séance?"

She nodded.

"It should be Emily," June said.

She looked at June sharply and opened her mouth to protest, but Lara was already shaking her head. "No, June, I'm sorry, but Emily has to be there." Lara met her eyes. "I've managed to talk to everyone about their experiences but you and Jim, Emily, and everyone else has more or less said the same thing—that the house is focused on you somehow. It's crucial for you to be there."

She was happy to have a reason to agree and nodded.

"Who, then?" June asked. Her face was spotted with color, and she was clearly fighting her own anger.

"Well, it can't be me, and it can't be Emily," Lara said. "And ideally, we would have four people at the table. Less than that is supposed to be dangerous, at least according to what I've read."

"Only five of us here," June said. "How can we have two lookouts if we need four people at the table?"

"Jim," Lara said. "Someone needs to talk to him."

Emily and the others looked at each other guiltily. Things had gotten progressively worse for Jim the last few days, and everyone knew it. She had seen the changes in him even before they'd been locked in her bedroom together. He was drinking too much and obviously hadn't been sleeping well, if at all. He was on the verge of a nervous breakdown, and they all knew it. They should have talked to him days ago, if not sooner, but everyone, like her, had avoided him.

"I'll talk to him," Mark said, resigned.

Emily shook her head. "No. I'll do it. It has to be me."

"Why?"

She paused, unable to explain easily. "He's got something against you now, Mark. You saw it last night. If you'd tried to stop him, he would have taken a swing at you." She remembered, suddenly, that he'd actually become violent with her before, that night outside his room, and some of her certainty drained away. She made herself go on, though. "I think he'll take it better from me."

"What will you say?" June demanded. "What could you possibly do? Get him to stop drinking?"

She took June's hand. "I don't think that's possible, but I can try to talk some sense into him. He's part of this. He just doesn't want to admit it. He's fighting it for some reason. Maybe I can make him accept things. We're stronger together, all of us."

They walked back to the house, going in via the front door in order to check in briefly with the searchers. After a quick greeting, June, Lara, and Emily went inside and left Chris and Mark to talk to the men and women in the search party. Emily was surprised to see the doors to the sitting room propped open again, and when she looked in there, she saw Jim staring out the front window, drinking already despite the hour. She gestured for Lara and June to leave her alone with him, and June reluctantly followed Lara into the dining room. She took a deep breath and walked into the sitting room.

Jim must have heard her, but he didn't turn around. He continued to stare out the window, standing in profile to her. She took a few steps closer but kept a cushion of space between them. Even from here, she could smell his sour stink. His clothes and hair were a mess. The hand that lifted his drink to his mouth was trembling, and an overwhelming pity swept through her.

"Jim, we need your help."

He laughed, bitterly, and finally turned toward her. The pity she'd felt evaporated in a sweeping blaze of horror. His eyes were completely crazed, the grin on his lips crooked and false.

"You don't need my help, Emily. None of you do. I saw you all outside together. You seemed to be getting along fine without me."

"Jim, we wanted you out there. You didn't have to stay inside—"

Again he laughed, and a sneer replaced his grin. He turned and took a step toward her. "Like I said, I saw you guys. You're like one big, happy, multi-racial family. You were happy I wasn't there. Relieved, even."

She couldn't help but take a small step backward to recover some space between them. Already, she knew this had been a mistake. She had to fight the temptation to turn and look behind her for the doorway.

"That's not true, Jim. I can't speak for the others, but I was wishing you were there the whole time."

His sickly grin returned, his bloodshot eyes narrowing. "You actually expect me to believe that? You're here because you need something from me." His grin faded, once again replaced with a sneer of disgust. "I also saw you and June, holding hands, dashing out there late because you stayed in bed fucking around." He turned his head and spat on the carpet. "Disgusting. Nothing worse than dykes." He stepped closer, gesturing at her with his drink. "You don't need me for anything, Emily, when you've got that fine piece of ass to use." He shook his head, clucking his tongue. "Real shame that, but I guess you never can tell these days." Now he smiled. "Though I can see which side you butter your toast on, and it ain't with dick, that's for sure."

She risked a glance behind her and continued to back up. She raised her hands a little in a warding-off gesture. "Listen, Jim, you're drunk. I'm going. I don't think you mean any of this."

His broad smile made his chapped lips crack a little, and a tiny bead of blood formed at a corner of his mouth. "Oh, I mean it, all right. Every word."

He had erased most of the space between them and stood perhaps three feet away. She had to fight the urge to run away, but that might be an overreaction. At this point, he was simply being insulting, not physical.

"So tell me," he said, "what you want from me. It can't be this, after all." He grabbed himself between his legs and then laughed, his head thrown back.

She took the opportunity to turn, but she wasn't fast enough. He snatched her shoulder, spinning her toward him.

"Hey!" he said, his spittle hitting her face. "Don't leave when I'm talking to you, you cunt!"

She struggled, and he dropped his drink, the glass landing with a heavy clunk but not breaking. His hands now free, he held her by both shoulders, his fingers painful. He jerked her hard, twice, snapping her teeth, then stopped, dragging her toward him and leaning down into her face, close enough to kiss her.

When he spoke, he was almost screaming. "What do you want from me? Huh? What do you want?"

"Jim!" June called from the doorway. "Let her go!"

Jim was startled, and Emily pushed his chest as hard as she could. His fingers slipped off her shoulders, and she almost got away before his hands clamped down, this time on her throat.

The pain was immense and startling, closing off sense and thought, leaving only instinct and panic. She clawed at his face and arms and jerked back and forth until he squeezed hard enough to make her knees go weak with pain. His face was a mask of rage and stupid brutality, but his eyes were distant, unseeing.

She had a vague memory of a self-defense class she'd taken in college. She'd been taught how to get out of a choke hold but couldn't remember how. The pain and lack of air were making her stupid. Lara and June appeared on either side of him, yanking his arms to get his hands off her throat, but the knowledge and understanding of what that meant was starting to slide away into the haze of pain.

Tiny pinpricks of light appeared in her vision, and her chest started to feel tight and hot. In a final effort to push him away from herself before she lost consciousness, she put her hands on his chest and felt something in his pocket: the little lead soldier. Her fingers were too weak and uncoordinated to get it out, so she pulled down on the pocket until it ripped off, the toy falling to the ground.

Jim let go immediately, and everyone fell into a pile of limbs on the ground. She scooted away as fast as she could, clutching her throat. June gave Jim one more push away and then came to her, folding her into her arms and howling in fright and relief. Lara had gotten back on her feet and was bent at the waist, trying to catch her breath.

"You monster!" June screamed at him. "You fucking animal!"

"June," Emily tried to say, but her voice came out in an almost inaudible croak, the pain so intense she stopped trying to talk. She clutched at her throat again, tears springing to her eyes.

Jim was sobbing, his knees clenched to his chest, almost fetal. His pale face was streaked with blood from her scratches. He held out one hand toward her. "Emily, oh God, Emily! I'm so sorry!"

"You're fucking right you're going to be sorry," June said, still almost screaming. "You're going to spend the rest of your life in prison, you asshole. Attempted murder! Assault!"

"I don't know why I did that! Emily, you have to believe me! I couldn't stop myself!"

He had moved forward a little, and June maneuvered her body in front of Emily's. "Don't you touch her! Don't you go near her!"

She swallowed painfully, and when she spoke, it was still barely above a whisper. "June—listen to him. It wasn't him."

June stared at her, her face a mask or horror and incredulity. "Don't tell me you believe him!"

She was fighting an overwhelming fatigue now. More than anything, she wanted to go back upstairs and lie down and let June take care of her. But it was important for everyone to understand what had happened. She grabbed June's shoulder. "It wasn't him," she croaked, making her voice as loud as she could despite the pain. She pointed at the lead soldier. "It was that."

Lara followed the direction of her finger and walked over to the lead soldier lying on the floor. "What? This thing?"

Before Emily could call out a warning, Lara reached down to pick it up, and when her hand enclosed the toy she cried out in pain and flung it from herself. It hit a wall and fell to the floor behind the sofa.

"Jesus Christ!" Lara said, clutching her hand. She was bent double in pain, and when she stood up again and held out her hand, everyone could see a dark-red imprint on her palm. "It burned me!"

Jim was still sobbing, rocking back and forth, and Emily took June's distraction as an opportunity to scoot over to him on the floor. She held out her arms, and he launched himself at her, making June cry out in fright. This time, however, he was simply hugging her, crying into her hair.

"Shhhh, Jim," she whispered. "It's okay. You're okay."

"I thought I was lost, Emily. I thought I was lost," he kept saying, over and over again.

"You're here now. You're with us again," she said. "You're safe."

CHAPTER TWENTY-THREE

With the summer sunlight blazing into Emily's bedroom, the setting for the séance was the least likely imaginable. Any outsider seeing the four of them seated at the table might think they were sitting down for the most competitive game of canasta ever devised. Their faces were grim and determined, pale and drawn.

Because Mark and Chris had become the de facto points of contact for the search teams still outside, the only man at the table was Jim. The scratches on his face had been cleaned up, but they were still angry and painful-looking. Emily had spent a great deal of time cleaning his skin from beneath her fingernails, the horror and disgust of it enough to make her gag. June had helped both of them, dabbing at Jim's face with alcohol and gauze and gently icing the skin on Emily's throat. Neither she nor Jim blamed the other for what had happened, and for her, having him here at the table seemed natural and somehow right, almost as if it had been fated for the four of them to be sitting there together this afternoon.

They'd decided to hold the séance in her bedroom for a few reasons. The first was the most obvious, at least according to Lara: things happened in Emily's room. They could, however, just as easily have used the pool house or the bathroom, except the pool house was too public, the bathroom was too small, and Emily's bedroom door locked, so if anyone outside came knocking, they'd have warning. Right now, Chris was downstairs near the front door, and Mark was right outside the bedroom door. Should anyone insist on seeing them, Chris would text Mark's phone, and Mark would knock. They'd also given Mark the only key to the bedroom.

Lara had placed the Celtic hanging bowl in the center of the table. She'd also used a glove to pick up the lead soldier and placed it in the center of the bowl. Jim was staring at it uneasily, almost as if he expected it to take control of him again, but Lara had insisted that they have a few artifacts from the family to act as focal points for spiritual energy.

One of Margot Lewis's journals also lay on the table, under the hanging bowl. Regardless of the content, Lara argued that Margot had spent enough time with the journal to imbue it with at least a little of her energy, and they were all fairly certain the soldier had been Nathan's at one time. They had no way to know of anything that belonged to Julia, but they'd included the bowl in the circle since it might have been important to the family.

Lara's phone chimed, and she turned off the alarm. It was now ten minutes to four. "Okay," she said. "It's time to start."

She held out her hands, one to Jim and one to June. Emily likewise extended her hands to June and Jim, and they were all connected. Lara met each of their eyes, and one by one they nodded, ready. Lara took a deep breath and closed her eyes before beginning.

"Spirits of Gnarled Hollow, we call you. Margot Lewis, we call you. Nathan Lewis, we call you. Julia Lewis, we call you. Other spirits in this house, we call you. Reveal your secrets to us. Show us how to help you. Show us what you will."

After a long, tense pause, the hair rose on the back of Emily's neck. June and Jim's fingers tightened in hers, and she squeezed back. Lara spoke again a moment later.

"Spirits of Gnarled Hollow, we call you. We seek answers. We seek to understand. Margot Lewis, help us understand. Nathan Lewis, help us understand. Julia Lewis, help us understand. Other spirits in this house, help us understand. We beseech you to show us what you know."

The air around them seemed to grow denser, and the light in the room dimmed. Emily squeezed her eyes shut, suddenly too frightened to see what was coming. Jim and June's grips were now viselike and painful, and everyone was breathing heavily. When Lara spoke again, her voice sounded strained and frightened.

"Spirits of Gnarled Hollow, we call you. You sought us, and we came. You wanted us, and here we are. Margot Lewis, use us. Nathan Lewis, use us. Julia Lewis, use us. Other spirits in this house, use us. We are ready to be used for your purposes."

A strange, audible pop, as in an airplane, sounded, and Emily couldn't help but flinch and duck a little in her chair, hunching her shoulders. She could hear herself breathing, hard, but as the initial fright passed, she realized she could no longer hear the others.

Instead, she was aware of the sound of birds somewhere close by, and then a gust of wind brushed her face, as if from an open window. June and Jim had relaxed their grips, and even straining, she still couldn't hear them breathing. She waited for a long, tense pause, aware the whole time that the sunlight on her face was warm and hot, bright beneath her eyelids. She took a few deep breaths and finally opened her eyes.

The room around them had entirely transformed. The table and the chairs they sat in were still here, as they'd always been, but the rest of the room was completely different. Instead of the large, canopied bed she slept in every night, a smaller day bed squatted in the corner of the room farthest from the table. The bed hadn't been made, and the sheets and blankets were bunched in a wild tangle. The room was strangely decorated, with several paintings she didn't recognize on the walls. Two life-sized statues of naked women stood a few feet away, the style reminiscent of Rodin. Cups and saucers, plates and silverware were strewn haphazardly on the floor and two tiny tables, and discarded clothing littered the floor. It was the bedroom of an incredible slob.

The curtains here were drawn back, but they were heavy and velvet, a deep gold. A gauze scrim hung down each of the windows, blocking the harshest of the light, but the room was still incredibly bright with sunlight. The walls were strangely silver, from paint or paper, she couldn't tell, and the floor beneath the mess was now a bare, golden wood. All the windows on the front side of the house were wide open, a warm breeze blowing in and occasionally rustling the scrims.

She looked back at the others in order to tell them to open their eyes, but one glance at their faces and her voice died in her throat.

Something was strangely still about the three of them—unnaturally so.

"June?" she asked, pulling her hand a little. June didn't respond, that same waxen stillness seeming to immobilize her. Her eyes were closed, but her face was calm, almost slack. Jim and Lara were similarly waxen.

"Jim? Lara?" She jiggled her hand in Jim's loose grip, horrified when hers slipped out. Lara had told them not to let go of each other's hands for fear of breaking the spell. Jim's hand stayed exactly as she left it, slightly open as if it still held hers. She pushed on his shoulder. "Jim? Jim!" She pushed harder, but he didn't move. His body felt stiff and cold.

She looked back at June on her right and touched her face. It was cold and dry, and she jerked her hand away. June felt neither waxy nor wooden, but rather fake and artificial—almost rubbery. She was reminded of the hands that had held her underwater in the bathtub. She slipped her right hand out of June's and stood up quickly, her chair falling backward onto the ground. Fighting her instinct to avoid touching the unnatural bodies of her friends, she went around the table and shook each of them, one by one, by the shoulders. They were frozen, their stillness so complete she couldn't move them even an inch. They felt like soft stone, rooted in place.

Again, she was aware of her own rapid breathing, which made their stillness and quiet that much eerier. Fighting an almost overwhelming disgust, she bent her head close to Lara's face and realized she could detect no breath coming from her slightly open mouth. She placed two shaking fingers on Lara's throat and then ripped them away a moment later. Lara had no pulse.

Reeling, she backed away from the table, stopping only when the window hit her back, the gauze scrim brushing her skin and making her jump away, startled. She stood there, staring at the three people still seated at the table, putting her hand to her mouth to stifle a scream.

She heard the click of a door and spun in that direction, cringing with fright. The door that opened was in the center of the wall she normally shared with the bathroom—a door that didn't exist as far as she knew. It opened a fraction of an inch and paused, as if waiting for something, and then opened farther, about a foot. A moment later, a face appeared, peeking around the door at her, much lower than she'd expected. It was a young girl.

At the sight of the girl, her fright drained away, and her breathing and heart rate slowed almost at once. The girl eased one shoulder into the room, revealing the corner of a white, old-fashioned dress. She looked directly at Emily and then motioned for her to follow before slipping back behind the door again. She left it open.

"Wait!" Emily called out, then put her hand over her mouth, startled by how loud it had been in the room. Gingerly, she touched her throat, amazed that it no longer hurt. Her voice had sounded normal because it apparently wasn't injured.

She walked toward the open door and then paused, glancing back at the others still seated at the table, eyes closed. Before she could lose her nerve, she went directly to June and bent down to kiss her cold, dead lips.

"I'll come back to you, June. I swear it."

She turned and faced the partially open door, squaring her shoulders. She took another deep breath and walked toward it, flinging it open, ready for anything.

CHAPTER TWENTY-FOUR

The room behind the door was an artists' studio. Easels were set up in several places, and a drafting table took up one corner. Paintings were propped on the easels, each a work in progress. Emily recognized a few as paintings that normally hung in the sitting room downstairs and elsewhere in the house, but some were wholly unfamiliar. A chaise lounge dominated the middle of the room, draped with a velvet blanket despite the summer weather. A few pillows were arranged on it, and others had fallen to the floor. She stepped farther into the room to examine one of the paintings and then heard the door to the balcony opening to her left. She spun in that direction, heart leaping.

Two young people entered the room, both of them laughing. The girl wore a high-necked, lacy white dress and high leather ankle shoes. The boy was in loose velvet trousers and an open-necked, cream-colored shirt. His hair was unkempt and wild, hers tied up almost primly in braids pinned on top of her head. Their clothes and hair immediately suggested another time period, as the careworn clothes were clearly not costumes.

They were laughing so hard they had to clutch each other for balance, and both of them collapsed on the chaise lounge, still laughing. The girl looked briefly in her direction, but if she saw her standing there, some ten feet away, she said nothing. Emily moved an arm wildly, and when neither of them reacted, she felt safe to assume they couldn't see her. She cleared her throat loudly, and again they didn't react. Her anxiety eased. They couldn't see or hear her.

The boy calmed first, wiping his eyes and chuckling lightly. He was handsome, with wavy, light-brown hair and startlingly blue eyes. He was perhaps in his mid-to-late teens, something like her freshman college students, though perhaps a little younger. He had clearly tried to grow a mustache, but the patchy, pathetic thing barely dusted the top of his lip. When he'd fully calmed, he watched the girl continue to laugh, his grin slowly fading and replaced with a sneer.

The girl looked to be about his age, and her face caused a dim bell of recognition to ring in Emily's mind. She'd seen this girl somewhere. Unlike the boy, acne marred her face, which was also a little too long and pale to be attractive. Her nose was oversized and hooked, and her teeth were slightly crooked.

"Stop it," the boy suddenly said.

The girl stopped laughing, her face falling slightly when she met his eyes. Haughty anger replaced her disappointment a moment later, and she frowned.

"Stop trying to boss me around, Nathan. You thought it was funny, too."

Nathan's smile returned and he laughed, once. "You're right. I'm sorry."

The girl seemed to accept this apology, as her expression cleared a little. "That'll be the last of Aunt Mildred, I hope."

Nathan was still grinning. "She was dad's final cousin. If I'm not mistaken, we don't have any more relatives for her to call on. No more replacement parents."

"Maybe they'll leave us alone now." Her voice was wistful.

Nathan sighed and got to his feet, stuffing his hands into his pockets. "Somehow I doubt that. Especially as I'm leaving next month."

The girl groaned dramatically and lay back on the chaise, throwing one arm across her eyes. "Do you have to go?"

Nathan laughed, but Emily could see that his expression was humorless, bitter. "You know I have to, Margot."

Margot flung her arm off her face and groaned louder. "Curse Father and his stupid rules." She sat up, pouting. "I don't want you to go."

Nathan frowned, shaking his head. "And I don't want to leave you. But I have to. I don't inherit if I don't finish school."

The girl grabbed his hand in both of hers. "But can't you fight it? In court, I mean?"

Nathan shook his head, slowly. "The lawyers said it wasn't any use and would end up wasting a lot of money. At least they agreed to let me go to art school and not to some stupid business program."

Margot flung his hand away and started pouting again, her color high. Nathan knelt in front of her and took both of her hands. "You know I love you, Margot, and I always will. I'll be back between terms—more often if I can."

She continued to frown, and he let go of her hands and got up on the chaise with her. A moment later, he was unfastening the little hooks on her dress at the back. Margot's eyes closed, her face twisted in triumph. He slid her dress down to her shoulders and started kissing her neck and shoulders. Emily turned away in disgust.

The door opened, and the same little girl she had seen earlier came into the room, freezing when she caught sight of the two on the chaise.

Nathan cursed and threw a pillow at her. "Get out of here, Julia!"

Margot laughed. "Yes—get out. Get out, or we'll lock you in the attic again."

Julia turned and fled, running out of the room as fast as she could, slamming the door behind her. Nathan and Margot started laughing, but a moment later the laughter turned into passionate kisses. Again, Emily turned away, tempted to go back into the bedroom she'd started in. The last thing she wanted to do was watch two teenage siblings making out.

The door to the balcony opened again, and Emily was certain Nathan and Margot would stop. They didn't seem to hear the sound, continuing in their furious passion. Julia stood in the doorway again, but she had changed from the little girl that had just fled. She looked quite a bit older. She glanced at her siblings on the chaise and once again gestured for Emily to follow her, appearing almost desperate now. Emily took one last look at Margot and Nathan and left hurriedly, afraid if she waited any longer she would see too much.

When she stepped through the doorway, however, things shifted dramatically. The popping pressure in her ears returned, and she closed her eyes, suddenly disoriented and dizzy. When she opened them again, she wasn't on the balcony outside the bedrooms. Instead, it appeared that she'd walked through the library door and into the sitting room. She turned around to verify this had happened and saw only blackness through the doorway behind her—an impenetrable shroud of swirling shadow. She looked away, quickly, too frightened to stare into that horror any longer. It took her a moment more to get her bearings and for the room to stop spinning.

The paintings on the walls of the sitting room more or less matched what hung on them in Emily's era, though the Turner was notably absent. The furniture, walls, and curtains were completely different from her time, however. The walls were painted yellow instead of papered, and most of the wooden furniture was heavy and Victorian. Two side tables, more modern, were completely mismatched with the large, long couch. More than the furniture, however, something about the room was disorienting. The space seemed much larger than it was in her era—roomier somehow—but it was hard to tell with all the chairs and tables in here.

Though Emily had followed her in here, the girl Julia was not in the sitting room, but Margot was. She sat on the overly large, uncomfortable-looking sofa, dressed in something similar to the outfit she'd been in before. Like Julia, she was older than she'd been before upstairs—her late teens now. Her skin was clear and her hairstyle less severe than it had been, and she'd grown into her strong facial features more fully. Emily could recognize her now more easily than she had upstairs, her face almost matching the handsome woman she would become in the next few years, the one Emily had seen in photographs from the 1920s and '30s. This Margot seemed expectant, excited even, and the cause was revealed a moment later when Nathan walked into the sitting room.

He had filled out significantly in the time between now and when Emily had last seen him, his body no longer slim and boyish. His mustache was luxuriant and thick, matching his hair exactly in color and body. His clothes were smart and dandyish, almost absurdly colorful, if formal. His eyes swept the room with something like disdain before he nodded briefly at his sister. He stood inside the double doorway to the room, looking around with a frown.

"I don't know why you've kept all these paintings," he said to her, his tone harsh and superior. He gestured at the walls. "I'm far beyond this derivative junk now."

"I like them," Margot said, likewise haughty. "They remind me of better times."

Nathan colored slightly and then turned, his eyes sweeping the room until he saw the bar stand, located in the same corner it stood in today. He walked over quickly and poured himself a tall glass of clear liquor.

"Father and his parents loved that Romantic garbage," he said, his back still toward her.

Margot leapt to her feet, her face contorted, her hands clenched. If Nathan heard her get up, he didn't let on, and Emily watched as Margot forced herself to calm down again, her expression gradually becoming disinterested and placid once more.

"You used to like that garbage yourself, Nathan," she said lightly. "But you can replace it all, if it no longer suits you. You certainly have the money, now, to buy new things." Emily wasn't sure, but she thought she detected some bitterness in this last remark.

Nathan turned toward her, smiling for the first time since entering the room. "I do, don't I?"

The indifference melted from Margot's face, and she rushed toward him. They clasped hands, their faces excited and happy.

"It's all yours now, Nathan. Every penny. We—I mean, you can do whatever you want with it. Europe, Asia, it's all open to you now."

He laughed, the sound boyish and loud, reminding Emily of the younger version of him she'd seen upstairs. Margot seemed to see this too, and her face transformed with joy. She released one of his hands to touch his jawline. For a moment, he let her run her fingers along it, and then he jerked away, his smile replaced with a disgusted sneer.

"I told you last night we wouldn't do that anymore," he said, stepping away from her.

"Why?" She sounded heartbroken, forlorn, her eyes pleading.

"Because it's disgusting. You know it as well as I do. We knew it before I left. If anyone ever found out—"

"They already know!" Margot said. "You should hear the awful things they say about us in the village. Once that bitch Mary told everyone what she saw, and then that gardener, what's his name—"

"Who cares what they say in the village? I meant elsewhere, in the real world. Boston, New York—real places. If it ever got out, I'd be ruined, and so would you."

"Is that the only thing stopping you?" Margot took a step toward him. "We could be careful, we could—"

This time, Nathan slapped her, hard. The sound was like a gunshot, and Emily jumped. Margot's hand went to her face, her eyes wide with horror and pain. Nathan grabbed Margot's wrist, squeezing it hard enough to make her wince and crumple toward him. He dragged her close enough to whisper into her ear.

"It's over, Margot. And if you ever come into my bedroom again like you did last night, I'll kill you." He flung her arm away from him and went back to the bar for his drink. His back still to her, he said, "You'll have to find someone else to fuck, sister of mine. You're all out of brothers."

Margot's expression was murderous. For a moment, Emily was certain she would attack him, here and now. Then something curious happened. A chill seemed to sweep through her. She shivered and then straightened up, and her face drained of expression. Except for the angry red handprint on her face, the whole incident might not have happened.

Movement caught Emily's eye, and she turned toward the doorway. Julia stood there, a wooden box in her arms. She seemed uncertain, afraid even, but she straightened her shoulders as if determined to go through with whatever she'd planned. She walked into the room, and both of her siblings turned toward her.

"Wait, now," Nathan said, grinning. "Is this little Julia?"

Julia nodded, her face coloring.

He laughed, throwing his head back. "My God! I barely recognize you. You've grown up so much."

"You might recognize her if you'd ever visited. Three years is a long time." Margot turned her back to them and sat down on the couch.

Nathan gave Margot a nasty sneer and then turned back to Julia. "You've grown into a real lady! You got the looks in the family."

Margot's face colored slightly, but she said nothing, and neither did Julia. Julia was indeed quite striking. Unlike her brother and sister, her hair was dark, almost black. She was pale, but not sickly like her sister. She had the same crystalline blue eyes as her brother, and her face was pretty with delicate, sharp features. She was tall and slim.

"What have you got there?" Nathan said, pointing at the box.

"She can't talk, you imbecile," Margot said, "or had you forgotten?" Nathan opened his mouth as if to reply and then shook his head, sighing. He gave Julia a gentle smile. "Is that a homecoming present? For me?"

Julia bobbed her head up and down, smiling widely, then held the box out in front of her, not stepping any closer. Nathan grinned and set his drink down, then walked closer to take the box. "How lovely, Julia. It was so nice of you to do this."

"You don't even know what it is," Margot said.

"Quiet!" Nathan snapped, his cool finally breaking. Margot grinned, clearly satisfied she'd finally riled him. Nathan turned and sneered at her before looking back down at the box in his hands. He took it over to one of the heavy tables and set it down. He had to fiddle with it for a moment before he found the clasp holding it closed, and when he opened it, his eyebrows knitted, his expression puzzled. He looked up at Julia. "What is this?"

Julia blushed slightly, her face falling. Nathan took out a lead soldier, holding it up. He peered at it closely for a moment, still puzzled, and then suddenly his face cleared, and the ghost of a smile rose to his lips.

"Wait a minute!" he said. "I remember these. I played with them as a boy. But they're different, somehow." He examined the toy he held a while longer and then beamed at her. "You repainted them, didn't you?"

Julia was smiling happily now, and she finally moved closer to him. She started taking the soldiers out, pointing at the ones she was most proud of, Nathan laughing and delighted with each of them. Margot watched them, her face rigid with hatred. A moment later, Emily saw why.

As Julia continued to pull out toys to display them, Nathan's attention gradually shifted from the soldiers to the girl next to him. Something distasteful suddenly glinted in his eyes as he watched her. As if unable to stop himself, he reached out and set his hand on the back of Julia's neck. If she noticed, she didn't let on, as she seemed focused on the gift. Nathan's face was soft and slightly red, his eyes fixed on the side of Julia's face as if willing her to turn his way.

As if suddenly sensing something strange, Julia stopped gesturing at the toys and looked up at him. Emily saw the moment Julia recognized what was happening, and then the girl cringed before stepping a short distance away. She was staring at him in horror and dread, and her pale face twisted with grief.

Margot had seen this entire exchange, and she laughed, once, bitterly. "What a love triangle we are, the three of us."

"Shut up," Nathan said, but Margot only laughed again.

Julia looked back and forth between them, her eyes filling with tears, and then she dashed from the room.

The two remaining Lewises bickered for a while longer, but Emily already knew what to expect. She watched the door Julia had gone through until she reappeared, poking her head around one corner. Again, she seemed slightly older than the girl that had dashed out the door a few moments before, but the change was subtler this time—a few months or a year, perhaps, divided this Julia from the last. She met Emily's eyes and gestured once again, and Emily followed her immediately.

This time, on the threshold of the door, Emily closed her eyes before she stepped through, and the disorienting sensation she'd experienced before was less severe. Her ears popped, but she didn't experience that same whirling dizziness like last time. She kept her eyes closed, and a smell suddenly assaulted her nose: dank, fetid water. Finally, she opened them, unsurprised to find herself in the pool house.

The water was a little murky, and the furniture that the pool house held in Emily's time was almost completely absent. A few heavy, uncomfortable-looking chairs were set up around the edges of the pool, and the entire place had yet to be tiled. From the smell, Emily thought that the pool must have been installed before the use of chlorine, as the odor reminded her of a lake or pond. Almost instinctually, she glanced in the direction of the steam room, but nothing was there, not even a door. It must have been installed later.

Margot Lewis was swimming laps in the pool, her hair under a rubber cap. She was just recognizable from this distance, and Emily hesitated before walking over to the edge of the pool to watch her more closely. Emily was standing in the exact spot she'd been in yesterday, when she'd seen Harry's body floating in the water, and she looked that way, afraid of what she'd see. He wasn't there. She started watching Margot swim again, wondering what to expect.

A moment later Nathan opened the pool-house door. He was dressed in old-fashioned swimwear, covered from neck to thigh, but it was nevertheless obvious that he had a nice, athletic physique under his red and black suit. His face, however, was a little more lined than it had been in the sitting room, a little tired and mottled, possibly from drink. Judging from the Julia she'd seen in this timeframe, only a year, perhaps, had passed from the scene in the sitting room, but he seemed much older than before. He paused for a moment upon seeing Margot, clearly surprised, and then he seemed to marshal his face into indifference. He walked over to one of the chairs, set his towel on it, and removed his light boat shoes before standing at the edge of the pool, hands on his hips.

Margot finally seemed to notice him, and she stopped her laps, swimming over to the edge of the pool farthest from him. She slid her bathing cap up to free her ears and put her elbows up on the edge of the pool, kicking lightly in the water.

"What do you think of the place?" she asked, her voice echoing strangely in the large room.

He looked around and then shrugged. "I said you can spend your money however you like, but I don't understand why you would waste it like this. I thought you'd take a trip somewhere."

"The money was a gift, to spend however I chose. I chose to spend it on a pool."

"I suppose it's better than those stupid gardens Julia planted," Nathan said, grinning.

"Or that bizarre Celtic crap she's so obsessed with," Margot added. "Father liked that stuff too, though I can't imagine why."

"She was out there this morning in the gardens watching the sun rise, if you can believe it," Nathan said, laughing and shaking his head.

They smiled at each other, the tension between them seemingly forgotten in their shared disdain. Nathan crouched and then eased into the pool. He swam a lap or two and then stopped a few feet from Margot. He mimicked her posture, his elbows up on the edge of the pool, and they both stayed there, kicking their feet slightly.

"It is nice," Nathan said, "the pool, I mean. I went to a public pool in New York, but this is much better. Private." He grinned at her. "It's just the thing, too. Very modern of you, Margot. Even the Rockefellers don't have a pool this grand."

Her face brightened, but her smile died almost at once. She turned away from him and stared at the water. He frowned, still watching her for a moment before speaking again.

"I wish you'd get over it, Margot. It's not as if you've been innocent yourself. I hear all sorts of things about you from the boys in town, and I'm fairly certain most of it is true."

She snorted. "No—I wouldn't say I'm innocent. But I also wasn't stupid like you were. I'm always careful to avoid…accidents of that kind."

He frowned more deeply. "Yes, it was stupid. But what would you have me do? She insisted on keeping it. I couldn't force her to get rid of it."

Margot looked at him sharply. "Couldn't you?"

He didn't reply, his expression stubborn and dark. Margot continued to stare at him before she laughed. "I think you actually wanted it. I think you decided not to interfere so you could have a child." When he didn't reply, she shook her head, almost imperceptibly, her guess confirmed.

"What was it, by the way?" she asked after a quiet pause. "Boy or girl?"

He glanced at her and then away, color in his cheeks. "A girl. Hilda."

Margot scoffed, but Emily could tell she was more upset than she let on. She looked, in fact, as if she were on the verge of tears. Nathan seemed to sense her reaction, and he let go of the wall and swam the few feet to her, pulling her into his arms. They kissed, deeply, and when they pulled away, Margot was crying. Nathan shushed her, running his hand over her back and hugging her more tightly. Finally, Margot moved away, snuffling, her tears finally finished. She seemed embarrassed now, but still hurt.

"I'm sorry, Margot. I know when we decided to start this up again, we both agreed we needed to cover our tracks. But I didn't mean for it to happen, even if I like the child."

Margot sneered at him and pushed away, out of his arms, swimming back to the edge of the pool. "What's that supposed to mean? She was born yesterday. How you could know if you like her or not?"

He raised his hands and then ran them through his hair before dropping them back into the water at his sides. "It's hard to explain. But when they brought her out of the house to show me, I don't know, something about her made me happy. Looking at her was like seeing into my own heart—the best part of my own heart." He shook his head. "You wouldn't understand."

She snorted again. "You're right—I wouldn't. You knock up the mailman's daughter, and now you're father of the year. Haven't you ever heard of paying someone off?"

He seemed angry now, but he took a long breath before speaking. "Look, I wanted to tell you something so you wouldn't be surprised. My lawyer is coming to the house tomorrow."

"What? Why?"

Nathan squared his shoulders. "I've redrawn my will. I want to make sure that if something happens to me, little Hilda will be taken care of. And now that we've talked, I know you would never think of helping her, so I want it official."

Margot didn't reply, but bright points of color showed in her wan cheeks. Her eyes blazed as she stared at him. Nathan either didn't notice her reaction or chose to ignore it. "Anyway, it's happening. It's my money, and I'll do as I like."

With that, he plunged into the water, swimming back and forth along the length with ease. Margot watched him for a long spell, rage still fixed in her eyes, unmoving, unblinking. Finally, as if snapping out of it, she looked around herself with a slightly dazed expression. A pitcher of lemonade was perched on a small table near the edge of the pool, and she levered herself out of the water to get it. She emptied the contents onto the ground and then stood watching her brother swim for a few moments longer before she got back in the water.

Nathan continued to do his laps, and Emily thought it likely that he was swimming to avoid an argument. His face remained in the water with most of his strokes, so he never saw it coming. Margot didn't hesitate. The next time he swam by her, she raised the pitcher high into the air and brought it down onto the back of his head with all her might. The water immediately filled with blood, and he plunged under, his hands going to his head. Margot was viper-quick, flinging the pitcher away and pushing him under when he tried to come up. He must have been at least partially stunned, as she was able to hold him under with what looked like very little effort. He thrashed beneath her, and her expression remained blank and cold the whole time, her mouth a thin line of determination. More blood spread out around her in rippling waves, dyeing the water around her a sickly pink.

It wasn't long before the thrashing grew weaker, and not long after that it stopped completely. Still, Margot continued to hold him down, her face blank and colorless. She didn't even react when the door opened and Julia walked inside. Julia took one look at the water and her sister and seemed to know instantly what had happened. Her hands went to her mouth, and she bent double in a silent scream. This movement seemed to finally snap Margot out of her murderous stupor. Life came back into her eyes, and she released her brother's body. He bobbed up to the surface, and she pushed him away impatiently.

"Get out of here, you creep!" Margot yelled.

Julia turned and ran for the door, almost running into it before flinging it open. She dashed outside and disappeared.

"Goddamn it," Margot said to the empty room. "What a mess."

Emily watched her swim to the edge of the pool and crawl out. Margot stood there, surveying her work, but Emily turned her attention to the door again. She didn't have long to wait. The door to the pool house opened again, and the Julia that had appeared in the doorway a moment later was identical to the one that had just dashed out in fright. She gestured for Emily to follow her, and Emily walked as quickly as she could, impatient now to see what would happen.

This time, Emily stepped across the threshold into the attic room she and the others had discovered last week. Similar to when they'd found it, the room was trashed with broken, splintered furniture. Emily even saw the box of lead soldiers on the ground where Jim had found them decades later.

This time, however, Julia was seated in the center of the room on the only chair left intact. Margot was standing near her, her eyes red as if from crying. Two police officers stood in the room as well as a man in a lab coat, possibly a doctor. Julia was staring at the floor, her shoulders almost bent double, hunched in on herself. It took a moment for Emily to realize she was tied to the chair with thick rope. Margot was snuffling, and the policemen seemed embarrassed, not sure where to look. Margot smiled weakly. "I'm so sorry. I don't mean to make a scene. I don't want to be a nuisance."

"Of course not," the younger policemen said, smiling. "You have every right to be upset after..." His eyes fell on Julia. "After what happened."

"I never expected she would do something like this," Margot said. "We've been treating her here at home, but she never seemed violent before."

The doctor nodded. "She's certainly never hurt anyone before today."

"What's the matter with her?" the older policeman said, staring at Julia with clear revulsion.

"Acute mania brought on by psychosexual hysteria," the doctor replied without a pause.

"Psycho—what?" the policeman asked, his face creased with apparent confusion.

The doctor shook his head and rolled his eyes, obviously impatient with the need to dumb things down. "She suffers from an overwhelming sexual attraction to her siblings."

Both policemen reacted with horror, blanching and flinching and physically stepping away from the girl in the chair.

"Christ," the older one muttered and then blushed. "My apologies, Miss Margot. Please forgive my language." He turned back to the doctor. "And you say Julia never acted out like this before?"

The doctor shook his head. "No. She's been caught watching her older brother and sister a few times, spying on them, if you will, when they were changing, that kind of thing, and she had all sorts of fantasies about them—unfounded, disgusting things."

"How do you know?" the younger one asked. "I thought she couldn't talk."

The doctor looked at the policeman as if he'd just crawled out of the primordial goo. "She can read and write, Officer." He rolled his eyes again. "Anyway, as I was saying, she was a Peeping Tom, and she had fantasies about them, but she never did anything physical, nothing violent, until now." He sighed. "Still, I might have seen this coming. We should have institutionalized her long ago."

"No!" Margot said. The men stared at her in obvious surprise, and she paled. "I mean, can't we continue to treat her here?"

The policemen were clearly dumbfounded. The older one spoke slowly, as if to a child. "She committed murder, Miss Lewis. Your brother, Nathan, is dead because of her. How can you expect her to remain in your house?"

"Isn't there a way? The publicity would be awful! It would ruin our family name!" She looked at each man in turn, and each refused to hold her gaze. Margot's eyes lost some of their phony fright and terror, the expression in them now calculating and cold. "If it's a matter of payment..."

All three men looked up in startled shock, but Emily already knew the outcome of this conversation. Despite their current denial and surprise, Margot would eventually convince all of them to go along with her plan, which was to keep her sister locked up in the family attic for the rest of her life. The public would hear that Nathan had drowned in an accident, and Margot would disappear for over a decade, long enough for things to be forgotten in town. Emily turned her back to them, ready to watch for the next Julia to appear in the doorway behind her.

As if her lack of attention had turned off the show, Emily was suddenly aware that the room had fallen quiet behind her. That same popping sensation came and went in her ears, and the room dimmed, but both sensations were less severe than before. When Emily turned around, she saw Julia standing on the far side of the same attic room, her back to Emily. Some of the broken furniture had been pushed to the side to create a bigger empty space, and a small bed was in here now. The windows now had bars on them.

Julia turned toward her, and Emily was startled to see her transformation. She was older by years, pale and so thin it was hard to know how she was able to walk. Her feet and lower legs were bare and scratched, and her wrists were chafed and red. She was wearing what amounted to a long, shapeless cotton sack, stained brown with age. This was the Julia Emily had seen in the window the first day she'd come to Gnarled Hollow.

Something furtive crept into Julia's expression, and she walked toward the door and toward Emily. Emily jumped out of the way at the last second, horrified to discover what would happen if they touched. Julia leant close to the door, pressing her ear against it, and then turned around and went back to the far side of the room where she'd been. She knelt and removed a floor board, then dug around for a moment and pulled a box from the hole. She sat back on her heels, her face triumphant as she held the box, and then she opened it.

She pulled out a few folded papers and a journal. Emily watched her set everything except this journal aside on the ground and then stand up with it in her hands. Julia opened it and did something curious. Instead of reading the journal normally, she turned it in her hands and seemed to be reading it on its side. For a moment, Emily was worried that she had lost her mind up here on her own. She seemed completely deranged holding the journal that way.

Julia continued to read, a smile gradually warming her wan face, and then she jerked, her head snapping toward the door. Emily could hear it now, too: a noise in the hall. Moving quickly, Julia put the papers and journals back into the box and then slid everything in the hole again. She managed to slip the wooden plank over it and move away before the door opened.

A young woman appeared in the doorway, a nurse's cap perched on her red, curly hair. She smiled when she saw Julia.

"Up and about, are you?" she asked needlessly. "I came up to see if you were awake, and I find you actually moving around. What a nice change of pace."

Julia gave her a warm smile and walked toward her, holding out her hands. The nurse took both of them in hers and gave her a quick hug. "And you're feeling friendly, too. Isn't that lovely? You haven't gotten out of bed a single time in almost a week! You had me and the doctor very worried."

She gave Julia a reproving pout, and Julia shrugged apologetically. The nurse grinned. "But you're okay now, and the doctor's out for the day. Do you know what that means? It means, if you're very good, we can sneak downstairs for a bit. I know you like looking outside, and I'll let you do that for a while if you're good. Will you be good for me?"

Julia nodded vigorously and the nurse laughed. "There's my little woodchuck. Tell you what—if you're good downstairs, I'll give you a second treat: a real bath. How about that?"

Julia smiled even further, but Emily, who was looking right into her eyes, thought she saw something sad and miserable underneath that smile. As she watched Julia follow the nurse into the hallway, holding her hand like a child, Emily knew once again what she would see if she followed them. Julia would look out the window that was currently in Emily's bedroom, staring down at the lawn as if her heart was breaking, and then she would be taken to the bathroom where Emily herself was attacked and nearly drowned. Is that what had happened to Julia? Or had she done it herself? Emily wasn't sure it mattered anymore—either way, Julia had died, alone and forgotten, labelled a murderer by her homicidal sister.

When Emily walked through the door to finally follow, she wasn't expecting another shift, but it happened, and she reeled, almost falling over before she regained her balance again. June, Lara, and Jim were seated at the table in her bedroom, eyes closed. Her chair was still tipped over on the ground, just as she had left it. Likewise, her bedroom had returned. It was the same as she remembered, down to her coffee cup and the sock she'd forgotten to pick up this morning. She moved closer to the table, almost holding her breath, and thought she detected movement beneath each of her companion's eyelids, almost as if they were sleeping.

Before she could look at them any closer, she heard the grandfather clock chiming far off in a different part of the house and the more distant sound of dogs barking outside. She set her chair upright again and sat back down. She grabbed June and Jim's hands before the fourth chime on the clock stopped ringing.

June opened her eyes and blinked a few times before turning and smiling at her. "That's funny. I think I fell asleep for a second. Did you?"

CHAPTER TWENTY-FIVE

M ark and Chris were bent over some folded papers, delicate with age and damaged with damp. Unlike the journals and other papers they'd found in the desk in the library, the box had been kept in a terrible atmosphere for paper. The attic was less insulated than the rest of the house, and the space under the floorboards was even worse. Chris was seated so close to Mark that their shoulders were flush and touching, but neither man seemed to notice.

They'd all waited until the searchers went home to retrieve the box from the attic. After the séance, when the four of them left her bedroom, they gathered with Mark and Chris in the sitting room, and Emily had given all of them the entire story of what she'd experienced. Lara had wanted to search for the box immediately, but Jim had prudently pointed out that it might provoke suspicion should the police want to question them further.

They'd all spent the evening impatiently waiting for everyone outside to leave, which, luckily, was much sooner than the night before. Clearly the search-and-rescue officials and volunteers were starting to lose hope. With no sign that Harry had even gone onto the grounds or into the woods, they were now beginning to wonder if they should bother to search them beyond what they'd already done.

The woods of Gnarled Hollow estate were enormous and, given the landscape, a dangerous place, with untamed foliage and steep, rising hills in most directions. A final decision regarding the continuation of the search would be discussed during a conference in town, and the six of them would be phoned in the morning with an update.

When the taillights of the final searcher had disappeared around the corner of the driveway, they'd all gone at once, wordlessly, up to the attic. Without asking the others, Emily removed the floorboard and pulled out the wooden box. It was filthy with age, clearly untouched after all this time. The others stood inside the doorway or out in the hall, their faces identically serious and grim. Here, for the first time, was proof.

Relatively sure they wouldn't be interrupted, they'd all gone back downstairs and removed the contents, one by one, onto the coffee table in the sitting room. June was seated near Emily, her face white and lined. Jim and Lara were likewise drained, as if the séance had taken something out of all of them. Only Emily had come back from the experience energized and excited, recharged, in a way.

"Interesting." Mark leaned back and away from the papers he'd been inspecting.

"Very," Chris said.

"What is it?" Emily asked.

Mark held it out for her. "The last will and testament of Mr. Nathan Lewis. He left everything to his illegitimate daughter, Hilda Grossman. It was written on June 21, 1919. According to this, the little girl was born two days before."

"There's that date again," Lara said quietly. "Today's date."

Emily took it from him and scanned it briefly. More than simply willing his money and estate to his daughter, Nathan had gone so far as to leave very clear instructions to disinherit his two younger sisters, mentioning an earlier, previous will that had split the estate between them. She looked at the date again and realized she'd forgotten something when she was telling them everything she'd witnessed during the séance. She held up the will and waved it. "He must have written this the morning he died."

Mark leaned forward, frowning. "What makes you think that?"

"I forgot to mention, but he and Margot were joking about the gardens right before he got in the pool, right before she killed him. He said Julia had been up that morning watching the sun rise on her new gardens."

Mark shook his head. "But his obituary said he didn't die until July. July 8th, in fact, according to my notes from the archive."

Emily held up her hands. "We know they covered it up and put out that he was drowned by accident. Maybe the date was part of the cover-up."

Mark raised his eyebrows. "Could be."

"It would certainly explain why today is so important to the presence in this house," Lara said. "I don't think the séance would have worked any other day. It had to be today."

Emily returned her attention to the will, rereading it one more time. When she was finished, she held it out for Mark, surprised by what she'd just read. "It looks like he even had witnesses." She pointed to the signatures.

"If he'd given that to his lawyer, as he intended, we wouldn't be sitting here right now." Mark paused for a moment, eyebrows lowering. "In fact, it might be legal even now, considering it was witnessed. I'm not sure."

"Why would he disinherit his sisters?" June asked.

Mark shrugged. "I don't know. It seems from what Emily told us that the baby meant something to him. Or maybe he was angry with Margot for some reason, or disgusted with her and what they were doing together."

Everyone turned to Emily as if for explanation, and this role was beginning to seem automatic and natural to her. Her throat hurt again, and her neck was painful to the touch, but her voice was a little stronger than it had been this morning. Still, she had to clear her throat and keep her voice low to avoid straining it further. "I don't know. I mean, from what I saw, it looked like he and Margot started having an affair again after he came back from school, but I think he was always ashamed of it. Maybe cutting her off was his way of cleaning the slate."

"But what about Julia?" June asked. "She was innocent in all of this, wasn't she?"

Emily shook her head again. "I don't know. She seemed to be, but then again, I only saw what she showed me. She was certainly innocent of his murder, but who knows what happened before, after Nathan came back from school."

"We should contact a lawyer," Mark suggested, glancing at Lara. "And a private investigator. This Hilda Grossman could be tracked down. We know her birthday and where she was born, so it shouldn't be too hard to find her if she's still alive, or her family if she isn't."

"Yes, we should," Lara said. "The estate should go to the real descendants, if possible." Everyone was surprised, and Lara, seeing their expressions, grinned. "I know what you're thinking, but believe me, my aunt would be relieved to get rid of it." She grinned more broadly. "Except for the money, of course."

Jim finally seemed to stir to life. He stretched and yawned with a little yodel, shaking his head as if to wake himself. He pointed at the contents of the box on the table. "What else was in there?"

"Another journal," Mark said, handing it to Emily. He riffled through the other papers briefly. "Here's some kind of letter. The first paragraph mentions the Turner." He handed it to June and again opened some more of the folded papers, setting each aside after he glanced at them. "We'll have to read the rest of this more closely, but I think they're legal documents. A lawyer might make more of them than I can."

June laughed a moment later, and everyone looked at her. She held up the letter Mark had given her. "This explains one thing, anyway."

"What?" Chris asked.

"The Turner was bought from Aris Rilke—a famous art dealer in the early twentieth century." She smiled. "Or a famous thief, to be more accurate. The painting must be one of the Turners she stole from a private collection in 1918, during the Great War. The original owner died in battle, and he never catalogued anything, so no one knows what went missing, and no one ever came forward to tell anyone about what they'd bought from Rilke. She was caught selling a painting one of the heirs recognized, but she never revealed anything else she'd stolen." June pointed at the Turner on the wall. "Now we know at least one of them. Even in 1919, when this letter is dated, it would have been nearly impossible to get a real Turner. It seems like Margot found a way to do that." She set the letter down on the table, almost reverently. "This is the first piece of evidence that has ever been found regarding the stolen collection, and it mentions the names of other pieces Rilke had for sale. I can hardly believe I'm actually seeing this."

"Going to be a great publication," Mark said, grinning.

June's eyebrows rose, as if she hadn't thought of this possibility before. "You're right. It is."

"No doubt going to ruffle some feathers, too," Jim said, grinning. "Some of the owners of those works might still have them."

June laughed. "Some of them will be surprised to know they have stolen goods."

She got up to examine the Turner more closely, letter still in hand, and Emily had a momentary longing for her so deep and so strong, she had to stop herself from rising to join her. She would have given anything to be alone with her for a while, just holding her hand. This morning already seemed like a thousand years ago.

When June turned around, her smile was gone. "That's one mystery solved, anyway. Too bad there are more."

"What are the others?" Jim asked. "We know who painted the rest of these, after all—Nathan."

June shook her head. "No—not quite. Not all of them, anyway." She looked at Emily. "When Emily told me that Nathan died in 1919, I knew there was more to it."

"Why?"

June walked over to a painting between two windows and pointed at it. "This one was painted later."

"How can you tell?" Mark asked.

"The skyline of the city. And the paint." She pointed at two other paintings. "That one over there is from the twenties, at the earliest, and so is that. And I'm pretty sure there are other paintings in the house from after 1919." She held up her hands. "I have no idea who did them."

Emily frowned, trying to recall the paintings she'd seen during the séance. She couldn't remember for certain, but she was fairly sure those places on the walls had been empty. She and June shared a long look, and Emily shook her head, not willing to comment. She couldn't be certain if the paintings were there or not. She'd been focused on the siblings, not the room.

Chris and Mark offered to cook dinner, and Emily realized as they suggested it that she hadn't eaten in a long time—sometime yesterday, perhaps. Almost as if their suggestion spoke to her body, she was suddenly pierced with a hunger so deep and clenching, she almost moaned. Everyone else seemed to have a similar reaction, and June and Lara offered to help them in order to speed up the process.

They left her and Jim alone, and Jim moved his chair closer to hers so they could read the journal together. They puzzled over the first few lines together, heads close. After a few minutes, she looked over at him, and something warm and deep spread through her heart. Despite her claw marks down his face and his clear fatigue, he seemed in better shape than he had in days. Now that he was back to normal, she realized how much she'd missed him, and how fond of him she'd become. It was incredible to have close friends. She couldn't remember the last time she'd liked people as much as she liked the people in this house, nor could she remember the last time she'd felt so accepted. Jim was unaware of her gaze, eyes rooted to the journal. She looked back at it, still smiling slightly with pleasure.

Soon after this, Jim pulled a little notebook from his front pocket and flipped through it. After reviewing for a moment, he turned to her, grinning. "I recognize this code. I already broke this one."

She was surprised. So far, they hadn't seen an example of a repeated code. "Oh? That's strange."

"It is. But look." He pointed to the dates on the inside cover: 1918–1919. "It's the earliest journal we've seen. Margot must have thought she lost it and saved herself the effort of coming up with a new code. I'd bet money Julia hid it from her."

"I wish we could find some kind of key for all these journals. She must have written them down somewhere, or she wouldn't have remembered this one. Our work would go much quicker if we had it."

Jim nodded absently. They'd said the same thing to each other a few times, but so far had discovered nothing of the sort. He returned his attention to the journal a moment later, his face creased with concentration. She handed it to him, fully, perfectly happy to let him decode it. As he worked, he wrote down what he read inside his little journal, flipping from the key to his translation every other word or so. He finished the first entry and leaned back, pushing the journal away from him in disgust.

"Goddamn it. It's more of the same shit. This entry was about a dressmaker's visit."

Her face heated with impatient temper, and she pulled the journal back to take another look. "But it can't be! Or at least not all of it. She must mention something in here about Nathan or something else, or Julia wouldn't have hidden it."

"Well, if Margot did mention something, it's not here at the beginning. We'll have to read the whole thing to see if anything worthwhile is hidden in here." He sounded defeated, and even she felt like the whole thing would likely give them nothing of value. They were missing something.

She thought back to the scene in the attic room and remembered something she'd almost forgotten: Julia had turned the journal on its side to read it. Suddenly excited, she did the same thing and was dimly aware of Jim leaning forward to see what she was doing. Using the same code, she started reading the lines along the side. It was difficult work, as the letters and symbols were written as if meant to be read upright on the page, but after she'd decoded the first line with the journal on its side, she knew she was onto something.

"Holy shit," she said, leaning back away from the page.

"What?" Jim asked. He read what she'd written and then looked at her, shocked. "Oh my God. How did you know to do that?"

She explained about seeing Julia turn the journal on its side in the attic room during the séance. "It was almost like she was showing me how to read it—almost like she knew I was there."

His face, if possible, went even whiter than before. "Maybe she did. Maybe some part of her knew you would see her." He suddenly got to his feet, the movement so quick it startled her. He started pacing, rubbing his hands together.

"Do you know what this means, Emily?"

She beamed at him. "The other journals. We have to go through them again. We have to start over."

The idea, though daunting, was exhilarating. Now that they'd figured out what Margot had done, she was certain they would find something incredible in the journals, though what exactly, she didn't know.

Jim stopped pacing and looked down at her. "She must have been some kind of genius—Margot, I mean. First, she comes up with all these codes. Then she writes out what she wants to write out, then figures out a way for it to make sense written in either direction, upright or on the side." He shook his head. "It's incredible. I don't even know if you could do that very easily with a computer."

She tapped the journal again with her fingers. "And she started this one when she was what, nineteen?"

"Amazing."

"She should have worked for the War Office as a code writer."

Jim laughed. "Hell—maybe she did. Everything about her has been a complete mystery until now. Just think, before today, no one knew she was in an incestuous affair with her brother, a brother she later killed. Imagine what that will do for Lewis scholarship."

They were both positively gleeful, and when June came back into the room a moment later to call them to dinner, she laughed.

"You two look like the cat with the canary," she said.

Emily rose to her feet and raced toward June before pulling her into an embrace and giving her a long, deep kiss. June pulled away a moment later, blushing and glancing at Jim. "That was unexpected. I thought you wanted to keep us a secret."

She laughed. "What? I thought you did."

June shook her head, grinning. "I was following your lead. I would have been holding your hand this whole time if I'd thought you were okay with it."

She laughed again, so pleased she could feel happy tears pricking her eyes. She blinked them away, glanced at Jim, and then winked at June. "Anyway, I think he knew all along."

Jim laughed. "We all did. You guys weren't exactly…discreet. And anyway, you can tell."

"Tell what?" June asked.

Jim shrugged, his face reddening slightly. "Tell that you like each other, I guess. I saw it the first day Mark and I got here."

June and she smiled at each other, and Emily took her hand in hers. "Let's go eat. Jim and I have something really important to tell the rest of you."

CHAPTER TWENTY-SIX

The next morning, Lara called her family lawyer and hired a private-detective agency. She'd told her aunt what they'd found, and her aunt had been all too grateful to rid herself of the estate, if possible, giving Lara full permission to look into tracing the lost heirs.

By Thursday, Lara decided that she wanted to have a more active role in the search and had left to join the detectives already on the hunt. Although she'd been at the house for only a few days, her departure made the place seem emptier, their adventure almost over. Everyone seemed to feel this way.

Cocktail hour that evening was quieter, sadder somehow, as if what they'd experienced was already in the past. This, of course, was not the case, as Emily knew that she, June, Jim, and Mark would be here for a few weeks yet, and Chris wasn't leaving until early July, but the loss of one member of the party already seemed to suggest the end.

The search for Harry was called off on Friday, much to the relief of everyone in the house. The police seemed to suspect something the first day he was gone, but that suspicion, if it had ever actually been there, disappeared the longer Harry was gone. The police and search parties were just as baffled as the people inside. Harry seemed to have simply disappeared.

The house was quiet during this time. At first, Emily had braced for something to happen, and she was fairly certain the others had too, but by the weekend after the séance, they'd started to relax. No one said it, but Emily thought they all believed that now that the solstice had passed, things were quieting down again. They'd even started leaving the doors open, as they never closed on their own anymore.

Still, the lingering worry over Harry's disappearance coupled with the fact that the house still had missing rooms made them certain that things weren't quite finished yet. As to the solution of both these remaining problems, no one had any ideas.

Jim and Emily had gone into town and made scans of the first three journals—the one from the attic and the ones they'd already decoded. They printed out copies for everyone and divided them to speed up the work. She and Jim kept the bulk of the pages and worked on them during the day, but now the whole household would sit down and decode a page or two while they were in the sitting room together at the end of the day. Things went fairly quickly at first. Since Jim and she already had the solutions for the codes, it was simply a matter of transcribing the journals when they were turned on their sides.

She looked up from the page she'd been working on, her eyes automatically going to June. She smiled, heart swelling, at the sight of her. When June read anything, a tiny concentration line appeared between her eyebrows. She also wore reading glasses, which, rather than making her seem dowdy, were adorable. She had her hair piled on top of her head in a messy, loose bun held in place by a pencil. She was a brilliant, gorgeous woman made all the more attractive when in deep thought. She was focused too fully to notice Emily's gaze, so Emily took the opportunity and continued to stare, wanting very much to go over and brush a loose lock of hair off her face.

Emily, however, soon felt eyes on her and turned to see Mark smiling at her. He'd clearly watched her staring, and noticed whom she was staring at, and she couldn't help but color. Since Tuesday night, she and June had been open about their relationship. They sat next to each other, held hands, and didn't bother to hide the fact that they were going upstairs together at night anymore. Everyone seemed happy for them, and no one had been in the least surprised. It was obvious they'd already known or suspected.

She gave Mark a quick grin, stretched, and glanced at the clock, surprised to see the hour. She clapped her hands once, making everyone jump.

"Hey, all! That's it for today. Don't strain yourself. Jim and I are the ones that are supposed to be doing all this."

Chris pushed his pages away and got to his feet before stretching, touching his toes, and rotating a few times side to side.

"It's interesting, at least, but man, am I ever glad this is your project and not mine. I like being outside, not cooped up."

"How long do you think it'll take to do all the journals?" June asked. She'd taken her glasses off, and Emily could see that her eyes were strained with fatigue.

She glanced at Jim and they both shrugged. Jim sighed. "Even with your help, it'll still take all summer and most of the fall. It's tedious, as you've all seen, even now that we're reading interesting things."

Emily had decided and asked the others to wait on the earliest journal, the one from the attic, and suggested that they go back to the ones she and Jim had already started on from 1934 and 1935, the year Margot came back from Europe and the year immediately following. So far, from the hundred or so pages they'd reexamined, it appeared that every third or fourth page had a secondary reading when turned on its side. Pages with poetry, for example, could only be read in the regular way, as did others that revealed nothing with the alternate orientation. She wasn't sure, but she thought this was simply another way for Margot to confuse her readers.

In the pages that did have a secondary reading, they had found what appeared to be a new, previously unknown novel. The style was quintessentially Lewis, the story so far so much like her last novel, published in 1933, that it might have acted as a kind of sequel. Once they'd realized what they were reading, Jim had contacted the editor at a scholarly press, and when he'd told her what they'd found, the editor immediately sent them a contract to publish their findings. The novel, once it was assembled and edited, would come out next year with Jim and Emily's names as editors, and the others as assistant editors.

Neither she nor Jim, however, had decided what to do about the biographical information they'd learned. So far, they had found no evidence for what Emily had seen during the séance, and aside from a few old rumors generations removed, they had no proof that Nathan and Margot had ever been intimate with each other.

Margot had possibly recorded some of this in her earliest journal—again, this might explain why Julia hid it—but, considering Margot was known as a fiction writer, even if she basically spelled out what had happened, it wouldn't necessarily be taken as truth. This was, of course, one of the reasons Emily wanted to wait to translate the 1918-1919 journal. Seeing what she'd experienced during the séance in print would mean fulfilling a kind of obligation, to Julia at least, to set the record straight. She wasn't sure she was ready for that or what, if anything, it would accomplish.

June suddenly stood in front of her with a gin and tonic, and Emily took it from her gratefully. The last few days had been scorching hot, the natural coolness of the house finally incapable of keeping up with the heat. The house was stuffy and almost fetid, the humidity very high despite the lack of rain. Even in her lightest clothes, she felt overwhelmingly hot. The others had taken to wearing extremely light clothing as well, so that the five of them sitting here looked like they were ready for the beach.

June moved her chair closer to Emily's and sat down heavily, her drink almost sloshing out of her glass. She held the cool drink to her face for a moment before taking a sip and closing her eyes.

Emily squeezed her hand. "You seem tired. Are you okay?"

June opened her eyes and blinked a few times before giving her a weak smile. "I'm fine. It's the heat. I'm not used to it. I've been thinking of running home for a few days to have a break. I have some things in the office I need to take care of, too."

Emily's stomach dropped at the thought. More than simply leaving for a few days, eventually, at the end of the summer, June would be leaving for good. She worked at a university in Seattle, almost as far from where they were now as you could get in the continental US. Emily had a hard time imagining the day that June and the others would leave, going back to their lives, while she did what?

Every time the notion arose, she repressed it, wishing her problems would resolve on their own, but she needed to start making inquiries to get her life back on track. It was much too late to get a position for the fall semester, though she might be able to find something temporary for the spring. Visiting positions to cover sabbatical or maternity leaves were sometimes available, after all. The idea of looking was daunting, however, and every time she thought about it, she felt a little nervous and sick. Getting her last job had been an enormous undertaking, and the idea of searching for a new one made her want to shut down and give up.

June, as if reading her thoughts, took her drink from her and set them both down. She turned in her chair, leaned forward, and took her hands. June made her meet her eyes.

"I know what you're thinking, but you don't have to worry. We'll still talk. Every day. And we'll visit each other. I know you're worried about finding work, but something will turn up. I promise."

She had finally confessed to June and the others that she was now unemployed, and their responses had been supportive and empathetic. Everyone in academia knew that a lot of positions were tenuous now, even with tenure, especially with conservative state governments in charge in many places. With money cut from educational budgets at whim, no one in the public sector could avoid hearing about it. Jobs that had been nearly impossible to lose were now evaporating at the stroke of a pen, and lots of academics were becoming more and more careful about what they said or published to avoid censure and dismissal.

Not able to stop herself, she asked, "But what if nothing comes up? What if I never find a position again?"

June smiled and pulled her into a quick hug. "You will. And anyway, didn't Ruth say she was paying us for all of this? There's enough work here to keep you busy for a long time. I've only worked on the journals a few hours this week, and even I can tell it will take months to finish." She frowned. "But I wouldn't want you to do it here alone, after we all leave."

"Why not?"

June shook her head. "I would hate for you to be here by yourself. It's not safe." She looked away, her cheeks flushing. Her eyes darted back to Emily's and then away. "Maybe..." She shook her head. "Never mind."

"What?"

Still clearly nervous, June couldn't meet her eyes. She laughed lightly. "I was going to say maybe you could come back to Seattle with me at the end of the summer. Work on the Lewis project there. You could adjunct, too, if you wanted." She shook her head again. "I'm sorry. That's stupid."

Her heart was pounding, and her eyes felt dangerously close to tears. She squeezed June's hands, making her meet her eyes finally. "I'd love to, June. I'll go wherever you want."

They were grinning at each other stupidly, both of them near tears, so wrapped up in each other they'd forgotten the other people in the room. She snapped back into reality when Chris accidently dropped the platter he had been carrying onto the table. She and June jumped slightly at the thunk, June yelping.

"Sorry," Chris said. He indicated the cheese platter. "Thought I'd bring in some snacks since no one's eaten yet."

"Good," Jim said, grabbing a wedge of cheddar. "Watching these two was giving me a toothache."

June blushed and laughed, and Emily's heart soared even higher. June wasn't embarrassed to be overheard. In fact, from the set of her shoulders and her fierce expression, Emily would say she was proud, as proud as Emily was of her.

"Oh, gosh!" June said, slapping her forehead. "I forgot. When we were all in town yesterday, I bought some champagne. I wanted to open it last night, but I left it in the fridge."

"What's the occasion?" Jim asked.

June frowned as though she was thinking. "Nothing specific. We made so much progress this week. We know so much more than before. Not everything, but we're getting there." She shrugged. "And it's always a good time for champagne."

"Well then, by all means!" Jim said. "There are glasses in the dining room, too. I can get them if you want help."

Emily had started to get up, but June waved her down. "No. That's fine. I'll get it. You guys relax."

Now that the doors stayed open on their own, it was possible to see into the dining room from here, and she watched June until she turned beyond the far doorway. When she looked back at the others, Jim gave her a knowing grin and winked.

She moved closer to the cheese, grabbing a small plate and filling it. She half-listened to the others, who were discussing the upcoming election, still focused on June and what she'd said. Emily could hardly believe it. Never in her wildest dreams would she have hoped, after meeting June, that they would reach the point of moving in together. June was so far above her level it was still hard to believe. Sex, yes, but this? Out of all the beautiful people in the world she could have had, June had somehow chosen her, instead. It was unfathomable.

She smiled at the thought of telling her sister or her parents that she was moving to Seattle to live with a woman she'd just met. They knew she was gay, and they had met some of her earlier girlfriends, but as none of them had been very serious, no one in her family had taken them seriously, either. Now here she was, fulfilling a lesbian stereotype and possibly moving in with a woman she'd known for mere weeks. She'd made fun of friends who had done that, but that had been jealousy, obviously. Sometimes you simply knew you were meant to be with someone.

She'd spaced out enough to lose track of time, coming out of her daydream only when Jim said, "What's taking her so long?"

"What? Who?"

"June. She's been gone at least ten minutes."

"Maybe she's having trouble finding the glasses," Chris suggested. "I'll go help her."

"No. That's fine," Emily said. "I'll go."

She went into the dining room, switching on the light as she entered. It stayed light out quite late now, but the house was situated in such a way that this side of the house was always a little darker than the other.

The dining room was empty, and she frowned. She could see the champagne glasses in the little sideboard in the corner of the room, untouched. Perhaps June was searching for them in the kitchen. She might not have heard Jim correctly.

A nervous dread twisted her stomach, and she hurried across the dining room and through the door to the pantry and kitchen. It was dark, but she already knew what she would find when she turned on the light.

The room was empty.

Her anxiety deepened. The room was bathed in a sickly light from the inadequate single bulb, but even with better lighting, looking in here would be fruitless. She walked over to the fridge and opened it, immediately seeing the champagne still on the shelf. She closed the door and took a few deep breaths. She didn't need to panic. June might have gone to the bathroom or upstairs to change. It would be strange for her not to tell them this when they were waiting, but not unheard of.

Repressing her rising panic, she walked as quickly and calmly as she could into the entry room again and knocked on the little bathroom door. She opened it a moment later, finding it dark. Her stomach clenched with fear, and again, she forced herself to calm down in order to think rationally.

She went upstairs next, making herself walk. June was not in her own bedroom or in Emily's. Neither was she in either of the upstairs bathrooms. Emily stood on the balcony, peering down into the foyer, her heart racing painfully. It was all well and good to tell herself that things were fine, but not if they weren't. She knew. She'd known the moment she saw the champagne in the fridge.

Like Harry, June had disappeared.

CHAPTER TWENTY-SEVEN

The blood rushed to Emily's head, and she swayed. She shuddered once, shaking so hard her knees went weak. She grabbed the top of the railing to hold herself up, and a wild, piercing horror rose from within. Something close to a scream escaped her lips, and she sank to the floor, clutching the bars of the railing like they formed a personal prison.

She was screaming so loud it didn't take the others long to find her, but it did take them a while to figure out what was wrong. Emily, incapable of speech, had been led, sobbing, downstairs to the sitting room, held up and nearly carried there by Mark. Jim and Chris had gone off to search for June and had come back some time later with the same conclusion as Emily: June was gone.

By the time they returned, she had stopped sobbing and screaming, and she sat there on the sofa, Mark's arm around her shoulders, stiff and silent and staring ahead. She was beyond tears; she felt numb and dead. She couldn't get the image of Harry's body out of her mind. He was the last person to disappear, and he'd died, his corpse lost somewhere in time. The same thing was happening to June, and no one could do anything about it.

"Should we call the police?" Chris asked.

Jim laughed. "And what? Report another missing person? No way they'd let that slide. They'd think we're serial killers or something."

"Even if we called them first?"

Jim shook his head. "What did it get us last time? It's not like they found Harry."

Mark made a quieting motion with his free hand, but it was too late. Emily looked at Jim, eyes filling with tears. He was, after all, exactly right. Searching would be futile.

"Well, what should we do?" Chris asked, his voice harsh and broken. "Just let her go?"

"Of course not," Mark said. He squeezed Emily's shoulders. "We'll look, and we'll do it together. There must be a way to get through to wherever, whenever they are. Both she and Harry found a way there, but not how to get back. We have to figure out how to get there ourselves."

He sounded confident, but Emily knew that his attitude was all for her benefit. None of them had a clue as to how to go about their search or to make it a success. It would take too long. Even if they did find a way to contact that other place, that other time, it would be too late. June was already lost.

"Where should we start?" Chris asked.

Mark slowly got to his feet. "The attic. Emily felt things there, and June did, too. And the box was there."

Emily stayed where she was on the couch, still unable to move, and unwilling to go on a wild goose chase. It was hopeless.

"I'll stay with her," Jim offered. "You guys go on."

Mark and Chris left without arguing, neither of them moving very quickly. They knew, like she, that there was no point in rushing around. There was really no point to try to find her, but she wouldn't say so. Let them have their petty hope. For her, hope was dead.

Jim, who had been abstaining the last few days, walked over to the bar and fixed himself a drink. She watched him with dazed surprise, amazed that he could move around like a normal person. If she tried to, her limbs wouldn't function. She'd fall on the floor and never budge again. At least here, she was sitting upright.

Jim took his drink and walked over to the window, looking outside at the lawn. She remembered that, for him, it had all started there. He'd seen the piece of trash outside and run to get it, only to turn around and see Julia Lewis in the upstairs window. To a certain extent, everything that had happened had happened after that for him. He'd finally started to believe.

This idea made some of the fog in her head lift a little. Something similar had happened to her, too. She'd had that strange experience on the road on the way here, and that awful feeling when she first saw the house, but the mystery of it all had really started when she saw Julia up in the window. Up in her bedroom window.

She frowned, and more of the bleak dread that had been closing her down faded as her understanding grew. Why that window? In Julia's day, it had been a bedroom, Nathan's, or at least it had been his when the Lewis children were younger. So why would Julia appear there? What significance did it hold for her? The nurse had apparently taken her downstairs to let her look outside, but was that the only explanation?

During the séance, Emily had walked from Nathan's bedroom— her bedroom now—into the artists' studio. The sound in the wall had come from there, right where the door had been in the past. Harry had been talking to Jim in her bedroom before he disappeared. It all came back to that room somehow. Julia had been showing them things from that room since the beginning. It was, it seemed, the only place she could contact them, the only place she could come through.

Emily rose, surprised to find herself steady and calm. Jim had his back to her, and with the day's dying sunlight so bright in here, he must not have seen her reflection in the window. Walking quietly, she left the sitting room and went upstairs as quickly as she could, thankful now that these stairs were carpeted. She didn't make a sound all the way up to her bedroom.

She stood outside the door, amazed again to find herself so cool and composed. When she opened the door, something was going to happen—something permanent and important. She wouldn't survive it, whatever it was, but she felt at ease. Life, after all, would mean very little now that June was gone, and she might possibly find her.

After she unlocked and opened the door, however, she found the room just as she and June had left it this morning. The bed was unmade, a few articles of clothing lay on the floor, and two cups of coffee sat at the little work table beside a pile of journals.

She frowned, closing the door behind her. She'd been certain, was still certain, in fact, that the answer lay somewhere in here. Julia had been giving them clues all along, helping them find the answers. She had to find the newest one.

She walked slowly through the room, examining everything. Something should be out of place, something should reveal itself, but nothing did. Walking over to the wall that her bedroom now shared with the bathroom, she stood before it, eyes closed, but when she opened them again, it was still only a wall. She ran her fingers over it, expecting to feel something, but it was, as it appeared, simply a wall covered in thick, silk wallpaper.

Thinking suddenly that the wallpaper might be covering the door, she turned to see if she could find a knife, and then she heard something strange at her feet. She looked down and had to move to the side to see what she'd stepped on: a small puddle on the floor below her feet. When she moved a little more to let the light fall on the floor more clearly, she saw that, rather than a single puddle, there were several of them a foot or so apart. They led to the bedroom door.

Footprints.

Without hesitating, she followed them. They disappeared, of course, on the carpeted balcony and stairs, but she found them again downstairs in the marble foyer leading to the front door. It was difficult to tell whether they were going or coming, but she somehow understood that they had gone from inside out.

Jim had come to the doorway of the sitting room when he heard her, and he frowned when he saw the water on the floor. "Say, what's that?"

Without answering, she flung open the front door and started running. Jim shouted in surprise behind her, but she kept going. She'd put on flip-flops this morning, and she slowed very briefly to kick them off before running again with all her might. Jim's steps were behind her, but they sounded farther and farther away the longer she ran. If she slowed down, if she wavered for even a moment, he would catch her, and this whole thing would be over. She was being given one chance, one single chance, and she would never get it again. She ran and ran, the ground tearing into her feet, past the gardens, and down the path into the woods.

When it came into view, the door to the pool house gave her a moment's fright. She was certain Jim would catch up if she had to stop and unlock it. Then, as she came closer, a strange calm certainty ran through her, and she knew she would find it unlocked. She threw the door open and continued, running at the water, pausing only to launch herself into a graceful dive.

The water was shockingly cold, making her body clench and seize. Rather than pool water, she might have dived into an icy lake. She fought against her instinct to get out of the water and swam toward the bottom of the pool. She hadn't been in a pool in years, but the rhythm of swimming returned at once. She swam with strength and ease.

She continued to go down, deep enough that her ears popped. She kept her eyes clenched for fear of stinging them with chlorine but was finally compelled to open them to get her bearings. Around her was deep darkness, and for a moment she was completely disoriented, with no idea which way was up or down. She jerked her head around, peering into the swirling gloom, panic rising, and finally saw, far off in the distance, a tiny pinprick of light. She moved toward it, the light growing stronger the longer she swam. A few moments later she was surfacing, pulling in a great lungful of air and sputtering for breath.

She put her feet down and stood up. The water barely hit her waist, the depths she'd been swimming in now gone. She wiped her eyes before looking around.

Margot Lewis sat on the edge of the pool in a lounge chair, alone. Her eyes were closed as if she were either sleeping or trying to sleep, her head tilted back and away from Emily. Unlike the last time Emily had seen her swimming, her swimsuit seemed nearly contemporary, tight and red and revealing. With her face angled upward, it was hard to see how it had changed with time, but her hair was entirely different than during the séance—shoulder-length and curled.

The room had also changed, appearing now almost as it had in Emily's era. More chairs sat around the edges of the pool, and the bottom of the pool was tiled, as it was in the future. As Emily brushed the rest of water out of her eyes, she could taste and smell chlorine. She wasn't sure when chlorine began to be widely used for pools, but all of these things—the tiles, Margot herself, and the chlorine— suggested that a significant amount of time had passed since the murder of Nathan Lewis. If she had to guess, it might be the 1930s or '40s now.

She swam to the edge of the pool, frightened that Margot would hear her, but the woman didn't move. Like last time, no one in this time could hear or see her.

She pushed herself out of the water and sat on the edge, trembling. Her lungs still felt a little tight and hot from holding her breath so long, and she wasn't used to that kind of exertion. Between her exercise and her worry for June, she felt an exhaustion so deep and so overwhelming, she wanted to lie down and sleep.

She eventually made herself stand up, water dripping everywhere. During the séance, Julia had acted as her guide, showing her exactly what she needed to see. Now, though Julia had clearly shown her how to get here through the wet footprints, she wasn't here. Emily wasn't sure what she should do or where she should go.

The door to the pool house opened, and she flinched, startled. Two men in coveralls walked in and paused near the door. Margot sat up, stretching and thrusting her chest out, and Emily watched the men stare at her from across the pool.

"Gentlemen?" Margot said eventually, tossing her hair back.

The oldest man removed his hat. "We have the electricity set up, Miss Lewis. We need to run some tests now."

"Good. Please, do whatever you need to. Don't mind me."

She leaned back, closing her eyes again, and the men exchanged bemused glances. They turned and walked to the far wall, where Emily saw, for the first time, that a door was there—the door that led to the steam room. The younger man couldn't keep his eyes off Margot, and not watching where he was going, he almost tripped over a small pile of construction materials as he walked. The older man turned and gave him a dirty look, and they continued toward the steam-room door.

Emily walked over in their direction, still wet and dripping, so she could hear what they were whispering about. From their glances in her direction, they were trying not to bother Margot.

"We should have asked Steve to come along," the older man whispered, shaking his head. "It'll be hard to do this without him."

The younger man paused, then, also speaking quietly, replied:, "Still, it's possible. We'll have to be in there together when it starts up, and then one of us can go outside and make adjustments."

The older man sighed. "It'll take longer that way, but I guess you're right—it can be done." He plucked at the canvas coverall. "We should have dressed better, too. Going to sweat our brains out."

The younger man glanced at Margot again. "She might not mind if we take 'em off. Seems pretty lonely out here." He raised his eyebrows up and down a few times and leered.

The older man grinned in return. "Get your mind out of the gutter, Don. Let's finish this job before you go all Romeo on me."

They opened the steam-room door and went inside. Even now, weeks after being trapped in there, Emily stood outside, peering in at them, unwilling to cross the threshold. The men had apparently left a ladder in there for their use, and the younger man, Don, climbed up it in order to fiddle with something on the ceiling. The older man handed him tools as he worked, calling out advice about adjustments.

She was so wrapped up in what she was watching, she hadn't noticed Margot's approach until she was right behind her. Frightened, she jumped a little and ducked out of the way. Margot stood in precisely the spot where Emily had been a moment before, watching the men work. It took them a moment to realize she was there, and they both smiled at her, uncertain.

"Anything I can do to help?" Margot asked.

The men shared a look, and the older one shook his head. "No, miss. Don't worry. We've got this handled."

"I couldn't help but overhear you earlier," Margot said. "It sounded like you said you needed a third set of hands. I'm no expert, but I can do something if it's easy."

Again, the men shared a look. Like Emily, they seemed startled to realize that she'd overheard them, and judging from their guilty expressions, they were wondering if she'd heard what Don had said about her earlier.

Don, still up on the ladder, shrugged. "Okay, if you don't mind, miss. See the three knobs out there by the door?"

Margot peered around. "Yes."

"The red one is for temperature, the black one is for pressure, and the last one, the green one, is a timer."

"Okay."

"When we're ready, I want you to turn the black one, and I'll tell you how far. I have to adjust the pressure valve up here, and Paul can tell me if I'm doing it right better from in here than out there. Please don't touch the other knobs. We have the temperature pretty low now so we won't get burned, and it heats up real quick if you turn the red knob."

Margot laughed. "Is that all? Even silly old me can turn a knob."

The older man, Paul, grinned stupidly. "Of course, Miss Lewis."

The men continued to work inside, and Margot stood there watching them. This was the first time Emily had gotten a good look at her face, and she studied it intently. Margot had aged significantly since the last time Emily had seen her. She had lines around her mouth and eyes but had aged beautifully, overall. She was much more attractive in this era than in any period Emily had seen her in the past. She seemed to have grown into her long features. She wasn't what anyone would call pretty, but, like the pictures Emily had seen from that period, she was strangely beautiful in a handsome, hard way. Her eyes, however, were empty and dead. She was smiling, ostensibly for the men, but the smile didn't rise beyond her mouth. Emily was likely projecting a little, but she couldn't help but shiver at the coldness in her eyes.

After a while, a long, low hiss came from within the steam room. "Miss Lewis, please twist the black knob to the left about halfway!" Don said, raising his voice.

"Like this?" Margot replied, turning the knob. The hissing grew louder.

"Yes!" Don shouted, his voice muffled by the sound. He was adjusting things on the ceiling, and water was dripping from the pipes that ran the length of the room. After he turned a few screws, the water was replaced with steam, which started issuing from the pipes in little bursts of white clouds. Paul, the older man, was frantically handing Don different tools, and Don continued to adjust several screws and knobs on the ceiling. A moment later, he was obscured by the steam.

"Twist it to about three-quarters to the left!" Don shouted.

By now, the men were essentially invisible, and Margot turned the knob again as requested. "How's that?"

"Perfect!" Don said. His voice was almost inaudible, dampened by the hissing steam. The steam room was now simply a wall of white swirls, completely impenetrable.

The next time Don spoke, his voice was so distant, Emily had to lean forward to catch the last of his words. "All the way to the left!"

Margot turned it all the way, and the hissing, which was already very loud, became even louder, almost painful to her ears. The steam pouring out of the room was dense and hot, and Emily took a few steps away from it, sweat pouring down her face. Had she waited a moment longer, she might have seen something in Margot's eyes, a warning perhaps, but as it was, she saw only what happened next.

Margot pushed the steam room closed. She didn't move quickly or slowly, her action at first seemingly innocent. She was, however, careful to close the door quietly, and it clicked, echoing across the tiled pool room. Her face was still calm, and she moved away from the door toward the construction materials on the floor. A couple of boxes of tile, some covered buckets, and several tools were there, one of which was a tall hoe. Margot bent, picked it up, and walked back to the door. She lodged the pole of the hoe under the handle to the door, effectively locking it. Then she stood there a long time, doing nothing, before she turned to study the knobs again. She twisted the red one all the way to the left.

Seconds later, a muffled scream came from within, along with the sound of something metal falling onto the ground—the ladder, if Emily had to guess. She could hear vague, distant shouts and screams inside, and then the door started rattling as Don or Paul tried to open it. Someone was pounding inside, and she could hear him crying for help, his screams frantic and pleading but significantly muffled.

Margot had backed away, and Emily, who had watched all of this in a daze, finally saw her face. Her expression was still calm, but a slight smile twisted her lips, and for once, the smile shone in her eyes. She'd backed away from the door a few steps, almost as if she were afraid it would open, but, seeing that the pole was working to hold it closed, she widened her smile and edged closer. She tested the door and then leaned forward, pressing her ear to it. As she did, her smile brightened even further. She looked happier than Emily had ever seen her.

Already, the shouts inside were growing fainter, the pounding on the door more erratic, weaker, and less frequent. She couldn't be sure, but the sounds seemed to be coming from lower down, as if one of the men was on the floor now as he pounded to get out.

All of this had taken very little time. Even in her shocked daze, Emily would have guessed that perhaps one or two minutes had passed since Margot locked the door, maybe less. Emily had backed away from the door about ten feet, too horrified to stand and watch any of this closely. The smile on Margot's face chilled her straight through. It was like seeing the face of evil itself.

She turned, ready to run away, but after a step toward the pool, she stopped, turning back to the on-going horror. Margot still bent close to the door, her hands and ear pressed against it. From Emily's current position, it would be possible to remove the pole of the hoe simply by pushing it aside. She wasn't sure what would happen if she tried. So far, her physical interaction with these different timelines had been minimal. She was, however, wet from the pool, and the steam had been hot, so she might have some corporeal presence here. Something else occurred to her. Twice now she'd almost touched one of the Lewises, and some instinct deep within her made her leap aside both times to avoid it.

Trembling now, she made herself retrace her steps, stopping a few feet behind Margot. Her every instinct told her to leave, to run back to the pool and swim to safety. That same part of her, some deep calm feeling from within, told her she would be allowed to leave, to go back to her own time. She knew then what she had to do.

Emily pushed the hoe to the side, releasing the door.

The hoe clattered onto the ground, making Margot jump. A second later, the door handle moved, and Margot had to push it with her hands to keep it closed. A voice from within escaped, a startled "Help!" but Margot managed to close the door again using the weight of her body. She dug her heels in, her back braced against the steam-room door, her mouth twisted in a determined snarl.

The door behind her slid open again for a second, and another shout escaped, but once again Margot managed to slam it closed. She grabbed the door handle and pulled it, keeping the mechanism from opening from within, and when she realized that this worked better than holding the door with her body, she turned and braced herself to continue to hold it closed. She was clearly struggling, her face distorted and strained with effort, and Emily saw her hands go white with the effort to keep the handle from moving.

Efforts inside eventually weakened. After a while, little sound came from within. An occasional bang on the door was followed by the handle jiggling in Margot's hands, but never once did Margot relax. She stayed there, pulling the handle, her feet braced at the bottom of the door, trembling with effort.

Again, Emily wanted to leave. She could feel an almost physical pull toward the pool, toward escape. After all, she remembered how this turned out. Harry had told them that two men had died in an accident in the steam room—this must be them. Harry hadn't given them any details, hadn't known them, but Emily was certain that her suspicions were correct.

Margot had killed these men, or rather, she was killing them now. Still, Emily had been able to move the hoe, and if she didn't try one more thing, she'd never forgive herself. Her next effort went against every instinct she had. The very idea made her skin crawl, but she had to try. Emily placed her hands on Margot Lewis's shoulders.

It was all she could do not to let go immediately. At first, a deep, penetrating cold went through her, a chill so cold it burned with intensity. She fought it and squeezed harder, and finally, as if she could barely reach across the small distance between them, she felt the skin on Margot's bare shoulders. Again, she almost let go, the sensation so repulsive she would have given anything to stop touching her. She didn't.

Margot screamed and spun around, crumpling to the ground a moment later. Her hands went to her shoulders, and her eyes rolled around in wild panic. Emily could see two red marks on her shoulders, and from the way Margot clutched at herself, Emily could tell she was in pain. She snatched at one of Margot's wrists, and again, Margot howled on contact. Bracing herself on the ground, Emily started to drag her away from the door. Margot fought, hard, twisting and screaming, so Emily used her second hand to get a better grip on the same arm. When she touched Margot's forearm with her second hand, Margot screamed again, this time relaxing enough for Emily to drag her a few feet before she came to her senses again. Margot struggled into a crouching position, pulling back and away from Emily so hard she slipped out of Emily's grasp. Margot wasn't ready to be released, and she fell onto the ground, her mouth snapping closed. Emily saw a trail of blood start to drip down her chin. She'd bitten her own tongue.

Released now, Margot sprang to her feet and backed away quickly, her eyes darting around, looking for her attacker. She'd lost what fright she'd had, her face now contorted with rage. She was clutching her wrist to her chest with her other hand and crouched low as if to ward off assault.

"You can't stop me, Julia," Margot hissed, her eyes still darting around. "You couldn't stop me before, and you can't stop me now."

"Maybe Julia can't, but I can," Emily said.

Margot froze, her face pointed in Emily's direction. She narrowed her eyes, but her gaze still looked beyond where Emily stood, unseeing. "Who said that?"

Emily was startled. She hadn't expected Margot to hear her. Before, any sound she made in any part of the past had been seemingly inaudible. Something had changed, perhaps through the physical contact they'd shared. Still, it appeared Margot couldn't see her, so she took a step toward her.

She took a deep breath and raised her voice to a shout. "Leave. Now."

Margot flinched, still clutching her injured wrist to her body. A moment later, she tried to pretend she hadn't been frightened. Her face grew nonchalant and calm, and she stood up straighter. Emily had seen her do this a few times—cover up her real feelings—so she knew it was pure bravado.

"Make me," Margot said, her voice calm.

Without hesitating, Emily charged her and pushed her down with both hands. Margot fell to the ground with a bone-rattling crunch, calling out in fright and pain. Emily kicked her once, hard, in the ribs, and Margot screamed. She was quick to move aside, as a moment later Margot groped around blindly, trying to grab Emily's leg.

Again, she raised her voice to a shout. "Leave. Now. Leave or I'll kill you."

Margot's lips were still screwed into an angry snarl, but Emily thought she saw real fright in her eyes now. She was losing the ability to pretend she wasn't affected by what was happening. Slowly, she crawled to her feet, cringing. She stood for a moment in a kind of half-crouch, panting. She threw one last look at the steam-room door, and then, without another word, she left, walking neither slowly nor quickly to the pool-house door. She opened it and left without turning around.

Emily went to the steam-room door a moment later and threw it open. Instead of steam, however, the doorway revealed that strange, swirling blackness she had seen during the séance, the one that seemed to separate the different time periods she'd experienced. Without hesitating, she plunged into its depths.

She was almost overcome and staggered once she'd reached the other side. As it was, she had to sink onto one knee to keep from falling. She was deafened for a moment before her ears popped, and then the room tilted and shuddered into existence around her. Finally, some kind of reality came into focus, and she found herself, once again, inside the steam room.

She heard something to her right and turned in time to see June launching herself across the room. June bowled her over in an embrace, and they both hit the floor, clasped together and crying.

"You came for me, you came for me," June kept repeating, kissing her lips and face over and over again.

Emily kissed her and then pulled back a little, meeting her tear-stained eyes. "Of course. I'd never leave you here. And I'll never leave you again, June. Never."

June nodded and started crying harder, and Emily hugged her again, letting her cry onto her shoulder. Tears were falling, unheeded, from her own eyes, and she squeezed June, nearly overwhelmed by the depths of her relief.

Eventually they moved apart, both of them sitting on the floor of the steam room. Emily couldn't keep her eyes off June. She still couldn't believe what she was seeing. Still, it was strangely cold in here, and June was shivering. She rubbed June's arms briskly, frightened to feel the chill in her skin. June looked both wonderful and terrible at the same time. Wonderful, because she was here, but terrible, physically. They'd been separated, at most, a little over an hour, but June's appearance had completely altered. Her face was sunken, the skin stretched tight on her cheekbones, her lips cracked and bleeding. Her light summer clothes were tattered and grimy, her skin dull and pale.

"How long have you been here?"

June shook her head, tears welling in her eyes. "Days? A week? Longer? I don't know. I lost all track of time. I managed to get one of the pipes to open a little, so we've had water, but it's hard to get enough to drink unless you sit there sucking on it."

"We?"

June gestured behind Emily, who turned to see Harry, lying on the tiled shelf that functioned as a seat. He was strangely motionless.

"Is he alive?"

"Barely. He lost consciousness yesterday, I think, but he's still breathing. He's been here without food, like me, but much longer."

Emily struggled to stand before helping June. She led her over to the seat next to Harry, helping her sit. June sank down with relief, clearly weak enough that walking was an effort. Emily leaned down and put her face close to Harry's mouth. She could faintly detect breath coming from it, and when she checked his pulse, it was weak and fluttering, the skin on his wrist worryingly cold.

She turned to say something to June and then stopped when she saw her face. June was staring straight ahead, clearly terrified, her eyes fixed on something behind Emily, who spun, quickly, but relaxed a moment later. The doorway out of the steam room was open, and once again it was filled with the swirling blackness she'd come through several times before.

She put a hand on June's shoulder. "It's okay. That's how we get out of here."

June still appeared frightened. "Can we? Can we go now? Please? I can't stand it in here any longer."

"Of course. Help me with Harry."

It took some effort. Emily was a weakling on a good day, and this wasn't one of those. She shook with the strain. Beyond the swim and the panic she'd felt at losing June, the experience with Margot before she'd come in here had taken something out of her. She felt as if she'd done hard manual labor all day, her body sore and aching. She was also significantly shorter than either Harry or June, so trying to brace him between the two of them under his arms wouldn't work. Eventually, she and June decided to carry him between them, Emily taking his feet, June lifting him under his arms, and, before she could let June hesitate, they walked together through the doorway.

Emily had forgotten to warn June about the disorientation, and June staggered the moment she stepped through into the pool house, dropping Harry's upper half and falling down with a little cry. Emily released Harry's feet and crouched next to her, gripping her shoulder.

"It's okay. Close your eyes and take deep breaths. It will go away soon."

June took several, one hand on her forehead as if dizzy. Finally, she opened her eyes, smiling weakly. "I'm okay. Check on Harry."

Emily left her and moved down next to Harry's face again, putting her ear close enough to detect his breathing. It seemed, though she couldn't be sure, a little stronger, surer, as did his pulse. His skin was still cold, however, and she wondered if they could find a blanket to wrap him in. She was about to share this idea with June, when June let out a strangled moan. She had one hand over her mouth and was pointing behind Emily. Emily spun around, almost slipping on the tile in her haste.

Nathan and Julia stood about ten feet away. Unlike any time in history, they looked to be about the same age. Nathan was wearing the red, old-fashioned swimsuit Emily recognized, but unlike the svelte, tanned body he'd had that fateful afternoon when he was drowned, he was so white now he could have been bleached. His hair was wet, plastered to his head, his mustache moist with water. His eyes, however, were the most disconcerting thing about him. Rather than the piercing blue they'd been in life, they were so bloodshot the whites were entirely red, and both eyes bulged from their sockets. Julia was likewise altered from what she'd been in life. Like Nathan, she was grossly pale. She wore the sack-like dress Emily had seen her in before, but it was wet and stained pink at the bottom. She too was soaking wet, her hair falling in damp snarls around her face. Two jagged, open cuts ran the length of her forearms, so deep Emily was certain she could see bone.

Nathan and Julia had come to them as they were in death, or, at least, at the moment of their deaths. Seeing him as he was now, Nathan appeared to have drowned moments ago. Julia likewise looked as if she had recently cut her wrists. Neither of them said a word—they simply stared at her. During a long, quiet pause, the tension was so biting she could barely breathe.

Finally, she made herself get to her feet and take a hesitant step toward them. "I'm sorry. For what happened to you. I'm sorry she killed you, Nathan, and I'm sorry she blamed you for it, Julia."

Neither of them reacted.

Emily gave June a quick glance and then took another step toward them. "I'll do whatever I can to help you move on. I'll let people know the truth. I swear it, even if it takes the rest of my life to prove it. Everyone will know what Margot did to you."

These words had a greater effect on Nathan and Julia than her previous statement. They moved for the first time, looking at each other and then back at her. After a long moment, Julia nodded slightly, her eyes fixed on Emily. Nathan, however, took a step toward her, putting out a hand as if to touch her face, but Julia moved forward and grabbed his other one, pulling it frantically before he got too close. He looked back at his sister, appearing troubled, but eventually his expression calmed, and he put his arm down and stepped back to Julia's side.

The two of them continued to stare at Emily, Nathan's eyes searching, his brow furrowed. Finally, his expression cleared, and he took Julia's hand. They turned around and walked away. About ten feet from where they'd stood, they took on a strange, faded translucence, and a few feet later, they disappeared entirely.

June gave a startled cry, and Emily turned to join her, crouching on the floor again. They embraced, and a feeling of absolute joy and relief swept through her like a warm wind. June clutched her, as if she'd felt it too, and they drew back far enough to kiss, deeply.

Suddenly Harry was coughing, and they immediately moved apart. A moment later, he'd gotten himself up on his elbows and was looking around. He spotted them and smiled, and June laughed with loud, sweet joy.

"God, am I glad to be out of there," he said. His voice was hoarse, almost broken, but it sounded steady and calm, nonetheless.

Emily moved next to him and took his wrist again to check his pulse. Not only was it beating more strongly, but warmth had come back into his skin.

She was about to suggest that she and June help him to one of the lounge chairs so she could go get help, when the door opened. Jim stumbled in a moment later, almost falling. He spun around wildly, and then, spotting them, his body relaxed and his hands went to his eyes.

It took a moment to realize he was sobbing.

CHAPTER TWENTY-EIGHT

Seattle did more good for Emily than she'd thought possible. After everything that had happened, June had insisted on a break from Gnarled Hollow, and Emily was unwilling to let her go alone—unwilling, really, to let her out of her sight. The thought of being apart, even for a few days, was too much to bear after almost losing her. June had been relieved when Emily agreed to go.

They spent the first two days in June's apartment, alone with her cats or walking to get drinks or dinner nearby. June lived in the Capitol Hill neighborhood, close enough to walk to campus. Emily had been in the city once before at a conference, but she was still impressed by its beauty, especially in the summer. She'd never spent much time by the water, and the salty bay air kept them cool, even in early July.

On Wednesday, they finally went to campus, ostensibly the reason they'd come to Seattle in the first place. June had some paperwork to file for a grant and some interlibrary books to pick up and return. She could probably have done all her errands via snail mail or phone calls, but June had insisted that she needed to go there in person, and they had needed it, but for other reasons. Spending time together outside of the house reassured both of them that what they had wasn't simply a product of close quarters and terrifying events. They liked being together, and the time alone also allowed them to talk, for once, about themselves and not their work or the house.

June introduced Emily to a friend in the English department, and by the next day, this friend had managed to help her line up a position as an adjunct instructor for the fall semester. She would teach composition and the occasional sophomore literature class, which she'd done many times. The pay was dismal, and she would receive no benefits to speak of, but she thought she might squeak by and pay what bills she had, at least for now, especially as she wouldn't have any rent while staying with June. She could use the upcoming school year to find something more permanent.

On Thursday, she met several of June's friends at a bar, including an ex-boyfriend and two ex-girlfriends. June had prepared her beforehand, but Emily still found the experience unnerving. The exes were all incredibly attractive, like June, and all of them seemed to be staring at her as if they didn't see the appeal. If she was aware of this reaction, June didn't let on, holding Emily's hand and touching her back frequently, almost proprietarily. By the end of the night, the exes didn't bother her anymore, and she couldn't help but feel a strange, smug satisfaction as she and June left together, hands linked.

The visit overall was incredibly restful and restorative. She hadn't slept so well or eaten so much in weeks. Still, by the time they left Seattle, she was impatient to get back to Gnarled Hollow. They had a lot of loose ends to tie up before they could take a longer break and had left somewhat abruptly. The fall semester would begin in only six weeks, and her desire to finish her work was creating an increased sense of urgency.

June, on the other hand, was reluctant to return. By the time they'd retrieved her car at the airport and started driving back, she had nearly shut down. Two hours later, closer to the estate, she still wasn't speaking, and the few times Emily saw her hold something, a coffee or a snack, her hands were shaking.

"You could have stayed there, you know," Emily finally said. "In Seattle, I mean. You already have a lot to work with. Maybe a break would do some good. You could always come back in January, or next summer."

June gave her a long look and then turned away, staring out the passenger window. "I couldn't do that." Her voice was so quiet, Emily almost didn't hear her.

"Why not?"

June shook her head. "I couldn't let you..." She shook her head again, and Emily was alarmed to see tears in her eyes. She flipped on the turn signal and pulled over onto the side of the road. No one was out here on this road in the woods, but she put on the hazards anyway.

They sat there for a long time, June quietly crying and refusing to meet her eyes. Emily had turned in her seat toward her, and she waited, patiently, for June to stop. Finally, she did, and Emily saw a deep, abject terror in her eyes.

June clasped Emily's hands, desperately. "I couldn't let you go there on your own. I just couldn't. I-I never want you to be alone there. It isn't safe for you."

"Mark and Jim are still there. I wouldn't be alone."

June shook her head. "That isn't enough. That house…wants you, I think. It wants you to stay there. Forever."

Emily sat for a while in silence. She'd never had this impression, but on the other hand, everyone kept telling her that she was different from the others somehow, singled out from them, and sometimes she could see that herself. During the séance, Julia had revealed some of the mysteries of the house to her and her alone. Also, only she had been capable of crossing that divide between time periods on her own. But why?

She squeezed June's hands. "Listen to me. Nothing's going to happen. I don't know why I'm different from the rest of you, but I am. What you said proves it. I think…I think it does want me, the house, I mean, but I think it wants to use me, not hurt me. It wants the real story to come out, and I'm the one to do it."

The violence of June's reply startled her. June launched herself at her, squeezing her, sobbing. "Why? Why does it have to be you?"

Having asked herself that question, she had no reply, and she hugged June back just as fiercely. Eventually, they pulled apart, June looking sheepish and embarrassed. They sat there staring at each other for a long time before Emily spoke again.

"I don't know why it has to be me, June, but it does. We all know that." She hesitated. She didn't like to bring up the vision they'd shared of Nathan and Julia in the pool house. June always seemed terrified when she mentioned it, but she had to now. "I promised them, June. I swore I'd share their real story."

June continued to stare at her, her expression grave. Finally, she let out a long sigh and turned in her seat to face the front. "Okay. Let's finish this, then."

Emily started the car, and June was silent for the remainder of the trip. Emily could sense June was still upset, angry even, but none of them, Emily included, would be able to move on until this was finished, until the world knew what had happened at Gnarled Hollow.

When they arrived at the estate, they drove directly to the garage. They'd brought only backpacks, so they had no reason to unload at the front door. By the time they approached the house, Mark and Jim had come outside and were waiting for them. Seeing their faces, Emily knew something had happened.

Jim was grinning wildly, almost maniacally. He seemed to have recovered some of his vitality. The scratches on his face were almost gone, and his color was normal again. He looked, in fact, as if he'd been tanning, his skin golden and healthy. Mark's face was likewise altered. The rings around his eyes had disappeared, the lines on his face were a little less severe, and he seemed to be standing taller again, as if a weight had been taken off his shoulders.

Everyone hugged hello, and seconds later, Jim, clearly impatient, said, "You're never going to believe it."

"What?" Emily asked.

Jim shook his head. "It's too much to go in to here. But first of all, Lara and Ruth are on their way. They should be here in a couple of hours."

Emily stopped walking. "Both of them? Why?"

Jim laughed, a deep belly laugh, throwing his head back. "That's part of it, but I'll let them tell you. Lara wanted to call you right away when she found out, but I told her it would be better in person, so she waited."

Emily looked back and forth between them, seeing nearly identical grins of mischievous joy, then at June. June was smiling, vaguely, clearly lost herself, but enjoying the men's cheerful excitement.

She raised her shoulders at Emily and then spoke to Jim. "Okay—we can wait. What else is new? What's the other part?"

He laughed again and shook his head. "You have to see it."

Mark was grinning. "He's right—you really need to see."

Still confused, but game, Emily followed them into the house through the door to the kitchen. Immediately upon stepping inside, she knew something had changed. She and June shared a puzzled look and peered around the room. Everything appeared to be in the right spot, nothing had obviously changed or moved, but something in the room was wrong somehow. Jim and Mark were watching them, grinning like children.

"Do you see it?" Mark finally asked.

Emily started to shake her head and then stopped. The counter, which went around the length of two of the walls in the kitchen, had changed. Normally a dark, sealed wood, now a few sections of it seemed almost cloudy, the color no longer uniform. She walked over to one part of the changed counter and ran her fingers across it. She held it up for June: dust.

"I don't get it," June said, coming closer. She didn't get near enough to touch it, eyeing the change warily from a few feet away.

"Open the cabinet above that part of the counter," Mark suggested.

Emily looked up, surprised she hadn't noticed. The cabinet door, like the counter, was grimy with dust, the wood almost obscured beneath filth. She reached up to open it and heard June's quick, frightened intake of breath. Her hand on the handle, Emily pulled it open.

The inside of the cabinet was curious. Instead of containing dust and grime, it was completely preserved, identical, perhaps, to the last time it had been opened. The shelves held boxes and cans, and even without getting anything out, Emily could tell that they were old, antiques even. Old cereals, soups, and tin ingredient canisters sat there, neatly arranged, almost as if they'd been put in there recently.

She turned back to the others. June had taken a step back, her expression frightened, but Jim and Mark, still grinning, seemed thrilled. Emily looked around the room, spotting three more places that were dusty and grimed.

She smiled at Mark. "Are you saying...?"

He nodded, vigorously. "It came back."

"What? What came back?" June asked.

"Everything," Jim answered.

Mark laughed and grabbed one of June's hands. "Look. It's easier to show you, like I said. And it's more obvious on the other side of the house, and upstairs."

June let herself be led from the kitchen to the foyer, and Jim and Emily followed. Even here, it was obvious something had changed, but it was difficult to see with the naked eye. June paused, clearly confused, but Mark laughed and pulled her hand again, leading her to the library. When he opened the door, it was suddenly very obvious.

The library had grown.

June screamed and put her hands to her mouth. Mark put an arm around her shoulder. "I'm sorry, June. I thought you understood."

June spun around, eyes wide and terrified, her hands still on her mouth. Emily stepped forward, and June rushed into her arms, squeezing her so tight it almost hurt. Emily met Jim and Mark's eyes, both of them troubled, and she ran her hand up and down June's back.

"Shhhh, June, it's okay. Don't you see? The house is back to normal. It came back—all of it. All that lost space."

June drew back, meeting Emily's eyes. Something in Emily's expression must have calmed her a little, as her own expression softened. She stepped away and took a wary look around her, and then, as if the explanation had finally sunk in, she seemed to relax. A moment later, she was peering around, her fright now replaced with curiosity. At least three new sections of bookcases were in here, all of them, like the cabinets, dusty with age.

"How much bigger is it in here?" June asked.

"About two yards on each wall," Jim replied.

Emily frowned at him. "That's not enough."

He grinned. "Exactly. Come see the sitting room. It's even more obvious in there."

They followed him in, and a curious thrill of déjà vu swept through Emily. The last time she'd stepped through that door, Margot had been sitting in there waiting for Nathan. Seeing the room as it was now, even with the different furniture, it was difficult to forget she wasn't in the past.

The room was much longer, the front wall so removed from where it had been, they could have been in a different room altogether. The furniture was the strangest part of what she saw. Rather than sitting, as it had, in the center of the room, it was off-center, much too close to this end. Yards and yards of empty space stretched beyond the edge of the sofa and chairs. Further, the wallpaper stopped past the edge of the sofa, exactly where the wall used to end. Beyond the edge of the paper, the wall was yellow, the paint peeling with age. There were, however, paintings on the yellow walls, and June gave a startled cry when she saw them, rushing toward them immediately. She looked at them for a moment and then turned back to Emily and the others, eyes wide.

"These paintings are new. I mean—they're old, but I've never seen them before."

Mark was grinning again.

Emily walked closer so she could see them herself and then took a long moment to view the room. It had seemed much larger when she'd seen it during the séance, and now her suspicion was confirmed: like the library, it had grown.

She smiled at Mark, her heart racing with excitement. "You said it changed upstairs, too?"

"Boy, did it!" Jim said. "You should see your room now, June. It's almost as big as Emily's. And my room actually looks like a real nursery, not some closet."

"What about mine?" Emily asked.

Mark shook his head. "It's identical. But there is something new right next door."

Almost racing, the four of them headed upstairs, Emily so curious she had to stop herself from running ahead. Even from the balcony, anyone could see that things had altered dramatically. Emily's door, which was the farthest from the stairs, looked very far away now. Another obvious change was the new door.

"June," Mark said, touching her hand, "I think you should go in first."

Jim was smiling so widely all of his teeth shone. "Yes. It should definitely be June."

June's fright had mostly dissipated downstairs, but she looked scared again. Emily took her hand, and the two of them walked to the new door together. They paused, tentative, and Mark made an opening gesture.

"Go ahead. It's not locked."

June met her eyes once, and then she opened the door.

It was the artists' studio Emily had seen before, but much altered. The chaise lounge, which had been in the center of the room, was gone, and the whole place had an air of decay—the floors dusty, the curtains tattered. The easels, however, were here, and although Emily couldn't be sure, it almost seemed as if there were more of them than the last time she'd been here. Each one had a painting in progress on it, and June strode to the nearest one to examine it, bending over so close her nose almost touched the canvas. Mark and Jim had come into the room by this point, and they were both smiling when June turned around, obviously stunned.

"These are by the same artist—the one I haven't identified yet, not Nathan."

Mark pointed at an enormous paint box on a table nearby. "Mystery solved."

June and Emily walked over to it, and there, in clear, bold letters, was a name: Julia Lewis. June let out a quick laugh and spun around to Mark.

"Julia? But how?"

Emily, however, suddenly remembered the gift. Julia had given her older brother his box of old lead soldiers, but she'd repainted them. She laughed at the memory and reminded the others about that part of her vision.

"Sure, but that doesn't explain all of this!" June said, gesturing around the room. "Painting toys is one thing, but these are masterpieces!"

Emily shrugged. "But remember—Nathan created most of the paintings that are still in the house *before* he went to art school. Maybe Julia learned how to do it too, or he might have taught her."

June seemed thoughtful. "I've also been thinking, from what you told me, that their father, and maybe their grandfather, were also painters. I'd almost put money on it." She shook her head, clearly dumbfounded. "It's almost hard to believe."

"But when?" Emily asked Jim and Mark. "When did she have time to do all this? She was locked in the attic for years."

Jim shrugged. "She might have done it before they put her up there."

"Or that friendly nurse might have let her in here once in a while, or maybe her doctor. Art therapy—something like that."

"Amazing," June said. She was, like Mark and Jim, clearly excited now, the remains of her fear discarded in the thrill of the find. June would most likely devote the rest of the summer to tracking down the rest of the proof she needed to publish a paper on the talented Lewis family. Their art had been essentially lost out here in the woods, and now the world would know about them. There was, in fact, enough work here for a book, and the shiny gleam in June's eyes suggested that she realized this fact. The revelation of this find would be incredible, earth-shaking in her field. June could easily curate show after show of these paintings in museums and galleries around the world. It would be a sensation.

"When did all of this happen?" Emily suddenly asked. "When June and I left, the house was like it used to be."

Jim and Mark shared a look, and something like guilt replaced their smiles. After a moment, Mark gestured for Jim to explain. Jim still seemed worried, but he finally sighed.

"You won't like it."

"We didn't want to tell you, actually," Mark added.

"What?" June asked.

They shared another guilty look, and again, Mark indicated that Jim could go on. Jim met both of their eyes before speaking. "It will sound crazy, at first. But on the other hand, it worked, so who are we to say it was crazy?"

A low anxiety began to build inside Emily. Obviously they'd done something dangerous and were ashamed of themselves.

Again, Jim hesitated, and finally Mark spoke. "We had another séance."

"In the steam room," Jim added.

June flushed with anger. "Are you fucking insane! You did that without anyone here? What if something had happened? What if you'd gotten locked in there!"

Jim held his hands up. "Wait, June, let me finish. I should have said we *tried* to have a séance."

"It didn't work."

"Or, at least we thought it didn't. We were out there, just the two of us. We went out around four in the afternoon, like last time."

Mark sighed. "We took the hanging bowl with us, and the lead soldier, like last time, and we closed the door."

"Are you kidding me?" June said, almost screaming.

Again, Jim held up his hands. "Jesus, June, let me finish."

June looked as if she might yell again, but she shut her mouth, face red with the effort of holding her tongue. Finally, Jim spoke again. "We wanted to ask about the house, ask what could be done to make it return to normal."

Mark said, "I called on Julia, mostly, and Nathan, but nothing happened. I asked them to show us how to heal the house. I asked them what was wrong with it. Jim told me some of the phrases Lara had used during her séance, so I tried to make myself sound like her when I asked for their guidance. I called on them three times, like she did."

Jim shrugged. "Nothing happened. I didn't even feel weird. A little scared, maybe, but that was all."

"So how did it change? The house, I mean?" Emily asked.

Jim grinned again. "It just changed. After the séance, Mark and I walked back to the house, and it had gone back to the way it was before, back to normal."

"That's all?" June asked. She sounded a little calmer, but she still appeared upset.

Mark shook his head. "I can't explain it, but yes."

"A little anticlimactic," she said, her expression finally losing some of its anger.

"I know!" Jim laughed. "That's a first for this place. Usually the house seems to like a bit of drama. Some flair."

"When do you suppose it changed? Became smaller?" Emily asked.

Mark held up a finger. "That, at least, I can answer." He went over to the coffee table, which was covered in stacks of papers. He riffled through them and then held two small paperclipped piles out for Emily. "These took me forever to find, but I knew they had to be somewhere. I found them in different part of the archive this week at the library."

"What are they?" she asked, taking the two stacks.

"Fire-insurance forms. One from 1920 and the other from 1930. The house had to be surveyed both times."

Emily scanned the older one, noted the square footage, and then scanned the next. The house had shrunk. There was even a short paragraph in the later, 1930 document, that noted the change, but the surveyor seemed to suggest that the previous person had simply made mistakes, or, at least, that's what he wrote on the form. Goodness knows what he thought when he realized how much smaller the interior of the house was from the outside, or the fact that rooms were missing.

She met Mark's eyes. "So you think—"

"I think the house shrank, closed in on itself, if you will, when Julia killed herself. I think it's been hiding all this time, or maybe Julia's been hiding it, until the truth could come out."

"She was waiting for us," June said. Everyone turned to her, and Emily was scared by the strange, distant look in her eyes. June's face was white, pupils dilated. She seemed dazed, almost in a trance. Emily was afraid to reach out to her, but when she did, touching June's shoulder, the expression faded almost immediately, and June shook her head a couple of times as if to clear it. She frowned. "What's wrong?"

Emily and the others shared a look. She held out a hand, and June took it and squeezed her fingers.

"Nothing," Emily said.

A moment later, everyone jumped when the front door opened. The doors to the sitting room were wide open, and Lara and an older woman came inside. The older woman was red-faced, waving a paper fan on her face. Her clothes were raucous and vivid, but clearly well-made, maybe even designer.

"Jesus, this heat!" she said, and Emily recognized her voice. It was Ruth Bigsby.

Ruth spotted them and brightened. She held her arms up and came into the room, hugging each of the others before stopping in front of Emily. Emily had braced herself for a hug and was puzzled that Ruth didn't offer her one right away. Instead, Ruth stared at her critically, almost as if she were searching for something in Emily's face. Finally, she smiled and pulled her into a bone-crunching embrace.

"Sorry about that," Ruth said after she stepped away. "I meant to be a good sport, but it's hard. I can't believe it. At first, I thought I should be angry. And I was, for all of a minute—Lara will tell you. I even broke my favorite mug when I heard. But like I said, with the government on my back like it is, I realized that maybe it's a good thing. Those taxes were going to kill me."

Emily was baffled, and June seemed lost as well. Lara suddenly laughed. "Oh gosh, that's right. You don't know yet. I thought these guys would have let you in on it by now."

"We wanted you to tell them," Mark said, grinning.

Ruth was clearly confused, and then her eyebrows shot into her hair. Ruth stared at her, clearly stunned. "My God! Do you mean to say you don't know?"

"Know what?"

Ruth laughed and then held up a hand. She went back to the large purse she'd dropped and bent down, digging around in it. After mumbling and fumbling through it, she threw aside a silk scarf and then pulled out a large file folder, stuffed with paper. She stood straight and returned to Emily, holding out the file. Emily took it, still confused, and then Ruth dug in her pocket. A moment later, her hand came out, holding a ring of keys. Again, Emily took them, confused.

"What are these for? What's in this folder?"

Mark stepped closer and put a hand on her shoulder. "It's your inheritance."

Ruth held up her hands. "Well, technically, it's your mother's inheritance, at least while she's alive."

June's eyes had grown huge, and her hand went to her mouth. Emily, however, was still lost. "I don't understand."

Mark put both his hands on her shoulders and squeezed them, lightly. "This is your house, Emily. Nathan Lewis, your great-great-grandfather, left it to your great-grandmother, Hilda, your mother's grandmother. You're the heir to Gnarled Hollow."

EPILOGUE

The applause was thunderous. People leapt to their feet as if they'd just watched an opera. The five of them had spoken for about twenty minutes each, but June's stunning presentation on the Lewis family artwork had thrilled their audience the most.

Eight months ago, when they'd all parted at the end of summer, Emily had felt homesick for the others. She and June were together, of course, making June's little apartment their new home, but she often wondered what the others were doing. Even Chris, who'd been at the house only a short while, seemed like family now. She'd been afraid that, given enough time, the connection among the five of them would be lost, the drama and excitement of the summer gradually forgotten. The academic school year, with its chaos of activity, had a way of erasing the past.

Then, in November, Mark called her. They'd emailed once or twice since they'd parted in August, but they hadn't spoken, so she was thrilled to hear his voice again, and even more excited at his proposal. He wanted to hold a series of lectures at various academic venues around the country. All five of them could present their current work on the Lewis family and Gnarled Hollow. The lectures would act, in part, as a means of introducing their forthcoming publications and get people excited about them.

The series had been an immediate success. They'd started in January, first in Los Angeles, on Jim's campus. The lecture had been so well received, they'd been asked to give it again the next day. They'd moved on from there to Seattle in February, and already by then, acclaim had spread. Once again, they'd given their lecture twice, back-to-back, to a full house of a few hundred students and scholars.

For their lecture today in New York, the last one of the tour, they'd reserved a much-larger venue, hoping to circumvent the need to do it twice. The end of the academic year was near, and she, June, and Jim could ill afford more than a weekend away from their jobs on the West Coast. Even with the additional space and seating, however, people were standing at the back of the room, and some had to sit in the aisles. Students and scholars were in attendance, as well as the general public.

They'd decided to end, rather than begin, their tour here, partly because June's first curated exhibit of the Lewis artwork would be here in the city this summer. It was opening in mid-May at a large American art museum. Once she and Emily finished grading their students' finals back in Seattle, they would return to New York for the opening reception before going to their second home at Gnarled Hollow for the summer. Many of the people in the audience that day had come specifically for a preview of the art, none of which had been shown to the public before that day.

June, still at the podium, was flushed with happiness at the applause, and she took a slight bow before returning to her seat at the table with Emily and the others. They'd asked everyone to hold their questions until the end of the lectures, so it came as no surprise that most of the questions from the audience were directed at June, who'd spoken last.

She explained that she had been able to detect the work of four different artists, one from the era in which the house had first been built, one in the later nineteenth century, and those she'd already known—Nathan and Julia. She'd initially believed that the oldest paintings had been created by Nathan and Julia's paternal grandfather, Roger Lewis, but subsequent research had revealed that, in fact, it was their paternal grand*mother*, Claudia, who had been the first Lewis artist. She had trained her son, Nathan and Julia's father, and he in turn trained Nathan. How Julia came to be such a prolific and sensational painter was still a mystery June had to solve, but she suggested to the audience that she might have been self-taught.

After some silence, June had to field some technical questions about paint types and carbon dating before someone finally remembered the other people sitting next to June.

Mark answered several questions about the house, including more detailed answers about the architect, whom he had finally tracked down. While some of Mark's conclusions about the house were theoretical, he did have proof now that the architect had made similar mistakes when he'd designed other houses. Roger Lewis had requested a Queen Anne home in the American style, and the architect had, instead, interpreted the request as a British-style home. The house had been mostly completed by the time the mistake was caught, and the subsequent lawsuit had bankrupted the bumbling architect. He'd died a pauper in Rochester, humiliated and forgotten despite leaving a legacy of gorgeous homes, including his masterpiece at Gnarled Hollow.

After this, Chris fielded a couple of questions related to the gardens, and then Emily and Jim were asked, at length, about the new Lewis novel coming out next autumn. Jim projected his slides of the journals up on the large overheard screen again, showing once more how he and Emily had decoded them. Even now, he explained, they'd only gotten through about half of the Margot Lewis journals, which suggested that yet another novel might be hidden in the others.

Twenty minutes later, after the chair of their panel had suggested they start wrapping up, she asked for one final question. Emily saw plenty of arms go into the air, but the student helper, who had been walking around with a microphone, clearly worn out or bored, passed it to the nearest arm.

The man stood, and Emily was stunned to see her old boss, the chair of her previous department.

"Hi, Emily," he said. Even from across the room, she could tell that his face had gone beet red from all the eyes turned his way.

She leaned forward to her mic. "Hi, Greg."

The crowd gave a light, awkward chuckle at their informality, and Greg's face remained bright with embarrassment. He cleared his throat. "Um, from what you and Jim Peters have suggested, most of your upcoming publications pertain to the new fiction you've found in the Lewis journals."

"Correct. That's our focus for now."

"Are you thinking of writing a biography of Margot Lewis? It seems, in some ways, like you're the ideal candidate. After all, you're related."

The crowd engaged in a lot of hushed and whispered conversation, and the room filled with a confused buzz of voices. Emily waited until it had died down a little, raising her hand for silence.

"For those of you that don't know, I found out last summer that I am in fact related to Margot Lewis."

Jim eagerly leaned forward to his mic. "That's right, people. You're looking at the descendent of Nathan Lewis."

Emily elbowed him playfully during more quiet laughter. A light patter of applause broke out at their silliness, and Emily rolled her eyes at him before leaning into her mic again.

"To answer your question, Greg, yes, I am working on a biography. However, my focus is not just Margot, but also her siblings."

She and Jim had translated Margot's earliest, 1918-1919 journal together last summer before the school year began. As expected, they found a wealth of information detailing the twisted actions of Margot Lewis—a full confession of everything that had happened between when her brother returned from university, the resumption of their affair, and the murder after learning about the baby.

Further research had revealed more evidence of what they found in the journal. Mark had uncovered a coroner's report for Nathan, some psychiatric records on Julia, and a letter detailing some payments Margot Lewis had provided to keep her sister locked up despite the doctor's eventual misgivings. Emily had also managed to track down the descendants of the two servants that had witnessed the siblings' incestuous affair. As far as Emily and the others were concerned, they had all the evidence they needed to prove Margot Lewis was a psychopathic killer.

Greg seemed confused. "Why? I mean, why include them in the biography?"

Emily grinned and glanced at the others seated next to her. They all smiled, knowingly, and she laughed before speaking again.

"You'll see."

About the Author

Charlotte was born in a tiny mountain town and spent most of her childhood and young adulthood in a small city in northern Colorado. While she is usually what one might generously call "indoorsy," early exposure to the Rocky Mountains led to a lifelong love of nature, hiking, and camping.

After a lengthy education in Denver, New Orleans, Washington, DC, and New York, she earned a doctorate in literature and women and gender studies.

An early career academic, Charlotte has moved several times since her latest graduation. She currently lives and teaches in a small Southern city with her wife and their cat.

Website: http://charlottegreeneauthor.com.

Books Available from Bold Strokes Books

A Fighting Chance by T. L. Hayes. Will Lou be able to come to terms with her past to give love a fighting chance? (978-1-163555-257-7)

Chosen by Brey Willows. When the choice is adapt or die, can love save us all? (978-1-163555-110-5)

Death Checks In by David S. Pederson. Despite Heath's promises to Alan to not get involved, Heath can't resist investigating a shopkeeper's murder in Chicago, which dashes their plans for a romantic weekend getaway. (978-1-163555-329-1)

Gnarled Hollow by Charlotte Greene. After they are invited to study a secluded nineteenth-century estate, a former English professor and a group of historians discover that they will have to fight against the unknown if they have any hope of staying alive. (978-1-163555-235-5)

Jacob's Grace by C.P. Rowlands. Captain Tag Becket wants to keep her head down and her past behind her, but her feelings for AJ's second-in-command, Grace Fields, makes keeping secrets next to impossible. (978-1-163555-187-7)

On the Fly by PJ Trebelhorn. Hockey player Courtney Abbott is content with her solitary life until visiting concert violinist Lana Caruso makes her second-guess everything she always thought she wanted. (978-1-163555-255-3)

Passionate Rivals by Radclyffe. Professional rivalry and long-simmering passions create a combustible combination when Emmett McCabe and Sydney Stevens are forced to work together, especially when past attractions won't stay buried. (978-1-163555-231-7)

Proxima Five by Missouri Vaun. When geologist Leah Warren crash-lands on a preindustrial planet and is claimed by its tyrant, Tiago, will clan warrior Keegan's love for Leah give her the strength to defeat him? (978-1-163555-122-8)

Racing Hearts by Dena Blake. When you cross a hot-tempered race car mechanic with a reckless cop, the result can only be spontaneous combustion. (978-1-163555-251-5)

Shadowboxer by Jessica L. Webb. Jordan McAddie is prepared to keep her street kids safe from a dangerous underground protest group, but she isn't prepared for her first love to walk back into her life. (978-1-163555-267-6)

The Tattered Lands by Barbara Ann Wright. As Vandra and Lilani strive to make peace, they slowly fall in love. With mistrust and murder surrounding them, only their faith in each other can keep their plan to save the world from falling apart. (978-1-163555-108-2)

Captive by Donna K. Ford. To escape a human trafficking ring, Greyson Cooper and Olivia Danner become players in a game of deceit and violence. Will their love stand a chance? (978-1-63555-215-7)

Crossing the Line by CF Frizzell. The Mob discovers a nemesis within its ranks, and in the ultimate retaliation, draws Stick McLaughlin from anonymity by threatening everything she holds dear. (978-1-63555-161-7)

Love's Verdict by Carsen Taite. Attorneys Landon Holt and Carly Pachett want the exact same thing: the only open partnership spot at their prestigious criminal defense firm. But will they compromise their careers for love? (978-1-63555-042-9)

Precipice of Doubt by Mardi Alexander & Laurie Eichler. Can Cole Jameson resist her attraction to her boss, veterinarian Jodi Bowman, or will she risk a workplace romance and her heart? (978-1-63555-128-0)

Savage Horizons by CJ Birch. Captain Jordan Kellow's feelings for Lt. Ali Ash have her past and future colliding, setting in motion a series of events that strands her crew in an unknown galaxy thousands of light years from home. (978-1-63555-250-8)

Secrets of the Last Castle by A. Rose Mathieu. When Elizabeth Campbell represents a young man accused of murdering an elderly woman, her investigation leads to an abandoned plantation that reveals many dark Southern secrets. (978-1-63555-240-9)

Take Your Time by VK Powell. A neurotic parrot brings police officer Grace Booker and temporary veterinarian Dr. Dani Wingate together in the tiny town of Pine Cone, but their unexpected attraction keeps the sparks flying. (978-1-63555-130-3)

The Last Seduction by Ronica Black. When you allow true love to elude you once and you desperately regret it, are you brave enough to grab it when it comes around again? (978-1-63555-211-9)

The Shape of You by Georgia Beers. Rebecca McCall doesn't play it safe, but when sexy Spencer Thompson joins her workout class, their non-stop sparring forces her to face her ultimate challenge—a chance at love. (978-1-63555-217-1)

Exposed by MJ Williamz. The closet is no place to live if you want to find true love. (978-1-62639-989-1)

Force of Fire: Toujours a Vous by Ali Vali. Immortals Kendal and Piper welcome their new child and celebrate the defeat of an old enemy, but another ancient evil is about to awaken deep in the jungles of Costa Rica. (978-1-63555-047-4)

Holding Their Place by Kelly A. Wacker. Together Dr. Helen Connery and ambulance driver Julia March, discover that goodness, love, and passion can be found in the most unlikely and even dangerous places during WWI. (978-1-63555-338-3)

Landing Zone by Erin Dutton. Can a career veteran finally discover a love stronger than even her pride? (978-1-63555-199-0)

Love at Last Call by M. Ullrich. Is balancing business, friendship, and love more than any willing woman can handle? (978-1-63555-197-6)

Pleasure Cruise by Yolanda Wallace. Spencer Collins and Amy Donovan have few things in common, but a Caribbean cruise offers both women an unexpected chance to face one of their greatest fears: falling in love. (978-1-63555-219-5)

Running Off Radar by MB Austin. Maji's plans to win Rose back are interrupted when work intrudes and duty calls her to help a SEAL team stop a Russian mobster from harvesting gold from the bottom of Sitka Sound. (978-1-63555-152-5)

Shadow of the Phoenix by Rebecca Harwell. In the final battle for the fate of Storm's Quarry, even Nadya's and Shay's powers may not be enough. (978-1-63555-181-5)

Take a Chance by D. Jackson Leigh. There's hardly a woman within fifty miles of Pine Cone that veterinarian Trip Beaumont can't charm, except for the irritating new cop, Jamie Grant, who keeps leaving parking tickets on her truck. (978-1-63555-118-1)

The Outcasts by Alexa Black. Spacebus driver Sue Jones is running from her past. When she crash-lands on a faraway world, the Outcast Kara might be her chance for redemption. (978-1-63555-242-3)

Alias by Cari Hunter. A car crash leaves a woman with no memory and no identity. Together with Detective Bronwen Pryce, she fights to uncover a truth that might just kill them both. (978-1-63555-221-8)

Death in Time by Robyn Nyx. Working in the past is hell on your future. (978-1-63555-053-5)

Hers to Protect by Nicole Disney. High school sweethearts Kaia and Adrienne will have to see past their differences and survive the vengeance of a brutal gang if they want to be together. (978-1-63555-229-4)

Of Echoes Born by 'Nathan Burgoine. A collection of queer fantasy short stories set in Canada from Lambda Literary Award finalist 'Nathan Burgoine. (978-1-63555-096-2)

Perfect Little Worlds by Clifford Mae Henderson. Lucy can't hold the secret any longer. Twenty-six years ago, her sister did the unthinkable. (978-1-63555-164-8)

Room Service by Fiona Riley. Interior designer Olivia likes stability, but when work brings footloose Savannah into her world and into a new city every month, Olivia must decide if what makes her comfortable is what makes her happy. (978-1-63555-120-4)

Sparks Like Ours by Melissa Brayden. Professional surfers Gia Malone and Elle Britton can't deny their chemistry on and off the beach. But only one can win... (978-1-63555-016-0)

Take My Hand by Missouri Vaun. River Hemsworth arrives in Georgia intent on escaping quickly, but when she crashes her Mercedes into the Clip 'n Curl, sexy Clay Cahill ends up rescuing more than her car. (978-1-63555-104-4)

The Last Time I Saw Her by Kathleen Knowles. Lane Hudson only has twelve days to win back Alison's heart. That is if she can gather the courage to try. (978-1-63555-067-2)

Wayworn Lovers by Gun Brooke. Will agoraphobic composer Giselle Bonnaire and Tierney Edwards, a wandering soul who can't remain in one place for long, trust in the passionate love destiny hands them? (978-1-62639-995-2)

Breakthrough by Kris Bryant. Falling for a sexy ranger is one thing, but is the possibility of love worth giving up the career Kennedy Wells has always dreamed of? (978-1-63555-179-2)

Certain Requirements by Elinor Zimmerman. Phoenix has always kept her love of kinky submission strictly behind the bedroom door and inside the bounds of romantic relationships, until she meets Kris Andersen. (978-1-63555-195-2)

Dark Euphoria by Ronica Black. When a high-profile case drops in Detective Maria Diaz's lap, she forges ahead only to discover this case, and her main suspect, aren't like any other. (978-1-63555-141-9)

Fore Play by Julie Cannon. Executive Leigh Marshall falls hard for Peyton Broader, her golf pro…and an ex-con. Will she risk sabotaging her career for love? (978-1-63555-102-0)

Love Came Calling by CA Popovich. Can a romantic looking for a long-term, committed relationship and a jaded cynic too busy for love conquer life's struggles and find their way to what matters most? (978-1-63555-205-8)

Outside the Law by Carsen Taite. Former sweethearts Tanner Cohen and Sydney Braswell must work together on a federal task force to see justice served, but will they choose to embrace their second chance at love? (978-1-63555-039-9)

The Princess Deception by Nell Stark. When journalist Missy Duke realizes Prince Sebastian is really his twin sister Viola in disguise, she plays along, but when sparks flare between them, will the double deception doom their fairy-tale romance? (978-1-62639-979-2)

The Smell of Rain by Cameron MacElvee. Reyha Arslan, a wise and elegant woman with a tragic past, shows Chrys that there's still beauty to embrace and reason to hope despite the world's cruelty. (978-1-63555-166-2)

The Talebearer by Sheri Lewis Wohl. Liz's visions show her the faces of the lost and the killers who took their lives. As one by one, the murdered are found, a stranger works to stop Liz before the serial killer is brought to justice. (978-1-635550-126-6)

White Wings Weeping by Lesley Davis. The world is full of discord and hatred, but how much of it is just human nature when an evil with sinister intent is invading people's hearts? (978-1-63555-191-4)

CPSIA information can be obtained
at www.ICGtesting.com
Printed in the USA
BVHW08s0956180918
527830BV00001B/68/P

9 781635 552355